What Child Is This?

RANDY BURBA

PAGE PUBLISHING, INC.
Conneaut Lake, PA

First originally published by Page Publishing 2020

ISBN 978-1-64628-249-4 (pbk)
ISBN 978-1-66241-794-8 (hc)
ISBN 978-1-64628-250-0 (digital)

Printed in the United States of America

CHAPTER 1

Dec. 23, 1999, Chicago, Illinois

Melanie Russell leaned heavily against the customer service counter in Carlson Department Store. Her legs ached, and two packages pulled at her left arm like deadweights as she finished making out the check. Forty-two dollars and thirty-seven cents.

The dull throb from the front of her head had worked its way down her neck and was now spreading slowly through her shoulders. Still, she managed to smile as she handed the check to an elderly salesclerk.

Wanda, as her name tag boldly proclaimed, put the check through the cash register endorser.

"A gift for your husband?" Wanda asked cheerily as she folded the thick red sweater and placed it in a shopping bag, along with a large box.

"Yes, it is," Melanie answered, holding onto her smile despite the fatigue she felt at the end of yet another busy shopping day. "This was the last item on my list."

Wanda slipped the receipt in the bag and slid it across the counter.

"Is Santa coming to see the kids? You really are in great shape if Santa's shopping is done too."

Even though Melanie had heard the question—and others like it—many times since her marriage to Jack three years ago, she still winced.

God, how she hated these questions. Why was it that at age thirty-five, with a wedding band and elegant engagement ring adorning her left hand, people always assumed she was a mother with a house full of children?

The fact that strangers asked these questions, especially at Christmastime, still amazed her. And the question still hurt.

"Uh…I, we, don't have any children," Melanie answered. The salesclerk frowned slightly. "I mean, we don't have any yet. We might, though. Someday. Maybe."

The silence seemed to last forever as she picked up the Carlson's bag and gripped it tightly along with the rest of the day's purchases.

Wanda the salesclerk seemed troubled, even a bit embarrassed, but she recovered quickly. It was a trait she had honed effectively after more than thirty-two years in the customer service industry.

"Oh, there's no hurry for that sort of thing, at least not anymore. You're still young. There's plenty of time to start a family. And there's nothing like children to add some real excitement to the holidays."

Her words were followed by another long pause.

"Best of luck to you and your husband," she said while turning to ring up another customer's merchandise. "I hope he likes the sweater."

Melanie managed another smile. She tossed her purse over her right shoulder, lifted the shopping bags with her left hand, and trudged toward the store's huge front entrance.

The memories came flooding back as she walked, like a zombie, through the crush of people milling about the store like army ants.

She thought about the wonderful courtship she had shared with Jack. They were introduced by her best friend, Theresa, during an office party at Lakeview Hospital in Louisville, Kentucky, almost four years earlier. Theresa, a registered nurse in the hospital's emergency room, was still recovering from a messy divorce and hadn't wanted to attend the Christmas party alone. Melanie accompanied her, and the party was starting to wind down when she met her future husband, Dr. Jack Russell.

The introduction had been brief. "Dr. Russell, this is my best friend, Melanie Wade. Melanie, this is Dr. Russell. Jack Russell."

WHAT CHILD IS THIS?

Melanie, still working her way through the crowd at Carlson's, smiled as she replayed the scene in her tired mind.

"It's a pleasure to meet you," Jack had said as he took her hand and smiled warmly. "I was beginning to think I'd never meet an interesting person at this party. I was wrong."

Theresa smiled coyly as she slipped away. "Be back in a sec," she said, making her way toward the restroom. "Try not to bore her to death, Dr. Russell. And please, no emergency-room war stories. Melanie has a weak stomach."

Hearing her name spoken finally brought Melanie out of her trance. She had been mesmerized by Jack Russell's deep gaze. He was still holding her hand.

"Pleased to meet you too, Dr. Russell," she managed, feeling the rush of blood to her face from either embarrassment, excitement, or both. "Really, though, my stomach's not that weak. I mean, I teach kindergarten, so I'm tougher than I look."

"Jack. Please call me Jack," he said, slowly releasing her hand. Then he laughed heartily. "If there's one thing I can think of that's scarier than being an ER doc, it's teaching kindergarten. You have my admiration already."

The cold Chicago wind caught Melanie off guard, snapping her back to the present and away from the warm feeling of that first encounter with Jack.

If possible, the sidewalk and street before her were even more crowded than the store. *The Windy City is living up to its name*, she thought as she turned left and headed down Muir Street toward the corner of Lincoln Avenue.

As she walked briskly down the street, she again drifted back to the Louisville office party and her first night with Dr. Jack Russell.

After their introduction and the quick abandonment by Theresa, Jack and Melanie were left to talk the night away. And they did. The conversation had come so easily, Melanie would say later. Jack Russell was just everything you expected a man to be.

Tall, dark, and handsome, as her mother would say. With gentle features, deep green eyes, and a dazzling smile, he was intelligent, friendly, interesting, and much to her surprise, very humble. *For a man who has it all*, Melanie had thought, *he doesn't seem to know it.*

By the time Theresa finally returned and pulled Melanie away, Jack had already asked for her telephone number.

"If you think it would be okay, I'd like to call you sometime soon. Theresa talks about you a lot, and she mentioned that you weren't involved with anyone. I'd love to invite you to dinner…you know, if you think it would be okay."

"It would be okay." Melanie had laughed. "In fact, I look forward to it. I'm usually home from school by four thirty each day. I probably shouldn't say it, but my nights are generally pretty quiet. Call whenever it's convenient for you."

Melanie was startled as she bumped into a man pulling a young boy along by the hand. "Excuse me," she said. "I'm sorry."

"No problem," the man, clad in a heavy brown coat, said from behind a scarf that covered most of his face. "It's a hell of a crowd out here today." He walked quickly away, pulling the boy behind him.

Fully alert now, Melanie's mind slowly let go of the past. The first date had happened, of course, followed by many, many more. She fell in love with Jack almost instantly, and the love had grown with each passing day.

By October of the next year, they were married. In January of 1997, he was transferred to the large regional medical center here in Chicago. Naturally, she came with him and had been very fortunate to find a teaching job at Mercy Elementary School, located just a few miles south of the hospital.

A beautiful home in the suburbs was purchased by summer, after just five months of apartment living, and the life she and Jack had started together seemed almost too good to be true—everything, that is, except the baby, the baby they both so desperately wanted, the one they had been trying to conceive since their wedding day more than three years earlier, and the one that, according to the ob-gyn the two had been working with for the past six months, was never going to come.

"I'm sorry," Dr. Jan Stewart, a friend of Jack's and an expert in the field of fertility, had told the couple as they sat anxiously inside her inner office. "All the tests are complete. I've checked them and rechecked them. Jack, I'm afraid you suffer from sterility. It's not something that can be corrected. Jack, Melanie…I'm so sorry."

It was the first time she had ever seen her husband cry. He didn't cry, exactly, but rather, he sat there, stunned, holding Melanie's hand and looking at Dr. Stewart. He remained silent, but his eyes grew moist. His head dropped slowly, and he turned slightly away from his wife.

Melanie was devastated. Her heart ached for a baby. Really, it always had. Growing up as an only child, she had always dreamed of one day raising a large robust family. Her eagerness to be a mom had only increased after meeting Jack. *What a wonderful father he will make*, she had thought, even as the two stood before God, the priest, and family and friends inside St. Dominic's Cathedral on their wedding day.

Now, according to this woman, a friend of her husband's and one of the most respected specialists in Chicago, it was never going to happen.

Even in her grief, as the disappointment began to soak in like nothing she had felt before, she thought of her husband, the man she loved so deeply, the man who was still holding her hand but who continued to look away as if ashamed.

"Can we have a minute, Dr. Stewart?" Melanie asked.

"Certainly. I'll be right outside if you need me. I have much more to talk to you about… Perhaps a little later. And I have some wonderful information to share with you concerning adoption."

It was at the sound of the word *adoption*—a word that seemed to fill the room—that Jack finally released his wife's hand. He stood and slowly walked to the back of the large office.

Dr. Stewart also stood, opened her mouth as if to say something else, then stopped. "I want to give you some time together first," she said. "Stay here as long as you like." Then she walked through the office door and gently pulled it closed behind her.

Melanie went immediately to her husband. "Please, Jack. Don't do this," she cried. "Look at me."

Jack turned to her, his eyes still moist, and she buried her head into his chest. "I'm...so...sorry," he said. "I didn't know about this. I never—"

Melanie squeezed him as hard as she could, cutting off his words. There was great strength in her blue eyes, and they blazed with warmth and compassion as she looked up at her husband.

"Stop it, Jack. Do you hear me? Stop it right now. We are not going to do this. We are not going to lay blame, and we are not going to feel guilt. This is not our fault. This is in God's hands. We're in God's hands. And we're going to deal with this, together. You and I. Together. Do you understand me?"

Jack nodded slowly, stunned at the fierceness of his wife's resolve.

"I love you, Jack. I love you more than life itself, and nothing will ever change that. But you can't turn away from me. Not now, Jack. I need you now more than ever."

The sharp, long blast of a car horn made Melanie jump and brought her back to the present. She was standing at the corner of Lincoln and Broadway, and a taxi slipped across the street in front of her, the tires just inches away from her favorite brown walking shoes.

"Geez, lady," the cab driver grumbled through the open window as he moved by, "you really ought to take your naps at home."

Melanie sighed deeply, then stepped back onto the curb to wait for the light.

That was smart, she thought. *Killed by a rude taxi driver two days before Christmas. That would make for a wonderful holiday, now wouldn't it?*

"Just one more block to go," she murmured to herself, thinking of the cold gray parking garage ahead. She'd left her Toyota Camry there hours earlier, and now her weary limbs and tired feet were looking forward to settling into the soft front seat.

The light flashed walk, and she and dozens of others hustled across to the opposite curb. As she made her way down the final block to the garage, she smiled slightly.

We've handled this pretty darn well, Melanie thought to herself. *Jack and I. We've grown closer during the months since our meeting with Dr. Stewart. Jack is back to his old self again, and together, we're slowly putting the pain behind us. This isn't going to be such a bad Christmas after all.*

Suddenly, she longed for her husband. He was off today, a rare treat for an emergency-room doctor at this time of year, and she'd been shopping most of the day. *Gone too long*, she thought.

She picked up the pace despite the dull protest from her legs and hurried down the street.

"Ho, ho, ho! Merry Christmas, young lady," said the large man clad in a Santa Claus suit. He stood in front of a Salvation Army kettle, ringing a bell. The eyes behind the white, fluffy beard were dark, but they were kind, gentle eyes, and he smiled broadly as he walked closer to Melanie.

"I can see you're helping Santa with the shopping this year," he said. "Is there anything left for our needy children?"

Melanie couldn't recall if she'd ever turned a deaf ear to a Salvation Army volunteer. She guessed it had something to do with teaching children. She always stopped at the kettle, and she always donated, even that one time, two years ago, when she reached into her wallet and found it empty after a day of shopping. Even then, she'd made out a check for twenty dollars and handed it over to Santa.

"I should have something left for your kids," Melanie said as she shifted the packages from her left hand to her right and opened the purse that dangled from her shoulder. She found a loose ten-dollar bill and, despite the glove, was able to snatch it out, fold it, and deposit it in the kettle.

"Merry Christmas, Santa," she said, shifting the packages again and preparing to hurry off.

"Wait," he said, grasping her forearm gently and pulling her closer to him. "Santa has something for you too." Pulling a bright red-and-white candy cane out of his pocket, he smiled again and placed it in Melanie's empty hand. "Bless you, my child. I hope you and your husband have a very happy holiday."

Melanie looked at Santa. How did he know she had a husband? He couldn't see her rings with the gloves on. Then she braced herself, waiting for the inevitable question about her children. It never came.

Instead, Santa pulled her closer and whispered in her ear. "Merry Christmas, Melanie. Merry Christmas to you and Jack."

Melanie lurched backward. She stared into Santa's eyes, searching frantically for some sign of recognition, some indication that she knew this man. She had to know him, didn't she? He knew her name. He knew her husband's name.

"Do I know you?" Melanie shouted, trying not to sound hysterical on this busy street corner. "Are you someone I know?"

"I'm someone you know," he said softly. "I'm someone you've always known." He gently pulled Melanie closer again. "More importantly, I know you. You are a good person, a very special person. Because of that, you will be blessed with a warm, happy holiday. Merry Christmas to you and Jack."

Melanie wanted to pull away again, pull away and run for her car or perhaps to a police officer if she could find one on the busy street. But despite her anxiety, her fear, she did not run. She continued to gaze into the man's eyes.

"The new year, the millennium, will be a special time for you," he said. "It will be a time of great rejoice. It will be the year where you receive a great gift. Do you understand, Melanie? A great gift." She stood in a trance, unable to move or speak. "But it will also be a time of great sorrow—a time of hardship unlike any other, trial and tribulation no one else has endured, except one. Long ago. Do you understand me, Melanie?"

Santa rang the bell loudly and turned to look down the sidewalk. Melanie finally moved.

"Who are you?" she asked again. "What are you talking about? Why are you saying these things to me? Are you crazy?"

He turned back to Melanie. He smiled again, but there was anguish in his eyes. "No, I'm not crazy. I'm just not sure about the rest of the world. I guess we're going to find out. You and me, Jack, the others…and him."

Melanie shook her head in disbelief. Was she losing her mind? Could this really be happening? Right here, on a busy street corner? Two days before Christmas?

"You'll understand in time," he said. "But you'll need help. I'm one of many sent here to help you. I'll be here next year, at this exact spot, ringing the bell for Christmas. Come and see me. Please."

He turned away again, for the final time. "Ho, ho, ho! Merry Christmas, little fella," he called out to a small boy standing near the kettle with his parents. "Have you been a good boy this year?"

Melanie staggered away toward the garage, toward her car. She could think only of Jack and getting home to him and getting away from the insanity of this man dressed as Santa Claus.

But as she pulled out of the garage and turned north on River Road, toward home, his words were haunting her. How did he know her? How did he know Jack? And what did his words mean? What was it that he wanted her to understand?

A time of great rejoice, he had said. A time of great sorrow too.

"It's crazy talk, nothing more," Melanie said to herself, above the sound of the windshield wipers as she drove home toward the Highlands and her warm two-story house. Thick, wet snow was falling on the windshield, making the drive more difficult than usual.

"Enough of this nonsense," she said aloud, again in the quietness of her car. "It's all so stupid. I'm not even going to tell Jack about it."

But she did. And he was troubled by the account too. They talked about it all that night and most of the day Christmas Eve. But by nightfall, Jack's sister, Amy; her husband, Keith; and the children, Julie and Stacey, had arrived from St. Louis.

Their thoughts were pulled away from the bizarre meeting with the Salvation Army Santa, and Christmas Day dawned clear and cold. It was, in fact, a wonderful Christmas for the entire family. And by month's end, with the return to work by both Jack and Melanie fast approaching, the subject was dropped completely.

The year 2000 had arrived.

Doctor and Mrs. Jack Russell had managed to get a handle on the sorrow they shared over the news about sterility. Although they weren't quite ready to start talking about adoption yet, the future looked much brighter than it had just a few months earlier.

"I think 2000 is going to be a very good year," Jack said as he kissed his wife in the comfort of their den on New Year's Eve. A bright orange blaze flickered from the fireplace. The couple sat on the floor, sipped champagne, and watched television's Dick Clark lead the countdown to midnight live from Times Square.

"Me too," Melanie said as she set her glass aside. Slowly, she began to unbutton Jack's flannel shirt. "Call me crazy, but I just have a good feeling about things now. With you at my side, I feel like I can do anything."

The fire continued to burn, and the two became one.

In the morning, they awoke together and climbed groggily from the floor. They made their way toward the kitchen window, still holding each other, and looked out at the sunrise as the automatic coffee maker kicked on.

"I love you, Jack," Melanie said softly. "Promise me you will always love me."

"I promise," he replied, hugging her tighter. "Always."

They continued to gaze out the window, watching the huge golden sun as it inched higher in the sky. The kitchen floor was cold, and Melanie shivered slightly.

With dawn came the millennium. It was upon them.

CHAPTER 2

March 29, 2000, Louisville, Kentucky

The Joseph Nantz Nursing Home, located along Muhammad Ali Boulevard on the Louisville side of the Ohio River, was not an easy place to visit.

Melanie always felt a sense of dread as she entered the front gate and drove toward the spacious one-story facility. It was easier when Jack was along, but the ER was short-staffed, and he couldn't get away this trip. The burden of being an only child never got easier, she had heard a woman say on TV once. She couldn't remember who it was, some guest on the Oprah Winfrey show. But there was, she admitted, a lot of truth to the statement.

She parked, locked the car, and walked across the front lawn toward the visitor's entrance.

There's no better time than spring in Kentucky, Melanie thought as she stopped to observe the pink blooms on a redbud tree. Two robins sat perched near the top. In six weeks, they'd be running the Derby at nearby Churchill Downs, and she still embraced many fond memories of attending the racetrack with her parents.

Melanie glanced at her watch. Nine o'clock already. The morning was slipping by fast, as was the weekend. *I better get in to see Mother*, she thought. *I'll feel better once I see her.*

She stopped at the reception desk and found Geri Johnson, the day shift coordinator, making a fresh pot of coffee.

"Good morning," Melanie said. "And Happy Easter."

Johnson was a tiny woman, barely five feet tall and no more than a hundred pounds, at best. She had bright red hair, which she kept cut short, and always wore an abundance of makeup. From the high arching eyebrows to the dark eye shadow and ruby red lipstick, she had the appearance of an aging stage actress. As she walked to the counter to greet Melanie, her looks suffered greatly next to the visitor's simple, elegant beauty.

And there was no denying Melanie's beauty. Slim yet athletic, she had long legs, narrow hips, and breasts that were large but not too large, as Jack liked to say. Delicate features highlighted a face that needed little more than a brush or two of makeup and a quick touch of lipstick. Deep blue eyes and thick shoulder length hair, naturally curly and light brown in color, completed the package.

Although she never thought of herself as beautiful, she had to admit she could never remember having worried even as a teenager about her appearance. "I guess that's a good sign," she had once told a friend as they prepared for their class reunion at Assumption High School.

"No shit," her friend, Gloria Masden, had replied. "You haven't changed a bit in ten years, and no one will recognize me without a name tag. If I stand by you too long, people will think I'm your mother. Go away. You make me sick."

Melanie almost laughed at the memory.

"Happy Easter to you too, Mrs. Russell," Johnson said. "It's nice to see you again."

The two women shook hands, then hugged briefly. "Care for some hot coffee?" Johnson asked.

"No thanks," Melanie replied, smiling sheepishly. "I've had my limit. In fact, I'm already looking for a bathroom."

They laughed together.

"How's my mom? Is she still the same?"

"I'm afraid so. You know how it is with Alzheimer's. Miss Martha has her good days and bad. The last few, though, have been mostly bad."

Melanie frowned. "I was afraid of that. I called late the other night and talked to one of the nurses—Jacqueline, I think—while I was packing to come down here. She said Mother had been out of it lately, even more so than usual. She said she seemed troubled about something."

"Oh, honey, you know how it is," Johnson said. "It's just a wicked, wicked disease. And it goes from bad to worse. But Miss Martha seems okay. I mean, she's experiencing very little pain. And the night shift people say she's sleeping well."

Melanie nodded slowly.

"No use fretting about it," Johnson said. "Besides, you're here now. Quit wasting your time with me and go see your mother. I know in my heart she'll be glad to see you, even if she can't show it. She knows you always come on the holidays."

"Thanks, Geri. Thank you all for everything you do here. I'll go see her now. Still room 408, right?"

"Right as rain. I'll give you ten-to-one odds she's sitting by the window, watching those birds sing, just like always."

Melanie made her way to room 408. She had flown from Chicago's O'Hare Airport to Louisville to see her one and only living relative, yet she felt empty as she entered the room.

Martha Wade was sitting near the window, staring straight ahead.

An attendant, a large woman, had just finished making the bed. She nodded at Melanie and touched her hand lightly as she left the room.

"Thank you," Melanie whispered to the attendant.

"Happy Easter, Mother," Melanie called out to her mother, sounding as cheerful as possible. "I love you."

Her mother, seated in a wheelchair, did not move. Instead, she stared straight ahead, blinking her eyes occasionally, saying nothing.

Melanie stepped between the window and her mother, stooped down, and grasped her hands. "God, I miss you," she said, fighting back tears. "I miss you so much, Mother. I miss you and Daddy both."

She glanced at the nightstand near her mother's bed. There, as always, was the photo of her father, James Wade. The picture was ten years old, taken during the summer of 1990, just two years before his tragic death.

A lineman with Bluegrass Gas & Electric, James was killed while working to restore power during a severe thunderstorm in eastern Jefferson County. A hole the size of a pinhead in his rubber gloves, resulted in electrocution as he worked on an energized line. He was just fifty-one at the time. His only daughter, Melanie, had just turned twenty-eight.

And for those twenty-eight years, James Wade had been the love of his daughter's life. He was a large, gentle man who showered Melanie with affection. When he was not working, he was spending time with his wife and daughter.

Work and home—that was all that mattered to him.

The fact that he and Martha were unable to have more children didn't seem to trouble him greatly, though it sometimes did his wife. Instead, he put all his energy into playing with his daughter. From hide-and-seek to Barbie dolls to basketball, the two played together as Martha watched from the back porch with great pride and love.

"I have a feeling about you, sweetie," he had told his daughter when she graduated from nearby Bellarmine College. "You're a special person. Someday you'll leave your mark on this world. I'm so proud of you."

Six years later, he was gone.

Martha never recovered from her husband's death. Although she experienced very few medical problems prior to the accident, her health declined rapidly over the next several years. The Alzheimer's disease was diagnosed in 1994, and the nursing home became necessary just a few months before Melanie and Jack met at the hospital Christmas party.

For her part, Melanie had managed to move forward following the accident. Through her work at school and helping care for her mother, she stayed busy, and that helped. But not a day went by when she didn't think about her father.

Subconsciously, that was probably why she had put romance on hold until meeting Jack during the Christmas break of 1995.

Jack's parents, Bob and Regina Russell, both enjoyed good health and still lived in Tucson. They were financially comfortable and able to visit Jack, his sister, and older brother, David, who lived in New York, on a regular basis.

Because of that, Melanie thought, *Jack sometimes feels guilty about my lack of immediate family.*

After he and Melanie were married and the transfer to Chicago followed, he insisted they take Martha with them.

"I have contacts through the hospital," he said. "We'll find her the best facility in the city."

Melanie was tempted at first. The prospect of being close to her mother despite her condition was reassuring. But in the end, she just couldn't do it. She couldn't break her word.

As Martha Wade's mental and emotional condition deteriorated, she had made a living will through an old family friend, Attorney John Hayburn. She also made her only daughter promise to never move her from the Louisville area.

"James and I were both born here. You were born here, Melanie," she'd said. "Now your father is buried here. This is home for me. I never want to leave, no matter what happens. You are still young, and you may want to move someday. You shouldn't worry about that. Enjoy your life. Go if you need to go. But please, let me stay here."

This was why the two now sat in room 408 at the Joseph Nantz Nursing Home. Melanie Russell always kept her word.

She stayed through the morning and had lunch with her mother. In the afternoon, she read some poetry aloud and talked to her about work, Jack, and Chicago. She cried as she told her mother about their inability to have a baby. Through it all, her mother stared out the window.

As she gathered her things and prepared to leave, Melanie went to her mother, bent over, and kissed her softly on the forehead.

"I love you, Mommy," she said. "You know I always will."

Her eyes were filling with tears as she turned to walk away. Suddenly, Martha Wade reached out and grabbed her daughter's arm. Melanie almost shrieked as her mother's fingers dug into her forearm.

"It's happening," her mother said. "The journey now begins. Your journey begins. Be strong, Melanie. My sweet Melanie, be strong." Then her eyes went blank again, and Martha released her daughter. Her breathing slowed, and her eyelids closed. Her head fell to her left shoulder.

Finally, Melanie was able to move. She ran into the hallway and screamed for help. Two orderlies, followed by Geri Johnson, came running from the front lobby.

"Something's wrong with Mother," Melanie gasped. "She's not breathing!"

As the four entered the room, they found Martha face up on the floor. Both her arms were extended out in a V shape from her sides, and her feet, covered in soft blue slippers, were crossed at the ankles.

She was dead.

Outside the window, the robins sang.

One of the orderlies glanced at the crucifix hanging above Martha's bed, then looked at his partner. "Look how she's lying," he whispered. "Let's get her on the bed. This is giving me the creeps."

Near the doorway, Melanie felt queasy, and she dropped to her knees on the carpeted floor. Despite her best efforts not to, she vomited. Rocking back and forth on her knees, she cried hysterically as Johnson tried to console her.

"Oh my god! What's happening to me?" she wailed. "What's happening to me?"

CHAPTER 3

May 24, 2000, Chicago, Illinois

Finally, the last day of school had arrived at Mercy Elementary. Melanie smiled as her kindergarten class shuffled out the doorway toward the buses, leaning forward to counterbalance the weight each of them carried in their backpacks.

There's always a lot for them to take home on the last day, she thought. *Those backpacks will only get heavier when they return in the fall to begin first grade.* By that time, Melanie and Doris McKenzie, the other kindergarten teacher at Mercy, would be breaking in another group of scared, homesick five-year-olds.

She felt a familiar pang as she watched this year's class head off for summer vacation. It was the same emotion she felt every year. Once again, she'd grown to love and appreciate these youngsters. They had warmed her heart with their energy and enthusiasm, and she felt pride as she watched them grow and develop during the school year.

Tears started to flow as Lisa and Lesley Zettel, the twins, turned and waved before filing out the door. Many of the others did the same, then giggled when their teacher waved back.

"I'm going to miss you guys," Melanie called out. "Don't forget me next year. Stop by and see me, or I'm gonna be mad."

"We will!" The children squealed as they broke and ran for the exit doors.

Melanie smiled and shook her head as she walked to the window and watched all the students from Mercy climb aboard the buses.

They always say that, she thought, *but they never come back to see me or Doris. Once they hit the first grade, they're on to bigger and better things. I guess that's the way it's supposed to be.*

She stood at the window, melancholic, for several minutes after the last bus pulled out of the large parking lot. Finally, she turned and began straightening her desk and filing away year-end papers. Slowly, her thoughts shifted away from the kindergarten class and toward a more immediate concern.

She glanced at her watch… three twenty already. Her appointment with the doctor was scheduled for four o'clock.

Better get a move on, she thought. Dr. William Bingham's office was a twenty-minute drive from the school. With the bus traffic in full force this time of day, the trip could take longer.

She hurriedly gathered her things and walked quickly to the principal's office down the hall. There she ducked her head in and found Karen Luckenbill, the receptionist, talking with Principal Alvin Nord, Doris, and fourth-grade teacher Samantha Mattingly.

"I'm heading out," Melanie said. "See you in the morning."

"That's right," Nord said, laughing. "Be here nine o'clock sharp, not a minute later. We've got a lot of important matters to discuss. Vacation plans—that sort of thing."

Everyone laughed.

"Heading home, Melanie?" Doris asked.

Melanie paused. Doris McKenzie was her best friend. They'd grown extremely close since Melanie had arrived during Christmas break three years ago. But she wasn't as close with Nord or Mattingly.

"Yes," she finally answered. "I'm going home. Just a stop or two to make and then home to the castle. I'll call you later."

"Good," Doris said. "I'll need a pep talk. I'm always a little blue when the kids leave us behind."

Melanie smiled and pulled the door closed. A frown creased her face as she walked to the car. *I'm nervous*, she suddenly realized. *I hate doctors. Except Jack, of course. And I'd feel better if he knew about this. But he doesn't, does he? Thanks to my sneaking around behind his back.*

Melanie pulled out of the parking lot and glanced at the Camry's digital clock... three thirty-one. *I should just make it*, she thought. *I hope Dr. Bingham is a nice man.*

He seemed like a nice man. Although his office was small, and a little on the dingy side, he smiled warmly as Melanie entered. She was accompanied by Carol Potts, a nurse in her midfifties with a large waistline, thick glasses, short gray hair, and a serious demeanor.

"Ah, Carol, I see you've brought in our new patient," Dr. Bingham said. "Welcome, Mrs. Russell. It's nice to finally meet you in person."

Melanie's heart raced. Her head throbbed. Suddenly, surprisingly, she had a bad feeling about being here. She was confused, scared, and couldn't understand why. Quickly, she retraced the events that had brought her before this stranger.

It began shortly after her mother's funeral in March. Depression had set in, followed by sleeplessness, loss of appetite, and fatigue. Jack kept a close eye on her, and the symptoms did begin to fade after a few weeks, just as he had predicted.

All but the nausea. It started just three weeks ago and had been with her every morning since. Sometimes it lasted only a few minutes and didn't affect her again until the next morning. Other days, it lasted for hours and resulted in not only retching but also dizziness. And in other ways, Melanie wasn't feeling right. She couldn't quite describe it, but it worried her—worried her enough that she secretly kept her condition from Jack. As a result, she'd let her fingers do the walking through Chicago's yellow pages, and she came upon the name of Dr. William Bingham, MD.

The appointment was made five days ago, and every day since, she had made plans to tell Jack about it. But each evening, when he came home from the hospital, she changed her mind. *He'll overreact*, she thought. *He'll make me go to one of his friends, probably a specialist, and they'll put me through the ringer with examinations and tests because Jack will insist that they do. No, this is best. I'll go see this man, and he can tell me I have the flu or whatever, and everything will be fine. No need to worry Jack about an occasional puke. Maybe I'm just going through the change a little early. When does menopause arrive, anyway? Can it hit you at thirty-five? Probably so, the way my luck's been running.*

"Melanie, are you okay?" Dr. Bingham asked. He walked from behind his desk and took her hands into his. His hands were damp, almost sticky. The touch brought Melanie out of her trance.

"Yes. Yes, Doctor. I'm fine. It's nice to meet you too." She pulled her hands away and stepped back slightly.

This is a mistake, Melanie thought. *I should not have come here. And I certainly shouldn't have come without Jack. But it's too late to grow brains now. The best thing to do is answer his questions and go home. From now on, I'll leave all my medical decisions to my husband.*

"Nurse Potts, is Mrs. Russell all caught up on her insurance premiums?" Dr. Bingham asked. Carol Potts, always the good soldier, held her tongue and nodded her head. Although she wanted to, she didn't roll her eyes in response to the crude question.

"Well then, little lady," he said lightly, turning back to Melanie, "I guess we'd better get started. Now, could you please describe your symptoms to me again?"

Melanie told him everything. She didn't want to. In fact, she didn't want to talk to Bingham at all. But she was here. There was something wrong with her. And he was, at least according to the Yellow Pages and the small diploma hanging on the wall behind him, a family doctor.

Bingham listened intently, nodding his head from time to time and taking notes as Melanie explained her condition. Nurse Potts sat stoically off to the side. Her presence was required by state law once the physical exam began.

It's a good thing too, the nurse realized as Bingham continued to ask questions of his new patient. *There's no telling what this nasty little man might try if left alone with a woman like Melanie Russell.*

Sleaze bucket was the term she used when describing Bingham to her husband, Ben. And if she wasn't six months away from retirement, she'd leave this idiot and catch on with a respectable practice or clinic somewhere in the city. But for six months, she could put up with anybody. Even Bingham.

After some twenty minutes, Bingham's questions mercifully ceased.

"We need to draw some blood, check your blood pressure, and get a chest X-ray," Bingham said, talking to both Melanie and Potts. "But before we do the X-ray, I need to perform a pelvic exam."

Melanie cringed at the thought of this man spreading her legs so that he could push and prod the contours of her intimacy.

"Why a pelvic exam?" she asked, sounding more shrill than she realized.

"I need to rule out pregnancy. Your nausea could be caused by morning sickness. That would also explain some of the other symptoms."

Melanie almost laughed out loud. Never had she imagined that she would find comfort in her husband's sterility, but the emotion she felt at this moment could only be described as relief. She could put the whammy on this diagnosis and keep her panties on at the same time.

"No, Doctor, I'm not pregnant," she said. "I can't have children."

"Are you certain? Has a physician told you that? Are you infertile?"

"Yes. We were told, my husband and I, that we can't have children. I mean, my husband is sterile, so we can't have any children."

Bingham stared at Melanie intently for a few seconds. His eyes seemed to linger on his patient a bit too long, and the slightest of smirks spread across his oily face. Melanie's neck grew warm, and anger flashed through her eyes. She fought to maintain a steadiness to her voice.

"I'm not pregnant, Dr. Bingham. I can assure you of that."

Bingham hesitated for a moment, then answered. Cheeriness had returned to his voice. "Certainly, certainly," he said. "I'm sure it must be something else. But the pelvic exam is still necessary, as are the other tests. Nurse Potts, take Mrs. Russell into the exam room, and let's get started."

Forty-five minutes later, Melanie was again seated in Bingham's office. This time, she was alone. And she was frightened. The doctor and his nurse had both behaved peculiarly during the exam. Neither had much to say. Bingham's tone had been somber when he asked Melanie to return to the office and wait for him.

The loathing she had felt as a result of his prying fingers had long since been replaced by fear and anxiety over what he might have found. Could it be cervical cancer? Cancer of the uterus? Problems with her ovaries? What was wrong with her?

Melanie reached inside her purse and put her fingers around the cell phone. She wanted to call Jack and tell him where she was. She wanted him to come and take her back to the safety of their home.

But she didn't. She released the phone and pulled her hand from the purse. *I've gone too far to turn back now,* she said to herself. *I'll know the verdict soon enough. And once I know I'm going straight home to tell him the truth, good or bad. That's what I should have done in the first place.*

Melanie looked at the large clock on the wall. It was already five ten. What could be taking so long?

A few minutes later, Bingham entered the room. He was alone. He smiled at Melanie and immediately some of her fear subsided.

"Mrs. Russell, this is going to sound like that old doctor's joke. But I'm going to say it anyway. After completing your exam I've got both good news and bad news."

Melanie felt sick as the fear returned with fervor. She stared blankly at the doctor.

Bingham searched for a smile from Melanie. Obviously, she had failed to see the humor in his remark. I'm not surprised, he thought. The pretty ones are always bitches.

He smiled again.

"The good news is, you are indeed pregnant," he said, abruptly. "The bad news is, I'm not quite sure how this pregnancy has come to pass. And I'm not just talking about any problems your husband is supposed to have. I'm talking about your current physical condition."

Melanie was speechless. The words she had so wanted to hear now left her bewildered. How could she be pregnant? Had Dr. Stewart misdiagnosed Jack's condition? That had to be it. But how? And what was the other thing this jerk had mentioned? What was wrong with her current physical condition?

"I…I don't understand what you're saying. You have to be mistaken. I told you Jack is sterile. We've had all the tests. His condition has been confirmed and reconfirmed. He cannot produce children."

The office fell silent. Bingham did not speak. He continued to watch Melanie's face.

"Listen, Dr. Bingham. I realize you don't know me. You don't know anything about me or my husband. And I really don't care what you think you might know about us. I'm just trying to understand what's going on here. So let me say this as plainly as I can. Jack cannot have children. He is my husband, and he is the only person I've been with since the day we first met, almost five years ago. So you must be mistaken. I *cannot* be pregnant."

Melanie looked at Bingham, waiting for an answer, waiting for an explanation to end this madness.

Bingham paused. He knew what he had to say but wasn't quite sure how to say it. He too was perplexed by what he'd discovered about Melanie Russell. Explaining it to anyone would not be easy.

"Mrs. Russell," he began. "I'm not passing judgment on you. And I'm not passing judgment on any doctor who told you and your husband that you could not have children. I'm certainly no expert in that area and don't pretend to be."

Again, he considered his words carefully.

"But I do know one thing. You are pregnant. Without a doubt. Your blood work shows it. The pelvic exam shows it. My best guess is that you are about seven weeks into your term. Ultrasound will give us a more exact estimate, but you are certainly well into your first trimester."

His words were starting to have an effect on Melanie. He stood up and walked around to the front of his desk, closer to his patient.

"You must feel it," Bingham said. "The morning sickness. A change in your hormone levels. A heaviness in your breasts. You are pregnant, Mrs. Russell. By the end of the year, you will have a child."

Melanie slumped forward and put her head in her hands. Her heart was pounding and emotions, conflicting emotions, were pouring out of her. She wanted to laugh and cry at the same time. Images were racing through her mind.

Would the baby be a boy or girl? Would he or she be healthy? Would he or she look like Jack? Or maybe even her dad?

She had felt different for some time now; there was no denying that. There was something growing inside her. She knew this doctor's words were true. But the burning question remained. How?

The joy she felt was tethered by apprehension. How could this be explained? To Jack? And to his family? To Doris and her other friends?

The apprehension was quickly turning to fear.

Before she could ask a question, Bingham broke the silence. "There's more, Mrs. Russell. Something else I have to tell you."

Melanie pulled her head from her hands and stood. Her knees felt weak, and Bingham's office walls seemed to be moving in on her. The small diploma behind his desk appeared to be growing larger.

She closed her eyes tightly. When she opened them, she looked directly at the doctor.

"I'm not sure how to say this, so I'm just going to say it," Bingham said. "Your hymen is intact."

Melanie continued to stare at the doctor. Blankness covered her face.

"The hymen is the membrane that covers your—"

"I know what it is," Melanie said slowly, her face void of expression.

"Yes, I'm sure you do. Then you must also know that it's impossible for a woman who is pregnant to have that membrane still intact. The hymen is broken during one's first encounter with intercourse. Sometimes the membrane is broken in other ways, especially in young girls."

Bingham waited for a response. Or at least some acknowledgment that his patient was listening. There was no recognition in Melanie's eyes. After a brief moment, he continued. "As I said, I'm not an expert, but I've examined a number of expectant mothers in this office. I've been a doctor for almost twenty-three years, and I've never seen anything like this. And I'll be damned if I've ever heard of a hymen growing back. But membrane or not, you're pregnant."

Melanie looked away from Bingham and refocused on the wall behind him. It continued to push in on her, and the heat from the incandescent lights in the ceiling was growing more intense. She felt sick to her stomach and reached down for the arms of the chair located directly behind her. The room was slowly starting to go dark.

Bingham lunged forward and caught Melanie before she hit the floor. She dangled lifelessly in his grasp.

"Nurse Potts!" Bingham shouted. "Get in here. Now, Carol. Hurry!"

CHAPTER 4

May 25, 2000

Melanie inhaled deeply and drew in the sweet aroma of fresh lilacs. Her eyes opened slowly, and she gazed straight ahead—through the rose colored glass on her favorite bathroom window and beyond to the deep blue, darkening sky outside.

She lifted her head gently off the bath pillow at the back of the tub and shifted her body slightly beneath the warm, soapy water that covered all but her head and shoulders.

The hot bath and fragrance created by lilac oil beads had combined to put her to sleep. Almost.

Too much had happened during the past twenty-four hours. There had been no sleep. *And I'm not sure*, Melanie wondered, *if I'll every sleep again.*

Groggily, she pushed her feet against the front end of the deep tub and slid her torso out of the water. A clean, white towel, wrapped efficiently around her head, kept her brown hair high and dry.

Despite every effort, her mind drifted back to yesterday—and Dr. Bingham's office—for the hundredth time.

It all seemed surreal, like something out of *The Twilight Zone.* Mostly though, it seemed like a really bad nightmare.

She had fainted in Dr. Bingham's office. In his arms, for God's sake! But at least he and Carol Potts had tended to her. Together they had carried her to an inexpensive vinyl-covered couch in the office.

One of them had placed a cold compress on her forehead, and within minutes, according to Potts, Melanie was awake.

As soon as she could, Melanie got to her feet. She thanked the nurse for her concern. She seems like a good person, Melanie thought, as she went to the desk to pick up her purse and jacket. Reluctantly, she also thanked Bingham, though her words lacked sincerity.

He had tried to get her to stay longer. "Let's make sure you're okay before you drive home," he said. Melanie said nothing. "Please, Mrs. Russell," Bingham added. "You seem upset."

Melanie bit her tongue. Hard. She fought the emotions building up in her again. *I can't afford to faint again*, she reasoned. She pulled on her jacket and turned to face Bingham.

"I am upset," she said. "And I don't think that's going to change in the next few minutes or hours or days. I'm pregnant. I don't know how or why. And according to you and your exam, I'm not only pregnant, but I'm apparently some kind of mutant freak. I'm thirty-five years old. I've had sex with my husband hundreds and hundreds of times. Yet you say my private parts resemble those of a virgin."

Melanie felt the room start to move again, so she paused and worked hard to slow her breathing.

"Look, I'm not a virgin. That's the one thing I'm sure of right now. If I am pregnant—and I believe you are right about that—then I've got to figure out how this happened. My husband and I will solve this puzzle together. Then we'll have our miracle baby and become the best parents God ever put on earth."

Melanie glared at Bingham for another moment or two, then opened her purse and pulled out her checkbook. She looked at the doctor. "Please, bill me now for this visit, the exam, tests, everything. I don't want any of this submitted to our insurance company. I need to pay you and get on my way. As soon as possible."

Melanie leaned forward in the tub and turned the hot water on. Her bath was beginning to cool, and she wasn't ready to get out yet. She was alone in the house and still had an hour or so before Jack arrived.

Poor Jack.

He was going to be a daddy, and he still didn't know it. Melanie was holding on to her secret. Holding on to all of them, really. The truth would come out. It had to. She wanted it to. But she needed more time to accept what was happening and to decide how to break the news to her husband.

Everything was moving so fast.

She had paid the bill at Bingham's and driven home. Twice she had pulled to the side of the road, sobbing uncontrollably, gripping the steering wheel tightly. When she finally arrived home there was a message on the machine from Jack. He was pulling a double shift in the ER and wouldn't be home until after midnight. An evening alone was just what Melanie needed to get her thoughts together.

By the time Jack unlocked the back door, climbed the stairs, and crawled wearily into bed beside her, Melanie had made some decisions. She turned in the spacious bed and leaned over to kiss him on the cheek.

"A long night?" she asked.

"Not too bad," he replied, wrapping his strong arms around her slender waist. "Not as bad as usual, anyway. I'm beginning to think violent crime is on the decline in Chicago."

He chuckled, then closed his eyes and started to drift away. Melanie relaxed a bit. She had hoped Jack would go right to sleep. He squeezed her gently again.

"I almost forgot," he said. "How was the last day of school? I bet you cried again, didn't you?"

Melanie was caught off guard by the question. Had this really been the last day of school for the Zettel twins and the other smiling children at Mercy Elementary? It felt like those goodbyes had occurred weeks ago instead of earlier in the day.

No wonder, Melanie thought. *My whole life has changed since I walked out of that building.*

"Everything went really well," she answered, as Jack's breathing fell into a familiar rhythm. "It was a good day, honey. No tears for me."

Jack slept deeply. Melanie didn't sleep at all. Her mind raced as she again focused on the decisions she'd reached on her own.

She'd decided against going to another doctor for a second opinion. Bingham might be a quack, but she was pregnant. She felt it now more than ever. She didn't need someone else to tell her that a baby was growing inside her.

And she didn't need a second opinion about the other part either. What was that talk about her hymen remaining intact? That was ridiculous. Maybe her vagina wasn't in textbook condition. Maybe every fold of skin wasn't exactly where it was supposed to be, but what difference did that make? It had nothing to do with the pregnancy, and the pregnancy was the key issue here.

No, she was going to pay a return visit to Dr. Jan Stewart. She was going to inform Jack's friend of the symptoms she'd been experiencing, just as she described them to Bingham. But she would not mention his diagnosis. She wouldn't mention him at all. To anyone. Ever. Instead she was going to let an expert, a respected physician, examine her and tell her what she already knew.

She was with child.

Then Melanie prayed Dr. Stewart would be able to explain to her—and more importantly, to Jack—how the pregnancy had occurred. Then, and only then, could the rejoicing begin. Melanie longed for that day. In fact, she thought about it throughout the night.

By the time Jack awakened, shortly after seven o'clock, Melanie had already called Doris.

"Doris, I'm not going to be able to make the meeting today. Please apologize to Mr. Nord for me, and tell him I'll get in tomorrow or the next day to catch up on everything I miss. Tell him that something urgent came up, and I'll fill him in on the details later."

Doris was worried. Melanie knew she would be.

"Is everything all right?" Doris asked. Then more directly, "What's wrong, Melanie?"

"Nothing, Doris, really. Nothing bad has happened. Something good, in fact. Something I want to talk to you about. If it's okay, I'll come over tonight and tell you about it. I need to talk to someone, or I'm going to bust."

The concern in Doris's voice remained. "Has Jack been transferred again? Is that it? Please don't tell me you're leaving town."

Melanie couldn't suppress a giggle. Doris was a true friend—one of a kind really. She had grown to love her mild-mannered, big-hearted colleague during their time together at Mercy. And she had leaned on her heavily at the time of her mother's passing. She could share things with Doris, about her mother, that only another woman could understand.

"I'm sorry, I don't mean to laugh, Doris. But you know I wouldn't be happy about leaving Chicago, about leaving you. This is our home now. You can't get rid of me that easy."

Doris laughed too. She sounded relieved. "Okay, I'll tell Big Al you couldn't grace us with your presence at the year-end meeting. But I can't believe you're doing this to me, making me wait to find out your news. You'd better be at the house early tonight. Right after dinner. Promise?"

"Promise," Melanie said. "I'll tell you what. I'll even help you do the dishes. So tell Reece and the kids to eat as much as they want. Aunt Melanie is on the way."

The two laughed again, then said their goodbyes.

It feels good to laugh, Melanie thought. *When this news is finally out, I'm going to laugh until my belly hurts*. It was a wonderful thought.

Jack and Melanie talked briefly over breakfast, then he headed back for the hospital. "I feel like that guy on the television show," Jack said as he donned a jacket, "you know, the doctor that works all the time."

"The ugly, bald one?" Melanie teased. "Or the brooding, handsome one all the nurses try to get in the sack?"

"I'm outta here," Jack said, walking toward his black Jeep Cherokee in the garage. "I'll call you later."

Melanie had tried to sleep during the afternoon, but sleep wouldn't come. She kept thinking about the baby. And despite the apprehension she felt about everything else, she was beginning to be elated about this unexpected turn of events.

The more she thought about becoming a mother, the more excited she became. Her mind raced with images, and her heart fluttered with emotion. Finally, in an attempt to relax and calm her nerves, she'd drawn the hot bath.

"I better get out now," Melanie said aloud, looking at her shriveled fingers and toes. "I'm starting to look like a prune." She smiled at the absurdity of talking to herself, thought again about the baby, and let her hands drop to her body.

She traced the contours of her breasts with her fingers. Maybe it was her imagination, but they did seem fuller, slightly larger than normal. Melanie moved her hands lower, down to her abdomen, and spread her fingers across her stomach. It was taut and flat.

Not for long, she thought, imagining her belly swollen three, four times its normal size. It made her back hurt just thinking about it. Yet the image brought another smile.

"Enough, already," Melanie said again, her voice sounding silly in the empty bathroom. "Get out. Jack will be home soon, and Doris is expecting me."

* * *

Reece McKenzie pulled open the door. The edges of his thick mustache moved closer to his nose as he grinned broadly and stepped out to greet Melanie. "Welcome, stranger," he said, gripping Melanie in a warm bear hug. His embrace reflected the strength of an urban fire fighter. After fifteen years on the job, he was still one of Chicago's finest.

Melanie's feet were barely touching the welcome mat on the back porch. "Put me down, you big ox. You're gonna break my ribs."

Reece laughed heartily and released the visitor gently to the concrete. "Gosh, it's good to see you, Melanie. It's been months since you and Jack have been by. How's Doc doing?"

Having pulled Melanie into the house, Reece shut the door and automatically locked it behind her.

"He's great, as always," Melanie said, looking around the kitchen for Doris and the children she had grown to love so much. "He wanted to come over too, but he's been pulling a lot of extra duty this week, so I told him to stay home and rest. Besides, if you guys got together and start talking about the current state of emergency services, we'd be here all night."

Reece laughed again. "Yeah, I guess you're right about that. Let me go get Doris. I think she's giving one of the boys a bath."

As she waited Melanie walked around the room. The day's last sunlight cast long shadows through the window. The sink, completely void of dishes, had been cleaned and shined. So had the stove and table. Melanie smiled as she stood in front of the side-by-side refrigerator. Three young handsome blond boys smiled back at her from a photograph held to the door by a magnet.

"The Three Stooges." That's how Reece affectionately referred to his sons.

Future heartbreakers, that's what they are, Melanie thought as she studied the photo closely. This picture was about six months old, she guessed.

Jacob, the oldest, was seven now, and she'd proudly served as his kindergarten teacher two years ago at Doris's request. "We're too much alike," Doris said at the time. "Both of us will do better if you take him this year."

It had been a wonderful experience for Melanie. Jacob was very intelligent, worked hard, and had a warm, caring personality. "The apple doesn't fall far from the tree," she told Doris, just two days after school opened. "Except he's much better looking than his mother."

Joshua, now four, was next in line. He was a typical second child. Quiet, more reserved, but almost breathtakingly beautiful with crystal blue eyes, curly hair, and porcelain skin. Melanie looked forward to teaching him next year.

Jordan, almost two, was the last of the litter. The name was an interesting part of his story. Doris would have friends and family believe Jordan, like his two brothers, had been named after strong, proud, biblical figures. Since both she and Reece hailed from large Irish Catholic families, the story contained some truth.

But it was also true she gave birth to her youngest son in July 1998, the same week the Chicago Bulls captured their sixth and final NBA championship. The team, as always, was led by the icon known as Michael Jordan.

"My baby doll is not named after a basketball player," Doris insisted whenever the subject came up. But it was difficult for her to suppress a grin. "That's my story, and I'm sticking to it."

Also on the refrigerator was a small prayer card, complete with a picture of the pope and a list of emergency telephone numbers. A computer-generated calendar containing important family dates was taped to the upper corner of the appliance. May 24, yesterday, was circled and marked as the last day of school. "Hooray!" was penciled across the entire block.

"Well now, you must be hungry, judging from the way you're staring at my refrigerator." Doris erupted into laughter as she entered the kitchen from the front part of the house. The sleeves of her wet sweatshirt, emblazoned with DePaul University across the front, were pushed to her elbows. Her long blonde hair was pulled back in a ponytail, and the sweatpants she had on were soggy at both knees.

"Josh and I have been having our regular battle of the bath. I try to wash some of the grime off him. He tries to swim from one end of the tub to the other, underwater. Thank God Reece has him now. I think Josh realizes the battle is over."

The friends laughed together.

"Really, can I get you something?" Doris asked. "I had Reece bring home some Chinese. The boys ate like birds, so there's plenty left."

Melanie shook her head, then feigned disappointment. "Awe, no dishes. I had my heart set on it."

"No way," Doris said, pulling out one of the five chairs surrounding the table and settling in. "I wanted to get straight to your news. Come sit. Reece and the boys know the kitchen is off limits for the next hour or so."

Melanie obeyed. Suddenly, she was a bit nervous. Doris knew about the frustrations she and Jack had faced while trying to conceive a child. Melanie had shared all the details with her following the many visits to Dr. Stewart's office. Yet here she was, in the home of her best friend, about to tell her that somehow, contrary to all medical know-how, she was pregnant.

She was confident Doris would stand by her, no matter how complicated the situation surrounding her pregnancy became. But she wanted Doris to understand and believe her, right away, with no hesitation. She needed confirmation desperately. So she looked at her friend. And she told most of the story.

Melanie was breathless, almost exhausted, as she finished spilling the news. It had taken almost thirty minutes, although both women had lost all track of time. The words had come pouring out. One friend talking, the other listening. Now came the moment of truth. Melanie lowered her eyes and gazed at the plaid place mat in front of her. The room was silent.

Suddenly Doris was up, reaching across the table and putting her arms around Melanie. "Congratulations!" she shrieked. "I knew it could happen. I just knew it."

Relief washed over Melanie and became a wave of pure joy. She reached out and embraced Doris, the two women stretched awkwardly across the table, jumping up and down as each straddled a chair.

"Melanie, you don't know how I've prayed for this, prayed for so long." Tears flowed down her face. "It broke my heart to watch you and Jack...to see the pain you both were going through. And now this. It's a miracle."

Doris walked around the table and pulled her friend into an emotional embrace. Tears flowed freely from both women now.

"What a wonderful mother you will make. And Jack, he'll be such a proud papa. I'll bet he's thrilled to death."

Melanie tensed. She pulled back from Doris and returned to her chair. She wiped away the tears of happiness and drew in a long, deep breath. "You better sit down," she said. "I have more to tell you." This time Melanie included every detail. She told of the visit to Bingham's office. She mentioned briefly his strange report concerning her condition, including the creep's dirty little looks. And finally, she revealed the most troubling part of all.

"Jack doesn't know yet. You're the first person I've told."

Doris' eyes widened slightly. Her lips parted as if to say something, but she didn't. Instead, she waited for Melanie.

"I'm a little nervous about all of this. He's a doctor, and in his mind, this will seem impossible. I'm not sure how to explain it to Jack."

Doris stood again and walked to her friend. "You don't have to. Make your appointment with Dr. Stewart. That's a great idea. She'll see that you're pregnant, then let her explain it to Jack from one doctor to another. That's the best way. Then I can share the news with Reece and the boys. We can tell everyone at school, the hospital, at the fire station—everywhere. It'll be great. Everyone will be so happy for you two."

Melanie stood too, preparing to leave. Doris was wonderful. Her excitement, the way she accepted the news—without a single question or glimpse of skepticism—made Melanie love her more than ever. But despite the warmth her friend was spreading, Melanie's heart felt heavy. In addition to her child, she was also carrying a strange feeling of emptiness and guilt. She bit her lip as the pair walked to the back door.

"I hope you're right," she said. "I need for this secrecy to end, and I need Jack with me again. I miss sharing everything with him."

But as she kissed Doris goodbye and made her way to the car, she was overcome with anxiety. For the first time in her married life, Melanie felt alone.

* * *

Doris watched from the kitchen window as Melanie backed down the drive, toward the street in front of the house. Quietly she bowed her head and put her hands together. "Dear Lord, help my friend," she whispered. "Help Melanie and Jack. Please be with them and give them strength in their time of need. See them through the rocky days ahead. Their love is deep. Let them keep that love in their heart. Together, through your grace, they can make it."

Doris paused for a moment and turned to see if Reece or the boys had wandered within earshot. Then she closed her eyes again. "And please bless this child, Lord. My prayer is that you will protect and keep this baby safe and well. In your name, I pray. Amen."

Doris pulled a paper towel off the rack by the sink and dabbed her eyes. She was crying again, crying for Melanie and Jack. After a few minutes, she tossed the damp towel in the trash can and went to her own family.

CHAPTER 5

May 28, 2000

Dr. William Bingham was seated at a desk in the study of his home. It wasn't a study really, just a glorified den. But he liked to refer to it as a study. It made the small room sound important. Made him sound important.

The pictures were back. Hot off the press from the little photography center he frequently visited. The shop, located on West 24th Street between a strip joint and an ugly hole-in-the-wall liquor store, was a haven for those with unusual photographic needs. The good doctor certainly fit that description.

Scattered on the desk in front of him were grainy black-and-white photographs. The pictures, like hundreds of others kept in a file in the bottom drawer, were close-ups of a woman's pelvic region. They were not porn pictures, and they certainly weren't the type that might be considered sexy by normal people. But then, normal people didn't frequent the 24th Street photography shop.

The woman in the photos was lying on an examination table. Each foot was placed in a metal cuff, in stirrup-like fixtures raised above the table. A thin paper gown was pushed to the woman's waist. Two hands, covered with rubber gloves, were touching the pubic area, examining private details, gently exposing the most intimate flesh of another unsuspecting patient. Those same hands now used a pen to write the woman's name on the back of each photo.

Bingham smiled as he neatly printed the name—Melanie Russell. "Congratulations, Billy boy," he said to himself. "You've outdone yourself this time."

For many years, Bingham had practiced more than medicine in his small private office. He also practiced perversion, and he was good at it. No one, including his ex-wife, his estranged daughters, even Carol Potts, knew about his naughty little collection.

He smiled again. Neither the patients nor any of the nurses who had worked at his side were wise to his game. He was proud of that. Yes, the tiny high-tech camera, the one that looked like an intricate lapel pin on his lab coat, had cost a small fortune. The special high-speed film used in the camera was extremely expensive, and so too were the developing costs. Add to that the price of blowing up the small prints to a size suitable for viewing, and the investment was considerable.

That was why Bingham only took shots of a precious few—the really special ones, women like Melanie Russell.

He reached in the middle drawer and pulled out a magnifying glass. Hunched over he held the glass inches away from the photo of Melanie and inspected it closely. The translucent membrane just inside the vagina was barely visible.

Although it was not a classic sample of a female hymen, it was close enough—close enough for smut work, at least. After a moment, Bingham put both picture and glass down, then leaned back in the chair.

"Jackpot," he said with delight.

This photo would be more than just another nice addition to my collection, he thought. This one would be worth some money to someone, maybe even the tabloids. He could see the cover story now: VIRGIN BIRTH! MIRACLE BABY! Maybe even MODERN-DAY MARY!

"Yes, ladies and gentlemen," he said, standing and dancing around the empty room. "Billy boy's ship has come in."

CHAPTER 6

June 2, 2000

The raspy voice of Bob Seeger drifted from the four speakers inside the Jeep Cherokee. As usual, Jack had the vehicle's stereo tuned to WEZR Easy Rock 106.5. While driving with his left hand, he held the right one, clenched in a tight fist, inches from his mouth. It was his microphone.

In a monotone, flat voice, Jack joined in with the legendary rocker, singing backup to the classic tune, "Night Moves."

"I woke last night to the sound of thunder. How far off I sat and wondered…"

Melanie, sitting in the bucket seat next to her husband's, laughed. She couldn't help herself. No matter how many times he did it—and Jack did it a lot—his corny lip syncing efforts always made her laugh. It wasn't just his bad voice. It was the facial expressions and the body language. Right now, for instance, he had his head tilted back, flipping it from side to side, as if he too had Seeger's shoulder-length hair.

Finally, mercifully, the song ended and was followed by a commercial break.

Jack leaned forward and turned the radio down. "I'm glad we didn't have to wait too long to get your appointment," he said, reaching over and taking Melanie's hand. "Jan's great about that. It was really nice of her to work us in."

Melanie squeezed his hand and nodded.

"We've been through a lot with her, but she's really made things easier for us, don't you think?" he asked. "Even though she's a friend and colleague, she's been very professional about everything. And she's an excellent doctor.

"I'm glad you wanted to see her this time too. I'm sure some of your symptoms are related to stress…you know, the emotional difficulties and grief we faced when trying to have a baby. And you're still recovering from your mom's death too. That's not something people get over easily, Melanie. I'll bet that's why you feel tired and still have some nausea."

Melanie looked out the passenger side window. Traffic was heavy this morning. The Jeep crawled along in the middle of the three-lane highway.

"I'll guess we'll know soon enough," she said, still looking out the window. "At least I feel comfortable with Dr. Stewart. You can't say that about every doctor."

"Hey, wait a minute," Jack protested, mock anger in his voice. "Don't beat up on my profession like that. Have you ever met a doctor you didn't like? And unless I'm mistaken, didn't you marry one?"

Melanie tried to smile. She didn't quite make it. "I don't think they're all like you, honey. And even though I like Dr. Stewart, I'll be glad when this is over."

Another classic tune was coming over the radio. Jack pumped up the volume and got his microphone ready. "Get ready, little lady," he said, using his announcer voice. "It's time to get down with Otis Redding."

* * *

Dr. Stewart walked into the office, smiled warmly, and greeted both Jack and Melanie with a hug. She had known Jack for years, going back to a residency the two shared at a small hospital in Bloomington, Indiana. Though they had worked closely together through one full rotation and had partied occasionally on the weekends, their relationship had never strayed beyond the professional level. Jack liked Jan Stewart, respected her intelligence and work ethic, but he'd never been attracted to her. Stewart, in turn, had neither the time nor inclination to interrupt her career with something as foolhardy as romance. Still didn't, for that matter.

Although her history with Melanie was much shorter and less defined, she'd made it a point to develop a professional relationship with her as well. She did with all the patients, but this was special. Jack was not only a friend but a colleague.

She viewed her work with Jack and Melanie as a professional courtesy. As a result, she was going the extra mile with the couple's infertility woes. In fact, that was why she had agreed to see Melanie again. Any problems she was having undoubtedly stemmed from grief. Grief was common when potential parents learned they couldn't have children. It was to be expected really. Symptoms typically included lack of energy, headaches, irritability, insomnia, and even guilt and feelings of inadequacy.

That was why Dr. Stewart didn't expect this session to last long. In fact, she had an ultrasound scheduled in forty-five minutes. *I could have made this diagnosis over the phone*, Stewart thought, even as she greeted Jack and Melanie. *But it's better to handle things this way. Counseling wounded couples is most effective when done in person.*

"All right then, Melanie. Jack tells me you're experiencing some medical problems," Dr. Stewart said as she opened a file folder on her desk. "Could you please describe your symptoms to me?"

Seated on the edge of the chair, Melanie looked at her husband. Jack nodded. "Go ahead, honey. Tell her what's the matter."

Melanie didn't like the tone she detected in Jack's voice. It had the sound of one of those game show contestants who already knew the answer to the final question. Dr. Stewart's voice had the same sound. Annoyed, Melanie made a quick decision. *Why wait?* she thought. *Let's just drop the bomb now.*

"I think I'm pregnant."

Melanie was looking at Dr. Stewart when she said it. The doctor, calling upon her professional training, hid her surprise well. This was not the answer she had expected, but when it came to medicine and dealing with patients, few things shocked her anymore. She simply looked to Jack for his reaction.

Melanie also shifted her gaze to meet that of her husband's. In his face, both women saw bewilderment.

"What are you talking about, Melanie? You know you aren't pregnant. You know that I…we can't make babies. Why on earth do you think you're pregnant?"

Dr. Stewart was back in control. "It's probably a phantom pregnancy. It's very unusual, but I have heard of cases before." She paused to gather her thoughts. Both Jack and Melanie sat in silence. "It's a natural instinct for most women to want to reproduce. Obviously, it's a shock when some find out they can't. And it doesn't really matter if the problem is with the woman or her husband. They still feel the need to create offspring. In some cases, it is incredibly strong. It is very rare, but in a few, isolated cases, I've heard of women developing a phantom, or false, pregnancy. They experience many of the symptoms, including morning sickness, fullness of the breasts, abrupt weight gain. Some women even stop having their period for a time.

"It is similar to a person who has lost a limb in an accident or had to undergo amputation. There have been many reports of patients complaining of pain in an arm or leg that is no longer there. No one knows for sure why this occurs. My answer is that the mind is an incredible thing, something that can leave emotional scars long after physical ones have healed." Dr. Stewart looked at Melanie. "I'm sorry, but I believe the symptoms you are experiencing are psychological rather than physical. And in all honesty, that's a field I know very little about."

Jack reached for his wife and put his hand lightly on her shoulder. "It's okay, Melanie. I know someone at the hospital. His name is Kevin Bickett. He has a good reputation. I'll talk to him and explain our situation. I'm sure he'll be willing to help us."

Melanie didn't speak for several moments. Instead, her mind raced back to Dr. Bingham, his diagnosis of her pregnancy, and the results of her exam.

Maybe I should tell them everything, she thought. *That would be the easiest way to sink the ship Dr. Stewart had christened and set sail… the* USS Phantom Pregnancy. *But no, there was a better way.*

"May I ask you a favor then before we go?" Melanie asked.

"Certainly. I'll do anything I can to help you and Jack."

"Examine me. Examine me, and tell me I'm not pregnant. Then we'll go."

Jack started to protest, but Dr. Stewart raised her hand, politely but effectively blocking his words.

"That's not a problem. In fact, I'm glad to do it. Let's go to an exam room, and, Jack, please come with us. You should be part of this too. And you can tell us more about Dr. Bickett while we're waiting on results from the blood test."

* * *

This time, there was no music in the Jeep. Only silence and the low hum of the air conditioner as Jack and Melanie made their way home from Dr. Stewart's office. Jack sat stiffly behind the wheel, looking straight ahead as he negotiated heavy traffic and drove past Grant Park. Melanie gazed out her window without noticing the famous landmark's majestic beauty. Her mind was elsewhere, replaying the series of events in Dr. Stewart's office.

The examination had gone according to plan. Everything else was in free fall. After they'd returned to Stewart's office, the three sat quietly for some time.

Confusion and disbelief had infiltrated the organized world of the two doctors. Melanie understood, even sympathized with them. She'd been dealing with confusion and disbelief for more than a week now.

Jack sat silently, keeping his thoughts to himself. Melanie fidgeted nervously in her seat. She felt better now that the secret was out. There was a certain sense of relief associated with the confirmation of her pregnancy, but anxiety remained. In fact, her concern was escalating. Both she and Jack were game show contestants now. And neither had the answer to the final question. How? How could she be pregnant?

They looked to Stewart for an answer. Melanie prayed it would be one Jack could understand. Yet even as she hoped for the best, she feared the worst. It was a fear shared by their doctor. As she prepared to address the desperate couple, she realized her answer would cause an old friend much pain.

"Let me begin with an apology. I'm sorry, Melanie. Sorry I gave you and Jack that speech about a possible false pregnancy. I rushed to judgment without giving you the benefit of the doubt and, more importantly, before I'd administered any tests to determine your condition. That was very unprofessional on my part."

Melanie nodded absently. At this point, she cared little about mistakes in procedure. Jack stared blankly ahead, his face void of any expression.

Stewart inhaled deeply. *Quit stalling*, she thought. *And get on with it.*

"Melanie. Jack. I find this very difficult to say. But as your doctor, it is my oath to tell you the truth about your condition, including how this pregnancy came to be. And it is my professional opinion that Jack is not the biological father of this baby."

Stewart could feel the red blotches spreading in jagged-shaped patterns on the skin around her neck. Since childhood, these irritations appeared whenever she was embarrassed or under stress. And right now she was experiencing those emotions and, more, including a deep feeling of sadness.

Neither Jack nor Melanie noticed the blotches. He was looking at the floor. Melanie was looking at her husband as tears streamed down her face and dropped silently onto her blouse.

Stewart shifted her attention to Jack. Her assessment was based on scientific evidence, nothing else. It was important to her that he understood that.

"About 13 percent of men suffer from untreatable sterility. Of those, most have no sperm in their semen because the tubules in the testes that produce sperm either do not develop or have been irreversibly damaged. You have no sperm in your semen. Because of that, it is medically impossible for you to produce a child." The doctor hesitated, then plunged ahead. "You are not the biological father of this baby."

Jack stood and walked to the farthest corner of the room, away from his wife. Melanie sobbed, her breaths coming in jerky, painful spurts. She tried to stand, to speak, but couldn't.

"I'm sorry," Stewart said. "I wish there was another explanation I could offer, a better way to tell you, but…I realize how difficult this must be."

The office was silent for several minutes. Stewart remained seated behind her desk. Jack walked in small circles near the back of the room, his head down, hands in his pockets. Slowly, Melanie regained control of her emotions. She stood and moved closer to her husband. In her mind, she searched for words to ease his pain and prayed that he could somehow see the truth.

"Jack, listen to me. I know what you must be thinking. You think I've betrayed you. But I haven't, Jack. I swear to you, I've never been with another man, not ever. I love you too much, Jack. And I love you too much to lie to you. I know it's impossible to explain, but this is not another man's baby. It's our baby."

Jack tried to respond, but the words wouldn't come. He looked at his wife, and his heart told him to go to her. He wanted to take Melanie in his arms, pull her close, and tell her he believed in her. But doubt pierced his thought process, numbing his mind and preventing him from moving.

With great effort he, looked at Stewart. "Are you absolutely sure I'm not the father?" he asked in a pleading voice.

"I'm certain. Biologically, it's impossible. If it were possible, even remotely, I'd certainly tell you. I wish there was something else I could say."

Jack looked at Melanie with sorrow in his eyes. He lifted his arms, palms toward the ceiling, in a gesture of helplessness. When he finally spoke, his voice was thin, cracking with emotion. "What can I do, Melanie? What do you want me to say? I'm trying to hold on, but I don't know how."

Melanie felt as if she were sliding down a long dark tunnel. She was fighting to slow the descent, but the sides of the tunnel were smooth, with nothing to grab onto. As she struggled to hold her marriage—and her life—together, she groped frantically in the blackness. Finally, her fingers touched something. After many years, it was still there. It was her faith.

"Do you believe in miracles? Either one of you?" she asked. "As doctors, have you ever seen something happen, a patient recover, that you couldn't explain? Couldn't that be considered a miracle?"

Jack didn't answer. He didn't know what to say. The question was left for Stewart.

"I'm the wrong person to answer that kind of question. I'm afraid I don't believe in a supreme being. I don't believe in God," she said. "I wish I did. People find comfort in their religion, in the struggle between good and evil. I respect that in others. But I've always been a believer in science. I'm a student of medicine, and even though I've seen things occur that could not be explained by either science or medicine, I believe an answer does exist. It's just that we haven't progressed to the point where we can answer all things. Some choose to call those events a miracle. I'm afraid I don't."

The couple remained in the office for several more minutes. Neither said a word. Stewart talked about the pregnancy and told Melanie to come back in thirty days for an ultrasound and complete workup. She also made mention of the thin membrane near Melanie's vagina and asked if it ever caused her pain during intercourse. Melanie shook head absently, and the question was followed by an awkward silence. The blotches on the doctor's neck grew larger while Jack continued his circular path, his face pale and troubled. There had been little more to say.

Melanie's thoughts returned to the present. The Jeep was turning in the driveway, and Jack parked it in the garage. They were home. Not a word had been spoken since they left Stewart's office. Not a word would be spoken the rest of the night.

* * *

For three days, Melanie approached Jack, trying to get him to talk about the pregnancy, about their marriage. He would have none of it. "I know this isn't going away," he said when fending off yet another attempt to break the silence. "But I need more time."

He was hurt. Deeply. Melanie understood his pain, yet his refusal to talk worried her. As the days and nights passed with no communication, Melanie sensed his pain turning to anger. And that troubled her more.

On the third night, sleeping alone in her bed, Melanie had the dream. It was a dream of redemption and revelation, and it was a dream that would change her life—and the direction of her family, forever.

CHAPTER 7

June 6, 2000

Melanie woke with start. At least it seemed like she was awake. She rolled over to reach for Jack and instead found her mother sitting on the side of the bed. Martha Wade looked much younger than her daughter remembered.

She looks a lot like me, Melanie thought.

"Hello, Mother," she said. "What are you doing here?"

Martha laughed. It was a wonderful, warm laugh, free of pain and confusion. It had been many years since Melanie had heard such sound come from her mother.

"It's time we talked, dear. Past time, really. You've carried this burden by yourself long enough. We felt it was time you had some help."

Melanie sat up in bed and rubbed her eyes. She looked at the digital clock on the bedside table. It read 3:16 a.m. "We?" she asked weakly, straining to see in the dark as she looked around the room.

A large figure walked, almost glided, to the foot of her bed. "It's me, sweetie. It's Daddy."

Melanie gasped and lunged from the bed. She threw her arms around James Wade's neck and squeezed mightily. "Oh, Daddy," she cried as he lifted her off the floor. "I've missed you so much. You've been gone so long."

The man held his daughter for several minutes, then reluctantly put her down. He took one hand, his wife the other, and together they led Melanie back to the edge of the bed.

"There's much we have to tell you," Martha said. "And much you need to understand."

Melanie shook her head, trying to wake up. She knew this was a dream, but it all seemed so real. She'd felt as light as a feather in her father's arms, just as she had when she was small, when she'd go running to him as he entered the house each night. But it was a sweet dream, the most wonderful dream of her life.

Why fight it? she asked herself. So she sat quietly on the bed and listened as her parents told her great stories.

They told Melanie of heaven and God and of his great glory. They told her of angels and saints and of the true believers, all of whom had their place in God's kingdom. Both spoke of peace and joy and a place where pain and suffering were no more. They were wonderful stories, and Melanie felt safe and warm as she listened to her mom and dad.

I wish Jack were here, she thought. *He believes in God. He would love to hear these things. And Doris. Doris has a deep faith, an honest faith in God and his wondrous deeds. How thrilled she would be to hear these stories.*

But now the stories were changing. Martha's face was less joyous, and her dad's voice took an ominous tone.

"There is another place, sweetie," James said, "a place without light or hope or glory of any kind. It is a dark place with dark forces. The leader of this place sends out his armies, and they come not in hundreds or thousands, but tens of thousands. They are many, and they are evil."

Melanie shivered. The sweetness of her dream was gone. It was turning ugly, and she was afraid, more afraid than she could ever remember being in the light of day. Martha kneeled at her daughter's feet and took her hands. James stopped for a moment and put his arm around Melanie's shoulders.

They seem so sad now, Melanie thought. *Do they feel sorry for me?*

James spoke again. "The dark forces are strong. They have made horrific gains on earth during the past thousand years, and they will continue to strike with every effort to bring an end to the world."

Silence filled the room for several minutes. Melanie glanced at the clock again, but the neon red numbers had not moved. The time was still 3:16.

That's odd, Melanie thought. *This is certainly a strange dream.*

Now Martha was talking to her only daughter. As she spoke, she wept. "It is now the beginning of another thousand years. It is time to discover the condition of the human race. Should the world continue as we have known it, or is it time to bring about the end so that it can begin anew?"

Melanie pulled back from her mother. "Are you asking me, Mother? Why are you asking me?"

Martha smiled. "No, dear. These are not questions for you. They are questions only one can answer. That's why God is sending his messenger again. He is sending his Son."

"Is he coming to save the world again?" Melanie asked. "Is he coming as the redeemer?"

Martha hesitated, looking at James.

Finally, he spoke. "It will be different this time. God's Son is coming for a different purpose. He is coming to evaluate the world. He will come for a time to live among the masses, then he will return to the right hand of the Father. Upon his return, the decision will be made. God will decide if hope exists, if the good still outnumber the evil. If there is hope, the world will continue for another thousand years."

Melanie was beginning to understand. Suddenly, her heart was racing. Her nightgown was damp with sweat. She was engulfed in fear.

"When will the Son come?" she asked. "How is he to come?"

Martha stood, reached to Melanie, and pulled her to her feet. Together they walked to the window and looked outside. The moon was full, high, and bright in the dark sky. Off in the distance, the tall buildings of downtown Chicago towered like soldiers in the night.

"You know, don't you, Melanie? You know how he is coming. He is coming to you, to you and Jack. He is to be your son during his time on earth. You have been chosen."

Melanie started to weep. Terrified, she touched her stomach as a wave of anguish washed over her. Memories of the past year came flooding forth. She remembered the Salvation Army Santa at Christmas and her mother's strange words before her death in the nursing home. Had those events been dreams too? Was she dreaming everything or nothing?

Maybe I've gone insane, she thought.

"Why me, Mother? Why am I to be the one?"

"The reason is as simple as it is certain. Before, when the Son came to save the world, the caretaker was also chosen carefully. She was a virgin, pure of heart and soul and body. She possessed great strength and holy character. These traits were necessary because of the tremendous responsibility placed upon her and because of the pain and suffering she had to endure when her Son was tortured and put to death. You have been chosen for similar yet different reasons. The world has changed dramatically in two thousand years. It has grown full of nonbelievers. Ridicule, doubt, hate, prejudice, fear, and loathing rule the day now. Because of that, the new caretaker will face obstacles more difficult than ever before.

"You have been chosen for a reason, Melanie. It is because of your great inner strength. You have always had the resolve to do the right thing, against all odds. You are kind and sincere in your feelings for others, yet you are fierce and protective of those unable to fend for themselves. In many ways, you are a warrior. And this time, a warrior is needed."

Martha led her daughter back to bed. As she crawled in, her father covered her with the sheet and blanket, tucking her in as he had many years before. He beamed at Melanie with great pride.

"I know you're afraid," he said. "You feel as if the weight of the world has been placed on your shoulders. And I know you feel alone." He sat next to Melanie and stroked her soft hair. "Remember when you were in junior high school and your friend Penny got sick?"

Melanie remembered. Penny had died of leukemia at thirteen. She fought long and hard against the disease, but in the end, it was not enough. Melanie was devastated, hurt, angry, and bitter all at the same time. She cried for hours in the arms of her father following the funeral.

"Remember what I told you then?" he asked. "I told you God would not place more on you than you could handle. I told you that with time, the pain would ease, you would recover, and life would go on. I was right, wasn't I?"

"Yes, Daddy. You were right."

"Then listen to me, Melanie. He places this burden on you now because you are the right one. You are the one he needs, the one we all need. You will prevail in this journey. It will be difficult, but you will prevail."

Melanie was growing restless. She was tired of the dream. It had been wonderful to see her parents again, so young and healthy in appearance. But she wanted it to end. She wanted to awaken, and she longed for Jack to shake her and tell her the dream was over.

Instead, her father spoke again. "You are not alone in this journey. There are many here to help you. Help will come to you in many different forms, and they will protect you and the son against all evil. Take comfort in that."

"What about Jack?" Melanie asked. "Will he be with me too?"

There was no answer.

"Will he be with me?" Melanie screamed. "I can't do it without him. Will he be with me?"

Melanie opened her eyes. She was in the middle of the bed, kneeling, with her hands clinched in tight fists. Her hair was matted, and her nightgown was soaking wet. Shaking, she was exhausted. Sunlight filtered through the window, revealing an empty room. Dawn had arrived.

She fell forward on the bed, face first into the blankets. Muffled sobs came from deep inside her.

"Please, God, no," she said, whimpering helplessly. "I can't do this. I can't do it alone."

CHAPTER 8

June 12, 2000

Almost a week had passed since Melanie's bizarre dream, yet details of the conversation she shared with her dead parents remained vivid. The images of her mom and dad coming to her in the middle of the night were crystal clear, and she recalled not only their words of prophecy but also their concern for the burden she now carried.

She had been unsuccessful in her efforts to dismiss the vision as just another nightmare, and with each passing day, she realized the significance of the visit.

More importantly, she recognized the truth. Something inside her kept rising to the surface, reinforcing what she already knew, making real what was once inconceivable. The baby inside her was the Son of God. He was coming again—this time, not to save the world but to judge the condition of the human race.

How or why was no longer important to Melanie. She had been chosen. This time, she was to be the mother, the caretaker, and the enormousness of the task was overwhelming her.

Melanie had wandered around the house in a stupor. Jack was gone most of the time, and when he was home, he avoided her as much as possible. Doris called three or four times a day, leaving messages on the answering machine. None of the calls had been returned. Bit by bit, Melanie was fading away. Not only was she losing hope, she was losing the will to live. No longer able to deny the truth about what was happening to her, Melanie's survival instincts, once so keen, were vanishing rapidly.

Some warrior I am, Melanie thought as she lay on the couch, staring blankly at the television. Alone in the house again, depression clouded her mind. She felt warm and safe on the couch and closed her eyes. Within minutes, she was asleep.

She was awakened by the doorbell. She could hear it ringing again and again, but it carried a distant, faraway sound. Melanie pulled the afghan tighter around her shoulders and closed her eyes. The numbing effect of sleep was creeping back over her when she felt a hand on her shoulder, followed by a quick, hard shake.

"Get up, Melanie. Enough is enough. Get off that couch and talk to me."

Melanie recognized both the voice and the tone. She'd heard it many times in the classroom next to hers, particularly when a young student had crossed the line at Mercy Elementary.

"Hello, Doris," she said, without opening her eyes. "Why don't you come on in? Make yourself at home? Wake me up and yell at me? That's just what I need right now."

Melanie felt a pair of hands grab the afghan just below each shoulder. She opened her eyes as Doris pulled her from the couch. The face of her friend was flushed, and her eyes flashed anger. Melanie had never seen her this upset.

"Maybe it is what you need," Doris shouted. "Maybe a swift kick is just what the doctor ordered. If that's what I need to do to get your attention, then I'll do it, Melanie. So help me, I'll do it."

Melanie burst into laughter—hysterical laughter. The sight of Doris, standing in her living room, eyes bulging and voice shaking with anger, was a rare image. Despite her depression, Melanie was enjoying it. For the first time in many days, she felt a little like her old self again.

Doris was still upset, but her anger was subsiding. In truth, she had been relieved to find her friend alive and well. The laughter was an unexpected bonus. Doris finally interrupted.

"Now that I know you're okay, I feel like killing you," she said, smiling at the absurdity of her words. "You scared me to death, Melanie. You really did. I've been worried sick about you."

The laughing ended, and a somber shadow returned to Melanie's face. "I'm scared too. And I don't know what to do."

"Just talk to me. I can't help if you don't tell me what's going on."

For the next several hours, the friends talked. Melanie told her everything in great detail. She even told Doris about the dream and what she had come to believe. As she said the words out loud for the first time, she realized how ridiculous it all sounded.

The feeling of complete helplessness returned, and she was growing sleepy again. Because she wanted Doris to leave, she concluded her tale of woe with a blunt, harsh conclusion.

"So not only has my husband disowned me, but I'm pregnant with the Son of God. And even if I survive this, he might determine the world as we know it should end, and all this pain and suffering will have been for nothing. So excuse me if I don't return every call or watch today's exciting episode of *Days of Our Lives*. It's just that I've got a few things on my mind, that's all."

Melanie looked at Doris for her reaction. What she saw in her friend's face surprised her. It wasn't shock or anger or even disbelief. It was sympathy, and her eyes brimmed with tears when she finally spoke.

"There's a reason why I've been so frantic to reach you," Doris said. "Something has happened to me too. Three nights ago, I had a dream, and in this dream, I was in heaven, talking with a beautiful angel. The angel told me what was happening to you, even told me about the baby. She asked me if I could help."

Melanie was no longer drowsy. Her heart raced with fear and anxiety and something else. For the first time in many days, another emotion was taking bloom inside her. Hope.

"Could this be true?" Melanie asked. "Do you think it could really be happening to me?"

Tears were no longer pooled in Doris's eyes. They were streaming down her face as she reached out and clutched Melanie's shoulders. This time the grip was tender.

"Before my dream ended, the angel told me her name. It was Katherine. She told me to remember her name, then she disappeared. A few seconds later, I woke up."

Doris paused to compose herself. "I climbed out of bed and went to the bathroom, and Reece was standing there, looking in the mirror. He had a strange look on his face. Before I could say a word, he told me about a dream he'd had. Melanie, he'd had the same dream."

Doris was trembling now. Melanie held her, trying to comfort her friend. "I asked Reece if the angel had told him her name. He nodded weakly, then whispered her name to me." Melanie and Doris locked eyes, then Doris spoke the name. "It was Katherine."

* * *

The two women were seated at a large oak table in one of the huge research rooms located on the second floor of the Chicago Public Library. Books, reference manuals, and a telephone directory were scattered on the table before them. A black tattered Bible also rested on the table. It was turned to page 4288, the book of Revelation. It was seven-thirty. Melanie and Doris had been researching in the library for more than six hours.

Having found strength in each other and a message in their dreams, the two decided on a course of action while at the house. Melanie showered, changed clothes, and came downstairs to find Doris in the kitchen, waiting with a bowl of soup and a chicken sandwich. Melanie was much too nervous to eat, but Doris insisted.

"That's a real baby inside you," she said, pouring a glass of milk. "He needs nourishment, and so do you."

After eating, Melanie had tried to reach Jack at the hospital. After a lengthy pause, Jeffrey, the unit coordinator at the ER desk, informed her that Dr. Russell was with a patient. Melanie hung up the phone, wrote a message, and left it on the kitchen table.

"I just hope he comes home tonight," she said sadly. "When he leaves the house each morning, I always have the feeling he's not coming back."

The words struck Doris hard. She'd never known two people more in love than Jack and Melanie. To see that love crumbling was painful. She could only imagine the pain and sorrow she and Jack must be experiencing. She walked behind Melanie as the two made their way to the car, and silently offered a quick prayer.

Bring Jack back to her, Doris asked. *Help her with this. Forgive me for my lack of humility, God, but is that asking too much?*

The trip to the library had been short, and the research was underway by one o'clock.

"I'm still not sure what we're looking for," Melanie said, closing one of the large books. "There's nothing in the Bible or anywhere else that talks about the Son of God being born again. When he comes again, it is to be in adult form, as he was when he died on the cross, and it will be the final sign of the apocalypse."

Doris nodded in agreement. "I know that's what the Catholic Church teaches, and most of the other religions too. But maybe something's changed. Maybe we're missing something. All the experts admit the book of Revelation is almost impossible to understand. One thing's for sure, we know the dreams were real. And we know the baby is real. Let's just keep looking."

At nine-fifty, a young man entered the room and told them the library was closing. He helped them put the books away. Doris had several pages of hand-scribbled notes on a yellow legal pad. She tore the pages off, folded them, and put the papers in her purse. They left together.

Outside, in the warm night air, Doris used her cell phone to call Reece. "Yes, we're okay," she said, smiling at Melanie. "She feels better knowing that if she's going crazy, at least she's not alone. We've been doing some research at the library. I'm going to drop her off and come straight home. I'll look in on the boys when I get there. Bye."

Doris drove in silence for a time, then started thinking aloud. "What we need is someone to help us. There has to be someone in the city of Chicago who knows more about this than we do."

Melanie felt like laughing, but was too tired. "No kidding. I could have told you that before we went to the library."

Doris continued to drive, her mind working feverishly. "I'll call the rectory tomorrow. I'm going to talk to Father Malone, hint around and see what he knows about the book of Revelation, the Second Coming. Maybe he'll know something that will help us or at least give us an idea of where to look for information. How does that sound?"

"It's better than anything I've got. I'm too tired to think."

They pulled into the driveway, and Doris gave Melanie a long, warm hug before letting her go. They'd both noticed the absence of the Jeep in the garage. "Hang in there, honey. Things will get better. Jack will come around. I just know he will."

Melanie nodded without much conviction. But the emptiness inside her was not as powerful as it had been at the beginning of the day. Thanks to her friend.

"It helps a lot to have you and Reece on my side. You've given me hope again, and that's enough for now. You'll never know how much your friendship means to me."

She closed the door quickly and walked to the house. She was crying again and didn't want Doris to see. She closed the door and locked it, then pushed a series of numbers to activate the security system.

The house was empty. She was alone. As she headed for the stairs, she placed her hand lovingly on her stomach. She stood silently in the darkness and, for the first time, thought of the life inside her. She thought of her son. And suddenly, she realized she was not alone.

CHAPTER 9

June 14, 2000

"Dr. Russell. Dr. Russell. Sorry to wake you, but you're needed in the ER. We've got a hot one on the way. Patient is critical. ETA is eight minutes. We're in trauma 2." Laura Underwood, a hospital intern, turned and left the doctors' lounge.

Jack, still lying on the sofa, rubbed his eyes and looked at his watch. It was 7:20 a.m. "Great," he said to himself. "Twenty minutes of sleep between shifts. That should hold me for another twelve hours."

He got up, stretched, grabbed his stethoscope, and followed Laura to the second of the hospital's four main emergency room areas. Three nurses were working feverishly around the trauma table in the center of the room, setting up supplies and preparing the crash cart and other equipment. Laura was in the adjoining washroom, sterilizing her hands. A fourth nurse helped her don a mask and rubber gloves.

Jack joined them. "Anybody else coming to the party?" he asked. He was already fully awake, his mind completely focused on the job ahead.

"Yes, Dr. Coen's coming," Laura said. "He always wants to be here when you take center stage. I think the old geezer has a thing for you."

Jack and the nurse laughed. "That's brave talk for an intern," he said. "Once you get to know him better, you'll appreciate what he brings to the table. Dr. Coen's seen it all and done most of it. I'm always glad to have his experience in the trauma room."

"Here they come," the nurse said, interrupting. "It looks like county EMS."

Jack's heart sank as the gurney, carrying the bloody body of a small boy, was pushed through the double doors. EMT Howard Crockett delivered the bullet, loaded with bad news, to the doctors.

"Eight-year-old boy, single gunshot wound to the neck. Pulse is 150 and thready. BP's 50 and palpable. We couldn't tube him, Doc. There's too much blood. He's about to code."

Jack and the nurses helped Crockett and another EMT lift the boy onto the trauma table. Jack, barking orders and exuding confidence, was already in the zone. "Notify the OR. Tell them what we've got. Call the blood bank, and tell them we need 8 units of O positive."

The EMTs were on their way out.

"What the hell happened to this kid, Howard?" Jack asked, anger in his voice. "Where are his parents?"

"They're outside with the police. Kid was shot at the bus stop over on Lakeshore Drive. The police think it may have been accidental. Another kid brought a gun from home. Good luck. I'm afraid you're going to need it."

Gilbert Coen entered the room, breathing heavily. "Sorry, I was on the sixth floor when I got the page. The elevator's out of order, if you can believe that. What have we got?"

"An 8-year-old kid who will never see nine. That's what we've got," Laura answered. "He's going down."

Jack's anger came roaring forth, but it didn't affect his work. Two of the nurses glared sharply at her, then resumed their duties, waiting for the doctors' commands.

"Don't ever let me hear you say that again, not in this ER," Jack said. "This is a place where miracles can happen, because where there's life, there's hope. Now quit standing there like a vulture, and help save this boy."

At the end of the table, Coen nodded his head approvingly. "What's the pulse ox?" he asked.

"Only 70," said a nurse, "and cyanotic."

"We've got no air way. Get the intubation tray," Jack said. As he tried to insert a narrow tube down the boy's throat, blood came spewing out. "We've got a full gusher. He'll be brain dead in another 90 seconds. I'm going to make a surgical airway. He's got to breathe."

A nurse handed Jack a scalpel. He quickly but carefully made an incision just below the bullet wound. Laura gave him a tracheotomy tube, followed by a syringe. "Give me the numbers as we go," he ordered.

"BP's 60 over 40. Pulse 160, Doctor."

The tube was in. A small gurgling noise emerged from the boy, and his chest ever so slightly started to move up and down.

Jack pulled a stethoscope from around his neck and put it to his ears. "Let's see what we've got."

Except for the sound of the heart monitor, the room was completely silent. Coen, without realizing it, was holding his breath. Beneath his mask, Jack was smiling.

"I like the way it sounds," he said. "What's his BP now?"

"Eighty over sixty—and getting stronger, Doctor."

Coen exhaled deeply. Jack, with his scrub top covered in blood, placed his hand gently on the boy's head. "Welcome back, little guy. I know two people in the waiting room who are going to be very happy to see you." He turned to the nurse. "Can you ventilate?"

"With pleasure, Doctor. That was great work."

"Thanks. Good job all around." Jack looked at Laura. "Call the OR and tell them we're on our way."

As he left the room, Dr. Coen slapped him on the back, shaking his head in admiration. He turned to Laura Underwood. "You can learn a great many things from him. But only if you keep a positive attitude."

"I'm sorry. I didn't mean to come across like I did," she said. "I realize he's the best doctor in the hospital."

Coen laughed. "I've worked at ten different hospitals in my career, and I've witnessed or assisted with emergency room cases in dozens of others, all across the country. He's the best I've ever seen.

Period. Because he never gives up. He takes it personally when he loses a patient. And Jack Russell doesn't like to lose."

She nodded, understanding the significance of Coen's words.

"Come on now, ladies, let's get this young lad up to the operating room. He's got a long life to look forward to."

CHAPTER 10

June 15, 2000

Eddie Weaver, a short fat, bald man with pink puffy skin, was asleep when the phone rang. Dressed only in a sweat stained T-shirt and striped boxer shorts, he was seated in a well-worn recliner inside a filthy apartment on Chicago's lower east side. It was shortly past seven o'clock, and Weaver had fallen asleep while watching Hard Copy on the tube.

He let the phone ring as he reached for a cigarette with nicotine stained fingers. He popped one in his mouth and lit it, drawing long and hard on the filter tip. He smiled, clenching the cigarette between yellow teeth as he fumbled to find his eyeglasses on the tray table beside the chair.

"Hold your damn horses," he said, laughing and talking to himself. "Only a dumb ass would call me in the middle of my show and let the phone ring for five frigging minutes."

Finally, after another dozen rings, Weaver picked up the receiver. As usual, he dispensed with the pleasantries. "This better be good," he snapped. "Who is it?"

"It's the president of the United States," came the reply. "Weren't you expecting my call today?"

Weaver was not amused. "I'm hanging up now, you jackass."

"No, no. Don't hang up. It's me. Bingham. I think I've got something for you...and this could be a big one."

Weaver took his glasses off and rubbed his hand across the beard stubble on his soft chin. He laughed again, but not happily.

"You always think you've got something big, Bingham. The only thing you ever have for me is smut. It's pretty good smut, I admit, but not the kind of thing the gossip rags can use. So do me a favor. Take your sales pitch to some other snitch. I'm trying to earn a living here."

As he moved to hang up the phone, he could hear Bingham's high-pitched whine. "This is different, Eddie. And real. I think it's something you could use, something that could score both of us some big money. Just give me thirty seconds."

"What the hell is it?"

"I've got a patient—well, had a patient—who came to see me. She's a top-ofthe-line beauty, a schoolteacher and a doctor's wife, and she's pregnant. But it's not her husband's baby. He's sterile, so he must know he's not the father. I've never met him, but I'm betting this whole thing is pretty messy by now."

On the other end of the phone, Weaver looked at his imaginary watch. "Unless this woman or her husband is a big star, you've got nothing," he said. "Besides, your thirty seconds are up."

"Wait," Bingham yelled. "Eddie… Are you there, Eddie? There's more. I haven't told you the best part. Eddie?"

"Quit saying my name, and spit it out, you idiot. What's the best part?"

"She's still a virgin, Eddie. Even though she's been having sex, a membrane is still intact inside her vagina. If nothing else, it's a medical miracle. The fact that her husband's not the father just makes it all the more juicy. A virgin birth story ought to be worth a few hundred thousand, and I've got four great photos to back up my story. Real photos."

There was silence on the phone.

"Eddie, you still there? What do you think?"

Weaver was holding the television remote in his hand and was now standing in front of his chair. He was no longer looking at the TV, having turned it off seconds earlier. For the first time in his life, he was glad to be talking to William Bingham.

"Bring me the pictures. Bring them as soon as you can."

CHAPTER 11

June 17, 2000

"Father will be right with you, Mrs. McKenzie. He's just finishing up with another parishioner. Can I get you some coffee or juice?"

"No, thank you," Doris answered. "I'm fine, thanks."

The secretary turned and left the large office located on the first floor of the rectory at St. Vincent's Catholic Church. The building was connected to the church by a covered walkway and the old three-story structure served as both a business office and residence for the four priests who attended to the religious needs of St. Vincent's three thousand parishioners. It was the same church where Doris and Reece had exchanged marriage vows ten years earlier, the place where each of the boys had been baptized, and the place where the entire family could be found every Sunday and on Holy Days.

Doris loved St. Vincent's. She felt safe and comfortable and at peace whenever she visited the church. But she felt none of those things this morning. She was worried and more than a little nervous. Today she'd come to St. Vincent's to see Father Clarence Malone, her favorite priest in all the world.

He'll be glad to see me, Doris thought. *He always is. I just hope he doesn't think I'm crazy by the time I leave.* Moments later she stood as the priest entered the room.

"Good morning, Father. Thanks for seeing me."

"Ah, it's always good to see you, Doris," he said, shaking her right hand with both of his. "You make the world a better place wherever you go. I've been looking forward to this visit since I received your call last week. I'm just sorry it's taken so long. But with Father Kelly on vacation and the wedding season upon us, it's been a carnival around here."

Priest and parishioner laughed together. Malone walked behind his desk and took a seat in a beautiful, high-backed chair. He brushed aside a few letters and papers that had been placed on his desk and turned his full attention to Doris, who was now seated in one of the two chairs opposite him.

Doris looked down at her hands and picked at the clear polish covering her nails. An awkward silence filled the room as Malone waited for his good friend to speak. She looked at him, started to say something, then stopped.

The priest was growing concerned. "What's the matter, Doris? Is someone sick? Are the children okay?"

"Everything's fine, Father. We're all doing well. But something has happened to a friend of mine, Melanie Russell, and I'm not sure how to tell you about it."

"Doris, this isn't like you. You've never been reluctant to tell me anything before, even during confession. Now please, tell me what's bothering you."

Still unsure of what to say and how to say it, Doris finally plunged ahead. "It's beyond belief, really, yet I do believe it. A miracle is happening to Melanie—to all of us, I guess. And, well, we need some help. I don't know where else to turn, Father, so I'm turning to you."

The floodgates were open now, and the words came rushing out. Several times Father Malone asked Doris to slow down, to repeat part of the story, but when he spoke, his words were kind and sincere.

If he thinks I've lost my mind, he's not showing it, Doris thought, even as she pushed ahead with more descriptions of Melanie's pregnancy, the dreams, and the many other strange events of the past six months.

Yet beneath the calm exterior, emotions were churning inside the priest. He'd seen and heard many unusual things during his lifetime in the clergy, but nothing had tested his faith, in both his church and in a friend, as much as the picture now painted by Doris McKenzie—schoolteacher, wife, and mother of three.

Clarence Malone was afraid. By the time Doris finished her account two hours later, his fear was escalating. What scared him most was a question that kept coming to him again and again during the narrative.

What if it was true?

* * *

Doris glanced at her speedometer. The red indicator bar rested between seventy-five and eighty. *Too fast*, she thought. *Slow down. And calm down. I'll be at Melanie's soon enough.*

The bar fell back to sixty-five, and Doris moved her car into the right lane of the Stevenson Expressway. The tension in her arms and shoulders subsided a bit, and she relaxed her grip on the wheel. In another fifteen minutes, she'd be at the Russell home in the Highlands.

All in all, the meeting with Father Malone had gone well. He'd postponed two appointments in order to spend more time with her, and he hadn't suggested that she was a candidate for the local loony bin. In fact, the priest had remained surprisingly calm.

It was hard to tell if he'd believed the story. He said all the right things, told Doris he trusted her judgment and respected her faith in the church. And they'd even talked at length about the book of Revelation. But there was little, if anything, in the church doctrine that could explain Melanie's pregnancy, the Second Coming of an infant Christ, or any of the visions the participants had experienced.

Malone had been honest with her; at least Doris was certain of that.

"If this is happening, if what you say is true, then I don't know how to explain it," he said. "Could this be a sign from God? My answer would be yes. Anything is possible. Could this be something else, a set of unusual physical or mental circumstances that has led to these dreams and your belief that Melanie Russell is carrying the Son of God? That is also possible, and I certainly don't have the expertise to tell you what might be causing it."

But the priest was leaving something out. Doris was sure of it, and considering what was at stake, she decided to take an aggressive stance with Malone.

"Father, is there something else you want to tell me? Do you have anything that might be of help to us?"

The priest nodded slowly. "There's another you should talk to, a priest I knew from long ago, when I was just a boy. He would be old now, probably in his late seventies, and I haven't heard from him in quite a while. He was born in France and may have returned there after retirement. Let me check around and see if I can get some information on where he might be now."

"Why should we talk to him, Father? What can he tell us?"

"I'm not sure. Maybe nothing. But he was a young priest when I was just a student in the seminary at Xavier in Cincinnati. He was a man of mystery, and all the boys loved talking with him. He'd tell us stories late at night, sitting up with us so we wouldn't be homesick. It was rumored he'd even witnessed an exorcism, performed in his homeland shortly after becoming a priest, but we could never get him to talk about it. Mostly, he liked to talk about the future. He liked to talk about the Second Coming of Christ, about the redeemer."

Doris remained silent. Father Malone had a faraway look in his eyes. He seemed uncomfortable revealing this information after so many years, and she dared not interrupt him. But already she sensed that Malone's old mentor might hold pieces to the puzzle she and Melanie needed.

"When he spoke of the Second Coming, he referred to Christ as a child, always as a child, born on earth as he was before, in a different time and place. To this day, he is still the only person to speak of Christ in that manner. We just thought he was making up stories, you know, something to entertain us and keep us interested in the seminary."

Father Malone did not speak again for several minutes. He was, Doris realized, back in the seminary, reliving early memories. For just a moment, at least, he was a young student again. A few minutes later, he stood. He was back to the present, back to the problem at hand.

"Give me a few minutes, Doris, and I'll see what I can dig up on Matthew Benoit. If he's still alive, I should be able to track him down for you. There's a very good website on former priests and nuns on the internet."

The traffic light was red, but Doris turned right onto Highlands Avenue anyway. Three-quarters of the way down the block, she pulled into Jack and Melanie's driveway. The Camry was alone in the garage. As she left the car, Doris snatched a plain folder from the passenger seat. The name Matthew Benoit was printed neatly on the front cover.

* * *

Melanie was sitting at the kitchen table, nibbling at a plate of pasta. She was eating because it was lunchtime, not because she was hungry. When Doris rang the doorbell, Melanie gratefully pushed the plate away. She'd been waiting all morning to hear from her friend.

Doris replayed the visit with Father Malone quickly, fast-forwarding to the parts that might be useful to Melanie.

"I'm telling you, Father Malone was not shocked by what I had to say. He might not believe everything I told him, but he feels like something is happening to you and to us. There's something about these events that frighten him, I think. And Father Malone is not easily frightened."

"What about the old priest?" Melanie asked. "Does Father really think he can help us?"

Doris poured herself a glass of iced tea and joined Melanie at the kitchen table. Her excitement was evident, and Melanie could feel a rush of adrenaline building in her as well.

"Yes. According to him, this Matthew Benoit is the only person to ever speak of the Christ child coming again to judge the world. Since that perspective went against the teachings of the Catholic Church, I think Father Malone just put it out of his mind, ignoring it for all these years. Until now."

The pair sat in silence for several minutes, each contemplating the next step.

Melanie opened the file folder. "Well, where is the priest now? Where can I find him?"

Doris smiled. "You're not going to believe this. You're going home. He's in Kentucky."

Melanie reviewed the fact file on Matthew Benoit. What she read amazed her, just as it had Doris and, to a certain degree, even Father Malone. The old priest was now seventy-eight, serving out the final phase of his Christian life as a Benedictine monk. He was living and working at the Abbey of Montessori, an order that had relocated from Burgundy, France, to central Kentucky in the mid-1800s. The abbey, home to some one hundred clergymen, was located just thirty miles south of Louisville. According to the file, Benoit joined the order in 1982, at age sixty. Thirty miles up Interstate 65, Melanie Russell was a fifteen-year-old sophomore at Assumption High School.

Melanie shook her head. "I've spent most of my life in Louisville and never even heard of this place. And there he was all along, that close to me. It's just so strange."

Doris pushed back the chair and stood from the table. She walked around and placed her hands on Melanie's shoulders, gently massaging the tense muscles she found there. "You could call it strange," she said. "Or you could call it another sign. You'll know for sure when you talk to him."

CHAPTER 12

June 20, 2000

Jack turned the water off and stepped out of the shower. He used a towel to dry his feet and legs, then wrapped it around his waist. He dried his upper body with a second towel, running it through his hair several times before placing it in the laundry bin. He put the finishing touches on his hair with a blow dryer and brush. He'd shaved in the shower and now splashed on a small amount of cologne, grimacing slightly at the familiar sting. After two quick blasts of deodorant, he made his way to the closet and started dressing.

He moved slowly, pausing several times along the way, rehearsing what he was going to say. Jack had been dreading this moment, putting it off for several weeks, and he still wasn't sure how to approach his wife. But it was time to talk. He loved her too much to keep ignoring her. It wasn't fair to Melanie and wasn't fair to the marriage.

Yet the pain he felt was taking a toll, slowly eating away his body from the inside. He'd lost weight, almost ten pounds, and secretly feared he was developing an ulcer. His allergies had worsened with the arrival of summer in the city, and he hardly ever slept anymore. Fatigue was starting to affect his performance at work, and his personality had changed drastically since Dr. Stewart told them about the baby. Gone was his boy-like charm and famous sense of humor. Jack was just a shell of the man he'd once been, and his marriage problems were becoming the talk of the hospital. He was aware of the gossip, but it didn't bother him. He had more important things to worry about.

It was the sense of betrayal that he couldn't shake. He wanted to believe Melanie and her claims of a miracle pregnancy, but the scientist inside wouldn't let him. Someone was the father of his wife's baby—and it wasn't him. Jack had asked himself often if he could live with that knowledge. The answer, much to his surprise, was yes. But only if Melanie told him the truth. He would try to forgive and forget, to put his life and marriage back together. He loved her enough to do that, to give it a try, but only if he could trust her from this point forward. In order to start again, he had to know the truth.

"She owes me that much," Jack said to himself as he tied his shoes. Dressed, he left the bedroom and walked down the stairs. His wife was in the kitchen.

* * *

Jack was furious. And wounded. Moments earlier, he'd stormed out of the house, hurt and angry and devastated, and now he wasn't sure where he was or where he was going. At least he'd had the good sense to leave the Jeep in the garage. He wasn't fit to drive in this condition, so instead he was walking—running, really—running away from a life that had once seemed so precious, so blessed.

He'd tried to talk with Melanie. At first, everything was fine. She had been so relieved he was ready to discuss things. She ran to him and hugged him tightly, tears of joy streaming down her face. Her body and its warmth felt good against his. Melanie still loved him; there was no denying that. So he'd closed his eyes and hugged her back. Jack wanted the embrace to last forever.

They were both emotional, so he'd waited until they'd regained their composure before talking about the baby. He told Melanie he loved her and would stay with her. He said he realized how they had longed for a child and how much having one meant to her. He even told her he was now willing to accept a son or daughter into their lives, and after much soul searching, he believed his words to be true.

"But I can't go forward without the truth," he said. "Who is the father, Melanie? I need to know."

Things had gone crazy after that. Melanie was hysterical. She refused to be honest. Instead she was sticking to her story, claiming the baby was a miracle child and talking out of her head. She started telling Jack about dreams she'd had, visions of her mother and father visiting her, and talking about the will of God, about angels visiting Doris and Reece and other wild tales. According to Melanie, she was pregnant with the Christ child, who was coming again to judge the condition of the human race.

His wife was going insane. He was sure of it. Maybe it was the guilt of an adulterous affair; maybe it was something else. Whatever was happening to her was painful to watch, and at one point, Jack stood in the center of his kitchen, eyes closed and holding his hands over his ears like a small boy. When that didn't work, he turned and fled the house, leaving his sobbing wife in his wake. Now twenty minutes later, he was still walking, dazed and confused, down a foreign street in a strange neighborhood.

He walked to a motel, checked in, and spent the night. After a sleepless night, he finally returned home shortly before noon. The house was empty. On the table, he found a note from his wife.

> Jack, I'll be gone for a few days. I'm going to a place where I hope to find some answers about what is happening to us and why. I've never lied to you, Jack, not once, and I'm not lying to you now. I love you more than ever. Believe that if you believe nothing else. I hope to see you soon. Melanie.

Jack let the paper fall to the table. He raised his hands and rubbed each temple with the tips of his fingers. "I know you do," he whispered. "I love you too."

CHAPTER 13

June 21, 2000

The plane ride from Chicago to Louisville was bumpy.

Mild turbulence—that was how the captain described it.

To Melanie and her fear of flying, the plane felt like a roller coaster. The sharp changes in altitude were met with concern, followed closely by fear, nausea, and panic. Melanie pushed a button on her armrest, and a flight attendant approached her from the front of the plane.

"Is there something I can get you?"

"On the ground would be nice."

The young attendant laughed. "Are you feeling ill?"

"No, I'm past that. I moved into the panic mode a few minutes ago. How much longer to Louisville?"

"Just another twenty minutes or so. The hot, humid weather is what's causing the bumpiness, but we'll be fine. The turbulence should subside once we start our descent. In another five minutes, we'll be below the clouds."

Melanie nodded her head. "Thank you," she said.

The attendant moved toward the back of the plane, collecting plastic cups and soda cans along the way. She closed her eyes and tried to relax. A morbid yet funny thought came to mind.

Why worry? she wondered. *If the plane goes down, at least all my problems are solved.* The ride was smoother now, and she was beginning to feel better.

Then the baby moved for the first time. It happened so suddenly Melanie wasn't sure if the movement in her stomach was real or just more turbulence. But a few seconds later, it happened again. A slight fluttering sensation. Not much, but real. There was life inside her. Three months' worth, if Dr. Stewart had things calculated correctly.

She opened her eyes and touched her stomach with both hands. The baby was beginning his second trimester. Sometime during the next six months, he would arrive. A bouncing baby boy. Her son. A very special baby.

The image was sobering. It filled Melanie with concern and anxiety, but it also made her feel good. made her feel complete.

I'll be a good mommy, she thought. *I'll do a good job, even if I have to do it alone.*

A few minutes later, the plane touched down in Louisville.

CHAPTER 14

June 22, 2000, Louisville, Kentucky

She thought about calling ahead. But moments before leaving her room at the Holiday Inn on Bardstown Road, Melanie decided against it. Her first words with Matthew Benoit should be in person. If he was the real deal—some sort of messenger assigned to help her with this odyssey—she wanted to see his face.

Melanie had always been a good judge of character, and she planned to use all her senses to form a first impression of this clergyman.

So she climbed in her rental car and headed south from Louisville. Forty-five minutes later, she drove through the entrance gate at the Abbey of Montessori. It was shortly after nine o'clock when she walked into the front office and was greeted by the monastery's information officer, Pat Melleray. He was dressed in a brown robe that came to his knees, and his feet were covered in old leather sandals. He smiled broadly and waved his hand as Melanie approached the desk. But he did not greet her verbally.

Melanie hesitated before speaking. Had the monks taken a vow of silence? She wasn't sure and didn't know if she should blurt out a question or not. The monk laughed.

"Hello, I'm Brother Pat. It's okay to talk, if that's what you're wondering."

Melanie grinned sheepishly. "I bet you get that a lot, don't you?"

"Yes, we do. People from the outside world often assume we've taken a vow of silence, but that's very rare these days. It's hard to perform charity work without talking to people. Now tell me, what brings you to Montessori?"

Melanie thought about her answer before giving it. "I've traveled from Chicago to meet one of the monks here, Matthew Benoit. He doesn't know me and isn't expecting me, but a friend of mine, Father Clarence Malone from St. Vincent's, told me I'd find him here. I need to speak with him, if that's permitted."

"So you want to see Brother Matthew? Well, that's a good choice if you're looking for information. Not much gets by Matthew, even at his age. We call him the Wizard, and it's a nickname borne out of respect, I assure you. We all go to Brother Matthew for advice from time to time, even the abbot."

The monk glanced at the digital clock on his desk. "Brother Matthew usually works in the fields on a pretty day like this, helping cut hay or tending to the dairy cattle. He always comes in by eleven for lunch and a short nap. You could see him then if you don't mind waiting."

Melanie nodded vigorously. "That would be wonderful. Thank you."

"I'll tell you what. Why don't you go across the courtyard and wait in the chapel? It's a beautiful place with comfortable seating, and you can look around at some of the memorabilia we've collected through the years. I'll send Brother Matthew over as soon as he comes in."

Melanie thanked the monk again, then left the office, and made her way to the chapel. She stopped near the entrance to read an inscription. It was part of a letter written by Pope Paul VI to the order on December 23, 1968. The words appeared on a bronze plaque bolted to the brick wall beside the chapel's double doors.

> The church has entrusted a mission to us, which
> we wish to fulfill by the response of our whole
> life...to give clear witness to that heavenly home
> for which everyone belongs and to keep alive in
> the heart of the human family the desire for his

home, as we bear witness to the majesty and love
of God and to the brotherhood of all in Christ.

I guess I'm going to find out a thing or two about missions, Melanie
said to herself as she entered the chapel. *I just hope Brother Matthew
can get me started in the right direction.*

Ninety minutes later, he followed Melanie through the doorway.

* * *

Matthew Benoit was a small man with dark skin and beautiful
charcoal eyes. Melanie noticed the eyes immediately. They were not
the eyes of an old man. They were crystal clear, sharp, and alert. His
hair was little more than white stubble cropped closely against his
tanned scalp. His face was weathered but friendly, and he walked
with a slight limp as he made his way to Melanie.

"You've come to see me?" he asked.

Melanie, spellbound, managed a slight nod. He reached out
and clasped her hands in his, and Melanie could feel the rough, hard
calluses that covered the monk's palms. The two gazed intently at
each other for several seconds. A feeling washed over Melanie. She
sensed greatness in this small man.

Finally, Matthew spoke again. "It's an honor to finally meet
you. I've been waiting a very long time."

Dozens of thoughts raced through Melanie's head. There were
so many things she wanted to say, so many questions she needed to
ask. But try as she might, the words wouldn't come out. She shook
her head in a gesture of helplessness.

"It's okay, my dear. There's no reason to fear me. I'm just an old
brother trying to hang on a few more years before I meet my maker.
I'm here to help you."

Melanie found his words reassuring. She also found comfort in
the quaint old chapel.

"Can we talk here?" she asked.

"Of course, we can. What better place to talk about you and
your most blessed son?"

The monk looked to the front of the chapel, where several of his brethren knelt in silent prayer. "Let's go up to the old choir loft. It's very private, and we can talk freely there." He took her hand and led her up the long spiraled staircase.

There were no pews or chairs in the loft, so Matthew gingerly crossed his legs and sat on the floor, placing his back against the loft's far wall for support. Melanie dropped easily and lightly to the floor in front of him.

"I see one thing already," he said, smiling at Melanie. "You are the picture of good health, eating right, keeping yourself in shape. My guess is, you are quite the athlete. Am I correct?"

Melanie was embarrassed. She hadn't come all this way to talk about herself. But she answered the monk with respectfulness. "Used to be, back in high school. Basketball and swimming. I was a sprinter on the track team. I gave it up when I went to college though. I thought it would be best to concentrate on my studies."

"It worked, didn't it? You were a good student? An honor graduate?"

"Yes."

"And you decided to devote your professional life to education. As a teacher? Is that right?"

"Yes, that's right," Melanie said. She was uncomfortable with this line of give and take, particularly with such pressing issues at stake. *I hope he knocks off the small talk,* she thought. *We need to discuss so many other things.*

Matthew smiled and looked at Melanie as if reading her mind. "Patience, young one. Patience is something you will need in the future. In order to move forward—day after day without always knowing or understanding the reasons why—takes great patience. Most of all, it takes great faith."

Melanie said nothing as she tried to keep other careless thoughts from popping into her head.

"But your faith is very strong, isn't it? It burns like a beam through your eyes, and it fills your heart. I feel tremendous strength radiating from your body and soul. The Father has chosen well, as I knew he would."

Melanie wanted to turn and flee the loft and chapel, even the abbey, and head for home. His ability to know things about her, to understand her thoughts, was disturbing. Yet she felt at peace with him, and that peace kept her calm. He smiled again, and the urge to flee was gone. Instead, she felt drawn to him, and edged closer.

He asked more questions—about her parents, Jack, her friendship with Doris, and more—and even as she replied, Melanie realized he already knew the answers. *Maybe he's lonely and just wants to talk to someone*, she thought. She grimaced and tried to pull the thought back, but it was too late.

This time they smiled together.

"I have very little interest in talking to most people. This, of course, is different. It is the greatest honor of my life—of any life—to meet and speak with the Blessed Mother. I will cherish this day, this moment, for all eternity."

Without warning, the old monk was crying. His bent shoulders shook up and down as he tried to control his sobs. Instinctively, Melanie leaned forward and put her arms around him. A few seconds later, he was in control again, wiping the tears from his face with the wide sleeve of his robe.

"I'm so sorry. That's the first time I've shed tears in…since I was a young man. I'm failing miserably in my duties as a messenger. I apologize for my weakness."

Melanie was dumbfounded. Try as she might, she could not understand why this man, a disciple of God and the church his entire life, was so moved by her presence. It made no sense. She was plain old Melanie, a wife and kindergarten teacher, a good old girl from the bluegrass state of Kentucky, and now a resident of Chicago. She was nothing special in the grand scheme of things, yet this man was moved to tears upon finally meeting her.

"You still don't completely understand, do you?" Matthew asked. "You are the one, the chosen one, the woman selected by God to bear his human son and raise him as your own. You must change the way you look at yourself. You have to, because from this point on, your life will never be the same."

She watched as he struggled to his feet. He reached for her and pulled Melanie to a standing position. Then he slowly lowered himself back to the floor, kneeling before her, placing a worn hand on each side of her stomach.

"If we are to have a future, if the world is to continue through another millennium, it will be decided by the life that grows inside you. And it will be decided rather quickly. Your son will gather information, draw out the true feelings and beliefs of the people on earth, and when the time is right, take that information back to the Holy Father. If he finds there is hope and love and goodness in people, then life as we know it will continue. If not, the apocalypse that is described in the book of Revelation will occur, and life will end."

Brother Matthew turned his head and put his right ear against Melanie's abdomen, as if listening for sounds from the Holy Child. Slowly he pulled himself up and stood face-to-face with his visitor from Chicago.

"I have known of this event my entire life. The Father came to me when I was a small boy in France, and told me this would occur. He has visited me many times, always reminding me of what was to come and preparing me for the day when I would meet you.

"He has allowed me to enjoy a wonderful life, taking me all around the world as a priest and monk and introducing me to many interesting people. But always, through everything, I've understood my primary purpose. It is simple really. I am to tell you as much as I can about the journey you are now beginning. The information I have is like a puzzle. I have some of the pieces, but not all. I will tell you everything I can. The rest will be left up to you. Do you understand?"

Melanie nodded.

"Are you ready to listen to all I have to say?"

"Yes. I think so. I hope so." She was nervous and fighting hard to hold back tears.

He smiled again. "I can't lie to you, Melanie. There is much to be concerned about. As the mother and protector of the Holy Child, your duties and responsibilities will be greater than you can even begin to comprehend. But there is room for optimism and hope.

Now that I've met you, my heart is no longer heavy. I like what I see in you. You are a strong, intelligent woman. He has chosen very, very well."

For the next two hours, Melanie listened as Matthew described, in great detail, the Second Coming of Christ. She was focused and intense, stopping the monk at times to ask questions. And as he talked, she realized she could no longer run from her destiny. Instinctively, she purged the desire to whine and complain from her mind and body.

Melanie had never been a quitter. This was no time to start.

Matthew was somber now, his words carrying not the weight but rather the fate of the world.

"The dark side will be after your son. They will be after you too, but you are not alone. Help will come to you in many forms, both expected and unexpected. And like you, those who come to help will be brave and strong. They will be soldiers, men and women who will one day sit at the right hand of God. They will defend you and the child to their death. And they will ask for nothing in return."

He looked at Melanie, and she nodded her head slightly. "I understand."

"Are you ready?"

"Yes. Ready as I'll ever be. I'm still not sure why I was selected. I keep asking myself if another choice would be better. I worry that he'll be disappointed in me. But I'm determined to do my best. If I fail, it won't be from lack of trying. I promise you that."

Moments later, the pair emerged from the chapel door, stepping out into the bright sunlight of another hot summer day. Brother Matthew and Melanie held hands as they walked to the parking lot and her car. She opened the door and started to slip inside, but then she turned abruptly and put her arms around the monk's neck, hugging him with all her might.

He surprised her by laughing heartily. "You're going to get rumors started with a hug like that. These old buzzards are a bunch of gossipmongers anyhow."

Melanie relaxed her grip and brought her arms from around his neck. Now she held his weathered face gently between her hands. "Thank you, Matthew, for everything."

Sadness crossed his face, for just a second, then the warm smile returned. "No, my angel. It is you who deserve thanks. My duties are almost complete. Your difficult journey is just beginning. No matter what happens, no matter how things turn out, I want you to know that I believe in you, Melanie. I will pray for you and hope that one day I will be allowed to join you in heaven."

Without another word, Melanie climbed behind the wheel and drove out the abbey's front gate. In her rear-view mirror, partially blocked by the rising dust from the gravel drive, Matthew was waving goodbye.

She wanted to cry but again held back the tears. "Here we go," she said to herself in a low, determined voice. "There's no turning back now."

CHAPTER 15

June 23, 2000, Chicago, Illinois

Doris and Reece McKenzie sat at the kitchen table. The breakfast dishes had been scraped and placed in the dishwasher, and the boys had moved outside to play in the yard. Husband and wife sipped a second cup of coffee, each staring vacantly out the back window.

"When does she get back?" Reece asked.

"Tonight. I'm supposed to pick her up at the airport between eight-thirty and nine. She said she'd call from Louisville if the flight is delayed or there is a change in plans." Doris stood up and walked across the kitchen. She set the cup, half full, in the sink, then turned to face her husband. "How do you feel, Reece? Do you still believe all of this is really happening?"

He pondered the question for a moment, then shook his head in exasperation. "Hell, yes, I believe it. I'm scared not to." He stood and walked to his wife, and they kissed softly. "Everything happens for a reason," he said. "I'm a firm believer in that. Why this is happening now to Melanie and to us is something I can't begin to explain. But I do know it's happening for a reason. God's reason."

The two kissed again. "I know something else too," Reece said.

"What's that?"

"I know I love you, and I know that together we can get through anything."

Doris smiled and hugged him. Yet even as she did, she felt a pang of guilt as her heart went out—through the distance—to her best friend.

"I pray that Jack comes around," she said. "This may all be impossible without him."

* * *

Melanie was almost home. She'd replayed her visit to Montessori with Doris while the two waited to claim her luggage. She filled in the rest of the details during the first ten minutes of the drive from the airport. Doris drove in silence now, absorbing the information she had received and leaving Melanie alone with her thoughts.

She'd put together a preliminary plan of action in the motel room last night. The most important thing, at least for the next several months, was to take care of herself, her body, and the baby. She was going to stay with Dr. Stewart and follow her prenatal instructions to the letter. Melanie felt good about the doctor's skills and dedication and hoped she would agree to deliver her son.

Until then, she would take it one day at a time. Doris was in the game, and so was Reece. Brother Matthew could always be reached in case of emergency, and she still hadn't forgotten about the Salvation Army Santa, the one she'd met last Christmas. He had told her he would see her again, and she no longer doubted his claim or his intentions. He was part of the team sent to help her and the child.

That was all Melanie knew for sure. She'd have to deal with new developments or associates as they appeared. And she would train herself to look for any sign of trouble, for any contact from members of the dark side. If they came for her unborn baby, they'd have a fight on their hands.

School was set to resume in six weeks, and Melanie looked forward to going back to work, getting her life in some form of order. It would be good to be back with the children, working again with her colleagues. She hoped Mercy Elementary would be a safe haven.

Only one question remained. Would Jack return to her? Or would he leave for good, divorce her, and abandon both mother and child? The thought of being alone, without Jack, made her sick, so sick that she quickly forced the thought from her mind.

Doris broke the silence. "Did you hear from him while you were gone?"

"No. I started to call a dozen times, but I thought the time alone might help him. I realize how hard this must be on Jack, and I don't hold it against him. I know he loves me, and I just keep holding on to that thought."

Doris nodded and turned into the driveway. She looked at her friend after putting the car in park. "I'm not a man, and God knows I'll never understand how they think. But I imagine this would be a very difficult thing for Jack or Reece or anyone to accept."

The car fell silent, then Doris continued, "And you have to remember something else. You've received signs about this. Reece and I shared the same dream. Jack's had nothing. He's hanging in on faith alone. If he didn't love you, didn't believe in you, he'd be gone already."

Melanie climbed out of the car, then pulled her suitcase from the back seat. Doris reached across and touched her gently on the arm. "Don't give up on him yet. I still don't think God would ask you to do this without including Jack as part of the plan."

"I hope you're right. I feel lost without him."

With nothing left to say, Doris watched Melanie enter the empty house and close the door behind her.

CHAPTER 16

June 27, 2000

Jack was seated at a long dining table in the hospital cafeteria. It was just past eight in the evening, and he was having dinner with Dr. Coen and Laura Underwood. Not that he was hungry. He'd lost two more pounds during the past week and was starting to worry about his health. As a result, he was eating just to be eating.

He and Melanie had talked twice since she'd returned from her mysterious trip to Louisville. No final decision had been reached, but as part of their conversations, he told her he loved her and would try to stand by her. Melanie displayed little emotion and seemed disconnected, almost oblivious to his voice.

"I understand," she said. "I'm glad you're staying here at the house."

Jack continued to sleep in the guest bedroom and was still spending a lot of time at work. But each day the situation was growing worse. Soon Melanie would begin to show signs of her pregnancy, and friends and coworkers would start to ask questions. In fact, rumors about his wife and a baby were already beginning to infiltrate the hospital.

He'd thought about telling Coen and some of his other friends, but somehow he couldn't. Not yet. He still wasn't ready to admit what was happening, at least not publicly. He wanted to call Reece and talk to him, try to explain things, but thought better of it. Reece was a good friend, a great guy, but how could he understand? He and his wife had three beautiful sons, and they'd had them together, the way it was supposed to be.

So instead Jack kept his frustrations and worries inside, preferring to pour his heart and soul into his craft. Saving lives was good therapy, he had to admit, even if he couldn't save his own.

Coen and Laura were in deep discussion concerning a surgery procedure that had taken place in the hospital yesterday. Doctors had taken a donor hand and replaced it on a patient. The man, a police officer, had lost his right hand three years earlier as the result of a car accident. The transplant operation, according to Coen, had taken more than sixteen hours.

"It's way too early to tell, but Dr. Edwards seemed pleased with the surgery," he said. "Just another medical miracle—that's what it is."

Laura was listening intently. Jack was not. "Can you imagine looking down at the end of your arm and seeing someone else's hand?" she asked. "How weird would that be?"

"Probably not as weird as the first time he looked down and saw nothing but a stump. What do you think, Jack?"

Jack came to attention, distracted for a moment from his tortured thoughts. "I think it's time we took our six good hands and went back to work. You guys going to eat forever?"

He stood up and headed for the cafeteria door. Coen laughed as he and Laura dropped their trays off at the kitchen counter. "Just when I think he can't possibly work any harder, he does. I don't know what's going on with Jack, but he's been a man possessed these last few weeks."

She nodded in agreement. "Look at it this way," she said. "If you're a citizen of Chicago, it's a good time to have an emergency. Superman's waiting for you in the ER."

The two hurried to catch up.

* * *

Jack was in the doctor's lounge, catching up on paperwork, when his pager sounded. He was up immediately and in the hallway, making his way toward the trauma center.

"What's up, Sheila?" he asked as he passed the charge nurse near the front desk.

"EMS just brought in a stabbing victim. Looks like a DOA, but they wheeled him into trauma one thirty seconds ago."

Jack broke stride and ran for the trauma room. Near the entrance, he passed two police officers and a detective assigned to investigate the case. They glanced at him briefly as he raced past. When he burst through the doors, he saw a young black man on the table, covered in blood and surrounded by a doctor and four nurses. Mina Jenkins, an EMT he knew well, was preparing to leave. She looked at Jack and, before he could ask, repeated the information she'd given to the others.

"Eighteen-year-old male stabbed twice in the chest and once in the abdomen. We responded to a radio call from city police and found him in an alley on Illinois Avenue. He wasn't breathing and had no pulse when we arrived. That was twelve minutes ago. We started CPR and continued until we came through these doors. No response. It looks like the knife penetrated the heart muscle at least once, maybe both times."

Dr. Tyler Stiles, the emergency room's chief of staff, climbed off the table, where he had been continuing CPR. His plastic protective gown was covered in blood, and his forehead glistened with sweat. "Let's call it, gang. Time of death: ten fourteen."

Jack stepped closer to the table. "Wait, Tyler," he pleaded. "Let me have a look."

Stiles laughed sarcastically, obviously annoyed. "Forget it, Doctor. He's been down too long, and the heart's sustained too much damage."

"Please, Tyler, if we can get to the heart maybe we can—"

Stiles was angry now. "I said no, Jack. I know you think you can save them all, but you can't. You sure as hell can't save this one. Now show some discipline."

The nurses and a second-year student who entered the room after Jack all frowned together. Few in the hospital liked the chief of staff. They liked him less when he talked down to the department's best physician.

Stiles, now in full eruption, continued to speak. As usual, his words were not only foolish, but prejudicial. "It's just one less gangbanger off the street. What's the big fuss anyway?"

EMT Jenkins, a black woman, was still in the room. She whirled and glared at Stiles. On many occasions, she'd bitten her tongue and ignored the doctor's remarks. But not tonight. She refused to let him spit on this young man's corpse.

"You're such a racist, such an idiot," she said. "Because he's young and black and was stabbed in an alley, you think he had it coming, don't you? In your mind, he's just another piece of street trash."

Stiles was furious. People didn't speak to him in this manner, especially not a lowly medical technician. But he was smart enough to realize his comment was out of bounds and potentially harmful to his career, so he let Jenkins have her say. Just this once.

She was near tears now and looked to Jack for support. He gave it with a gentle smile and a nod of admiration.

"You want to know why those three cops are waiting in the hallway? Or maybe I should tell you about the young woman being treated for cuts and bruises down the hall. The white woman was being attacked and sexually assaulted by a white man in that alley."

The room was silent. Stiles stood in the center, alone, without the respect or support of no one.

"That's right," Jenkins continued. "The police said this man—just a boy, really—passed by and saw the attack. He tried to help and got stabbed three times for his trouble. But he saved her life. You call him a gangbanger? She's calling him a hero. As we loaded him in the first ambulance, she was begging us to save him."

Jenkins was trembling with anger now. Two of the nurses—one black, one white—were weeping quietly as the emotional scene played out, and Jack was near the point of joining them. Stiles was as pale as a ghost and still speechless.

"It's not your fault he's dead. But he died saving a woman he didn't even know. The least you can do is show some respect, because in my book he's ten times the man you'll ever be."

With that, she turned and left the room. Through the window, Jack watched as the detective approached her and asked the obvious question. As she shook her head, the detective's shoulders slumped, and he went to tell the other officers.

Stiles left the trauma room without saying a word. One of the nurses pulled a sheet over the young man's body, covering him completely. "I'll call the morgue," said the medical student and left the room. The others joined him, leaving Jack alone with his thoughts.

He wanted to cry, not just for the lost patient or Jenkins or even for Stiles, the fool. It was everything, really. His marriage, his personal life, his professional life—everything seemed to be slipping away from him. Jack was emotionally drained. And there was no respite, no place he could go to recover and recharge his batteries.

He walked to a corner of the room and sat on a metal stool. He turned off the overhead lights and closed his eyes. The room was quiet and peaceful. Because it would be a while before a transporter from the morgue arrived, Jack decided to use the time and space to his advantage.

I'll take a few minutes to compose myself, he thought, *then I'll get back to my paperwork.*

He was comfortable with his back against the wall, but he wasn't asleep, and he wasn't dreaming, when he heard the sheet rustle. He opened his eyes and almost screamed when the corpse on the table sat up, uncovered himself, and turned to face him.

Despite the dried blood and gaping wounds—despite the fact he was dead—the young man smiled at Jack. It was a warm smile, the kind one old friend delivered to another. The patient, the dead man, seemed genuinely pleased.

"Don't worry, Doc. You're not losing your mind. I really am dead. And I'll be that way again in a few minutes. But I've got a message to deliver to you. It's about your wife and son. If you don't mind, listen closely. In my condition, I'm afraid I'll only be able to say it once."

* * *

Jack closed his eyes and rubbed them hard with the back of his hands. *He'll be gone when I open them again*, he thought. *Please, God, let him be gone.* But when he looked again the young man was still sitting on the table, still smiling.

Jack stood and looked through the double doors to the hallway. Men and women, members of the hospital staff, were walking past the doors, oblivious to the strange scene playing out inside trauma 1.

The impulse to run was growing in Jack, inching upward from his stomach and into his throat as it tried to escape his body in the form of a primal scream. If he could get to the hallway, he'd be safe. Safe from this…what? Zombie? Monster? Gruesome ghost? But despite his fear, or perhaps because of it, his body was refusing all commands from the brain.

Run! his mind screamed.

No, said the body.

This inner struggle continued for several seconds as Jack stood against the wall, eyes bulging and facial muscles twitching as a result of the strain being placed on his central nervous system.

Realizing his feet and legs had deserted him, Jack again looked to the hallway, hoping against hope that someone, anyone, would look into the room and come bursting in to help—bringing with them a cross, holy water, or maybe even a wooden stake.

No one stopped. No one even glanced in his direction. They simply continued to walk up and down the hall, scurrying to and fro like so many mice in a maze or like lambs being led to slaughter.

I'll yell for help, Jack thought. *A good scream will get some attention.* But again the signal was intercepted. The best he could manage was a long, dry swallow and a slight turn of the head, bringing his eyes back to the table, back to the dead man.

Jack was relieved to see the corpse still sitting on the table. At least he hadn't attacked, hadn't started toward him, Frankenstein-like, in an attempt to tear out his throat or do whatever it is that zombies and vampires did to their victims. Instead, the dead man laughed.

"Good gosh, Jack. You've been watching too many horror movies or reading too many of those Stephen King novels. I don't know about you, but when I think of someone rising from the dead, I sort of expect it to be a good thing. Haven't you ever read the Bible?"

Jack stared at the man, still unable to speak. But strangely, his terror was subsiding.

"No, it's the live ones you've got to keep your eye on. They cause plenty of trouble on their own. So don't worry. There's no reason to be afraid of me. I'm just a messenger, making a quick pit stop along my journey to a better place."

He walked over to Jack and put out his hand. Much to his dismay, Jack did likewise, and the two strangers—doctor and former patient—enjoyed a long, firm handshake.

"My name's Tommy Colbert. Or at least it was."

Jack's eyes narrowed slightly, causing the corpse to laugh again.

"Who were you expecting? Lazarus?"

Despite the intensity, the absurdity of the moment, Jack almost laughed. He was relaxed now. More importantly, he was listening. It was time, Colbert realized, to deliver his final message.

"I won't bore you with all the details of my life, short as it was, but let's just say I was put on this earth for a few very special reasons. I've accomplished all my missions and have enjoyed a very nice stay. This is my last stop before I return for my eternal reward."

Jack looked around the emergency room for hidden cameras and microphones. He felt like an actor, playing out a scene in a horror movie. But there was no producer, no director. And Tommy Colbert was no actor. He was, Jack suddenly realized, a messenger of God, sent here to tell him something of extreme importance. He looked at Colbert, the dearly departed, and tried to focus, because as the man said earlier, this message wouldn't be repeated.

"I died for a reason, Jack. Two reasons, really. One was to prevent a rape and murder. The other was to come to you in a form that was so shocking it would be impossible for you to ignore me. From the look on your face, I'd say I've at least gotten your attention."

Jack tried to speak and was not completely surprised to find that his voice had returned. "I'm still terrified. But not of you, so much as I am of losing my mind."

Colbert smiled. It was a kind, reassuring smile. "You know something special is happening, don't you? You don't know what it is or why it's happening to you and Melanie, but you are very much aware that a miracle is taking place. You feel it, don't you?"

Jack nodded. He had questions, lots of them, but didn't want to interrupt.

"Then let me explain this as simply as I can. You have been chosen by God to raise his son as your own. Melanie is pregnant with the Holy Child now. She will give birth to the baby in six months and will care and administer to his needs for as long as necessary. She has accepted the enormous responsibility that has been placed upon her, and she is prepared to raise her son—with or without you."

Tears were beginning to pool in Jack's eyes, and for the first time in his life, he felt real shame. He turned his gaze to the bloody trauma room floor.

"There's no need and no time to feel guilty. You've done nothing wrong, Jack. Take it from someone who knows. Melanie was not chosen randomly. She was not chosen without careful consideration. And she was not chosen for her individual strengths alone—great as they are. She was also selected because of you. Just as it was before, over two thousand years ago, God realized his son would need not only a good mother but also a good father. Melanie and you were selected together Jack, as a team."

Jack was crying now. Quietly the tears rolled down his cheeks. He was still afraid, yet he could feel a sense of pride, of accomplishment, welling up inside him. But most of all, the tears came from the love flowing from his heart. The love he felt for his wife...and his son.

For finally, the unknown was known. It was as if a dense fog had lifted from his confused world, his view no longer obstructed by guilt, worry, jealously, or false pride. More details would come later, he was sure, but for now Jack had only one thing on his mind. He needed to get to Melanie. He wanted to tell her he was sorry, tell her how much he loved her.

He looked at Colbert apologetically. Then his feet, no longer immobilized, started for the door. He was astonished to see the corpse—his messenger—back on the table. He grinned as he pulled the sheet over his torso, pausing before recovering his head.

"Go. It's okay," he said. "You're not the only one who has places to go, people to see. We'll talk again one day, you and me. And, brother, what stories we'll have to tell."

With that, he was gone. Jack wiped his eyes and plunged through the doors and into the hallway. Without a word, he rushed out the nearest exit and headed for the parking garage.

He was going home.

* * *

"Melanie. Melanie, where are you?" Jack scrambled through the back door and ran down the hallway, past the den to the kitchen. There was no answer, and he stood near the table, chest heaving as he tried to collect his thoughts.

Where could she be? The car was in the garage. Unless someone had picked Melanie up, she had to be here. Unless…unless something had happened to her. Suddenly Jack was filled with a sense of panic.

Not now, he thought. *Not when I've finally come to my senses.* He ran to the wall and grabbed the phone. Quickly he dialed a familiar number.

"Hello," said a voice on the other end of the line. It was Doris.

Jack tried to remain calm but wasn't having much success. "Doris, have you seen Melanie? Is she there now?"

"No, she's not here. I haven't talked to her today, Jack. Are you home? Is something wrong?"

He was engulfed in fear now, and his mind raced as he tried to imagine what had happened to his wife or where she might be.

"I don't know. I just got home, and she's not here. Her car's in the garage, there's no note, and I'm just worried—" From upstairs, Jack heard something. It was the sound of running water. Water was being drained from the bath in the master bedroom.

"It's okay. I mean, I think she's here. I forgot to check upstairs. Sorry to bother you, Doris. Bye."

Doris was still talking when Jack hung up the phone. He bounded back through the house and started up the steps, two at a time. Seconds later, he was in the bedroom, where he found his wife, standing near the closet with beads of water glistening from her naked body. Immediately he looked at her belly and noticed the slight round protrusion.

Melanie gasped when she saw him and instinctively covered herself with the towel she was holding. Jack came to her and lifted her from the floor.

"I love you," he whispered in her ear. "Please forgive me for the pain I've put you through. Forgive me for my weakness. And most of all, forgive me for not believing in you."

Melanie was already sobbing. She could feel the love in her husband's grasp, and it enveloped her like a safe, warm cocoon. Jack was back. Her soul mate had returned, and with him, she felt as if she could conquer the world.

"Hush, darling," she said. "There's no need to talk about that now. You know how much I love you, and that's all that matters. Your trust means everything to me. You mean everything to me."

The two fell to the bed, and Jack wrapped his wife in the warmth of a blanket.

They held each other tightly and talked for several hours. They talked about everything—about Doris and Reece, Father Malone, Brother Matthew, and even Tommy Colbert. But most of all, they talked about the future, about what it might bring and how they would stand together, side by side, to raise their son, the Son of God.

The conversation had slowed by the time the phone rang. Melanie reached for it and put it to her ear without moving from the bed. She continued to gaze into Jack's gentle eyes. She'd barely said hello when Doris's voice came screeching through the receiver.

"Melanie! What's going on over there? Jack scared me to death when he called earlier, and I haven't heard a word since. Are you okay? Is everything all right?"

Jack and Melanie smiled at each other.

"Yes, sweetie, everything's fine now. Jack's home. Really home."

CHAPTER 17

September 24, 2000

Melanie looked at the numbers on the scale and shook her head. Her weight was up eleven pounds, to one twenty-nine. Jan Stewart laughed. "You're being too hard on yourself. Eleven pounds at the end of the second trimester is not bad at all. In fact, it's better than I usually see. You'll probably gain another ten or fifteen pounds before delivery, which is just about perfect."

"I feel fat," Melanie said with a laugh. "But I feel good. I feel more healthy and alive than ever before. And I feel strong. Is that normal?"

"Absolutely. The six-month mark is a good time for most expectant mothers. The nausea is gone, the weight gain is still minimal, and you're probably sleeping well. Right?"

Melanie nodded.

"But don't worry, I'm sure you'll get to experience all the best parts of being pregnant—the swollen feet and hands, the aching back, sleepless nights and days, and the constant need, especially the last few weeks, to tinkle every few minutes."

The two women laughed together. They'd become close during the past few months. Dr. Stewart found Melanie to be a cooperative patient, following her orders and suggestions to the letter. And she wasn't a complainer. That was easy to understand, given the circumstances surrounding her pregnancy. Considering what she'd been through, the dilemma she'd faced with Jack, having the baby might be the easiest part.

At least everything seemed good now. Stewart noticed the change about three months ago. Things were much better between the couple, and she was glad to see it. Jack had accompanied Melanie on her last visit to the office, and the two seemed madly in love again.

She had no idea what facilitated the change, nor did she care. The chances of delivering a happy, healthy baby always improved when the mother was in good physical and emotional condition. Melanie Russell certainly fit that description.

And if things were going well with the dad-to-be, then all the better. "Everything is looking great," Stewart said. "Knock on wood, but it's my professional opinion that you'll be giving birth to a healthy baby boy in late December."

Melanie, now dressed, finished tying her shoes and stood, ready to leave the exam area. "There's no need to knock wood. First of all, I couldn't be in better hands as far as medical care goes. And secondly, I happen to have a little inside information. This baby is going to be very, very special."

"Is that right? And what is your source on this inside tip?"

"Let's just say a little birdie told me." Melanie turned and started for the outer office and the front lobby. "We'll see you next month, Doctor." Then she was gone.

Stewart smiled and walked back to the exam room. She couldn't put her finger on it, but there was something about Melanie that made her feel good about herself. The patient, through her actions and simple words, made her feel like the most important doctor in the world. It was a good feeling, and she found herself looking forward to the day when she would deliver Melanie's baby.

Maybe he'll be a Christmas baby, she thought. *Now how special would that be?*

CHAPTER 18

September 25, 2000

Melanie and Doris sat in the cafeteria at Mercy Elementary. Lunch break was almost over, and in another five minutes, they'd start the daily task of rounding up almost sixty kindergarten students. Doris looked on approvingly as Melanie choked down the last few drops from her milk carton.

"I'm really getting sick of milk," she said. "It tastes horrible with cafeteria food."

Doris laughed. "Everything tastes horrible with cafeteria food. At least your baby's going to be born with strong bones. And you know what they say about milk. It does a body good."

"Then why are you drinking tea?" Melanie asked, mock anger in her voice. "Don't you care about your body?"

"Sure I do. But not enough to drink that nasty milk every day."

Melanie shook her head in surrender. She stood and looked over the cafeteria, searching for her students to see if everyone had finished lunch. She walked to the door and raised her hand, just as she did every weekday during the school year. It was the signal for students to line up for the short walk back to the classroom. Doris joined her as they waited for the students to make their way from the lunchroom tables.

"It sure feels good to be back in a regular routine," Melanie said. "School gives normalcy to my life. Everything else has a supernatural feel to it, and sometimes I have to pinch myself to make sure I'm not having a very long, very realistic dream. Do you know what I mean?"

"Sort of. I mean, sometimes I try to put myself in your place, try to imagine what you're going through. But to tell you the truth, it's more than I can comprehend. I'm scared to death just knowing what my role is going to be. And that's just a drop in the bucket compared to the responsibilities you and Jack are taking on."

Melanie looked at her friend warily. "Are you trying to scare me? If you are, it's working."

"No, I'm trying to tell you how much I admire you. I'm in awe of your strength and courage. And while we're having this quiet little moment—here in the school cafeteria with all these unsuspecting people around us—let me tell you one more thing, just in case I don't get around to it later."

"What?" Melanie asked.

"I'm so proud to be your friend."

The two reached out and touched hands. The gesture was subtle and went unnoticed. It also ended quickly when five-year-old Mary Alice Thompson made a major announcement. "Come on, Mrs. Russell," she said, tugging at her teacher's hand. "I need to go to the bathroom."

* * *

The gray Volvo parked in the school lot did not belong to any member of the faculty. Nor was it a car driven by a parent. The tinted windows made it impossible to tell, but a lone figure occupied the driver's seat. Eddie Weaver puffed on another cigarette as he waited impatiently for Melanie to emerge from the building. It was after four, and he was agitated by the teacher's devotion to duty.

Ten minutes later, two women emerged from the school. Weaver didn't recognize the blonde, but the brown-haired beauty was the star of William Bingham's perverted photo collection. He lowered the tinted window about three inches and peered through the crevice with the help of binoculars. It was a warm fall day, and Melanie carried her jacket over her left forearm as she and Doris walked to their cars. Weaver had a clear view of her torso.

He grinned, still holding the cigarette in the corner of his mouth. The blouse was loose, but it was easy to see that Melanie Russell was pregnant. Not too big, but big enough. Big enough to close the deal with the editors of some of the least respected—and most widely read—tabloids in the country.

Weaver put the binoculars in the passenger seat and picked up a thirty-five millimeter camera. He pointed the telephoto lens at Melanie and zoomed in for a close-up. He snapped off eight pictures before she reached her car, then watched as she pulled out of the parking lot and drove away from the school.

"Be careful, my golden goose. We can't let anything happen to you, at least not until the baby's born and I collect my money. I don't give a rat's ass after that."

He started the engine and lit another smoke before shifting the car into drive. He'd return next month to check on the condition of his pet project.

CHAPTER 19

October 30, 2000

The waiter, a nice young man in shirt and tie, finished pouring coffee for Jack, Reece, and Doris. Melanie longed for a cup but held fast to her pledge to steer clear of caffeine during her pregnancy. Temptation, for the most part, had been easily avoided during the past seven months, but tonight the decision to wave off the waiter had been difficult. The aroma from the steaming pot made her mouth water, and besides, she was tired. She hadn't been sleeping well of late, and the coffee would have given her a boost of energy. She needed it because she certainly wasn't ready for the night to end. This was the first time the four of them had been out together for…well, Melanie couldn't remember the last time the Russells and McKenzies had gone out on the town for dinner and a movie.

She reached for a glass of ice water and squeezed a lemon wedge over the top. It wasn't coffee, but it was better than nothing.

A bus boy came by to clear away the plates. "Last call for dessert," he said. "I can't believe all of you are going to say no."

"None for me, my good man," said Reece. "I'm stuffed."

"Me too," said Doris.

"Ditto," said Jack.

All eyes turned to Melanie. The stares included grins from everyone except the bus boy.

"Why's everybody looking at me? Just because I look like a pig doesn't mean I am one. Besides, I've got my heart set on a big box of Milk Duds at the movies."

The bus boy laughed and turned to leave. "Jimmy will be right back with the check then. Thank you, and enjoy the rest of your evening."

Everyone finished their drinks and started for the exit. A tall, thin woman with dark hair, seated alone across the aisle and two tables down, stood and followed the foursome out the door. She stepped into the shadows of the large building, away from the restaurant's entrance, and watched as the two couples walked down Rush Street toward the cinema complex three blocks away.

"I'm glad we decided to walk," Reece said. "I need to burn off some of this dinner before I sit in the dark for two hours. I need some fresh air if I'm ever going to see the end of this movie."

Jack and Melanie laughed. Doris rolled her eyes. "You'll never see the end of it anyway. You can't sit still for more than ten minutes without dozing off. The last time we went to the movies, I had to poke you three different times."

The laughter was like medicine to the foursome. For a moment, the double date seemed like old times, and each was reminded of what life was like before Melanie became pregnant. The laughter and togetherness they felt transported them briefly to their former lives—to a time when things were much simpler and the future of the world rested in the hands of others.

"Well, I don't think anyone will be sleeping during this thriller," Melanie said. "Roger Ebert said you'll be on the edge of your seat before the opening credits finish rolling. I'm really looking forward to—"

Melanie's words were cut off when a man stepped abruptly onto the sidewalk, blocking their path. Reece tensed, and Jack instinctively stepped in front of the two women. It was a cold night, and the man wore a wide brimmed hat pulled down low on his head. The collar of his coat was turned up, making it hard to see his face even under the glow of overhead street lamps.

"Excuse me," said Reece, his hands clenched into fists. "Is there a problem?"

The man quickly lifted his right hand. In it was a large gray revolver. He laughed as Reece, and the others stepped back. "Yes, there's a problem. But not for long."

Reece gasped as he saw the man's index finger tighten on the trigger. Even as he lunged forward, he realized he was too late. If only he hadn't taken the step backward.

A shot rang out, stopping Reece in his tracks. It was followed quickly by two more sharp, loud bangs. Doris screamed and ran to Reece, but he was still standing. Incredibly, it was the gunman who jerked away, staggering to the right as he tried to make his way to the alley from where he had emerged. Blood poured from two holes near the breast pocket of his coat. One more shot rang out, striking the man just above the ear and driving him to the sidewalk, where he lay motionless.

Suddenly, the source of the gunfire emerged. The woman from the restaurant lowered her weapon and walked quickly to the fallen man. She stooped and placed her finger against the side of his neck.

The others stood in shocked silence. All but Jack. He was used to trauma, to seeing violence, although he usually wasn't in the middle of it. "Does he have a pulse?"

The woman stood and turned toward them. Her face was expressionless, her tone void of emotion. "No. He's dead."

"Who are you?" Melanie asked, her voice shaking with fear.

The woman surveyed the street. Other pedestrians were already approaching. And several cars had stopped in the middle of the busy street. She pulled open her coat and placed the revolver in a leather shoulder holster. From her left pocket, she produced a police badge.

"I'm an off-duty detective who witnessed a crime in progress. I'll take care of everything here. But you should leave. Now. You don't need this kind of publicity, and one of the *Tribune*'s crime reporters will hear this on the scanner and be here any minute."

The four stood still, too stunned to move. Their gaze shifted from the body to the detective and back again. Finally, Reece asked the obvious question. "He wasn't trying to rob us, was he? He was going to shoot us like dogs in the street. And you knew, didn't you? That's why you were able to stop him."

The detective looked at Melanie, and there was sympathy in her eyes. "He was here for you. But he would have killed you all to get to the baby."

Jack hugged his wife. The women were afraid, both of them near tears. He was experiencing a different emotion. He was angry. Very angry.

"Is this what she's got to look forward to, facing some gun-toting nut around every street corner? Is this the life God has planned for her? For me and our friends? Is this his plan?"

The stranger put her arm on Jack's shoulder and gently guided him and the others down the street in the direction of the restaurant.

"He has no plan," she said quietly. "Not even he knows how this will turn out. But he loves the child more than any of you will ever be able to understand. He loves you all and will protect you and the child as much as he can. He sent me, didn't he? And he will send others like me. You can count on that." She turned to walk back to the body. "Now go. Quickly. Get out of here."

Melanie pulled free from Jack and grabbed her by the shoulders. "Thank you, Detective. Thank you for saving our lives, for saving my baby."

They would never see her again.

* * *

Melanie, Jack, Doris, and Reece drove back to the McKenzie house. After Reece returned from taking the sitter home, the four gathered around the kitchen table. The events of the evening had blasted them forcefully from their comfortable lives. It was time, they realized, to face harsh reality. Forces, from two distinctly different camps, not only knew about the baby but were willing to die in order to secure his safety or terminate his life.

The focal point of the battle between good and evil, at least until the baby was born, was Melanie. Keeping her safe had always been a priority for Jack and the McKenzies, but the unknown gunman had suddenly upped the ante. The four now realized the Second Coming of the Holy Child was more than a spiritual struggle. It was a battle of life and death between real people. And at stake was the future of the world.

"We need a plan," Doris said. "We can't go around telling people what we know, because no one would believe us anyway. But there are some things we can do, together and individually, to help keep Melanie safe."

The others looked at her solemnly, their minds straining to think of ways to prepare for the most fearsome foe of all—the unknown. Ideas were tossed out, strategies discussed, and slowly a plan of action and reaction began to take shape.

"Okay, we all agree that Melanie should not be left alone, for any reason," Jack said. "And between the three of us, we should be able to manage that. Doris, you'll be with her at school each day. That's great. Plus, she's always surrounded by students and other faculty members while at work. I feel good about her being at school. When she's home, I'll be home. I can work my schedule to make sure I'm at the house by early afternoon, and we'll stay together until she leaves for work in the morning."

"And don't forget, I'm available too," Reece said. "I've got a ton of vacation time saved up, and I can cover any of the open spots. Weekends, nights, days, even emergencies. I can be available at a moment's notice."

The group fell silent for a moment. "What about the boys?" Jack asked. "It's not right for you to give up all your time with them."

Doris and Reece looked at each other and smiled. "I don't think you understand," Doris said. "Much of what we're doing is for our boys—our children and children everywhere. What happens during the next two months and after your son is born will decide their future or determine if they even have a future. Helping you protect Melanie is a small price to pay for us."

Jack reached out and took Doris's hand. He placed his left hand on Reece's shoulder. While still touching his friends, he looked at Melanie. She was fighting back tears.

"I don't know what we'd do without you two," he said, weariness and worry in his voice. "I really don't."

Melanie, unable to speak, nodded her head in agreement. She'd lost the battle with the tears. Silently they fell from her eyes and splashed in small droplets on the kitchen table.

CHAPTER 20

November 15, 2000

Eddie Weaver was losing his patience. He and William Bingham were seated at a corner booth in Angelo's Diner on Chicago's lower east side, and Weaver was trying to enjoy the last of his breakfast. It wasn't easy, not with Bingham's constant moaning.

"When are we going to get our money?" Bingham asked again. "When is the story going to break?"

Weaver slammed his fork against the countertop. He leaned forward and glared at his irritating business associate. "Godammit, can't you shut the hell up for just five seconds? Your mouth runs more than these eggs. Not that I've had the chance to eat them."

Bingham stopped in midsentence, frozen like a deer caught in headlights.

Without Weaver there was no deal. He didn't know anyone at the tabloids. In fact, he had no publication contacts at all. All he had were the photos of Melanie Russell, and Weaver was now in possession of those. Even the negatives. Like it or not, without Weaver, he had nothing.

"Calm down, Eddie. Just calm down. I didn't mean to push so hard. I'm just nervous. She'll be delivering in less than two months, and I'm worried about the cash. I don't see why we can't get the money before the baby's born."

Weaver sighed and pushed his plate back. His usual case of heartburn was burning a hole in his belly already, so he decided against shoving more of the greasy food down his gullet. Instead, he took a big gulp of milk, which always seemed to ease his stomach pain, then lit a cigarette, which only added to the discomfort.

If Willie the whiner says one more word, I'm walking out the door, he thought.

Fortunately for Bingham, he managed to hold his tongue a few more minutes.

When Weaver was satisfied that his perverted partner had suffered enough, he reopened the conversation. "This is the last time I'm going to tell you this. We can't collect squat until after the baby is born. What if Russell miscarries? What if she's hurt or killed before the baby is born? The story's no good until the baby arrives. That's why it's called a miracle birth, you idiot! Nobody's going to pay for the miracle pregnancy. Get it?"

Bingham nodded his head vigorously, like a caged monkey at the zoo. "Sure, I get it. Once the baby's born, all hell breaks loose, right? Then we get paid, man. Really paid. That's when our ship comes in, right?"

Weaver sneered at Bingham but said nothing. What good would it do? It was easy to see Doctor Dirt had already popped his cork.

"What are you going to do with your money?" Bingham asked. "I think I'll head down to Mexico for a while. Avoid the legal eagles and the lawsuits. Soak up some sun and some of that strong Mexican beer. Maybe soak me up a senorita or two. What about you?"

Weaver stood up to leave. As he did, a funny thought made him laugh. "If you leave, I might just stay here. This is a pretty big town, and nobody connected with the Russells knows my name. Maybe I'll just kick back and lay low in Chicago. Hell, with you out of my hair, it will seem like paradise." He turned and headed for the door. "Take care of that check, will you?" he shouted to Bingham. "And don't call me again for a while. Consider it my Thanksgiving holiday."

CHAPTER 21

November 26, 2000

A tall figure leaned against his car, casting a long shadow as the sun started its final descent below the horizon to the west. He was parked on a side street, one block over from the Russell home, but he had a good view of the garage and back entrance. He watched carefully as a tanned attractive couple exited the house amid hugs and waves from those standing at the back door.

The man recognized the older couple. Bob and Regina Russell, Jack's parents, had spent Thanksgiving day with their youngest son. Now they were leaving for the airport to catch a plane that would take them to the home of Jack's sister, Amy, in St. Louis. After spending the night and most of Friday with Amy, her husband, Keith, and grandchildren Julie and Stacey, the Russells would return to their warm, comfortable home in Tucson.

Even from a distance, the man could see the couple was excited about the impending birth of Melanie's baby. Regina hugged her daughter-in-law three times before finally leaving and even kissed Melanie's stomach for good luck.

Just inside the doorway, the man could make out two more members of the inner circle. Reece and Doris McKenzie were enjoying the holiday with their good friends. Toys scattered across the lawn told the watcher that the couple's sons—Jacob, Josh, and Jordan— were also somewhere inside. The door closed, and the others went back into the house.

The tall man pinched the bridge of his nose with his thumb and forefinger. His hands were big and strong. He rolled his head from side to side and heard the familiar crack from the top of his spinal cord. His long dark hair flowed freely to almost his shoulders, which were broad and thick. His intense face was covered with a neatly trimmed beard, and his blue eyes were the color of the Caribbean Sea.

He pushed himself away from the car and stretched his six-and-a-half-foot frame, extending his fingers toward the sky. His short blue-jean jacket rose above his waist, revealing a pearl-handled pistol tucked into the back of his jeans. He walked around to the driver's side of the car, opened the door and stuffed himself inside. On the seat next to him was a 12-gauge shotgun. On the floor was a high powered rifle, complete with a scope, and two boxes of ammunition.

The tall man positioned himself for a better view of the Russell home. Every member of the inner circle was inside. Together. Vulnerable. It was a dangerous situation, and the man was on full alert. He reached under the seat and pulled out a small cooler. Inside were two cans of Coke. He opened one and took a long cold drink. It burned his throat on the way down, and he could feel the effect of the caffeine almost immediately. He'd need it. It was going to be a long night.

* * *

Melanie woke with a start. Immediately she reached for Jack in the darkness and found him, sleeping deeply, beside her in bed. She turned her head to see the digital alarm, and the big red numbers displayed the time. It was four fifteen.

Doris, Reece, and the kids had stayed until almost eleven, and it was after midnight before Melanie and Jack retired for the night. Her back and legs ached, and she was exhausted.

So why am I awake? she thought.

Within seconds, it came to her. She was in danger. An inner alarm was blaring inside her head, warning her. Instinctively she was on her feet and shaking Jack awake.

"Get up," she whispered. "Someone's in the house. Someone's coming."

Jack stumbled out of bed. He'd grown to trust his wife's instincts. Without a word, he picked up the phone and punched 911. He put the receiver to his ear and could fill the panic rising in his throat. The phone was dead. Quietly he replaced the receiver in the cradle and, looking at Melanie, shook his head.

He pointed toward the bathroom. "Go, lock yourself in. Don't open the door unless you hear my voice."

Melanie was terrified. Her heart told her to stay with her husband, but she couldn't. The baby must be protected—at all costs. She felt helpless as Jack gently closed the door behind her. She locked it and moved to one corner of the bathroom. Melanie shivered and strained to hear in the darkness.

Jack was halfway down the stairwell before he saw the outline of a man standing at the bottom of the steps. In his hands, he could see the gleam of a blade. He squinted harder and made out a very large knife. Jack recoiled and started backing up the stairs. What could he use as a weapon? His mind raced, searching for an answer, but he was coming up empty and running out of time. If only he and Melanie kept a gun in the house.

He was at the top of the staircase now, and the dark figure was closing in. Jack braced himself. He was going to leap at the man, feet first, and pray that he could somehow avoid the blade. His only hope was that the ensuing fall would hurt the intruder more than it did him. It wasn't much of a plan, Jack realized, but at least his higher position on the stairs might be of some advantage.

The leap never occurred. Instead, Jack looked on—incredulously—as a hulking shadow followed the first intruder up the stairs. With one swift motion, the second man grabbed the first from behind, putting his forearm around his neck.

Before the knife-wielding intruder could even turn to face his attacker, the man used his other hand to violently twist the head in his grasp. Even in the darkness, Jack recognized the sickening sound that followed. The knife dropped to the stairs. The man, his neck broken, did the same.

Jack, still perched at the top of the steps, peered at the tall man in the darkness. Was he friend or foe? A miscalculation could mean death for him, his wife, and their unborn baby. He'd seen enough to know that, unarmed, none of them stood a chance against this man.

"It's okay, honey."

Jack whirled around to find Melanie standing behind him. "Go back!" he screamed, pushing his wife toward the bedroom. "Get out of here."

Melanie resisted. "Listen to me. Listen, Jack. It's okay. He's one of the good guys." She reached for a switch and turned on the light. The tall man stood silently on the stairs, looking up at the couple. As Jack stared in disbelief, Melanie walked to the man. Jack, feeling helpless, joined her.

"Mrs. Russell. Mr. Russell. My name's Michael. Matthew Benoit sent me. He thought I might be of some help to you." Michael looked down at the man he had killed. He was neither pleased nor displeased. "I guess he was right. He usually is."

"Who are you?" Jack asked. "How do you know Brother Matthew?"

"He's my late grandmother's brother. He called me from the abbey five days ago and asked me to come by for a visit. I drove up from Dallas and met with him on Sunday. Matthew keeps things pretty simple. He told me about you and the baby. Then he told me to get my big butt up here."

Michael looked at his watch, then glanced at the corpse again. "It will be daylight soon. I better take care of this. It's probably impossible, but you guys should try to get some sleep before morning. There will be no more trouble tonight. I'll come back tomorrow and properly introduce myself. I would imagine you might have some more questions for me."

With one hand, he pulled the dead man from the floor and slipped him over his right shoulder. He stooped and picked up the knife with the other hand, then started down the stairwell. "Mr. Russell, don't forget to lock the door behind me. And you'll need to call the alarm company, and the phone center first thing in the morning. Good night."

With that, he disappeared into the darkness.

When Jack returned to the bedroom, he found Melanie under the covers. "Are you okay?" he asked.

"I am now."

"What do you think about our new friend? You should have seen it, Melanie. He snapped that guy's neck like it was a pencil."

Melanie rolled onto her back and put her hands around her stomach, gently stroking her unborn child. "The chances of us completing this journey—of surviving to see it through to the end—just went up. That's what I think."

Then she turned to her side and pulled her feet up, curling into a ball beneath the covers. Within minutes, she was asleep. Sleep came easily now that Michael was standing guard.

CHAPTER 22

November 27, 2000

It was early afternoon, and five people occupied the den inside the Russell home. Melanie, Jack, and Doris were seated on the sofa, while Reece, about five feet away, sat in Jack's favorite chair. Standing in the center of the room, bashfully shifting his weight from one foot to the other, was Michael.

He'd returned to face the four people he knew only as members of a very special inner circle. For the past twenty minutes, he had talked about himself and answered questions asked by both the Russells and McKenzies. Michael liked them already. They were good people fighting a good cause, and as activities of the previous night clearly demonstrated, they were people in need of help—his kind of help.

Michael Starr was a young man, just twenty-seven years old. But he'd managed to cram a lot of life into those few years. A troubled teenager, he'd turned to drugs, alcohol, and women, and was going from bad to worse by the time he graduated—by the skin of his teeth—from high school.

At age nineteen, after kicking around between odd jobs for more than a year, he enlisted in the United States Marine Corps. After six weeks of basic training at Paris Island, South Carolina, he successfully completed a four-year tour of duty that included stops in California, Alaska, Japan, Australia, and Egypt. By the time he was discharged, honorably, Michael's mind had finally caught up with his body. Intellectually and physically, he was honed and razor sharp. He was also an expert in the areas of martial arts, demolitions, and weapons.

For the past three years, he had been employed as a US Marshal, working violent crimes in conjunction with the Dallas Police Department. To the law enforcement personnel he worked with on a daily basis, he was referred to simply as the Man. When the crime was too appalling, when the evidence was too thin, when conditions surrounding the case became too hideous, they always called Michael Starr.

He didn't enjoy the work or his role in it. He'd seen too many helpless victims during his stint in Dallas—children, the elderly, women, even people with physical and mental disabilities. Anyone who was an easy target. Easy prey.

These were the people Michael was assigned to help when he could. Usually, the victims of these crimes were beyond help, because when Dallas PD called the Man, it usually meant someone was dead.

It was a horrendous job, but Michael was ideally suited for it. By all accounts, he was a loner. No wife or children. His parents were deceased, killed in a car accident a year after he enlisted in the Marines. No brothers or sisters. No real friends. It made his assignments easier. There was no one else to answer to, except the victims.

He always remembered the victims, living and dead. And when he found those responsible for the most vicious of crimes, when he eventually tracked them down, Michael made them pay. The fortunate ones were arrested, jailed, and eventually brought to trial. Others weren't so lucky. Michael was rarely, if ever, second-guessed by his superiors. His was a dirty job, and he was good at it. Truth was, officials in Dallas were grateful to have him.

But now he was in Chicago, having taken leave from his duties in Texas. He respected and loved his uncle, Brother Matthew Benoit, more than any human on earth. Matthew had been the one to pull him through his drug-crazed days. He'd been the one to help Michael grieve and cope with the loss of his parents. And when Matthew finally asked Michael for help, there was no hesitation. He'd been asked to protect these four people, especially Melanie Russell and her unborn child. And that was what he planned to do.

Standing in the middle of the room, Michael was tired of talking. He'd said more in the past half hour than he sometimes said in weeks. But these people deserved some information. If they were going to trust him, place their lives in his hands, they needed to know something about him. He understood their curiosity. Even their fascination. But there was really only one thing Melanie and the inner circle needed to know. Michael would defend them at any cost, because Matthew had asked him to.

"Do you understand what is happening to me?" Melanie asked. "Do you know about our baby and what he means for the future?"

Michael hesitated before answering. It would be easier to lie. But these people, of all people, deserved the truth.

"I don't believe in God. I quit believing long ago. My parents were good people, snuffed out in the blink of an eye. No reason. No explanation. Just gone. The victims I see, on a daily basis, are helpless victims. They've done nothing to deserve the atrocities inflicted upon them. So I ask myself and you, if there is a God, why does he allow these things to happen?"

The room was silent as Michael paced back and forth. He was angry and struggled with his thoughts for a moment before continuing.

"But I do believe in my uncle. He told me about you. About your baby. Matthew says the baby you carry is the Son of God sent here to live on earth just as he did once before. He says this child will one day soon decide the fate of the world. I know Matthew believes this to be true. He believes it with his heart and soul. And that's good enough for me."

Doris stood up, staring intently into the eyes of the huge man before her. "But what do you believe?" she asked.

Michael pulled gently at his dark beard, pondering the question. He was surprised by his own answer. "Well, I know there's a hell. I've seen it up close. So maybe there is a heaven. Who am I to say?"

He smiled, revealing beautiful teeth. It was a shame so few people had witnessed a Michael Starr grin. "But even if there is a heaven, it doesn't mean you have to be in a hurry to get there now, does it? If you folks don't mind, I'm going to make sure you stay here among the living for a while longer. That baby's going to need a good family around him. And if what you say about the child is true, he's going to need all the help he can get."

Melanie stood and joined Doris in front of Michael. She reached out and took his massive hand into hers. "Thank you for coming, Michael. It's an honor to have you here. And it's comforting to have you on our side."

The men stood and joined their wives. Each of the others, in turn, shook hands with their newly assigned protector. A strong bond was already forming. It would only strengthen during the dangerous weeks and months ahead.

CHAPTER 23

December 10, 2000

Dr. Stewart slowly traced the ultrasound scanner across Melanie's abdomen.

She peered intently at the monitor which depicted a sonar image of the baby. Melanie and Jack shifted their gaze from the screen to the doctor, then back again. Everything looked good to them. The baby's heartbeat sounded strong. But then, what did they know? Stewart's opinion was the one that really counted.

She finally nodded her head approvingly, and the couple breathed a sigh of relief together. "The baby looks good, really good," she said, taking a paper towel and wiping off the lubrication gel she'd smeared onto Melanie's belly. "He looks completely normal in size and shape and is positioned perfectly for a traditional, vaginal delivery."

She put her arms out and helped Melanie pull herself from the exam table and into a sitting position. Melanie winced, trying hard not to urinate on herself. Her bladder was full after drinking several glasses of water in preparation for the ultrasound, but at least they'd had an unobstructed view of her womb.

"What about Mommy," Jack asked. "How's she holding up?"

Before Stewart could answer, Melanie responded in her most sarcastic tone, "Have you taken a good look at these ankles lately? And check out the muscles in my calves. If they cramp one more time, I think I'll set some kind of record for high jumping out of bed."

Everyone laughed, and Melanie carefully lowered herself to the floor. As usual, even the effort of sitting up and standing left her short of breath.

"Well, you may be falling apart on the outside, but your internal organs are in blue ribbon condition," Stewart said. "Your uterus, placenta, and even the umbilical cord looked great on the ultrasound. Your blood pressure is fine, as are all your other vitals. The baby has dropped considerably since your last checkup, so I think we're right on schedule. Just a couple more weeks of discomfort, then you two will be the proud parents of a bouncing baby boy."

Stewart opened the door to the exam room and called for a nurse. "Please see Mrs. Russell to the bathroom, then give her my card with all the emergency numbers on it. I think we're going to have a baby soon, and I certainly don't want to miss out on all the fun."

Melanie and the nurse shuffled down the hall, leaving Jack and the doctor together. "Have you guys decided on a name yet?" Stewart asked.

The question caught Jack off guard. "Uh, no. No, we haven't," he said. "We've been so busy with, well, with things…that we haven't even discussed names."

"You better hurry then," she said, walking quickly to the next exam room. "I know you're going to want to call him something besides Baby Boy Russell for the rest of his life."

Jack laughed nervously and went to wait for Melanie in the outer lobby.

Jan's right, he thought. *We definitely need to give this some thought. This isn't going to be an easy baby to name.*

* * *

"What kind of name would be right? You know, right for something like this?" Jack asked again. "I mean, we can't name this baby Carl or Al or Max."

Melanie laughed. She was sitting on the side of the bed, brushing her hair, once again amazed that so much of it seemed to be falling out. It was part of being pregnant, Dr. Stewart had said. Just one more way in which an unborn child sapped life out of the poor, expectant mother. Finally finished, she turned back to Jack, who was stretched across the bed, his head propped up by his elbow and right hand.

"Why not? Why can't we name him anything we want? He's our baby. It's our responsibility to care for him and raise him properly. It's up to us to give him a decent, respectable name, and if you like Carl or Al or Max, then let's talk about it. But you don't really like those names, do you?"

Jack was frustrated. Melanie wasn't grasping the importance of a name. She wasn't taking this seriously.

"Of course, I don't," he said. "We need to decide on a good name. Something strong and important. Don't you realize this is a name that might be remembered throughout history—by generations and generations of people who believe in the Word of God? Look at the name Jesus and what it has come to mean to people all over the world."

Melanie tried to suppress a giggle, but failed miserably. Instead, she erupted into laughter again. Jack frowned. He was growing angry. She rolled toward him and spooned herself against his body. "Correct me if I'm wrong, but I believe the name Jesus has already been taken," she said. "And besides, I believe our little boy would have a hard time walking around town with a name like that. Jesus Russell—it just doesn't sound right."

Jack rolled off the bed and stormed into the bathroom. By the time he returned, Melanie had regained her composure and was determined not to laugh again.

"I'm sorry, Jack. Really, I am. It's just that I've never seen you this uptight before. You really are concerned about what we should name our baby, aren't you?"

Still wounded, he returned to bed with his wife. "Of course, I am. And I would think you'd be a little more concerned too. Have you given this any thought at all?"

Melanie smiled and reached for the nightstand beside the bed. She pulled open the small drawer and took out a thick well-worn book. It was a reference book used by teachers of Bible study. She'd borrowed it from Doris six weeks earlier.

Jack looked at the book, then back at Melanie. "What's this?" he asked.

"This book has an entire section on names. It contains the names of prominent characters from the Bible. The characters are classified according to the meaning of their name. I found one I really like, Jack. It's on page 238. See if you can pick it out. If you can and you like it as much as I do, then I think that's the name we should give our baby."

Jack opened the book and turned to the page. Melanie had surprised him. It didn't happen often. He nervously used his index finger to scan down the list of names on the page.

Abel, Adam, Abraham, Cain, Caleb, David, Deborah, Eli, Enoch, Gideon…and Jack continued down the page. First he looked at the name, then the meaning.

When he came to the right one—the name he knew Melanie had chosen—he felt a lump in his throat, and a sense of calm come over him. The name and its meaning was perfect: Isaac, the long looked-for son.

Melanie leaned over and kissed Jack gently on the cheek. Then she whispered in his ear, keeping their secret safe from the rest of the world. "Isaac was a prominent character from the Old Testament. He was the son of Abraham and Sarah. The characteristics of the name include laughter, affection, peaceableness, and prayerfulness. The long looked-for son was a true man of faith."

Jack was speechless. Hearing his son's name for the first time seemed to bring everything into perspective. Despite all the circumstances surrounding this child—and they were monumental, to be sure—he was still going to be a father. His son would have a name, would be a real person, and would depend upon him and Melanie for almost everything for several years. Finally, he let the name roll off his tongue.

"Isaac. Isaac Russell. Mr. and Mrs. so-and-so, I'd like you to meet our son, Isaac Russell." He smiled. So did Melanie. "I like it," he said. "I really do."

"I have one more request," she said. "I think our son should have a middle name. And if it's okay with you, I'd like his other name to be one of our time, of our world." Melanie hesitated as she felt long-ago memories welling up inside her. She wanted to cry, but didn't. Instead, she shared the name with Jack. "I'd like to name him Isaac James Russell. James, after my father."

Jack reached for his wife and hugged her tightly. "Isaac James it is," he said. "It's a beautiful name, Melanie. It really is." He reached down and kissed his wife's belly, then turned his head slightly so that he could talk directly to their unborn son. "I love you, little Isaac James. And I can't wait for you to get here."

CHAPTER 24

December 12, 2000

Michael and Melanie were seated at the kitchen table, laughing as they watched Jack spin around the room with an old barbecue apron covering his shirt and tie. He was putting the finishing touches on a bountiful breakfast and was enjoying the attention he was receiving from his attentive audience.

"Tell me, old great chef Jack, what are you serving this morning?" Melanie asked. Then she leaned closer to Michael and whispered, "Play along."

"I'm but a poor visitor to this great place, and I am truly honored to be served by the greatest chef in the entire free world. I can't wait to see what you've prepared."

Jack approached the table with a steaming skillet in one hand, a spatula in the other, and a crazed look in his eyes. "Then wait no more," he said with mock zeal. "Behold, the golden flavor of my world-famous scrambled eggs."

The three of them laughed long and hard. Jack placed the now empty skillet in the sink, then tossed his apron on the counter, and joined the others at the table. Together they enjoyed sausage, eggs, toast and jelly, and orange juice.

"I was expecting room and board, but not all these wonderful meals too," said Michael. "I feel like I'm staying at a bed and breakfast. But really, I'm a pretty simple eater. You folks don't have to go to all this trouble."

Jack started to speak, but Melanie interrupted, "Are you kidding? It's about time Jack started waiting on me hand and foot. You'd better be like me and enjoy it while it lasts. Soon enough he'll turn back into the male chauvinist pig he really is, coming home at the end of the day and asking why his dinner isn't ready."

Michael cast a surprised look in Jack's direction. Melanie stifled a giggle as Jack jumped to his own defense. "That's a bunch of bull. Don't you believe her, Michael. I've treated this woman like a queen for years now. She's got it made and knows it. Not many women have the good fortune to marry a world-famous chef like me."

Laughter and light conversation continued as the trio finished breakfast. Plates, glasses and silverware were loaded into the dishwasher, then everyone prepared for the day's duties. Jack was off to the hospital while Melanie, with Michael serving as her driver, headed for Mercy Elementary. It was the last week of school before the Christmas recess, and Melanie was ready for a break. Once the baby was born, she planned to take at least six weeks maternity leave, maybe longer. It all depended on what happened following the birth. Both the expected and the unexpected. She was nervous, happy, fearful, excited, anxious, and joyful all at the same time. But one thing was certain. She couldn't wait to see and hold her son. It was something she'd been waiting for her whole life.

Jack backed out of the garage ahead of Michael and Melanie and turned right, heading for the expressway. Michael steered Melanie's car left, taking a shorter route to the school. After parking in a remote spot in the far corner of the lot, he watched Melanie enter the building. Then he settled in for another long day of watching and waiting. He opened the morning newspaper and turned quickly to the comic section. It was an old habit. In his line of work, the morning chuckle provided by Dagwood and the Peanuts gang was sometimes the day's only positive.

Every minute or two, Michael looked up to check on the school, his trained eyes searching for any signs of trouble, anything out of the ordinary. If need be, he could be inside the school within thirty seconds and could get to Melanie's classroom in another fifteen. He knew this because he'd timed himself on two separate occasions.

Michael Starr left nothing to chance. He couldn't afford to. Not now. The long-awaited son would arrive within the next two weeks. And with the very special birth, Michael suspected, the potential for danger would only increase.

He put down the paper for a moment and thought of Matthew. The image of his uncle made him smile. *I wonder if I'll live to see him again*, Michael thought. Quickly, he pushed the reflection from his mind and returned to the comics. He could use another bit of humor.

CHAPTER 25

December 22, 2000

Melanie and Doris were in the McKenzie's family room, listening to Christmas songs by Nat King Cole, Perry Como, Bing Crosby, and some of their other all-time favorite crooners. They wrapped presents and talked quietly as the three boys chased one another through the house, stoked to the gills on Christmas candy and thoughts of Santa Claus. Doris tried several times to slow them down, but her efforts were futile. Reece and Michael were in the kitchen, enjoying a cup of eggnog spiked with just a bit of Jim Beam's finest. Jack was at the hospital, pulling his last late shift until after the holidays. Three days before Christmas and all was well. Or at least seemed to be.

Emotionally, Melanie was hanging on. But physically, she was suffering.

Her back throbbed constantly, and her feet were tender and sore. She was constipated, exhausted from lack of sleep, and in a recently repulsive development, irritated by a raw red rash, which had spread across her neck and shoulders.

Yet Melanie accepted it all, without complaint, and would accept more if need be. Being pregnant was the greatest event of her life. She was nearing the end of a marathon. And once the baby was born, another race would begin—a race for life, not only for their son, but for all humanity. It was no place for the weak, only the strong. Melanie was prepared. And her inner strength—like rich cream—was beginning to rise to the top.

"I still can't believe how well you're holding up," Doris said. "I think I cried virtually nonstop the last two weeks of my pregnancies, all three of them. It never did get any easier for me. But the first one is always hardest, because everything is new and you just don't know what to expect."

Melanie was putting the finishing touches on a gift she'd purchased for Michael. It was a beautiful silver necklace with a religious medal attached. The medallion displayed the image of Saint Michael, the archangel. It was an easy choice. For obvious reasons, the gift seemed appropriate.

"I have aches and pains, just like all women do I'm sure, but I just feel so fortunate to be pregnant. We never dreamed it would happen, especially the way it has. Even though I've come to grips with who the baby is—and why he is coming—I still have moments of utter disbelief. But I don't dwell on it. I can't afford to. There's too much at stake and too many things to do. I'll never understand why we were chosen, yet I've accepted the fact that we were. My only choice is to do the very best I can."

The pair grew silent for a time, trimming wrapping paper and taping it securely around more packages. Finally, Melanie spoke again.

"Come on now, let's not get so serious. I'm surrounded by family and great friends. And even my own personal bodyguard. Now how many people get that kind of treatment? I feel like a Hollywood movie star."

Doris smiled, but it was a forced reaction. She still worried about her friend. "Maybe this will somehow get easier when little Isaac is born," she said.

Melanie nodded in agreement, and the conversation died again. Both women were busy with their thoughts, each realizing the birth of the baby, while wonderful, would only serve to increase the degree of difficulty they would face from here on out.

In the background, Crosby dreamed of a white Christmas.

CHAPTER 26

December 23, 2000

Melanie could hear voices coming from downstairs. Jack and Michael were talking. About what? She didn't know and didn't really care. She was tired, as tired as she could ever remember being.

Still in bed, Melanie was lying, as usual, on her back. She tossed aside the covers, pointed her toes, threw back her arms, and stretched. The muscles in her calves, bunched into tiny knots, relaxed a bit, and the tension in her neck and shoulders subsided. But the muscles in her abdomen, upper pelvis, and along her ribcage remained cramped. The entire middle portion of her body felt as tight as a drum.

It was morning and Melanie had made it through yet another difficult night.

She'd been up constantly, stretching her calves or going to the bathroom, and when sleep did overtake her, it never lasted long. Reluctantly she rolled onto her side and pushed her body from the bed. After washing her face and hands, brushing her teeth, and pulling her hair back into a short ponytail, she descended the steps in her robe and slippers.

She found the men in the kitchen, drinking coffee and eating fresh-baked donuts. "Where did you get these?" Melanie asked, reaching into the box for one. Jack went to the refrigerator and poured his wife a glass of milk. "Mrs. Anderson, from across the street, brought them over a while ago," he said. "She wanted to wish us a Merry Christmas and congratulate us on the baby."

Melanie accepted the glass from Jack, took a drink, then made her usual "yuck" face. "That's sweet," she said, reaching into the box for a second glazed. Jack and Michael looked at each other, each trying to hide a grin. "Go ahead, laugh. Make me feel more guilty than I already do. I swear I'm going to quit eating altogether once this baby comes. When I'm slim and trim again, you'll be sorry. So laugh now, while you still can."

Jack sat next to Melanie and kissed her on the cheek. "You're more beautiful now than you've ever been." And he meant it. Despite the swelling, despite the dark circles under his wife's eyes, she was absolutely radiant. She glowed with pride and love, and her radiance filled a room every time she entered it. Although he didn't say so, Michael was in complete agreement. Melanie Russell was a beautiful woman. And in the few weeks he'd known her, he realized her inner beauty was even more breathtaking than her outward appearance. Uncle Matthew had called her a special woman. He was right.

"So what are you doing today?" Jack asked. "Just two more days till Christmas, you know."

"Oh my god," Melanie said, pushing herself away from the table and walking to the refrigerator. There she looked at the calendar. "It's the twenty-third, isn't it? It's the day."

Both Jack and Michael looked at Melanie, confusion on their faces. "It's the twenty-third. One year ago, I met the Salvation Army Santa. He was the one who told me about the baby, about what was to come. Don't you remember, Jack?"

Jack nodded. He did remember. And he remembered something else. "Didn't he ask you to come back, to come and see him again this year? Today?"

While Melanie went upstairs to dress, Jack repeated the events of December 23, 1999, to Michael. The big man listened intently and was up to speed by the time Melanie returned.

"What do you think?" Jack asked. "Do you think she should go?"

"If what you say is true, this may be out of my league," Michael answered. "As I told you before, I'm not really a spiritual guy. But if we all go together, in broad daylight on a crowded downtown street, I think Melanie will be safe."

Melanie, feeling urgency now, took Jack's hand and pulled him toward the door. "Of course, I'll be safe. And of course, we're going. There is nothing to fear from the man I met last year. He had information for me then, and I believe he will have information for me again. Let's go guys. The traffic will be murder."

* * *

Melanie was disappointed. More than disappointed, really. In fact, she was experiencing feelings of betrayal. She and Jack and Michael were seated on a bench near the corner of Lincoln and Broadway. For almost an hour, the three had searched for a Salvation Army station, walking up and down both sides of the street where Melanie had encountered the strange messenger one year before. There were no signs of Santa or anyone else who might be of assistance to them.

"Are you sure this is the right place?" Jack asked. "Maybe you were shopping in another part of town when you met him. You know how crazy things get around the holidays. Even normal things are hard to keep up with."

Melanie was tired and irritable, not to mention disappointed. "I wish you'd quit asking me that. This is the spot. I was walking back to the parking garage after buying you that pretty red sweater at Carlson's. I remember it vividly. It's not the kind of thing that happens every day."

Michael and Jack looked at each other. She was right, of course. It had been a day, an event, that Melanie would surely remember the rest of her life.

The trio remained on the bench, watching as busy shoppers scurried back and forth, lugging packages and large shopping bags with them. It was unusually warm for December in Chicago, with the temperatures in the midfifties. Some of the shoppers even carried their coats.

Melanie grabbed Jack's arm. "What time is it?" Jack pulled back the sleeve of his jacket and looked at his watch. "Almost eleven thirty," he said. "Why?"

"That's it!" Melanie said, and both men could detect the hope in her voice. "It was late in the day when I passed here last year. "I'll bet we're too early. Maybe he'll be here if we come back later in the afternoon."

Jack was doubtful, but he wasn't going to argue. Finding the man meant a great deal to his wife. He'd wait all day if need be. He looked at her, slumped uncomfortably on the hard bench, anxiety and worry evident on her face and in her eyes. *It's the least I can do*, he thought and turned to tell her so.

But before he could speak, Michael stood and stretched his huge frame to its considerable limits. Both Jack and Melanie grimaced as he twisted his head from side to side, and they heard the now familiar popping sound that always followed. He grinned at their grimace.

"I've got an idea," he said. "How about we walk over to that pizzeria across the street and have a little lunch? My treat. I'll get us a window seat, and we can watch the street while we wait. How does that sound?"

Melanie raised her arms toward Michael, and he used them to pull her from the bench. "Fine with me," she said. "They're bound to have a seat more comfortable than this one."

Jack rose also, although reluctantly. He'd had two glazed donuts and three cups of coffee just two hours earlier. Pizza was the last thing on his mind. "All right. Let's go. But I can't believe you're hungry, Michael. You had a half a box of donuts before we left the house."

Michael said nothing as he led them across the street. Actually, Jack was right. He wasn't hungry. But being out on the street, alone with both Jack and Melanie, made him nervous. There were too many people to watch, coming at them from too many directions. And for all he knew, the request from last year's strange Santa could be a setup. The plan might have been to get Melanie on the street, alone and vulnerable, in her last few days of pregnancy. A public ambush on a crowded street. Michael trusted no one and took nothing for granted. Now was not the time to get sloppy. Melanie would be safer inside.

It was twenty minutes before a waiter could find seating for the threesome. It was another forty minutes before the steaming pepperoni pie and a side order of bread sticks arrived. Much to her dismay, Melanie was actually hungry by the time the food was served. She was halfway through her second slice of pepperoni when she saw him.

Santa was walking down the sidewalk across the street from where they were seated. In one arm, he carried the familiar red kettle and a small tripod. In the other, he held the bell and a green Salvation Army sign. About fifty feet past the bench where she and Jack and Michael had waited, he stopped and set up shop. Within minutes, he was ringing the bell, and pedestrians were stopping by to help out the world-famous charity.

The trio stared through the window at the man. Melanie was looking for signs of recognition. Jack, noncommittal, was simply looking. Michael was looking for danger.

"Let's go," Melanie said, standing quickly to leave. "I need to talk to him."

Jack glanced at Michael, seeking his approval. Michael shrugged his shoulders. "She seems to know these things," he said, rushing to catch up with Melanie. "Let's just stay close to her and see what happens." Jack dropped twenty five dollars on the table and caught up with Michael and Melanie as they waited to cross the street.

As they made their way across to the opposite curb, they could hear Santa's chant in a deep, friendly voice. "Ho, ho, ho! Merry Christmas! Merry Christmas, everyone. And don't forget the poor and needy. Help Santa buy food and clothes. Ho, ho, ho! Help Santa help the children."

Melanie waited as an elderly woman in well-worn clothes talked with Santa.

She dropped a few coins in the kettle, and Melanie smiled as she heard the bell ringer's reply. "Thank you, my dear. Thank you for helping the Salvation Army."

As the woman walked away, Melanie reached out and touched him on the shoulder as Jack and Michael stood beside her. "Hello, Santa. How have you been?"

He turned and the dark gentle eyes danced with delight. His brilliant smile was partially hidden behind the thick, fluffy beard, yet it still brightened the street corner, even in the early afternoon sun. He noticed the two men standing guard beside Melanie, nodded briefly, then stepped forward to take her hand. There was nothing threatening in his movements.

"Oh my, it's good to see you again. You look wonderful. Absolutely beautiful. You are not only a sight for sore eyes but a glorious treasure to behold. God bless you, my dear. God bless you."

Instinctively, both Michael and Jack relaxed. They were in the presence of goodness. Each man could feel it, although neither could explain it. There was no reason to fear this man.

Still holding Melanie's hand Santa turned to Michael, squinting against the sun as he looked up at the tall figure. "Michael, my good man. I wonder if you could do us a favor? I need to talk with Melanie for a moment, but I must keep ringing my bell. The donations come in twice as fast if someone is manning the kettle. Do you mind?"

The look on Michael's face made Jack laugh. The big man was not only surprised by the request; he was embarrassed. When Santa removed his hat and placed it atop Michael's head, his face was almost as red at the furry cap. "Go ahead, Michael," he said, placing the bell in his mammoth hand. "It's not hard. Just ring it a little and say, 'Ho, ho, ho!' every few seconds. People will give money. They always do."

Jack and Melanie were both laughing now. Sheepishly, Michael stepped over to the kettle. He looked over his shoulder at Melanie, and she nodded reassuringly. "I'm fine," she said. Then with a giggle, she added, "You go, Santa. Ring that bell."

The good soldier did as he was told. Later that evening, at home with Melanie and Jack, he would admit to enjoying his one and only bell-ringing experience.

With the light amenities out of the way, the mood grew serious as the mystery messenger huddled on the street with Melanie and Jack. The information he had for the couple was critically important and not particularly pleasant. Santa didn't mince words as he described the days ahead.

"Your baby will be born soon. Very soon. I want you to concentrate on the job at hand. Focus on the baby and the delivery. There's no need to worry about anything else. You have protection and should be safe, but there is always a certain amount of risk associated with the birth of a child. This baby is human, so you and he assume the same risks as any other mother and child."

The couple held hands as they listened. "We have a good doctor," Melanie said. "And Jack will be with me too. He's a very skilled physician."

Santa smiled. "I know he is," he said. "And you've been a great patient. You and the unborn infant are both very healthy. We expect the delivery to go well. We have the utmost confidence in you. In both of you."

Jack started to ask about the "we" reference but bit his lip instead. This wasn't the time or place to interrupt the messenger. Besides, he had a vague idea about the "we" part. God and his earthly army, no doubt.

Melanie pulled at Jack's hand, snapping him back to attention. The messenger continued, "The most difficult part for you—and the most dangerous time for the child—will be the first year of his life. That's when he will be most vulnerable. Just as it was before, members of the dark side will seek out the Holy Child and try to destroy him. They will come, as King Herod did, in an attempt to eliminate the child and all he stands for as quickly as possible."

The color was slowly draining from Melanie's face, and her legs were growing weak. This message was expected, really, but hearing the words out loud shocked her. People coming to destroy her child, a helpless newborn baby—the thought of it made her want to wretch.

"Will we have help?" Jack asked anxiously. "We've had help before." Santa glanced over his shoulder at Michael, who was still ringing the bell.

"You have a great protector in this man. Michael is a troubled, complicated soul, but he is a man of great courage and bravery. If you ask, he will stay with you, maybe even through the first year. You will need him."

Melanie wanted to cry. She was exhausted and frightened and was tired of hiding it. She wanted to drop to her knees on the sidewalk and scream at the top of her lungs. *I can't take this anymore*, she thought. *Please God, don't make me do this. Don't put all this on me. I'm not strong enough. Please make it stop.*

But she said not a word. Instead she looked into the messenger's eyes. "What else should we know?"

"First of all, let me give you some good news," he said. "Michael can't do it alone, and he won't have to. Besides yourselves and your friends Doris and Reece, others will step forward to assist you, especially during the early years. Keep your eyes open for allies, and they will come."

"What about the bad guys?" Jack asked. "They'll come too, won't they?"

"Yes. Stay on guard, at all times, especially where the baby is concerned. After his birth, you two will become less of a target. Instead, they will concentrate their efforts on the child."

"Any more bad news?" Jack asked.

The messenger hesitated, trying to decide if this last bit of information was too much, too soon. He wasn't sure how much more they could take. "I'm afraid there is more. The news of this birth and your special child is going to be made public…"

Melanie and Jack both gasped. "How?" she shrieked. "How could anyone else know about this? We've told no one."

The bell stopped ringing. Instantly Michael was at Melanie's side. "What's the matter?" he asked. "What's wrong?"

Melanie was crying now, unable to hold the tears back any longer. Jack put his arm around her, supporting much of her weight with his left shoulder and arm. The truth was, he was feeling a little wobbly himself.

The messenger looked at the trio before him, and there was wisdom in his dark eyes. He placed his hands on Melanie's shoulders and stared at her tear-streaked face. The scene of a hatless Salvation Army Santa—leaning on a pregnant lady—would have seemed odd to those passing by, but most were too busy to notice. The four people were an island unto themselves on the crowded street corner.

"You must listen to me. How it happens is not important. Why it happens is the key. The dark side wants to draw attention to your situation. The more attention you and the baby receive, the harder it will be to protect him. It will be difficult for you to distinguish between good and evil. Some will believe he is the Son of God, and they will want to see him, to touch him. Many others will deride him as a fake, a fraud, and they will also want to see him, but for a different reason. They will want to expose him and destroy your family. The human side of this situation will result in chaos, and it will expose the child to human forms of danger. But more importantly, it will create openings for the dark forces to slip in and do their work. That's where the real danger lies."

Melanie's eyes fluttered slightly, and she started to slump to the street.

Michael put his right arm around her waist, and together he and Jack held her up. "Melanie," Jack said. "Baby, are you all right?"

She fought to stay on her feet, fought hard. It took all the strength she could muster, but she remained standing. A few seconds later, she opened her eyes and stared into those of the messenger. The words she spoke were cold and harsh.

There was no easy way to ask the question. "Will he make it? Will my son survive?"

The messenger reached out and hugged Melanie tightly. "I don't know," he said. "But I pray that he will. I pray for you and your brave family with all my might."

Reluctantly, he pushed himself away. He took the Santa hat from Michael's hand and placed it on his head. He accepted the small gold bell from the guardian. "May the Holy Father shine his loving light on all of you. Trust in him, and he will show you the way."

With that, he returned to the kettle and began ringing the bell. As Jack and Michael helped Melanie back across the street, they could hear him continue the familiar chant. "Merry Christmas. Merry Christmas to all."

* * *

It was a little past eleven when Doris returned to bed. The wind outside the bedroom window whipped and moaned, and the sky was dark as clouds continued to roll across the city. Outside the temperatures plummeted as a strong cold front pushed through. Reece was awakened by the movement of his wife.

"Is anything wrong?" he asked.

"No, Jordan just needed a drink of water. He said his throat was dry. It's probably just sore due to the change in weather."

Doris snuggled close to her husband and put her hand against his cheek. "I'm scared, Reece. I don't know what's going to happen once the baby is born. I'm almost too frightened to even think about it."

The dark bedroom fell silent. "Reece? Reece, are you awake?"

He put his own hand against the one his wife still held to his cheek. "Yeah, I'm awake. I just don't know what to say. I'm scared too."

It was several more hours before either drifted into the warm confines of sleep.

CHAPTER 27

December 24, 2000

Christmas Eve dawned cloudy and cold. The temperature had dropped more than twenty degrees during the past twenty-four hours, and according to Chuck Munson, WCLN's chief meteorologist, Chicago would see single digits by nightfall. A mixture of sleet and snow was in the forecast, which seemed to delight Munson and the rest of the news gang at WCLN. "Winter arrives…just in time for Santa." That was how they kicked off the early morning newscast.

All the talk about the winter storm made Melanie uneasy. Chicago winters, unlike those in her hometown of Louisville, were usually brutal. A foot of snow was commonplace this time of year and could make driving conditions treacherous all across northern Illinois.

"What else can happen?" Melanie asked, anxiety in her voice. Both she and Jack were still in bed, watching the news on the bedroom television. "I don't want this baby to be born in the middle of a blizzard. What if I go into labor and we can't get to the hospital?"

Jack was determined to ease his wife's tension. "First of all, our friend Jan Stewart would be one disappointed physician." He waited for Melanie to laugh. When she didn't, he pressed on. "And secondly, you don't have to worry about that happening. That's why we bought the Jeep, remember? You can't get through winter in Chicago without four-wheel drive. And last but not least, I'm a pretty fair doctor myself. I've delivered at least a dozen babies in my career. I certainly think I could deliver one more if it comes to that. So all in all, I'd say you're in good hands."

Melanie didn't respond. Instead she rolled onto her side, although just barely, and closed her eyes. "I'm going back to sleep," she said. "Maybe this will all be over when I wake up."

Jack frowned. Melanie was clearly depressed. And even though she had every right to be, he was concerned. He hoped the baby would come soon. If they could just have a safe and healthy delivery, then maybe they'd have the strength to face everything else.

He kissed his wife on the forehead, then threw on a robe and headed downstairs. He wanted to talk with Michael. It was time for the two of them to form a game plan. There would be only one chance to bring this very special child into the world. And in all probability, there would be no margin for error.

"Help us, God," he said as he slowly descended the stairs. "Please help us through this."

* * *

It was ten in the morning when Melanie felt the first contraction. She was standing at the bedroom window, watching as the first drops of freezing rain splashed against the glass. The pain in her lower back was sharp and penetrating, as if someone were sticking a needle into her spine just above the buttocks. As she turned to make her way across the room, she felt a slight cramping sensation in her lower abdomen. It wasn't intense or particularly painful; rather, it felt out of place. The contraction was new, something she'd never felt before. And it scared her.

She went to the edge of the bed and sat down. Spreading her legs, she used her right hand to examine her vagina. Her pelvic region was damp, her white cotton panties stained by a pink mucous discharge. The discharge, she remembered from her many conversations with Dr. Stewart, was a very normal sign associated with the onset of labor. She sat on the bed and waited. Five minutes passed, then six, then seven. Melanie felt nothing except the searing pain in her back. The cramping sensation she'd felt earlier—or had it been her imagination—was gone.

I better go downstairs, she thought. *No sense sitting in my room all day.* At the top of the stairs, another labor pain arrived. She gripped the bannister tightly, holding on for dear life, because this time the cramping sensation was more painful and lasted almost a full minute. Melanie relaxed as the contraction finally subsided and purposely waited until her breathing returned to normal before calling for Jack.

"Jack. Can you help me for a second?"

Jack and Michael both appeared on the downstairs landing. "What's the matter, honey?" Jack asked. "Are you okay?"

Melanie, still holding onto the bannister, smiled nervously. "I'm fine. But I need you to come up and take a look at me. I think we're getting ready to have a baby."

Jack raced up the stairs, taking them two at a time. When he reached the top, he put his arms around Melanie. He could feel her shaking and was almost overcome with emotion himself. Only his years of training in emergency medicine prevented him from going into a full panic. "Are you sure? Are you having contractions?"

"No, I'm not sure. And yes, I'm having contractions. Or at least I think I am. I had one, followed by another about eight minutes later."

Then looking down at Michael still on the landing, she whispered so only Jack could hear, "My panties are soaking wet. But I can't see a thing down there, so I'm not really sure what's happening. I need you to take a look."

Michael, sensing privacy was in order, moved away from the stairs. "I'll be in the den. You guys call me if you need anything. I'll be right here—you know, out of the way." He laughed at the foolishness of his words as he left the couple alone.

Jack led Melanie into the bedroom and helped her onto the bed. Gently he pulled her panties off, and with her knees pointed to the ceiling and her legs apart, he examined her. A thick liquid was seeping from her vagina, and Jack was relieved to see it was pink in color instead of greenish brown or bright red.

"The wetness is coming from your amniotic fluid. It's perfectly normal. And you've started to dilate. It feels like your cervix is about three centimeters dilated. Let's wait and see if you have another contraction."

Jack went to Melanie's lingerie drawer and retrieved a pair of panties. He took a thick cotton pad from a special "surprise bag" Dr. Stewart had prepared for them, and he placed it in the underwear after helping Melanie pull them on. "That will help with the fluid," he said. "Jan put several of them in the bag, so we'll change it as often as you'd like."

Melanie smiled and took her husband's hand. This was the first time she'd had the chance to experience Dr. Jack Russell's bedside manner. "No wonder all your patients love you," she said. "You're quite the…"

Melanie didn't finish. She could feel another contraction building, this one just a bit stronger than the last. "Breathe, baby," Jack said. "Just breathe your way through it." He looked at his watch and timed the contraction. It lasted almost fifty seconds.

They sat together on the bed for the next half hour. Jack timing the length of each contraction and the intervals between them. They were coming every eight to ten minutes.

"You're in the first phase of labor, but the contractions are coming a little faster than normal. I don't think there's any reason to go to the hospital yet, but we better call Jan. Let's see what she says."

Jack opened the drawer on the nightstand and took out the card with the doctor's emergency numbers on it. But since it was Monday, he called the office first. The conversation between doctors was short and to the point. Yet it ended with a very personal touch.

"I'm sure Melanie's fine, but how are you doing, Jack? It's different when you're on the other end of the stethoscope, isn't it?"

"You better believe it. As the doctor, we always feel like we're in control, even when we're not. But being the patient, or the patient's husband, is a much tougher job. I just feel so helpless."

Stewart felt sympathy for her colleague and his wife. Real sympathy.

They'd endured much pain in their marriage, yet they had survived together. The sympathy she felt for Jack and Melanie was also mixed with a great sense of admiration. She respected them more than either would ever know.

"Now don't worry, everything is going well. Just keep Melanie calm and stay at the house. Watch some television, or do something else to occupy the time. I'll check back with you in a few hours and see how the labor is progressing. If anything happens in the meantime or if you have any other questions, call me back. I won't leave the office until we talk again."

After hanging up the phone, Jack relayed the information to Melanie. They sat on the bed for a while, easing their way through a few more contractions, and for just a moment, the couple felt like regular people, just a man and wife preparing to have a baby, their first. It all seemed so peaceful and natural and so right. But as quickly as it came, the feeling passed. This wasn't just any baby.

And Melanie was experiencing much more than the first stages of a simple labor and delivery. This was the Second Coming of the Christ child, the greatest event the world had ever known or would ever know. And the responsibility, awesome as it was, fell to her and Jack, simple people embarking on an extraordinary journey. They felt small. This was no cliché. The weight of the world was indeed upon their shoulders, and the responsibility they faced was truly real. In the solitude of their bedroom, deep emotions came crashing over them like waves.

"Do you think we can do this?" Melanie asked. "Everything up to this point has been like a rehearsal. But it's really happening now. Is there any way we can really do this?"

Jack wanted to give a simple answer, but couldn't. Instead he recalled a fond memory from their early years. "I remember once, shortly after we got married, when we were standing in line to see a movie. I was looking around at all the other people, and I suddenly felt very special inside. I felt lucky and wonderful and proud, all at the same time. I remember, at that moment, feeling invincible. Being with you gave me a sense of great strength. Together, I believed we could accomplish anything."

Melanie's eyes brimmed with tears as Jack knelt on the floor in front of her. "I still believe that. Although I admit, this is a little more than I ever bargained for." He smiled wistfully. "Can we do it? I can't say for sure. But I'd say our chances are as good as most. If God believes in us, we must have something going for us."

Silent tears fell from Melanie's eyes. Jack hugged her softly. It was a special moment, a dramatic scene of intense bonding between husband and wife. But it was soon interrupted by another contraction, and they were forced once again to face harsh reality. Their time was at hand. The child was coming.

As Jack timed the contraction, he thought of long ago, and another couple named Joseph and Mary. For the first time in his life, he thought of them as real people. Mary, the good, honest, loving mother. Joseph, her hardworking, devoted husband. How did they feel during those final hours before the birth of Christ? Did they too feel alone, afraid, and helpless? Of course, they did, Jack realized. Yet somehow, they survived with a special grace and dignity that even today was respected by millions and millions of people from all walks of life.

He looked at his wife, eyes closed and breathing easily now, and one emotion struck him like a runaway train. Love. God, how he loved her. He was willing to sacrifice anything, everything, to keep her and the baby safe. To give up now, to give in to his feelings of inadequacy and unworthiness, would be to abandon Melanie. That would never happen. So he would use his love for her and the baby as a shield against whatever came during the months and years ahead. Love would be his antidote, his salvation. It would get him through, he realized, and almost instantly, he felt better.

"Baby," he said, and Melanie opened her eyes. "We can do this. I truly believe we can."

She smiled softly and squeezed his hand. "I know," she said then closed her eyes again. "There's no other choice."

* * *

"Jan. It's Jack. The contractions are coming harder and faster, and she's a little more dilated than before. I think we need to go to the hospital."

Stewart, on the other end of the line, nodded in agreement. "Yes. Right away. A report on the radio said the roads are starting to get slick and hazardous, so why don't you two head on over? I'll meet you there in about thirty minutes, and we'll get set up for delivery."

Jack turned the television to the news channel and helped Melanie get dressed. She was in the bathroom when the traffic report came on. "Conditions are rapidly deteriorating," said a reporter standing—live—near the Lincoln Parkway. "Sleet and freezing rain are turning the roads into one long skating rink, and city police are already reporting numerous traffic accidents. With temperatures expected to continue falling during the evening, highway officials are urging all residents to stay…"

"What's the matter?" Melanie asked, emerging from the bathroom. "Is the weather getting worse?"

Jack muted the television. "A little bit. They're calling for several inches of snow later tonight. I'm glad we're going now before it gets dark and the roads get too slick."

He picked up Melanie's overnight bag and helped her slip on a warm, heavy coat. Then gently, he helped her down the steps. At the bottom of the stairs, she experienced another contraction, and they stood together until the pain subsided.

"Michael, are you ready? Let's get Melanie out to the Jeep."

There was no answer. Jack started to call out again, but suddenly the back door opened and Michael stepped inside. "I've got the black beauty all warmed up," he said. "You guys ready to ride?"

Melanie hesitated before walking out the door. "Wait. We've got to call Doris. I want to tell her and Reece that we're going to the hospital."

Michael grinned as he took the small suitcase from Jack. "Way ahead of you, little lady. I called ten minutes ago. Doris went crazy. She's so excited. Reece has been called out for some emergency runs, so she's at home with the boys. But she wants you to call her once we get to the hospital, if you feel like it."

"Thank you, Michael. You think of everything."

The trio walked toward the garage with Jack and Michael on either side of Melanie. "I hope Reece wasn't called out because of this weather," she said. "I don't like driving when the roads are slick."

Michael leaned back slightly and looked at Jack. Grimly, he nodded his head.

Jack understood but hid his concern. "I'm sure we'll be fine," he said. "We've got plenty of time. I'll drive slow and we'll stay on the expressway. We'll be there before you know it."

Jack looked at his watch as he pulled out of the driveway. It was five-thirty.

It would be dark in less than an hour.

* * *

The defroster on the Jeep was on full power, yet the fog on the inside of the window continued to spread across the glass. Especially on the sides. Melanie, seated on the passenger side, used her gloved hand to wipe away the cold condensation. The wiper blades on both the front and back of the vehicle were also working overtime, sweeping away the ice crystals as they formed on the windshield.

They were still three blocks from the expressway, and Jack was creeping along the side streets at just thirty miles per hour. Michael, seated directly behind Melanie, finally broke the tense silence. "The lights and holiday decorations are beautiful, aren't they? We've been holed up in your house so long, I'd almost forgotten it's Christmas Eve."

Jack followed Michael's lead. "Melanie and I always drive through this neighborhood at Christmastime. The folks here go all out with their decorations. I think they try to outdo each other, year after year."

He took his eyes off the road for half a second, sneaking a quick peek at Melanie. "That big brick on the corner, that's your favorite, isn't it?"

Melanie nodded absently. Her mind was not on Christmas or decorations. At the moment, she wasn't even focused on the baby.

The weather had her full attention. She frowned as they passed a vehicle on the side of the road. It was the third she'd noticed since leaving the house.

"I'm worried, Jack. It's ten miles to the hospital, even after we get to the Lincoln, and the roads seem to be getting worse. We should have left sooner."

Jack couldn't agree more, except he couldn't say it. Leaving sooner was no longer an option. So instead, he put on a brave face and tried to ease his wife's fears. "We'll be fine. Slow and easy, all the way to the hospital. The expressway will be in better condition than these side streets. It always is." He reached over and touched Melanie lightly on the thigh. She smiled, but not with much conviction.

Fifteen minutes later, Jack eased the Jeep down a ramp and onto the Lincoln Parkway. The muscles in his arms and hands were tense, and he cursed himself for not leaving home earlier in the day. Conditions on the expressway were no better than they'd encountered on the secondary route, and the four-lane highway was much more congested. To make matters worse, Jack realized, many vehicles were exceeding a safe speed.

Melanie started to protest but thought better of it. *What good would complaining do?* she thought. And besides, they were now out of options. The baby was coming, weather conditions would continue to deteriorate, and they were within eight miles away from the hospital. She felt another contraction coming on—they were about six minutes apart now—and she focused on the pain.

Just as the contraction ended, a tractor trailer eased past the Jeep and, having pulled far enough ahead, merged back into the slow lane. Jack slowed slightly to keep a safe distance between the two vehicles.

"He's going too fast," Melanie said. "Stay back, Jack."

Jack nodded. "Give a guy eighteen wheels, and he thinks he can go anywhere. But this is good, really. We'll follow him to the hospital exit. The weight of that truck will break up the ice and make our path a little smoother."

All was quiet in the Jeep for the next mile and a half. Then suddenly, it happened. The truck braked sharply, swerving back and forth in the road ahead of them. Jack tried to switch lanes, but couldn't. Another vehicle had inadvertently boxed them in, but it was the car behind them, a dark-blue Oldsmobile, that caused the accident.

It slammed into them from behind, forcing the back end of the Jeep into the emergency lane. Melanie screamed as Jack tried to check his vehicle and steer it back onto the highway. He was careful not to overcorrect and had almost brought the Jeep to a complete stop when the Olds slammed them again. Jack forced both feet onto the brake pedal with as much force as possible, but there was no stopping on the icy road. They skidded across the emergency lane, dropped over the shoulder, then slid down a sharp embankment. It finally stopped in a deep concrete culvert, balancing dangerously on two wheels.

The Olds never slowed. The driver, a middle-aged white male with bushy eyebrows and a burr haircut, smiled as he sped past and continued down the expressway. *Mission accomplished*, he thought, giving one last glance in the rear-view mirror.

Down in the culvert, Michael was already out of the back seat and standing on the ground. He was pulling the vehicle toward him, trying desperately to get the Jeep on all four wheels before it rolled over—on Melanie's side.

"Help me, Jack. We can't let it tip over."

Jack ripped off his seat belt, opened the door, and dropped three feet to the cold concrete. He too pulled at the vehicle, and together they were able to shift the weight to the left side of the Jeep. Metal groaned as the left tires finally touched down. The vehicle was safely balanced but was now jammed tightly between the wall of the large concrete drainage area and a support beam.

Michael and Jack opened the door and peered in at Melanie. "Are you okay?" Jack asked. "Are you hurt?"

Melanie was pale, and her eyes wide with fear. The accident, which had lasted mere seconds from start to finish, had seemed to go on forever. Neither air bag had deployed—thankfully—but the seat belt had pulled harshly against her abdomen, scaring her.

"I'm fine, but I can't get this stupid seat belt off. The door won't open. I'm trapped in here." Jack climbed in beside his wife and pushed hard on the release button. It wouldn't budge. He grabbed the strap with one hand, the buckle with the other, and pulled as hard as he could. The buckle would not release.

"Let me," Michael said. With one swift motion, he reached behind his back and pulled a knife and sheath from his waistband. The metal gleamed beneath the interior light as he carefully slipped it under the strap. Sliding the knife away from Melanie, it quickly sliced through the seat belt, and she was free.

"Another one's coming," she gasped. She gripped Jack's arm tightly until the pain subsided. Slowly, her breathing returned to normal. "What are we going to do? We're stuck, aren't we?"

"I think so," Jack answered. "We're jammed in here pretty tight, and these two wheels are barely touching the ground. Let's see if I can get it to move at all."

The engine was still running, and Jack shifted the Jeep from park into four-wheel drive. The tires churned furiously, but the vehicle remained still. "Wait," Michael said. "There's no way we're going forward, but maybe we can back it up a little. Give me a second."

He walked to the front and placed his massive frame against the bumper. "Okay, try it." Jack shifted into reverse and gunned the engine. Michael shoved against the bumper, using all his tremendous strength. Metal from the right side of the Jeep screeched against the concrete as they inched slowly backward. But three feet down the ditch, the culvert narrowed slightly—an obvious engineering flaw— and the vehicle jammed again. They weren't going anywhere without help.

Melanie was losing control of her emotions. A moment ago, she'd been afraid. Now she was terrified. "Call for help, Jack. I don't want to have our baby in this car. We need help."

Jack reached in the glove compartment and found the cell phone. He quickly dialed 911. After several anxious moments, a recorded voice came across the wireless device. All circuits were busy. "I was afraid of that," he said. "Too many people trying to use their cell phones at once."

Jack looked at Michael, then Melanie. "Here's what we do," he said. "First, let's lower the seats in the back and make a comfortable place for Melanie to lie down. I've got plenty of gas, so we'll crack the windows just a little and keep the heater running. That should keep it warm in here. I'll stay with Melanie and keep trying to reach someone with the phone. You walk back up to the highway and see if you can flag someone down. Maybe an emergency vehicle or tow truck will come by. Anything to help us get to the hospital."

Michael moved into action. The back hatch of the Jeep would not open—it had been damaged by the sinister Oldsmobile—but both doors on the driver's side were in good shape. He quickly lowered the seats in the back, making a flat surface for Melanie. After another contraction had come and gone, the two men helped her crawl gingerly into the back portion of the vehicle. Jack removed one of the headrests, and after wrapping it with two golf towels, he pulled from under the seat, placed it under his wife's head. Michael closed the doors and started up the steep embankment. He had a flashlight with him. Inside Jack tried to calm his wife and kept punching the redial button every few seconds.

"How long until the baby comes?" she asked. "I want the truth, Jack. I need to know."

"I think you're still several hours away from delivery. Two at least. The contractions are still steady, and the intervals between them have increased only slightly. But..."

"But what? Something has you worried. I can tell."

"It's hard to predict what the accident will do to your labor. Physically, you're fine. We were lucky we didn't roll over coming down this hill. But trauma sometimes affects labor and delivery, especially psychologically. It could speed the process up or slow it down. We'll just have to wait and see."

Melanie was shivering, and Jack took off his coat and placed it lovingly around her. The heater was set on high, and Jack was actually quite warm. Melanie was, too, in all probability. The trembling was more likely the result of fear, fatigue, and stress.

"If it comes to it, Jack, can you deliver our baby safely? Here in this car? With no instruments and no help?"

"Yes, without a doubt. But we haven't reached that stage yet. I know it's difficult, but try to relax. You need to rest and conserve your energy. Sooner or later, either here or at the hospital or somewhere in between, you're going to have this baby. And when the time comes, you're going to need all the strength you can muster. But please try not to worry. I'll do the worrying for both of us."

Melanie smiled. "I sometimes forget how much I love you. And I trust you completely. If you say everything is going to be okay, then I believe it. You always find a way to make me feel safe."

Jack set the phone aside for a second and kissed his wife tenderly. He pushed her hair back from her face and was once again struck by her beauty. "My god, you're gorgeous, even now with all this trouble heaped upon you. You are without question the most incredible woman I've ever met." He could feel a lump rising in his throat as he stroked Melanie's cheek. "It's no wonder you are the chosen one."

The words made Melanie feel special, but this was certainly no time to gloat. There was much work ahead—hard, difficult work. She closed her eyes and tried to rest.

Jack pressed the redial button again. Still there was no answer. Outside, Michael was nearing the top of the steep embankment. Ice made the climb extremely difficult, and his lungs were burning as he crawled over the crest and onto the edge of the emergency lane. Several minutes later, he stood and looked back at the vehicle pinned inside the culvert.

We'll never get Melanie to the top without help, he thought. *Not in these conditions. An attempt would be too dangerous.*

He turned and looked across the expressway. There was little traffic and no emergency vehicles in sight. "I hope Jack can reach someone," Michael said to himself. "I don't think we'll find much help up here."

* * *

Melanie screamed in pain. Jack, holding her hand, felt helpless. The contraction was long and hard, with the peak lasting almost twenty seconds. If only he had something to give her. Something besides words of encouragement.

It had been almost two hours since the Jeep was forced off the highway. The last time he examined Melanie, she was at least eight centimeters dilated. She'd thrown off Jack's coat and her own, too, and drops of sweat streamed down the sides of her face. The back of her blouse was soaked with sweat, and her pants, long since removed, were also wet.

The cell phone was off. In an attempt to prolong the battery supply, Jack was attempting to dial emergency services every ten minutes. All circuits were still busy. A blanket of wet snow now covered the Jeep, making it impossible to see out of the vehicle. He used the power control to lower the window slightly and looked through the dark night toward the lights on the expressway above. Jack had no idea where Michael was or if he was having any luck contacting help. He raised the window and turned back to Melanie.

One look at her husband, and Melanie knew. "It's just us, isn't it? We're going to have to do this by ourselves, aren't we?"

Jack wanted to lie, but didn't. Melanie deserved the truth. "I'm afraid so. Even when help arrives, it's going to take them quite a while to get this vehicle out of here. And we can't put you in an ambulance until we get you to the top of the hill. We can't risk that now, even with help. You're too close to delivery to be moved around like that."

Another contraction arrived, and Melanie, her entire body rigid, managed to hold back the scream. *This is only going to get worse,* she reasoned. *I'd better save the screaming for when the pain becomes unbearable.* When the contraction subsided, she relaxed. After catching her breath, she asked the question that had been worrying her since the accident, "After he's born, will the baby be okay? I mean, does he need anything immediately after he's delivered, or will he be all right until we can get him to the hospital?"

Jack smiled reassuringly. "Babies don't need a hospital to be healthy. They're born at home and many other places all the time. All we have to do is cut the umbilical cord, then keep him dry and warm. And eating won't be a problem. With you here, he's got a full supply of milk right at his disposal."

Melanie was relieved. Jack was being honest, and she felt better knowing the baby should be in good shape once the delivery was completed. Getting there—that was going to be the problem.

Jack helped her through another contraction, then checked her cervix again. It was now almost completely dilated. The contractions were coming every two or three minutes and were lasting almost ninety seconds, with very intense peaks.

Melanie was getting close. Very close. And Jack was nervous, more nervous than he could ever remember being. The life of his wife and his son was in his hands. He felt both alone and vulnerable.

He jumped as the driver-side door suddenly jerked open. Michael, his head and shoulders covered with ice and snow, climbed inside and closed the door behind him. He winced as he moved around in the cramped quarters of the front seat. His long legs, numb from exposure and weariness, were stiff, especially his knees. His feet felt like blocks of ice, and his nose and ears were burning. Frostbite, probably.

Despite it all, he was smiling. "You guys miss me?" he asked.

"You better believe it," Jack answered. "I was afraid something had happened to you."

"Almost did. Three cars nearly hit me. Every time they'd try to stop they'd slide right at me. I got pretty good at dodging them after a while."

He looked at Melanie and dropped the good humor. "How's our girl holding up?"

"Like a real champ. She's been working through the pain and doing a great job. She's handling this a whole lot better than I am."

Melanie lifted her arm in the air and waved it within the confines of the vehicle. "Hello. Remember me? You guys act like I'm not even here. I can still talk, you know."

Both men laughed. "See what I mean?" Jack asked. "When you get right down to it, she's as tough as nails."

Michael took off his overcoat and produced a small bag from the inside pocket. "I've got some good news," he said. "Not great, but better than nothing. A guy in a highway truck finally stopped. He's the county road engineer and had a two-way radio with him."

Melanie groaned and grabbed Jack's arm, cutting off Michael's news. She struggled through another long, difficult contraction. When it finally ended, Michael continued.

"Anyway, he got through to his dispatch station and told them about us. They're going to try and get some emergency help out here as soon as they can. I know that's going to be too late for the delivery, but at least now they know where we are, and we'll be able to get Melanie and the baby to the hospital tonight."

Suddenly, Michael felt bad. Standing out in the cold, his effort to secure help had seemed better. Now, watching Melanie suffer the pain of full labor, the news didn't seem so good.

"I'm sorry I couldn't do better."

Melanie turned her head and looked at him in the front seat. "Don't be ridiculous, Michael. That's the best news I've had since we left home. Really, it makes me feel much better knowing help is on the way. I've been worried sick about what would happen to us after the baby is born."

Jack smiled at his wife, then noticed the bag Michael was still holding. "What's that?"

"Oh, I almost forgot. This is the rest of my good news. The road engineer had a first-aid kit with him. This is it. It might have some things…"

Jack slapped his hands together. "Now we're talking," he said. "Let me have it."

Michael handed the small box over. Jack popped it open, letting the contents spill out. There was gauze, scissors, Band-Aids, tape, several large bandages, alcohol swabs, antiseptic spray, antibiotic ointment, a bottle of hydrogen peroxide, a can of spray-on blood clotter, an ice pack, and a pair of rubber gloves.

"This will work, Michael. This will definitely work. Now we've got the tools to get the job done."

Melanie could feel another contraction starting. "Well get them ready, Mr. Goodwrench. This baby wants out."

Jack helped her through the contraction, then turned to Michael. "Turn the ignition off. We need to save some gas, and it's hot as hell in here already. Then climb back here. I can use an extra set of hands."

After killing the engine, Michael squeezed into the back, staying close to Melanie's head. His massive frame seemed to fill the interior, but he hunkered down as best he could. "Hold out your hands," Jack demanded. When he did, Jack poured a small amount of peroxide into each palm. Then he poured some into his own palm and started rubbing them together. Michael followed his lead.

Jack then tore open several packages of the alcohol swabs and gave two of them to his new assistant. "Wipe your hands with them." He did the same. He handed the can of antiseptic spray to Michael. "Spray my hands," he said. "Then spray your own." Jack pulled on the rubber gloves and took the can from Michael.

"This is cold, baby," he said, spraying the area around Melanie's vagina. She gasped but said nothing. He also sprayed her inner thighs and even sprayed a large area of the floor beneath her. Jack then took out the scissors and wiped them with another alcohol swab. He opened a cotton bandage and carefully placed the scissors on the sterile dressing. Finally, he opened the package of gauze and the other bandages and placed them beside him on the floor.

"We're as ready as we'll ever be. The rest is up to Melanie." He smiled at his wife, and remarkably, she smiled back. "On the next contraction, I want you to push a little. Let's see what happens."

Sweat was dripping from Michael's face like rain. He wanted to wipe it away but was afraid to touch anything with his newly cleansed hands. Instead, he held them up in the air like a doctor preparing for surgery.

"It's okay to touch her," Jack said, noticing Michael's reluctance to do so. "In fact, I need you to prop her up a little. Hold her head and shoulders and make her comfortable. She's going to be working awfully hard for the next thirty or forty minutes. I want her to relax against you between contractions."

Michael twisted around and wedged his legs on either side of Melanie's shoulders. He lifted her easily and held much of her upper torso in his lap. Melanie reached out and took both of his hands. She squeezed them gently. "I'm sorry for putting you through this," she said. "But we're sure glad to have you here."

For a brief instant, Michael was almost overcome with emotion. When he could speak, he said two sentences that Melanie would never forget. "I've seen more than enough death. I can't wait to witness the miracle of life."

With the next contraction, Melanie pushed. With the go-ahead from Jack, she felt a renewed burst of energy. She was ready to give it all she had.

"Easy now. Not too hard," Jack said. "Let's just push a little until he starts to crown. Once I see his head, then you can really bear down."

Three contractions later, Jack saw his son for the first time. Not much, just a small patch of dark hair protruding from the birth canal. His heart was pounding. "It's time. Push, Melanie. Push as hard as you can."

Melanie grunted and pushed. She could feel her vagina stretching and then noticed a stinging sensation. The pain was intense, worse than she ever imagined, but she pushed anyway. She screamed and pushed, screamed and pushed, in what seemed like a never-ending cycle. She lost track of time and space. With each contraction, she pushed, and when the pain subsided, for a few precious moments, she fell back against Michael and rested.

Jack was coaching her, but she heard not a word. She was operating on instinct now. It seemed savage, but she was not that far removed from any other member of the animal kingdom. This was survival, pure and simple. She was fighting to bring her offspring into the world. She would push until she had succeeded. Or until she was dead. There was no stopping, no in-between.

Finally, through the haze of pain, she sensed a slippery, wet feeling. From some far-off place, she could hear Jack's voice. She couldn't tell if he was laughing or crying. "You did it, baby. You did it. Our boy is here."

Michael carefully lifted her shoulders and pushed her matted hair out of her eyes. Like Jack, there were tears in his eyes.

"Melanie, can you hear me?" Jack pleaded. "Please, Melanie. Say something."

She heard crying—loud, shrill crying—and felt a warm sensation on her stomach. With much difficulty, she finally managed to open her eyes. And for the first time, she looked at her son. He was wrinkled and purple and covered with slime and blood. But he was beautiful, even more beautiful than she had envisioned in her many dreams.

"Mrs. Russell, I'd like you to meet your son, Isaac James Russell," Jack said. "Isaac. This is your mom. I think you'll like her. She's some kind of special woman."

Melanie screamed, but this time, it was with a feeling of pure and utter joy.

She reached down where Jack was holding the baby and put her own hands around his tiny shivering body. Tears streamed down her face as she wailed in relief and celebration.

"He's perfect," Jack said. He'd already cut the umbilical cord, pinched it off with tape, and was in the process of delivering the placenta. "He looks as healthy as a horse. About eight pounds, I'd say."

Michael used his arms to steady Melanie's and carefully helped her control the squirming baby. He was overwhelmed by what he'd just witnessed. As the two men used their coats to cover mother and child, Melanie called out to the heavens.

"Thank you, God. Thank you for giving us this child."

Outside in the cold night air, snow continued to fall silently. A thought struck Michael, and he looked at his watch. It was five minutes past midnight. Christmas morning.

He looked at this special family—mother, father, and child—and shook his head, almost in disbelief. And for the first time in his life, he truly felt the presence of God.

* * *

Jack watched incredulously as his newborn son tried to suckle his mother's breast. He was holding Melanie from behind, supporting the weight of her body with his own, and keeping both mother and baby as warm and comfortable as possible. They were alone in the vehicle. Michael had departed ninety minutes ago, and by now was standing alongside the expressway, waiting for help to arrive.

The baby was now pink and healthy looking, having gotten past the initial shock of leaving his warm confines and spilling forth into the cold, cruel world. Jack had taken off his shirt and wrapped him carefully in it, and both mother and child had slept for a while. But he was up now—apparently hungry—and searching instinctively for his mother's nipple. He helped hold the baby to Melanie's breast and looked on in amazement as he naturally located the source of nourishment.

Jack knew from his medical training and from the information they'd received from Dr. Stewart, that there was no milk to be found in Melanie's breasts. At least not yet. Her breasts would fill with milk in three or four days. Until then, the baby would feed on colostrum, a clear premilk nutrient that would supply him with important antibodies. Just a teaspoon or two of colostrum would satisfy his hunger for now. And sure enough, moments after feeding, he was asleep again.

"Let me hold him," Jack said. He eased Melanie down on the makeshift pillow, then took the baby from her arms. He held him in his lap and marveled at the child's beauty. "I feel like I'm dreaming."

Melanie laughed. Carefully. Her mouth was dry, her throat sore. Her back was still throbbing and steady pain was beginning to set in now that the euphoria of the delivery was waning. She felt as if she'd been run over by a truck, but she'd never been happier. Or felt more alive. Finally, her dream had come true. She was a mother.

"Can you believe it, Jack? Can you believe we've been blessed with this child? And he's so precious. So beautiful. Are you as happy as I am?"

Happy didn't begin to describe his feelings. In fact, he couldn't think of a word or words that would do justice to his emotional state of being. He'd long wondered what it would be like to be a father. And now, he was a parent to the most special child in the world.

His joy was total and complete. He felt no confusion and, much to his surprise, no lingering doubts about being the father of this child. The fact that he had not supplied the sperm—had not actually fertilized the egg—did not affect his feelings of pride and happiness in any way. He loved this child as if he were part of his own flesh and blood. And in many ways, especially spiritually, he was.

Jack looked at the baby but spoke in a quiet voice to Melanie. "Many nights I've gone to sleep thinking about being a father, wondering what it would be like, how I'd feel once he was actually born. And as I'd drift off to sleep, I envisioned this being the greatest moment of my life."

Melanie waited several moments before asking the obvious question. "Well? Is it? Is it the greatest moment of your life?"

Jack placed his chin against the baby's neck, snuggling with his son. "It's more than that. It's the greatest moment of our lives. I know how badly you've wanted this, and I've wanted it for you. But I've always wanted it for me, too. This completes me. It completes us."

Husband and wife sat quietly in the back of the secluded vehicle. It was early in the morning, and the snow was beginning to taper off. It would be daylight in a few hours, and people all over Chicago—all over the world—would begin celebrating the day known for the birth of Jesus Christ.

Little did they realize a modern-day nativity scene had unfolded inside the confines of the Jeep, just a few hundred feet down a slippery embankment from the Lincoln Expressway. How could they know? There had been no trumpets or horns blaring the news, no angels or astronomical constellations pointing out their hidden location, no wise men coming to commemorate the wondrous occasion.

Just a simple man and his very special wife. The proud parents of the second Holy Child. The irony of the moment was not lost on Jack and Melanie. Neither was the staggering sense of responsibility that had engulfed them in the short time since the birth.

"Are you scared?" Jack asked. "Now that it's finally real, now that our baby is here, are you as scared as I am?"

Melanie nodded her head slowly. "Absolutely petrified. I've been lying here thinking about it, about the life we have ahead of us. I'm so nervous that it almost makes me ill, and that emotion comes at me like the surf at the beach. I'm nervous and sick for a few minutes, then it goes away, then it comes back again. But in between each anxiety attack, I feel good. Not just good, but confident. Energized, like I'm ready to go, ready to see this thing through to the end. And with that emotion comes calm. Serenity. Peace. I guess I feel like we're in the hands of the Lord, and He will help us and guide us during our journey."

Jack stared at his wife as she continued. "I know it sounds weird. It doesn't make much sense, really. But I'm ready, Jack. Scared but ready. I think we can do this. You and I together. For some reason, I have more hope right now than I've ever had before. Can you feel it? Or am I just crazy?"

He thought about it for a moment. The last twelve hours had been crazy, no doubt about it. Yet they had managed, with Michael's help, to overcome every obstacle and deliver a healthy baby boy. He looked down at his son, at Isaac, and he could feel the blood rushing through his veins as never before. He was alive. His wife and child were alive. And he was determined to keep it that way.

Jack reached down and softly rubbed his son's head. The hair was dark, resembling his own. Then he looked at his wife. "Yes, I can feel it. It's God's will. And God's will shall be done."

Five minutes later, the quietness was broken by loud voices outside the vehicle. It sounded like two men laughing. Both doors on the driver's side opened, and Jack and Melanie peered into the darkness. A head poked through each door. One was Michael's, as expected. The second was a wonderful surprise. It was Reece McKenzie.

"Merry Christmas!" he bellowed. "I ain't Santa Claus, but I've got a big red fire truck waiting for you at the top of this hill. Anybody interested?"

Melanie shrieked, and tears flowed again. Reece to the rescue—how appropriate. Jack, however, had other things on his mind.

"Look, Reece," he said. "It's my boy. Isn't he wonderful?"

Reece reached in and hugged his friend. Michael and Melanie couldn't see it, but they could sense it, the pride only one father could feel and share with another.

* * *

The rescue would be difficult yet simple and, hopefully, effective. Reece and the other three members of his fire and rescue crew had put together a plan as soon as they found Michael on the side of the road. They would use a wench to lower a rescue basket down the side of the embankment. They would secure Melanie and the baby with safety latches and straps, then pull the basket up the hill to the waiting rescue vehicle. The others could walk up. The Jeep would have to wait for another day.

"How did you know?" Jack asked as Reece and one of his team members, a short, stocky man named Samuel, waited for the basket.

"The call came through to our station, and I was in the office, talking to the captain, when he took down the information. When I heard the description of the vehicle and of the man standing in the emergency lane on the Lincoln, I thought about Michael. Then when the captain mentioned the part about a pregnant woman, I about went nuts. We've been so busy with the storm that our station is operating on split crews, but I begged him to let us come out and take care of this. He's a good guy, a decent man, and he gave us the go-ahead. We got here as soon as we could."

Minutes later, the rescue basket arrived, and the men helped ease Melanie out of the car and into the sturdy structure. They covered her and the baby with warm blankets. Then Reece radioed to the men above. Slowly they started towing the basket up the embankment. The ice and snow actually made the pull smooth and easy, and Melanie was fairly comfortable during the ride. The men struggled to walk beside her, and all four of them were huffing and puffing by the time they reached the top. Isaac slept the entire way.

Quickly Reece and the other rescue workers placed Melanie and the baby inside the vehicle. Jack and Samuel stayed in the back with the two patients, while Michael rode up front with Reece. The two other firemen headed back to the station with the larger truck.

As Reece slowly guided the van the remaining miles to the hospital, Michael filled him in on the details of the birth.

"Melanie looks pretty darn good, considering what happened," Reece said. "Did you guys have a bad time?"

Michael shook his head. "It was plenty scary, especially at first, but as the night wore on, it seemed like she just got stronger and more determined. I was gone most of the time, but I did get to help with the delivery. It was amazing. Absolutely amazing."

They rode in silence for a few minutes. Then Reece spoke again, quietly so the others couldn't hear. "This probably sounds silly, but I've just got to know. Did anything special happen? You know, like a divine light or something? Anything out of the ordinary, like you always see in the movies?"

Michael understood the question, even appreciated it. He'd wondered the same thing himself. "No, it was quiet really. But everything seemed to slow down, like time was standing still. To me, it felt like we were the only people in the world when that little baby was born."

He shook his head, trying to find other words to describe what he'd witnessed. "I don't know. It was like, you know, just perfect. No doctors, no nurses, not a bunch of people around. Just the husband and wife and then the baby. Except for me, they were completely isolated, together as a special family, in their only little world. Something about it just seemed natural, like it should be. It was like they were standing on their own, defying all odds."

Reece listened intently as he steered the vehicle off the expressway and down the ramp toward the hospital exit. They would pull into the emergency room center in a matter of seconds.

"It sounds beautiful," he said.

"The most beautiful thing I've ever seen. And I don't know why, but I believe I was there for a reason—not to help, because I really didn't do that much. It was almost as if someone was trying to tell me something, show me something. It was a weird feeling."

As he pulled into the emergency bay and put the van in park, Reece turned to Michael. "It was God, son. God's talking to you. He's going to make a believer out of you yet."

Michael smiled and, like Reece, climbed out of the van. As he did, he thought of Matthew Benoit. His uncle would be pleased. Then a second thought occurred to him. *Maybe that's why I'm here.*

* * *

The sun was just rising above the horizon of the city as they wheeled Melanie and her newborn baby into the hospital. After a quick inspection in the emergency room—performed by one of Jack's colleagues—they whisked mother and child to the maternity ward. There, still waiting for them, was Jan Stewart.

She came hustling down the hallway when she saw Melanie on the gurney. "Oh my goodness, I don't believe it!" she shouted. "You did it without me!" She took the baby from a hospital employee who was walking with Melanie and gave him a couple of bounces to wake him. "Wake up, Isaac. I need to see you."

The newborn opened his dark-blue eyes and looked right at Stewart, almost as if on command. He watched her for a moment, then closed his eyes, and went back to sleep. The doctor laughed long and hard.

"He looks fabulous. He really does. Melanie, Jack, you did a terrific job. I couldn't have done better myself. I'm almost jealous." As they neared Melanie's room, Stewart called for a nurse, then handed the baby to him. "Call pediatrics and have them check this baby from head to toe. Clean him and dress him, then bring him to the nursery. I'll be down to get him. If there's any problem, page me right away."

The nurse did as he was told. As he was leaving, he called back to Jack. "Congratulations, Dr. Russell, Mrs. Russell. The entire staff has been buzzing about your incredible night. You'll sure have some story to tell your little fella when he gets older, won't you?"

Jack looked at Stewart questioningly. "The call to emergency services came through our dispatch several hours ago. We quickly put two and two together, and the whole place has been on pins and needles waiting your arrival. Me included. I just can't believe everything happened this way and that I missed it all. I guess things happen for a reason despite our best-laid plans."

Reece and Michael, standing near the doorway, looked at each other and grinned like schoolboys. "I've got to go," Reece said. "My partner's waiting for me. I'll call Doris and give her the good news. She's probably crazy by now. I may have to admit her to the hospital. The psychiatric ward."

Michael left with Reece. He was going to the cafeteria for a well-earned breakfast. *Besides,* he thought, *Jack and Melanie need to rest.*

Inside the room, Stewart and Jack helped Melanie off the gurney. "Please, I've got to go to the bathroom," she said. "My bladder must be the size of a swimming pool."

When she came out, they helped undress her, and a nurse came in and cleaned her. The nurse had worked at the hospital for many years and had come to admire Jack's work in the ER. She gave Melanie a hospital gown and a pair of thick white socks. "These aren't hospital issue," she said, smiling at Melanie. "I save them for our really brave patients."

Melanie blushed. "Thank you so much," she said. "My feet are freezing."

Once Melanie was in bed, Stewart checked her thoroughly. She asked Melanie a number of questions and seemed pleased with all the answers. She wrote something on her chart and handed it to the nurse, who nodded and walked away.

"I'm going to give you something for the pain, just for a day or two, because you're going to need it. Natural childbirth, under any condition, is a pretty tall order. With all you've been through, you're going to be awfully sore. But all things considered, you look great. I'm impressed."

She pulled a chair from the corner of the private room and placed it beside Melanie's bed. She motioned for Jack to take a seat. "You two need to rest. I'm going to check on the baby, then I'll bring him back for a little visit—if I can get him away from the rest of the staff, that is."

As she prepared to close the door behind her, she turned back to look at the couple. Melanie was already asleep. Jack, as always, was still by her side. "Thank you, Jan," he whispered. "Honestly. Thank you for everything you've done. You've been a great friend."

She walked back and tapped Jack softly on the hand. "No, thank you. This has been the greatest experience of my professional life. I've learned more about honor, courage, love, and integrity than I could have ever imagined."

Jack was shocked to see tears in her eyes. "I don't know what's going on with you two—you three now—but I'm smart enough to know that it's something special. Maybe it is a miracle. I can't explain it, and don't need to. I'm just thankful to have been a part of it."

With that, she turned and quickly left the room.

Jack's thoughts were jumbled as his head dropped, and he drifted into unconsciousness. Was Jan still in the room? He couldn't remember. His last thought came in the form of a question, which he murmured aloud before fatigue finally overtook him. "I thought you said you didn't believe in God?"

* * *

Two men stood in a dark corner inside the hospital parking garage, each wrapped in a heavy coat as they tried to ward off the cold, harsh wind that whistled through the huge concrete structure. Both men smoked as they talked.

"Are you sure it's her, the Russell woman?" Eddie Weaver asked, glaring at the man. "I better not be freezing my balls off for nothing."

The second man, an administrative assistant on the hospital's graveyard shift, nodded emphatically. "Are you kidding? I admitted her. I saw her name right on the chart. Her husband—he's a hotshot doctor here. He gave me their insurance card and everything."

The man tossed away his cigarette. Then quickly lit another. "Besides, the whole damn hospital's talking about them. They were in an accident. The baby was born in the car. Can you believe that? On frigging Christmas Eve! It ought to be in the papers."

Weaver flicked his cigarette right in the man's face. It glanced off his head, and before he could complain, Weaver slapped him and grabbed him gruffly by the front of his coat. "It better not make the papers. You understand? You open your mouth to anyone else, and you'll be the one in the papers. Your own headline in the obituary section."

"Okay, okay," the man stammered. "I didn't mean nothing by it. I ain't going to tell nobody else. I'm dealing with you. You're my man. Take it easy for Christ's sake."

Weaver released the man and laughed. "Christ ain't got nothing to do with it. But by the time I'm through with the Russells, everyone will think the old boy does."

He took out a $100 bill and handed it to the man. He looked at it, then made a face. "Where's the other hundred?" he complained. "You promised me two."

"You'll get the rest when I get a copy of the admittance record. Now go get it. And hurry your ass up. I ain't got all day."

The man ran toward the garage elevator. Weaver fired up another cigarette, then put his hands in his pockets. "This is almost too good to be true," he said to himself. "And I owe it all to Bingham. Way to go, Billy boy. You sick little bastard."

CHAPTER 28

December 26, 2000

Although she was awake, Melanie's eyes remained closed. She was just too tired to open them. Too tired and too sore. It was early morning. She could tell because the sun was up, and she could feel flashes of light dancing across her face. And that meant she'd been sleeping for, what, at least twelve hours?

She'd had a light dinner about six o'clock Christmas night. She and Jack. Then a nurse had brought the baby in for a visit and feeding. After that, she just dozed off, expecting to take a quick nap. Now here it was, morning already. Time to get up and face the world. And a difficult future.

But not yet. In a few more minutes. Melanie smiled. *A couple more winks, and I'll feel better*, she thought. *I'll be ready to go.*

"Quit faking, you lazy dog. Open those eyes, and say hi to the best friend you ever had."

"Doris," Melanie said, surprised at the raspiness in her voice. She was fully awake now, and her eyes opened wide. In an instant, she was focused and alert, and reaching her hand out to the familiar slim figure standing beside her bed.

"Oh, Doris. I've got so much to tell you. You won't believe everything that's happened."

Doris reached over the bed railing and gave Melanie a long, warm hug. Then she kissed her on the forehead. "I won't believe? How can you say that to me after everything we've been through? I've reached the point where I'm not surprised by anything that happens to you. I wouldn't bat an eye if you told me Jack was really a little green alien and you're Cat Woman."

Melanie laughed despite trying not to. She held her abdomen and grimaced in pain. Doris laughed for both of them. "Don't do that to me," Melanie said, pretending to be angry. "I'm hurting all over."

Doris played along. "Spare me, please. I've pushed out three of those big headed boys, so don't try to con a con. You just like the attention, milking this for all it's worth. Now get out of bed, and let's go for a run. We've got to get the rest of that weight knocked off you before Jack starts ogling some young teenager."

Melanie laughed again, for several seconds, before getting it under control. "Would you stop already?" she pleaded. "You're killing me."

"Okay, okay. I'm sorry. Just wanted to make sure you still had your sense of humor. Lord knows you're going to need it during the next few weeks."

Melanie pushed a button on her bed control that raised her head and torso.

She and Doris were alone in the room.

"Where is everybody?" she asked. "And what time is it, anyway?"

"It's seven-thirty," Doris answered. "I got here about an hour ago. I just couldn't wait any longer. I had to see that baby. And I did, in the nursery. He's beautiful, Melanie. Absolutely beautiful. I can't wait to hold him."

Melanie smiled as she thought of her newborn son. Suddenly, she ached to hold him. "Is he still in the nursery?"

"Yes. I just came from there. Jack's down there with Reece and the boys. All five of them are standing at the window, staring at him like some exotic zoo animal. The boys are fascinated. And happy for you. All of us are, Melanie. I'm grateful everything turned out so well. I was worried sick until Reece finally called."

The thought of the previous night, their ordeal and the accident, reminded Melanie of the weather. She looked out the window and was amazed to see that the sun was indeed shining brightly. "The storm's over?"

"Reece said the snow stopped not long after you arrived at the hospital. About ten inches altogether, but the roads were in pretty good shape this morning. And the temperature is supposed to get above forty today. In fact, it looks like it's going to be a beautiful day."

Melanie shook her head in disbelief. Was she still asleep? Still dreaming? Had she really had the baby? Had she ever really been pregnant?

"It's weird, I know," Doris said. "But there's no sense trying to figure it out. It seems everything is happening for a reason, and the sudden storm is no exception. If you recall from religion class, there were unusual circumstances involved the last time this sort of event occurred. Maybe it's all part of the plan. If nothing else, it sure makes for a memorable birth, doesn't it?"

"You can say that again. It's something I'll never forget. Or Jack either. Or Michael. Poor Michael. I wouldn't blame him if he's on the next plane to Dallas."

Doris shook her head and motioned toward the door. "Well, he's not. He's standing out there in the hallway, watching over you. Been out there all night. Jack said he takes turns watching over you, then the baby. Constantly back and forth. I think he's driving the staff here crazy."

Melanie laughed. "But I'll tell you one thing, he's keeping them all on their toes. He's pretty intimidating just standing there quietly, watching everyone with those big bloodshot eyes. As I was coming in, one of the nurses asked me who he was."

"What'd you say?"

"I told her the truth. I told her Michael was a very dear friend of the family."

* * *

As Melanie spent the next several minutes recapping the previous night's events, two other people were also deep in conversation in a small office on the other side of town. Eddie Weaver was seated before Libby Elkington, regional copy editor for the *National Exposé*, a new and popular entry into the yellow journalism forum of tabloid newspapers.

Weaver was pleased with himself. He had Elkington's attention. That was obvious. Now it was time to close the deal.

"What separates your publication from most tabloids is your desire to publish the truth. I understand that your company enjoys the wild and shocking events of the day as much as the next paper, but you guys take the time and effort to gather facts and report an accurate story. In fact, that's why I've brought this information—"

"Save it, Weaver," Elkington said, interrupting her annoying visitor without a moment's remorse. "Flattery gets you nowhere with me. I know what we are, and you know what we are. We're tabloid trash. But at least we print interesting trash, and nine times out of ten, we get our stories straight and all the names spelled correctly. That's every bit as good as the big boys at the *Times* and *Post* do, yet we do it without all the moral posturing, whining rhetoric, and insulting pretense regarding honest, objective reporting.

"If it's interesting, shocking, titillating, exciting, and is at least close to the truth, we'll print it. If you've got pictures or supporting documentation, all the better. But if the story is good enough, we can live with it either way. That's why we spend millions on court settlements and attorney fees. We're so good we can buy our way out of trouble and still make money. Big money. After all, we give the people what they want."

Weaver grinned, exposing his bright yellow teeth. He liked a woman who cut right to the chase. In fact, this broad in her late forties wasn't half bad to look at. When this was all over, maybe he'd take a stab at getting her in the sack.

"Not a chance," Elkington said, easily reading the expression on Weaver's ruddy face. "Not in a million years. Your best bet is to keep grinding your little axe with the low-rate whores you've come to know and love down on the lower east side. Now tell me the rest of your story, and let's make a deal before I call the police and have them bounce your fat ass out of here."

* * *

It was a little past eight in the evening, and Doris was sitting on a chair inside Melanie's hospital room. In her arms was Isaac, wide awake and content after nursing from his mother. The two women were alone in the room with the baby, Reece having taken the boys out for hamburgers and fries. Jack had walked down to the vending machine for a candy bar and a cup of coffee after finally talking Michael into going home so that he could get a shower, some sleep, and a fresh change of clothes.

A nurse entered, gave Melanie a pill, and poured her a cup of water from the small pitcher on the hospital tray. "How's the pain?" she asked.

"Not bad. I'm feeling much better than I did this afternoon. Do you think Dr. Stewart will let us go home tomorrow?"

"Maybe," the nurse said, making a note on Melanie's chart then putting it back on the hook at the foot of her bed. "Normally, with an emergency delivery like you had, the doctor likes to keep you a little longer. But you're making amazing progress. And the baby looks great. She'll probably check on you again in the morning and make a decision then."

The nurse left the room to continue her rounds, closing the door softly behind her. Although the sound made by the door was almost silent, Isaac seemed to detect it. He squirmed in Doris's arms, and the movement caused him to spit up on the front of his little nightgown. She used a clean rag to wipe him off, then put him on her shoulder and patted his back. A loud burp followed. As she put the baby back in the cradle of her arm, she looked into his radiant face and began crying.

"What is it?" Melanie asked, alarmed. "What's wrong, Doris?"

"I can feel it, Melanie," she whispered. "It's like a magical glow, radiating from his spirit. The power of his soul is shooting through my body like electricity. Lord God Almighty. I am holding the Christ child!"

The women cried together until Jack walked in a few minutes later.

CHAPTER 29

December 27, 2000

Less than sixty hours after being rolled into the hospital with the help of Reece McKenzie and his band of merry men, the Russell family—Melanie, Jack, and Isaac—walked through the back door of their home. Jack held the baby as Melanie slowly shuffled through the doorway, still sore and tender but glad as all get out to be home. Michael parked the rental car, provided just this morning by the insurance company, in the garage and carried in the rest of Melanie's things.

A wonderful aroma drifted down the hallway, and Jack called out toward the kitchen. "Hey, Doris, we're home. And we're hungry. Is that some of your world-famous vegetable soup I smell?"

Reece pushed open the swinging door and smiled broadly as he greeted his friends. "No, it's some of my world-famous vegetable soup, you male chauvinist pig. Don't you know I'm the best cook in this group by far? Always have been, always will be."

Jack, Melanie, and Michael all laughed. Isaac squirmed in his daddy's arms.

"And the biggest blowhard too." Doris entered from the den, punched her husband playfully in the stomach, and gave Melanie a hug. "I've got a nice, comfortable bed set up for you in there, as well as a crib for the baby. And, Jack, I put a sheet and some pillows on the couch for you. You'll need to stay on the first floor for a few days, then you can all move back upstairs. The sooner the better, I'm sure you'll agree. I also changed your bed, and the nursery is open and ready for business."

Jack handed his son to Doris then kissed her on the cheek. "You're the best," he said before walking over to Reece and giving him a strong, warm handshake. "And you too, captain. You guys make quite a team."

"Yes, thank you both so much," Melanie said. "I can't find the words to tell you how much you mean to us."

The room grew silent for a moment as the four friends stood together, awkwardly, each unsure about what to say next. From behind Jack and Melanie came a low, rumbling sound. Michael, clearly embarrassed, smiled apologetically. His stomach was growling.

"I'm sorry," he said. "But that soup smells awfully good."

Everyone burst into laughter. As they moved into the kitchen, Doris looked down at Isaac in her arms. He, too, was laughing.

* * *

A distinguished man in an attractive dark suit stood at a newspaper stand on the corner of Twenty-Fourth Street and Baxter Avenue. His name was Lou Dodson.

Actually, Avery Douglas Dodson was his real name, given to him by loving parents on the day he was born fifty-eight years ago. Lou was simply a tag hung on him by his colleagues down at police headquarters. He'd served as lieutenant of the detective division at Chicago's Fourteenth Precinct for seventeen years, earning the prestigious position at the tender age of thirty-nine. He was called Lou out of respect for his rank but, more importantly, because he'd earned it.

It was a sad day at the Fourteenth when Dodson took early retirement. But his detectives understood. Lou wanted to spend more time with his wife, Trina, and together they planned to make the commute to Memphis more often to see their daughter, son-in-law, and two young grandchildren.

So he retired. Six months later, his wife was diagnosed with breast cancer.

Sixteen months later, in November of last year, Trina was gone. And Lou was alone. Fit and in excellent health, he was suddenly facing another twenty to thirty years of life with no partner, no job, no hobbies, and suddenly, not much enthusiasm. Isn't life just full of ironies?

"That'll be sixty cents, Grandpa," said the young man behind the counter.

Lou, who had been absently leafing through one of the tabloid rags—killing time as he so often did nowadays—glanced up at the newsstand salesman. He started to protest, to put this young punk in his place, then decided against it. Why bother?

Kids today have no respect for anyone, he thought. *Why try to make a difference now?*

He pulled a dollar bill from his front pocket, handed it to the young man, and walked away without a word, the newspaper rolled neatly under one arm.

Lou Dodson was a handsome man—black, about six feet tall, a solid 180 pounds. He looked a bit like his favorite actor, Morgan Freeman, only a little less gray and without any of the facial hair. He tried to grow a beard once, but Trina nixed the notion. As always, he'd honored her request and shaved. He'd thought about growing one since her passing but found he didn't have the heart.

Too old to change now, he thought. So he didn't. He still rose every day, weekends included, at precisely six o'clock. He showered, shaved, and dressed himself neatly in one of the dozen dark suits he owned. Except he picked out his own ties now and fixed his own breakfast. That part of his life and the wonderful morning conversations he'd shared with Trina were gone. As a result, he most often left his comfortable home near Soldier Field by seven thirty and made his way downtown, past the newsstand, to old friend Charlie Allen's coffee shop on Rush Street.

First he'd read the paper, drink coffee, and kill time with Charlie. Then he'd stop by the library to catch up on his reading, then perhaps take in a matinee at the movie complex, if he could find a film that wasn't full of filth, foul language, and sex. He was usually home by four, finished with dinner by six, and in bed no later than ten thirty—in bed, but not asleep. Sleep came agonizing slow to Lou, if it came at all. On more than one occasion since Trina's passing, he'd cried himself to sleep. Not that he'd ever mention that to Charlie Allen or any of his dear friends down at the precinct, several of whom still called him weekly. No, he was much too proud to ever admit he wept, even for his beloved Trina.

He found a seat in the coffee shop and was disappointed to learn that Charlie wasn't coming in today. A bad case of the flu, according to Charlie's son, Mark, who helped manage the place. "But it's a slow day, Mr. Dodson," he said. "Christmas letdown, I guess. I'd love to sit and chat with you awhile."

Dodson smiled at the young man. Old Charlie had certainly raised his boy right—polite, well-mannered, respectful of his elders, and a bright, intelligent businessman to boot. He liked Mark almost as much as his old friend. "No, no, son, you're much too busy to baby sit an old goat like me. I wouldn't think of it. I've got my paper here and need to catch up on a little reading anyway. Just have one of the ladies bring me a cup of coffee when they get a chance, and I'll be fine."

As he pulled the paper from under his arm and spread it across the square table, Mark laughed. "The *National Exposé*, Mr. Dodson. I never would of thought it."

Surprised and embarrassed, Dodson looked down at the newspaper. His frustration and annoyance with the clerk at the newsstand had caused him to buy the wrong paper. "Never you mind what I choose to read. This will help keep my mind off the bad taste of your daddy's coffee."

Mark roared with laughter and hit Lou affectionately on the shoulder. "That's a good one, Mr. Dodson. You got me. I'll have Lucy right over with a hot cup and a fresh cinnamon roll, on the house. You got me good with that one. I just wish Pop had been here to catch it."

Lou laughed and waved goodbye. While he waited, he scanned the front cover of the paper. As usual, it was full of gross, shocking headlines. One near the top caught his eye: CHICAGO'S OWN VIRGIN MOTHER GIVES BIRTH TO MIRACLE BABY. He turned to the center section and read the account, complete with censored yet very offensive photographs. By the time Lucy arrived with his coffee and roll, Lou was gone. The paper, ripped violently in half, was still on the table.

CHAPTER 30

December 28, 2000

Just one hour had passed since Melanie, Jack, and the others had received word about the scandalous article in the *Exposé*. As soon as they heard the ominous warning issued by the Salvation Army Santa just one week ago—all but forgotten during the exciting birth experience—came rushing back to them.

"The birth will be made public," he'd told them.

Reece rushed out and bought a copy of the paper and the feelings of shock, anger, and sheer bewilderment intensified as each member of the inner circle looked at it.

Melanie was sick, physically and emotionally. She threw up moments after seeing the first picture. As soon as she heard the news and saw the article, memories of her ill-advised visit to Dr. William Bingham's office came flooding back. The pictures—the awful, disgusting pictures—were taken by him. She was sure of it, because there was no other explanation and no one else twisted enough to do such a thing. She felt raped, violated, in full public view.

But the worst part was the picture of her beautiful baby boy stolen from the hospital, from her very room, and turned over to the barbarians at the tabloid rag. The photo of Isaac sent her into full panic. People read this kind of smut, enjoyed it even, and now they knew about her son—knew his name, approximate address, and what he looked like.

Melanie was hysterical by the time she and Doris finished telling Jack, Reece, and Michael about her brief encounter with Bingham. Jack wasn't hysterical. He was shaking with anger and headed out the door before Michael and Reece stopped him.

Jack turned on his friends like a raging animal. "He can't get away with this. Nobody can get away with this. It's criminal. It's evil. And when I find him, he'll pay and pay dearly. You two or no one else is going to stop me from doing the right thing."

Reece didn't know how to respond. He was angry too, and put in Jack's shoes, he was sure he'd feel the same way. Hell, he felt that way now. Maybe he'd go with Jack, and together that could stomp Bingham's ass in the ground before stopping by the *Exposé* office—wherever that was—and stomping a little more ass.

It was Michael who stopped them dead in their tracks, and he did it without lifting a finger. His words sent chills up their spines, cooling their temper and providing the whole group with a bitter dose of perspective.

"You leave now, and you leave me alone to protect the child. And make no mistake, he is in grave danger. Immediate danger. This article will do more than bring out the crazies and the fanatics and the well intentioned. It will surely bring out those who intend to do him harm."

Michael looked both men dead in the eye. "We're in trouble here. I can't do it alone. If you leave us, they'll get to Isaac. And when they get to him, they'll kill him."

Jack and Reece looked at Melanie seated on the floor and holding the baby in her arms. She was rocking back and forth, sobbing in great bursts, as Doris tried to comfort her. They looked at each other, then back at Michael, and nodded in agreement.

There would be no time for revenge or justice against Bingham and those who helped him. No, there was a more important war to wage. Suddenly, the battle plan had changed. The goal now was survival.

CHAPTER 31

December 31, 2000

It had been three days since the article on Melanie and her "miracle" baby had hit the streets. The phone had been ringing day and night. First came the concerned calls from Jack's parents and other family members. What in the world was going on? Jack explained things as best he could, then moved ahead. He was blessed with a good family. He knew that with time they'd trust his explanations and support him and his wife and their new baby through hell or high water.

Friends and colleagues called, many of them outraged over the slanderous allegations and doctored pictures that had been printed. Most of them had been supportive and understanding, while others were hesitant to offer much encouragement and did little to hide their skepticism when Jack tried to explain as best he could.

There were also calls from casual acquaintances and complete strangers—hate calls; love calls; calls from people who wanted to meet the baby, to touch him, and to bow down before him; calls from raving adults and even teenagers who insisted the child should be destroyed in the name of the real God. There had even been a dozen or so calls from attorneys from all over the country who wanted to represent the Russells in a lawsuit and civil action against the *National Exposé*.

By the third day, around midafternoon, the calls finally stopped. Not from a lack of interest or trying but because a field worker from the telephone company had finally made it to the house and changed the number.

Yet even the silent phone did little to ease the fear inside the Russell home. A sense of hopelessness had taken hold, with everyone in the group adopting a bunker-type mentality.

The three McKenzie children were staying with Reece's mother on the other side of town. Reece and Doris were living almost exclusively with Jack, Melanie, and Michael. The adults—except for Melanie—were taking turns standing guard inside the house, with Michael always manning the night shift.

"I don't need much sleep anyway," he said. "And I think we need to stay especially alert after the sun goes down."

Jack, Reece, and Doris were still off work because of the holiday break, but that would end after New Year's. The outside world would become suspicious, and their livelihood would be lost if the trio didn't return to work at some point. Melanie, of course, was on maternity leave for the next six weeks, and Michael had given his superiors no time frame for his return. But still, they were running out of time and options. And everyone knew it.

* * *

Isaac was asleep, resting comfortably on a thick, warm blanket placed in the corner of the kitchen, away from both the outside door and the window. His little body twitched occasionally but did nothing to disturb his deep breathing.

Melanie was seated at the table with the other four adults, each of them picking at the rib eyes Reece had grilled for them. She watched her sleeping baby and experienced a sad, sinking feeling at the image of him on the floor. *He ought to be in his crib*, she thought, *sleeping like a normal child in a beautiful nursery*. But she couldn't risk that, could she? She was terrified to let Isaac out of her sight for fear that if she turned away, he would be gone, stolen from them like the picture in her hospital room.

The thought of her baby deprived of so many precious moments sickened her. Would he ever have the opportunity to enjoy the things other children do? Birthday parties? Sleepovers? A simple walk in the park without armed guards? The thoughts made her want to cry. Again. But she didn't. She was too tired.

Jack touched her on the hand. "It won't always be this way, baby. I really believe that. I don't think God would put his Son on earth with no opportunity to enjoy life. That's not the kind of God I believe in. If we can get through this first year—the real danger period—then I think things will change. For the better."

Melanie continued to stare blankly at Isaac. "I know that seems like a long way off," he added. "But we'll find a way to make it."

She turned to the group at the table and shook her head. "Not without more help," she said. "Look at you guys. You all look like the walking dead."

The others stared at their plates.

"We could have sneaked by without that horrible tabloid article. No one knew us or knew what was happening. We had a chance to make it before the whole country was introduced to Melanie Russell, holy freak, and her new baby. People are already riding up and down the street day and night, gawking at us from a distance. It's just a matter of time before they get the nerve to walk right up. And what do we do then?"

There was bitterness in her voice, and the others suffered in silence. "Raising the baby would have been dangerous and difficult under any circumstances. I realize that. But at least it was possible. We could guard against the few who really know the truth about Isaac. We've done okay so far. But this…it's just too much. How can the five of us protect this sweet child from everyone? Everything? We'll try. We'll go down fighting. But now, because of my stupid mistake with Bingham, we're doomed to fail. You know it as well as I do."

Doris was crying, and the men were shaken too. Their reaction made Melanie want to take some of her words back. But she couldn't. Instead, she spoke another truth. "It was my mistake, not yours, and I'm the one who will have to live with it for the rest of my life. But it doesn't change the way I feel about you. I love you all."

The baby slept, and the inner circle sat silently at the table for several minutes. Jack was getting ready to speak when the front doorbell rang. In the stillness of the kitchen, it sounded like a gong from a large church steeple. All five adults, and even Isaac, jumped at the sound.

Michael was on his feet, weapon drawn from the holster under his jacket. Jack and Reece rushed to the hallway closet, each grabbing one of the shotguns Michael had provided. "Jack, come with me," Michael said. "Reece, stay with the baby. Guard the back door."

The doorbell rang again, and the two men made their way quickly down the hall. Michael peered through the peephole, frowned, then motioned for Jack to do the same. "Do you know him?" Michael whispered.

"No. Never laid eyes on him."

Michael looked out the windows for other intruders. Seeing none, he rushed back to the kitchen to check on the others. There were no signs of trouble in the backyard either. He walked back to Jack just as the doorbell rang for the third time. "This could go on forever. Get ready. Let's see what he wants."

As Jack pulled the door open, Michael stepped onto the front porch and shoved his revolver quickly into the visitor's chest. "Can I help you?" he asked in a voice that was both eerie and calm.

The man on the porch didn't flinch. Instead he looked at Michael, then around his massive frame at Jack in the doorway. He nodded politely then reached out his right hand.

"My name's Dodson. I'm here to help you."

* * *

It was late into the evening by the time Lou had convinced Michael that he was, indeed, one of the good guys. Melanie recognized his honesty and sincerity immediately. She'd developed an acute sixth sense when it came to meeting people and measuring their motives. It was a valuable defensive tool that had served her well and would continue to do so in the future.

Doris quickly sided with Melanie, followed soon afterward by Jack and Reece. But Michael, because of his past experience, was a tougher sell. He left no stone unturned while summing up Lou's intentions and reasons for being there.

"I've investigated some of the most hideous crimes you could ever imagine," he told Jack. "Mutilation, ritualistic slayings, even cases of cannibalism. And you'd be surprised at the number of times the killer was a nice, clean, respectable member of the community. I've booked doting mothers, best friends, teachers, members of the clergy, and yes, even police officers. After a while, you get to the point where you trust no one."

It was good to have a person like Michael around. They all realized it. Even Lou. So each of them waited patiently, seated in the den as he carried out his business.

First he called one of his most trusted colleagues at the Dallas crime center. A background check was performed on Avery Douglas Dodson. The profile report given to Michael was clean as a whistle. Then he called an old friend with the FBI, and again the check provided only positive information on what the friend described as a sterling, near-perfect career. Michael called several of the detective precincts in Chicago, at random, and mentioned the name of the retired lieutenant. Each time the response was the same. Great guy, even a better detective. Finally, he was able to reach Ralph Sunderland, the man who had replaced Lou at the 14th Precinct.

"I don't know what Lou's up to or why he asked you to call me, but I can assure you of one thing, Mr. Starr," Sunderland said, "if you're considering him for some type of position and it involves police work, look no further. You won't find a better man that Lou Dodson. He's brave and honest as the day is long. You can trust him with your life. I did on many occasions and wouldn't hesitate to do so again. If you need help, Lou's your guy."

Michael hung up the phone, turned, and looked at Lou. "I've got two more questions," he said. "How'd you come to know about Melanie and Jack and their baby? And why do you want to help?"

Lou put his hands together in his lap and carefully considered his response.

He knew the answer to both questions. Of course, he just didn't know if his answer would make sense to anyone in the room.

"Obviously, I was made aware of this situation through that awful article in the newspaper. How I happened to see it is something I can't even explain. It was an accident, more or less, except I now believe I was supposed to see it."

He then told them about his wife, her serious illness, and the way he lost her to the ravages of cancer. Trina's story was really the answer to Michael's question.

"We talked a lot before she died, spent hour after hour lying in bed and talking about all the wonderful times we'd had together. Sometimes Trina would talk about the future, about life without her. I didn't want to, but she insisted. She made me promise her things. I guess she wanted to know that I'd be all right without her. I tried to reassure her as best I could."

All eyes were on Lou as he spoke. He stared straight ahead, sifting through mental images of his wife during their last weeks together.

"One night she said a funny thing to me. We were talking and laughing about a show she'd watched on television when suddenly, she changed the subject and became very serious. Trina told me that one day, after she was gone, I'd see or hear something of great importance and consequence. She referred to it as 'my calling' and said it would be the last great challenge of my life. She said I'd receive a sign, and when I did, I should do the right thing."

He hesitated for several minutes before continuing. Only Melanie could sense the full deepness of sorrow etched across his face.

"She never spoke of it again, and I figured it was just a bit of confusion brought on by the pain medication. I'd forgotten all about it until this morning, when I saw the article in the paper. That article was my sign, and this—the task of assisting this family—is my calling. I want to help, if you'll let me. More importantly, I have a blessed angel in heaven who is counting on me to do the right thing."

Michael stood and smiled at his new partner. He walked over to the couch, where Lou was sitting comfortably between Jack and

Reece, and reached out his hand. Lou stood and gripped it firmly, and the two men shook hands.

"I'm sorry, Mr. Dodson. It's just that I…we can't afford to make a mistake. There's too much at stake. I guess you know that or you wouldn't be here."

"Please. Call me Lou. And there's no need to apologize, son. I'd have done the same thing, given your position. By the book. The way it should be done. To tell you the truth, I like your style. Take nothing for granted. Leave nothing to chance. Suspect everyone. That's the way all the great ones operate."

The others stood and came, one by one, to formally introduce themselves to the newest member of their team. Melanie was last in line. When she came to Lou, he surprised them all by dropping to his knees and kissing each of her hands.

Melanie, embarrassed, urged him to stand. As he did, Melanie noticed his lip was quivering ever so slightly. He bit it and managed to smile.

"Are you okay?" she asked.

Lou looked at the others in the room, then back at Melanie. "My life has been pretty empty since Trina passed. I've tried to keep busy, stay useful, but it's difficult when you have no family near and you've given up your career. Now in one day I go from hanging out at the coffee shop to this—serving the chosen one, the one sent by God himself to help decide the future of the world."

Suddenly, he laughed, breaking the silence in the room. "I guess you could say it's been a big day, especially for an old gumshoe like me. This morning, the biggest decision of my day was whether to have bacon or sausage with my breakfast. Now I'm committed to help protect the Son of God. Like I said, it's been a big day."

The others laughed with him, and Melanie kissed him on the cheek. Her spirits, so low just hours earlier, were definitely on the upswing. With Lou's arrival came more help, potential reinforcement through his contacts with local law enforcement, and most of all, renewed hope.

Yet somehow, she felt badly for Lou. Did he have any idea what he was getting into? She feared for his safety, his well-being, and abruptly she had a horrible thought. What were his odds for survival? An older gentleman who should be enjoying his retirement years. Was it right for them to steal that away from him? The answer, she realized, was yes. The baby must come first. Without Isaac, none of them had a future anyway. Quickly, she put the feelings of guilt out of her mind.

Lou, still standing before her, was experiencing a wide range of emotions as well. His calm exterior hid the excitement he felt, the feelings of worth and purpose that he'd somehow lost after leaving his job and losing Trina. He was alive again—alive and on the most important mission of his life.

In his prayers, he would thank the Lord for this special opportunity. Even as he wondered why God and these very special people would place their trust in him. Their confidence would fuel his fire over the weeks and months ahead. Their goodness and dedication to the difficult task at hand inspired him.

"May I see the Holy Child?" he finally asked. "It would be the greatest honor of my life."

Melanie walked across the room and lifted the sleeping Isaac from his crib. Lovingly, she placed him in Lou's arms.

Within seconds, Lou was doing something he'd never done before, at least not in full public view, not even at Trina's funeral, bad as he'd wanted to.

When Isaac opened his eyes and looked up at his new protector, Lou Dodson wept.

They were tears of joy.

CHAPTER 32

January 1, 2001

Lou spent most of the first day of the new year on the telephone. Since it was a holiday, the majority of law enforcement personnel he needed to reach were at home, watching football games and enjoying time with their families.

The plan, as laid out with Michael and the others the night before, was to expand the protection team slightly with outsiders who could be trusted. They needed reinforcements, but not at the expense of revealing every detail concerning Isaac and his reason for being. Lou told them he could round up a half-dozen people and, by calling in a few old favors, get them to help without asking too many questions.

The first call he placed was to his predecessor, Ralph Sunderland. He told the lieutenant about the Russell family and explained how he'd contacted them to offer assistance against any potential threat they would face as a result of the inflammatory article in the national tabloid.

"I wondered what that call was about last night. I figured those people were in some kind of trouble. It's good of you to help, Lou. They'll probably need it until this firestorm blows over, and the vultures jump on some other poor, unfortunate soul."

"I'm going to contact Nichols and Donahue, and maybe a few more of the detectives who still like to do a little moonlighting," Lou said. "We can't offer them much, but I'm hoping they'll be willing to help anyway."

"No problem, old friend. Touch base with anyone you think can help. And I'll see to it that we make some overtime pay available to them as well. After all, it's our job to protect all the people of this fair city—and that includes the Russells. I'll talk to some of the uniform guys downstairs and ask them to make that neighborhood a priority patrol area for the next several weeks. If there's anything else I can do, just holler."

Lou smiled as he hung up the phone. He'd left the precinct in good hands. At least he felt good about that. The smile quickly faded, however, as he punched in Donahue's number. The past was gone. It was time to concentrate on the future. There was much work to be done, and every second counted.

CHAPTER 33

Jan. 3, 2001

It was half past midnight, and Detective George Nichols radioed Lou from his car, parked one block down from the Russell home.

"Everything's quiet out here, boss. If it's okay with you, I'm heading home. I'm pulling a seven-to-three shift at the station tomorrow or, rather, later today."

Lou laughed. Nichols was always in a good mood. And he could go for days with little or no sleep. He was perfect for the night shift, which was why his old leader had selected him.

"That's fine, George. I appreciate you staying as long as you have. You gave me an extra hour of nap time. We'll be fine here for the rest of the night. Drive carefully."

The radio crackled again. "Will do, boss. I'll see you about six tomorrow—I mean, tonight. Then Donahue will be here the next two nights. If anything comes up, you know where to reach me. Good night, Lou."

"Good night, George. And thanks again."

Nichols started his car, did a U turn in the quiet street, then drove slowly past the Russell house on his way home. He saw Lou's silhouette in the front window. He did not see the three young men crouched low to the ground, about two hundred yards from where he'd been parked.

But they'd seen him. As soon as the gray sedan disappeared from sight, they stood. Each was dressed in black, from their boots to the knit caps covering their heads. Weapons were tucked carefully into their wide belts. Each had a knife and a pair of handguns. Wilson, the leader, carried a flashlight, and slung over his right shoulder was a semiautomatic machine gun, just in case the element of surprise was not enough to finish off their prey.

The attack the trio had carefully planned would be swift and violent. It would not be quiet, nor did it have to be.

There was no need for a covert operation. The three men cared little about being seen, heard, or even apprehended. Once the child was dead, their appointment was over. If it was time to meet their maker, so be it. The Dark One would provide for them. He always had.

The three separated slightly, then headed for the house. Within minutes, they would surround it and position themselves for an unobstructed view of all potential exits. Their plan called for no survivors, and that included any last-ditch effort by the mother or father to flee with the child.

Wilson, crouched low in the shadows on the north side of the garage, looked for signs of movement inside the home. Seeing none, he grinned and looked at his military watch. The strike was set for one o'clock. Ten more minutes, he thought, and we're on our way. He smiled. "A piece of cake," he said to himself. With any luck, they wouldn't even need the automatic weapon.

* * *

Lou flushed the toilet and grimaced. The sound of the rushing water sounded like a waterfall in the stillness of the dark house. He'd waited as long as he could, but that wasn't long anymore. He had no idea how many times he urinated during the course of a day, but it had probably tripled in the last five years, especially at night. Getting older was a bitch, even with reasonably good health.

He could almost hear his buddy Charlie Allen making fun of him now. "I don't know how the hell you ever made it as a cop," he'd once said. "You've got to have the smallest bladder in the state of Illinois. I bet you made half your arrests with your pecker in your hand, taking a leak at the end of some alley. It's a wonder they didn't find you killed that way."

Lou almost laughed, but didn't. Instead he stretched and walked down the hall. All was quiet. Melanie, Jack, and the baby were asleep upstairs. Reece and Doris were home tonight, trying to keep some semblance of order with their three young children. Michael should be resting on the couch in the den. He peeked around the corner to check on his new partner—and saw nothing. The big guy was gone, and Lou could feel his heart start to beat a little faster.

He resisted turning on the light and instead walked across the dimly lit room to the couch. The covers were thrown back from the makeshift bed, and Lou felt under them, putting his hand against the middle cushion. It was still warm.

Michael hadn't been gone long.

Lou picked up the telephone and was alarmed to find it already dead. It was a bad sign. He walked quickly to the back door and checked it. Finding it secure, he made his way to the front door. As he passed a mirror in the hallway, his heart skipped a beat, then tried to jump out of his chest. The message, scribbled hastily in soap on the large mirror, was blunt but effective: "Danger outside. Three at least. Stay with the family."

His weapon pulled out, Lou slipped off the safety and started up the stairs. "Where are you, Michael?" he asked himself as he made his way to the master bedroom. "Where are you?"

Melanie was awake before Lou walked into the room. She'd awakened abruptly, sensing danger. She was alert and on her feet immediately. Isaac was sleeping soundly in the crib next to the bed. Jack was also asleep.

"What is it?" she whispered. "Is someone here?"

Lou nodded, and together they shook Jack, waking him quickly. Lou held his index finger over his lips, reminding Jack to speak quietly.

"There's trouble of some kind, danger outside the house," Lou said. "Michael's gone. I believe he's already out there, and we need to be prepared for anything. Let's move."

Without another word, the trio sprang into action. Jack helped Melanie slide the crib into the bathroom. He took a handgun from the nightstand, rechecked it for ammo, then handed it to his wife. He kissed her and his son then closed the door. Melanie locked it behind him.

He then went to the closet and took another handgun from the top shelf. He also pulled down a shotgun and quickly pushed in three 12-gauge shells. Lou motioned for Jack to stop just inside the bedroom door. He went out of the room and positioned himself low and against a wall near the top of the stairs, creating three lines of defense.

The first line, Michael, was outside somewhere in the dark—alone against at least three intruders. *It's the smart move*, Lou realized, *attacking the attackers, taking the offensive, shifting the element of surprise from their side to your side.* But it was dangerous, and he feared for Michael's safety, almost as much as he feared for that of the sleeping child.

Wilson, still crouched near the garage in the Russell backyard, glanced at his watch again. Two minutes to ground zero and victory. His knees were aching. He was ready to go. But he held his place.

No need to rush, he thought. *Move on the mark. Make it last. Enjoy it.* As leader of the black hit squad, this was to be his shining moment.

Suddenly, he felt cold steel against the back of his neck. He froze, and despite his best efforts, panic rushed in. This was not part of the plan.

"Stand up," Michael said. "Slowly. And leave your weapons, all of them, on the ground."

Wilson did as he was told. There was something in the tone of the voice behind him that made him reject the impulse to turn and fight. His captor would be ready for that—ready for anything, probably. So Wilson decided to do as he was told and stall. If nothing else, at least the others would have a good opportunity to make the kill.

After laying each weapon on the ground, he stood and slowly started to turn and face Michael.

"Don't. Just answer my questions. How many others, and where are they?"

Wilson chuckled. "Come on, white knight. You know I can't tell you that, at least not for free. Maybe we can work out some kind of deal. You know, I'll tell you—"

The leader saw only a blinding flash of light a split second before hitting the ground, face first and unconscious. Michael had cracked him in the back of the head with the butt of his gun. For a fleeting moment, he thought of getting some rope and securing his captive, then decided against it. Why bother? This guy would never talk. He would only live to come and kill again. Michael took out his knife and drove it straight through the back of Wilson's skull.

He wiped the blood off the blade by swiping it against the man's dark shirt. He picked up the semiautomatic weapon, stood, and prepared to search for the others. As he did, the watch on the dead man's wrist beeped.

Michael grimaced and cursed under his breath. That was the signal. The others were already moving. He headed around the far side of the house. "Here they come, Lou," he said to himself. "You better be ready."

* * *

From his position above the stairs, Lou heard the back door crash in, and the home security system sounded an alarm. He glanced back at Jack, who stood wide-eyed but firm against the bedroom entrance. Then he turned his attention to the bottom stairwell. It was dark and difficult to see, but Lou knew what to look for. The gleam of a gun barrel. His ability to spot an attacker in the dark had saved his life on more than one occasion. He prayed it would help save this family now.

Seconds later, another crash sounded from the front of the house. A second shrouded figure climbed in through a shattered window. They were coming in, dead ahead, having thrown caution to the wind. This was now a full frontal assault, a search-and-destroy mission.

As the pair swept the downstairs portion of the house, each wondered about their leader. But his mysterious absence did not slow them. Rather, it incensed them, making their hate for the child and what he represented burn even hotter.

Inside the master bath, Melanie was shaking. Despite the noise and destruction below, Isaac was still sleeping peacefully. Alone in the dark with her baby, Melanie was afraid. She was also angry. How dare anyone come into their house, strangers sent on a twisted mission to snuff out the life of a sweet, innocent baby boy. She gripped the pistol tighter and pointed it toward the door.

As she waited and worried, a thought repeated itself over and over in her mind. *Not tonight. You won't get him tonight.*

As the first figure ascended the stairs, Lou took dead aim and opened fire.

Three rounds pierced the darkness, each finding its target—the torso of the attacker. He lurched and staggered on the steps, yet he kept coming. Jack looked on in disbelief, but Lou recognized the problem immediately. He felt what he could not see. The intruder was wearing a bullet-proof vest.

Lou strained for a better look in the darkness and waited patiently for his target to draw closer. Jack ducked behind the bedroom wall as the man opened fire, shooting blindly in the blackness. Lou held his position, then his breath, as he aimed at the center of the attacker's head. As he pulled the trigger, he realized his aim, thankfully, was still true. The bullet found its mark, and the man's head snapped back. As he fell down the steps, his revolver fell from his lifeless hand and came to rest on the bottom landing.

The other attacker screamed, then spewed profanities and bullets as he charged up the steps.

Jack dove across the narrow hallway and slid into Lou's feet. The old detective, low on ammo, calmly directed Jack. "The legs," he said. "Take out his legs."

Jack discharged the shotgun in the darkness, pumped in a fresh shell, then fired again. He pumped in the third shell and was about to pull the trigger again when Lou grabbed the barrel and gently pushed it to the floor.

"He's down," Lou whispered. "Save your ammo. Let's see if there are others."

The two protectors waited together in the darkness. The second intruder was moaning softly, fatally wounded by the two blasts from

197

Jack's shotgun. He was bleeding profusely from both legs, and his right arm was nearly gone. He was alive but unconscious, no longer a threat to anyone in the house.

After what seemed like an eternity, Lou and Jack heard another noise coming from downstairs. They braced themselves, pointing their weapons down the steps. Lou had reloaded, hoping for the best but expecting the worst. Jack had the one shell, plus a full clip in his revolver. He was prepared to empty them all.

Then a familiar voice called out in the darkness.

"Hey, guys, it's me. Everybody okay up there?" He flipped a switch beside the battered back door, and the three men squinted as they were suddenly engulfed in bright light. Michael looked at the fallen intruders and nodded his head in approval. "And to think I was worried about you guys."

Seeing the carnage scattered across what had once been a peaceful, beautiful home made Jack sick to his stomach. The thought of killing another man, even this man, was almost more than he could bear. Tears filled his eyes and bile rose in his throat as he turned away.

Lou touched him on the shoulder. "Go check on Melanie and the baby," he said. "We'll take care of this."

Michael, now halfway up the stairs, understood the emotions that were welling up inside his civilian friend. He'd experienced them too, long ago. "You're a brave man, Jack. You did what you had to do to protect your family. But I know that doesn't make it any easier."

Jack did not look back. He nodded his head slowly, wiped away the tears with the back of his hand, and slowly walked toward the bedroom.

"Were there any others?" Lou asked.

"One more. He's out by the garage. He was the leader but wouldn't talk. Neither will these two, apparently."

Michael put his foot against the unconscious attacker and rolled him onto his back. The man, his knit cap still in place, moaned but didn't open his eyes. As Lou looked on in horror, Michael took out his revolver and put a bullet between the man's eyes.

Lou rushed down the stairs, shock and anger evident on his face and in his voice. He grabbed Michael's massive shoulders and shook him as best he could. ·

"What's wrong with you?" he shouted. "Are you insane? That's murder, and it makes you no better than them!"

Michael remained calm, but it wasn't easy. He holstered his weapon, easily brushed off Lou's grip, then pushed him arm's length away.

"First of all, it's not murder. I don't let anyone, even scum like him, suffer needlessly. He was already dead. I just put him out of his misery. Secondly, this is not the kind of battle you see in the movies. There's not two sides to this story. There's only our side. We win, or the world ends. So in case you haven't caught on yet, we won't be taking any prisoners. It's kill or be killed. Sooner or later, you'll get a chance to look one of these thugs in the eye. And if you blink or hesitate, they will kill you. You'll die because they won't hesitate. They're on a mission—a mission to kill. You need to think about that."

Lou was less angry now. Michael's words rang true now that he heard them spoken out loud. He was sorry he had rushed to judge this great protector.

"And one more thing, old friend. I am extremely happy to have you on this team. Your wisdom, experience, and courage make us a more formidable foe for these Antichrist soldiers. But don't ever second-guess me again. I understand these people. I know how they think and how they act. And they are not the kind of people you show mercy to."

"I'm sorry," Lou said. "It's just that I'm not used to doing business this way."

Michael smiled, but there was sadness in his eyes. "I know," he said. "You're not like me and should be thankful for it. Nobody should be like me."

Lou felt badly and wanted to say more. After all, Michael's uncanny detection of the intruders had probably saved all their lives, and he was a brave and brutally honest man. But before he could think of anything to say, Michael waved him off.

"You better radio your friends at the station in case they're not already on their way. And pull all the strings you can muster. This is a helluva mess, and we're going to be asked a lot of difficult questions about what went on here tonight."

Lou passed him on the stairs and headed for the telephone. "You just let me take care of the police," he said. "You've done enough, big fella. Most of all, you've given that baby another chance."

* * *

Inside the bathroom, Jack was fighting back tears as he told Melanie about the bloody encounter. He spared her the details but told her the intruders were dead and that both Michael and Lou were unharmed.

"Thank God," Melanie said, hugging her husband tightly. She looked over Jack's right shoulder, at Isaac, still just nine days old, who was now awake in his crib. She could see his face in the moonlight as it streamed through the small bathroom window, and he seemed to smile at her.

She gently turned Jack toward the crib and addressed their son. "Here's your brave daddy," she cooed. "He's strong and brave and such a good man. I want you to grow up to be just like him, Isaac. Can you do that for me?"

Jack squeezed his wife's hand, then released it, and bent over the crib to be closer to his son. He rubbed Isaac's belly with the tips of his fingers, and the baby laughed at the tingling sensation. Jack laughed too and picked up his son. He felt better.

From down the street, they could hear the sirens wailing as police made their way to the Russell home. It would be a long and difficult night.

But they were still alive.

* * *

Fallout from the January 3 massacre at the Russell home lasted for months. Lou Dodson pulled every string known to mankind in keeping police authorities at bay. Still, it wasn't easy, especially when the FBI intervened.

Wilson and the other attackers were well-known within the office walls at the bureau. Despite their young age, all three had earned lofty status on the FBI's Most Wanted list. Wilson alone was suspected in at least three murders, all brutal ritualistic slayings. No one was sorry to see them dead. But the crime scene at Jack and Melanie's house certainly raised questions.

Wilson, found face down outside the home with a large knife hole through the back of his head, was rather difficult to explain—not to mention the condition of the third attacker, shot point-blank between the eyes.

Michael, when questioned, was polite and honest. His calm demeanor seemed to frustrate the agent assigned to the case. Finally, with Lou's help and urging, authorities closed the case. After all, no one was pushing too hard for the civil rights of these three.

Media coverage was a different obstacle and much more difficult to overcome.

The Russells, along with Michael and Lou, simply hunkered down and did their best to avoid the spotlight. They ignored hundreds of interview requests—both locally and from television stations and newspapers all across the country. When they were contacted, they declined comment.

In time the public's attention was diverted to other tragedies—twenty senior citizens were killed and forty-five more injured in a chartered bus accident on the north side of Chicago, and a prominent businessman and his celebrity wife were murdered while leaving the United Center after a Bulls' game.

Slowly, the death and bloodshed at the Russell home were pushed to the background and forgotten—forgotten by everyone but members of the team. The doors and windows were repaired, and the home security system was reinstalled, but the emotional scars remained.

Fortunately for Isaac, his parents, and his protectors, the publicity and notoriety associated with the break-in slowed the assault on the chosen one. It would be several months before trouble resurfaced. And during that time, there were many happy moments for the holy family.

For a while at least they were able to live as normal people.

CHAPTER 34

January 23, 2001

Melanie and Jack stood proudly inside the mostly empty St. Gabriel Catholic Church. Jack wore his most distinguished suit, while Melanie donned a beautiful midnight-blue dress. In her arms was Isaac, crying loudly as he fought against the long, flowing baptismal gown Melanie had borrowed from Doris. All three of the McKenzie boys had been baptized in the gown. Doris was deeply moved that Melanie wanted her own son to wear it now.

Father John Creed, the pastor at St. Gabriel's, was almost finished with the ceremony. It was one in the afternoon, and the private event was attended by less than fifteen people. Jack's mother and father, his sister and her family, and both of his brothers and their wives—they, along with Michael and Lou, were seated in the first few pews inside the large church. Jacob, Josh, and Jordan were seated between the two men.

Doris and Reece stood alongside Jack and Melanie. Isaac was now their godson.

The baptism went quickly and quietly. There were no disturbances, but as Father Creed poured holy water over Isaac's head, his cries seemed to rise into the rafters of the church and beyond.

When the ceremony ended, family members left the church and headed to the Russell home for Sunday brunch and a small celebration. Jack, Melanie, Doris, and Reece stayed behind to thank

Father Creed, and each of them offered their own prayers after the priest departed.

As he prayed, Jack looked at the large mural of Christ on the crucifix, and as he did, his head and heart filled with emotion. Isaac had met his true father today. Eventually, father and son would meet again. Would Isaac's life end on the same brutal and tragic note as the one who came before him?

Jack closed his eyes and asked for a better final scene. The others, at the same time, were praying for the same thing.

CHAPTER 35

February 14, 2001

"I'm not your sweetheart, but I think she'd like that."

Dr. Coen laughed and poked Jack in the side. The two men stood inside the hospital gift shop, looking over a wide selection of flowers, candy, and cards.

Coen was pointing at a beautiful arrangement of red roses, white carnations, greenery, and baby's breath. The price tag was forty-nine dollars.

"Unless, of course, it's a little too rich for your blood."

Jack shook his head and smiled at his friend. "No, it's not too much. If anything, it's not nearly enough. She deserves more, much more considering what she's been through."

The elderly doctor patted Jack on the shoulder. Jack didn't talk much about his wife and son, and when he did, it was with guarded words. But like everyone else, Coen had heard about the break-in. An attempted robbery, they'd called it, but he knew better. He knew Jack was hiding important secrets, but he was wise enough and kind enough not to pry. He knew all he needed to know about Jack Russell. He was a great doctor—and an even better human being.

Instead, Coen tried to reassure his friend with easy conversation.

"My Alice always loved Valentine's Day, still does actually, although our idea of a romantic evening now is a good meal, a little wine, a comfortable bed—and eight good hours of sleep."

Jack laughed. Coen always seemed to know just what to say. "Do you really think she'd like it?" he asked.

"It's a gorgeous bouquet. And the colors are perfect for the occasion. Maybe throw in a box of chocolates to cover all your bases."

"I'm sold," Jack said. He lifted the arrangement and carefully walked toward the cashier. "Pick me out a big box of candy. Maybe I'll have a piece or two myself."

* * *

Lou and Michael spent most of the evening in the den, watching the Blackhawks take on the Dallas Stars in hockey action. Michael, of course, was pulling for the Stars, while Lou was strictly a Chicago man. In reality, they wanted to give Jack and Melanie some space. It was, after all, a lovers' holiday.

That was why Isaac, resting comfortably in his portable carrier, was seated directly between them.

"Who's going to win, Isaac?" Michael asked, talking playfully with the baby. "Tell Lou. Dallas is just too tough, right?"

Lou chuckled. "You know, if he was old enough to talk, he could tell us. And the scary thing is, he'd be right."

The two men looked at each other for a moment. It was a light yet sobering thought. And both wondered to themselves for a brief second what it would be like to carry such a burden—knowledge of the future. The thought saddened them, and they quickly turned their attention back to the game.

* * *

Upstairs, Jack made passionate love to his wife. It had been a long time since the two had enjoyed even a brief moment together. And even when they were alone, the worry and mental stress of protecting their son left them exhausted. Their whole life had been turned upside down, and their individual needs had been overwhelmed by those of their son.

Both parents accepted the burden without hesitation, and neither had even once complained about a lack of time for themselves. But they'd missed it, their time together. And to have it back, even for a few hours, was wonderful.

Jack held Melanie in his arms, and they talked quietly in the privacy of their bedroom.

"I've missed you so much," she said. "I'd almost forgotten how much I love being with you, how good we are together."

He rubbed Melanie's flat stomach with the palm of his hand and marveled at the full roundness of her breasts. "I can't believe how physically fit you are, after just six weeks. I'm worried you're not eating enough, not taking good care of yourself."

Melanie rolled onto Jack and pushed the mussed hair from his forehead. "Actually, I'm eating great, better than ever before. I'm making sure I get a lot of protein and calcium and even started taking vitamins. Plus, I work out every day. There's nothing else to do around here, especially when Isaac is asleep, so I pop in a Jane Fonda tape and let it rip. Doris has been helping me, and I even caught Lou doing a few aerobics one day. He was so embarrassed that I caught him."

They laughed together, and the laughter reminded them of easier times. Jack kissed her softly on the lips, then harder, and they made love again.

Thirty minutes later, freshly showered, they dressed to go back downstairs. They couldn't become too selfish, even on Valentine's Day.

"I hope you're not working so hard on my account," Jack said. "I'd love you even if you weren't so beautiful."

"Well, that's good to know. But don't get too carried away with that male ego of yours. I take pride in how I look too. Yet it goes much deeper than that. I want to maintain a healthy lifestyle so I can be here, you know, for Isaac. I'm no spring chicken, and I don't know how long he'll need me, but I plan on protecting him as long as it takes. And to do that, I need to stay in shape."

Jack tucked his shirt in his pants and walked across the room to his wife. "You're always thinking, aren't you? Beauty and brains. How'd I get so lucky?"

They embraced for several long, meaningful seconds.

"Happy Valentine's Day, baby," he said. "Now come on down and find Jane Fonda for me. I guess I should get in better shape myself. And we'll give the candy to Michael. Big as he is, he'll eat the whole box and never gain an ounce."

There was a bounce in their step as they walked down to the first floor. And a gleam in their eyes. Being dutiful soldiers, Michael and Lou pretended not to notice.

CHAPTER 36

March 1, 2001

With the decision made, Melanie felt better. So did Jack. So did everyone. A few minutes earlier, Melanie had returned from Mercy Elementary after having had a heart-to-heart with Principal Alvin Nord. She was taking a leave of absence for the remainder of the school year.

"How'd he take it?" Jack asked.

"Very well, really. He didn't seem upset at all. Of course, Doris had already softened him up a bit. And like everyone else, he's aware of the trouble we had in January. He told me not to worry about a thing, said Victoria, my sub, was doing a good job and would be fine until the summer break. Mr. Nord didn't make me feel guilty at all."

Lou looked at Michael and nodded his head. Melanie noticed the gesture. "What's that all about? You two keeping secrets?" There was concern in her voice.

Lou smiled to reassure her. "No. It's just that Michael was right."

Both Jack and Melanie looked puzzled. "Right?" Jack asked. "About what?"

"When Michael told me about your decision last night, about taking the leave of absence, he said the principal would be fine with it. Looks like he was right. Again."

"Why did you say that, Michael?" Melanie asked. "You don't even know Mr. Nord."

Michael was uncomfortable. He wished Lou had kept his not-so-discreet nod of the head and his comments to himself. He stared at the floor.

"Fess up," Jack said. "How'd you know?"

Michael raised his eyes and looked at Melanie. "You can't see it, can you? The way everyone looks at you. The way they respect you. You don't realize it, and they don't either. But it's there, all the time. People sense the good in you. They trust you and believe in you… automatically. You could walk up to a stranger on the street, tell them they'd just won the lottery, and they would believe you. Even if they didn't play the lottery."

Melanie stood, mouth open, looking at Michael. "You're crazy," she finally blurted out. "You act as if I have some sort of power over people."

When Michael said nothing, she looked at Lou for support. He shook his head and smiled sheepishly. "It does sound crazy, I know. But I think he's on to something. I've noticed it too."

She shifted her gaze to her husband. Jack didn't smile. He knew better than that. Instead, he simply shrugged his shoulders. His body language spoke volumes.

Count me among the believers, it said.

Could it be true? Melanie was shocked and more than a little alarmed. Were people more receptive to her than before? Did they know somehow that she had given birth to the Son of God and was now in the process of trying to raise him?

She thought about it for a moment, then shook off the notion. If it was true, she didn't want to know it. Melanie felt more than enough burden already.

Michael came to her and took her hands into his. "Let's put it this way," he said. "Old Mr. Nord never had a chance with you." Then, in a more solemn tone, he added, "With any luck, neither do the bad guys."

CHAPTER 34

March 29, 2001

It was late in the evening, and Jack and Melanie lay in bed, absently watching television. Isaac, now more than three months old, slept quietly in the crib near them.

It had been a sad day for Melanie. The one-year anniversary of her mother's bizarre death in the Louisville nursing home. She understood her mother's passing much better now, but it didn't make the sadness go away. Melanie missed her mother more than ever. She'd learned there are some voids in life only a mother could fill.

"I know what today is," Jack said. "And I can see it's been tough on you. But at least you know, beyond any doubt, that there is a heaven and that Martha and James are both there, watching over you."

Melanie turned in bed and hugged her husband. Quiet tears quickly turned into heaving sobs as she let the pain of the past year wash over her.

Jack held her and whispered in her ear, "I know, baby. I know it hurts. It's okay. Let it all out."

And she did. Melanie cried long and hard, and when she finally stopped, she felt better. At least good enough to talk.

"I know she's watching over me, over us and the baby. She and Daddy together. But I miss her so much, miss her being here with us. I just wish she could have lived long enough to see her grandson, to spend a little time with him. She was never really happy after Daddy died. I think this would have made her happy."

Jack could feel a lump rising in his throat. He'd loved Martha Wade too. She was a good woman.

Finally, he found words he hoped would give Melanie comfort. "I could be wrong, but I look at it like this," he said. "I think Martha's death was the real starting point for this grand miracle. I can't explain it, but I think she had to die in order for this to take place. She's the one who told you what was happening, explained it to you, and made you believe. In my mind, Martha was God's chief messenger."

Melanie was crying again, but this time, the tears were happy ones. "What a lovely thought, Jack. That Mother was God's messenger, bringing the news of Isaac to me. Thank you, Jack. Thank you for giving me that wonderful thought."

She hugged him tighter and slowly closed her eyes. "I love you so much," she said. "You are my rock. You and Isaac are my entire life. Now and forever."

CHAPTER 37

April 2, 2001, Fort Lauderdale, Florida

It was Sunday afternoon, and William Bingham was enjoying the sights and sounds of one of the world's most crowded beaches. It was spring break month in the sunshine state, and what better place for an admitted pervert to experience a little rest and relaxation?

He'd seen seven wet T-shirt contests already—not to mention the Ft. Lauderdale "Bikini Games," and he'd arrived only three days ago. "I feel like a hog in shit heaven," he said to himself as he watched a pair of young beautiful girls walk past in suits that left less than little to the imagination.

He relaxed in his beach chair for another hour, salivating at each passing female, but the day was growing long and hot. Bingham didn't get out much, and despite his best efforts with sunscreen, a hat, and dark glasses, the big gold globe in the sky was beginning to take a toll on his fair skin. Besides, he was thirsty. As always. He looked in the small cooler at his feet and cursed himself for bringing only three Coronas.

So what if they cost two bucks apiece in the market across the street? He wasn't exactly running low on cash after receiving his share of money from the *National Exposé*. Eddie Weaver had met with him and given him the money in cold, hard cash shortly after the article and photos of Melanie Russell appeared.

He'd been on the run—or on vacation, as he liked to call it—ever since.

First, Las Vegas, then Los Angeles, and finally north to New York for two weeks in the Big Apple. By the time he hit Florida, he was riding high and still had more than $80,000 tucked beneath the spare tire in the trunk of his old car. He'd thought about purchasing a new one, but what was the point, especially when he could spend the money on more important things, like booze, cheeseburgers, and even women?

He might just buy himself a hooker tonight. But he needed more beer first. Bingham wasn't all that good in bed—or so he'd been told—and as a result, he needed all the courage he could get. Another six-pack should do the trick. So he picked up his cooler, left the chair in the sand, and headed for Sharkey's Food Mart located across the street and about three hundred yards away from his beach front motel room.

As he walked across the hot sand, his head began to throb. "Damn. Maybe I better get something to eat too," he muttered. "This frigging sun isn't everything it's cracked up to be."

By the time he reached the street, he was sweating profusely. The cheap sandals he was sporting had already rubbed a blister on his left heel, and his sunglasses were fogging up. He thought about walking down to the intersection and waiting for the light to change, but the burning blister told him no.

I'll just shoot across here, Bingham thought. *No harm, no foul. That's my motto.*

He watched several cars whiz past, waiting for an opening. Finally, one came. He hurried across the street and pushed through the door at Sharkey's. Bingham took off his glasses, wiped his forehead with the back of his sweaty hand, and soaked in the welcome relief of air conditioning. He headed straight for the beverage coolers and pulled out a carrier of six long-neck Coronas. He grabbed a bag of chips and small jar of salsa, then made his way to the cashier station. At the front counter, he also picked up another bottle of sunscreen.

"Better safe than sorry," he said to the young clerk. "That's my motto."

He paid with a fifty carefully counted his change, then took the plastic bag from the woman. As he pushed out the door and into the midafternoon heat, Bingham's sunglasses fogged again. He removed them, squinting as he stood on the sidewalk, and quickly wiped them off with a dirty handkerchief.

Better get these beers into the cooler, he thought. *Nothing worse than hot beer.*

With four of the beers pressed into the chipped ice inside the small cooler, Bingham picked up all his belongings and stepped off the sidewalk. A horn sounded sharply, startling him, and he looked up in time to see a red BMW roll past with four teenage girls hanging out the sides of the car. They were laughing at him, but Bingham didn't care. Hot chicks with hot young bods. He stared after them as they continued down the street, laughing and waving.

He was still smiling and drooling on himself when the car struck him from the left side. The driver, a fifty-something woman with dark leathery skin, never saw him as he stepped into the street. Her dog, a slim freshly sheared collie sitting in the front seat next to her, had completely blocked her view.

The silver convertible connected with Bingham at waist level, driving him forward and violently onto the pavement. The vehicle rolled over him, actually dragging him almost twenty feet, before the woman was able to push the dog away and come to a stop.

Of course, it was much too late for Billy Bingham.

The driver, looking back at the carnage in the street, screamed. Several pedestrians ran to the accident victim, while the clerk from Sharkey's ran to the door, looked out, then rushed back inside to call 911.

None of it mattered. Bingham was dead even before the rear tires rolled over him. Death due to trauma, including massive head injuries—that was what the coroner's report would say.

In the street, beside his bloody body, the broken jar of salsa and two beers seeped across the blacktop. The sunscreen bottle had been flattened, and white cream was splattered across Bingham's twisted right arm and his shattered sunglasses. Inside the cooler, the four

Coronas were still nice and cold. In less than one hour, so too was Bingham's body.

* * *

One month later, at her home in Nashville, Tennessee, Bingham's ex-wife, Betty, would find $80,000 in the trunk of the not-so-dearlydeparted's old car. The vehicle had been turned over to her because Bingham had no will and no living relatives other than their two daughters. She contacted her attorney, and he had a private eye look at the bills and run a check on the serial numbers. When the bills came up clean, he told her to keep them.

She did and put the money into a trust fund for the children, ages twelve and fourteen. A few years later, the money was used to pay for a pair of college educations at prestigious Vanderbilt University.

Melanie and Jack would never know it, but Bingham's share of blood money was eventually put to good use. It was all part of the grand plan.

CHAPTER 38

June 23, 2001, Chicago, Illinois

Doris and Melanie were seated at the kitchen table inside the McKenzie home.

It was Saturday, a little past seven in the evening, and the two had just finished putting away dinner dishes. It was Jordan's birthday, and Doris had decided to celebrate by having Jack, Melanie, and Isaac over for a barbecue cookout.

Michael, as usual, had accompanied the Russells, but Lou, feeling tired and drained from his constant night-shift duties, had begged off. He was home, getting a much-deserved good night's sleep.

Reece, Jack, Michael, Josh, Jacob, and the birthday boy himself, Jordan, were still outside, laughing and playing with the water balloons Josh had filled. Isaac, now six months old, was pulling himself along slowly on the floor of a playpen situated just a few feet from the table.

Doris counted the candles again that had earlier been removed from Jordan's chocolate cake. "I still can't believe my baby's three," she said. "It just doesn't seem possible."

She stood, tossed them into the wastebasket under the kitchen sink, then walked to the playpen, and scooped Isaac into her arms. The baby looked at her and grinned from ear to ear. "How you doing, big boy? How'd you like your first birthday party?"

She plopped back into her chair and sat Isaac on the table before her. He grinned again.

"I swear he has the bluest eyes I've ever seen, even for a baby," she said to Melanie. "They look like two little swimming pools."

Melanie smiled. She enjoyed watching her friend with Isaac. She was so good with children, and not just her own. Whenever students at school had a problem, they always came to Mrs. McKenzie. She had some sort of kinship with them. They trusted her, which was rare when it came to children and adults. Isaac had already taken to Doris, and each time she picked him up, he grinned.

"You better enjoy this little guy while you can. Before you know it, he'll be three, like Jordan. Then when you turn around again, he'll be grown, then gone."

They were innocent words spoken in earnest, the type of thing one parent says to another all the time. But suddenly, and with horror, Doris realized what she'd said. Hadn't the messenger, the Salvation Army Santa, told Melanie her son would be with them for just a short time?

She looked at Melanie, and even though her friend was smiling, she felt sick to her stomach.

"I'm so sorry, Melanie. I didn't mean it like that. You know that's not what I meant."

Melanie stood and took Isaac into her arms. But before she did, she reached over and kissed Doris on the forehead.

"Of course, you didn't. What you meant is that time passes quickly, for all of us. And that if we've got any sense at all, we need to cherish each and every precious moment.

"Come on," she said to both Doris and Isaac. "Let's go outside and see what the guys are up to. We can't miss out on all the fun."

* * *

Later that evening, after dark, a man in a white sedan watched as the Russells and Michael emerged from the back door and waved goodbye to the McKenzies.

He continued to watch as they climbed into Melanie's Camry, then drove away.

He followed them—from a safe distance—all the way home, carefully noting each turn, traffic light, and busy intersection. The trip took twenty-two minutes, covering a little more than ten miles. The watcher paid special attention to two dark, isolated intersections that were part of the route between households.

As Melanie and the others entered the house, disappearing from sight, he picked up a cell phone and placed a call. "Go," said a voice at the other end.

"It will work," the watcher said. "There's at least two spots that are perfect—secluded and out of the way, and very little they can use for protection. Tell the others we're set for the fourth. And tell them to bring all their fireworks."

CHAPTER 39

July 3, 2001

Michael, Lou, Jack, and Isaac were all staring at the television. Baseball's Major League All-Star Game, played for the first time in many years at Chicago's venerable Wrigley Field, was tied seven all in the bottom of the ninth. Two out, two on, and Cubs' hero Slammin' Sammy Sosa was at the plate.

"Come on, Sammy. Jack another one," Lou said. "Put it out on Waveland Avenue, and let's end this thing. I'm old and tired and ready for bed."

Michael looked at Lou and grinned. He'd grown very close to his special partner and really enjoyed spending time with him. Lou was a great guy, was a thoughtful man, and surprisingly, possessed a fine sense of humor. He also loved his sports, especially anything involving Chicago teams or players.

Jack was grinning too, while Isaac simply stared at the screen, mesmerized by the movement and the sound, which Lou kept pumping up as Sosa went deeper and deeper into the count. Melanie, asleep upstairs, had given up on the game hours earlier. She loved sports, but enough was enough. Besides, tomorrow was going to be a long, hot day.

It was the annual Fourth of July party at the McKenzie house. Firemen, school teachers, hospital workers, church associates, all kinds of friends and acquaintances would be there. And she was worried about Isaac. With all those people and the noise and commotion, it would be harder to concentrate on protecting the baby and a perfect time for someone at the party—someone Melanie might not know—to have easy access to him.

She'd discussed the party at length with Jack. Finally, they'd decided to attend. "We can't hide Isaac from the entire world," she said. "It's just not normal. He needs to meet people too. At least a few people."

Jack agreed. So had Michael and Lou, although reluctantly. Doris and Reece were also very concerned, but if Melanie and Jack were up to it, so were they.

Doris said she'd pay special attention to the guest list this year, dropping anyone she or Reece didn't know personally. Anyway, the decision was made. Everyone was on for the fourth.

The three-two pitch came Sosa's way, and even though he didn't drive it over the left field fence, he did the next best thing. He poked a single into center field, driving in Atlanta's Brett Boone from second base with the winning run.

"Ball game!" shouted Lou, standing and clapping his hands.

"Bedtime," said Jack. "Goodnight, guys." He left with Isaac and headed for the nursery, where he hoped he could successfully rock the baby asleep before putting him in his crib in the master bedroom.

Lou yawned, stretched, and slumped on the couch. "I'll take just a little nap, then be good to go," he said to Michael. "Then you can get a decent night's sleep for a change."

Michael stood and prepared to make his regular check of all the doors and windows. "Haven't you figured me out yet, Lou? I don't need sleep. I'm an insomniac. I've got too many things on my mind to worry about sleep."

Lou shook his head and snapped off the lamp at the end of the couch. "What's on your mind tonight, big guy?"

Although he didn't answer as he headed down the hall, a strange and sobering thought came to Michael. In fact, two images rushed through his tired brain. One was death. The other was the loving face of his uncle, Matthew Benoit.

He pushed the thoughts away and checked the locks. Every single one of them.

CHAPTER 40

July 4, 2001

Independence Day was a scorcher—ninety-eight degrees, high humidity, and not a cloud in the sky. Then again, what did one expect on the Fourth of July?

Wasn't it supposed to be hot?

Despite the heat and the large crowd, the McKenzie party was great fun. Even Jack and Melanie enjoyed it. Immensely. It was good to see old friends, happy faces, and spend time as they used to, laughing and talking and taking a brief respite from the constant pressures that came with Isaac and the dangers he faced.

The festivities went off without a hitch. Reece and Doris provided the meat—fried chicken and country ham—while everyone else brought a side dish. Baked beans, coleslaw, potato salad, corn on the cob, watermelon, fresh strawberries, and homemade chocolate chip cookies highlighted the menu. Lemonade and iced tea flowed from more than a half-dozen coolers, and by sunset, all the food and drink had been consumed.

Even Michael and Lou—special invitees—had a good time. Lou had a blast playing with all the children. It made it easier to keep a wary eye on Isaac and kept him from having to talk about himself with the adults. He kept a low profile, as his police buddies would say.

Michael tried the low-key approach as well but didn't have much luck. It was impossible for a guy his size to blend in with the rest of the crowd. Everyone wanted to know about the dark stranger, especially Rhonda Jackson, the recently divorced fourth-grade teacher at Mercy Elementary.

"You've just got to tell me about him," she said to Doris shortly after spotting him standing with Jack and Melanie. "My god, I've never seen such a body. And he's so rugged looking. Nothing like Frankie, my ex. He's such a puss."

Doris tried to discourage Rhonda. Truth was, she didn't like her much anyway. But her primary concern was Michael. The last thing he needed right now was a bitter, horny female nipping at his heels. "He's from out of town. Just a really close friend of the Russells. He'll probably be heading home to Dallas soon, so put your claws back in."

Rhonda expressed dismay at Doris's description of her intentions, then flipped her dark hair behind her ears, and headed straight for Michael. She kept him cornered for almost two hours, which wasn't all bad. Listening to her mindless banter at least gave him the appearance of being occupied while keeping other potential conversationalists at bay. More importantly, it also kept him close to Isaac and Melanie.

Finally, as the evening wound down and many of the guests were starting to leave, Michael decided it was time to put his admirer out of her misery, or at least him out of his.

"Did I tell you?" he said, looking down at the diminutive Ms. Jackson. "I've been accepted into the seminary. I hope to become a priest."

He almost laughed at Rhonda's reaction. She was crestfallen, not to mention pissed.

"It might have been nice if you'd mentioned that earlier," she said, her face flushed with anger. "Now I've wasted my entire day and ruined a chance to meet some nice, eligible men."

"What? You don't think I'm nice?"

"Sure...I do," she stammered. "I mean nice...men...who are interested in women. Real men, if you get my drift."

Michael couldn't contain his laughter any longer. "Oh, I see. Real men. Not me. Well, sorry to disappoint you. Best of luck in catching, I mean, meeting one. And happy Fourth of July."

Rhonda stormed off, but before she did, she made a point to get the last word in. "Me? Disappointed? Get real. You're the one who doesn't know what he's missing."

He watched her walk away. She did have a sweet body, he admitted. But that mouth. Who could stand listening to that on a regular basis?

He shook his head and returned his attention to Melanie and the baby. They were with Jack and Lou, sitting on the ground as Reece and a couple of his firemen friends were getting ready to set off a few small fireworks. The green and red and purple colors were beautiful against the backdrop of the night sky. Most of the children had remained for the holiday display, and they sat in the laps of their moms and dads and clapped gleefully as each rocket whistled into the air.

How blessed these children are, he thought, *to have their parents with them, enjoying precious time together*. For a brief instant, the image returned him to his own childhood. But the pangs of loneliness and the difficulties he faced growing up brought back the all-to-familiar pain. Michael quickly blocked the memories and focused on the splendor of the fireworks.

It was the perfect ending to a perfect day. He looked toward the heaven as bright streaks crisscrossed through the night. And he clapped along with the children.

* * *

Lou put the remainder of the baby's things in the trunk of his navy Lincoln, closed it, and walked around to the driver's side. He poked his head in and looked at Melanie, Jack, and Isaac in the back seat. "Everybody set?"

"We're all buckled in," Melanie said. "Ready if you guys are."

Michael, sitting on the passenger's side, nodded in agreement. Lou stood, waved one last time to Doris and Reece, then hopped in, and turned the ignition. Carefully, he backed out the drive and turned north toward the Russell home. One block down, the white sedan pulled into traffic, completed a sharp U turn, and fell in line about two hundred yards behind the big Lincoln.

"Thank you guys for coming," Melanie said. "We had a great time. I think even Isaac had a big day."

Jack reached forward and patted both men on the shoulder. "Really, guys, it was wonderful. Thanks to you two, we were able to relax and have some real family fun. We can't thank you enough. And not just for today." In the front seat, Michael was smiling.

"Don't mention it," Lou said. "We had fun too, right, big fella? I think Michael might have met his future wife. That teacher friend of yours seemed awfully sweet on him."

Michael pretended not to hear, but he couldn't make the grin go away. "Rhonda Jackson?" said Jack. "Man, oh man. Let me warn you about her right away. Her elevator doesn't go to the top, if you know what I mean. Plus, the word is, she has trouble keeping her panties on."

Melanie didn't approve of her husband's description or his choice of words, but she couldn't disagree with his conclusion. Rhonda Jackson was the queen of shock and seemed to enjoy her aggressive reputation.

"I hope she didn't come on too strong, Michael. I'm sorry if she ruined your day."

Michael turned in the seat, still amused. "It wasn't a problem, really. In fact, she helped me."

Suddenly, his voice trailed off. He peered through the back windshield, carefully observing a pair of headlights several hundred yards behind Lou's car.

"What is it?" Lou asked, instinctively looking for trouble in the rear-view mirror. "You got someone tailing us?"

Jack started to turn and look out the window. "Don't," Michael commanded, turning back to face the road in front of them. "Everybody, stay relaxed. It's just a feeling, probably nothing. Lou can keep an eye on things while he's driving."

Yet even as he spoke, he slowly withdrew his revolver from beneath the seat.

Lou casually pointed to the glove box. Michael opened it, took out Lou's pistol, and set it on the seat between them. He then reached down, pulled the right leg of his blue jeans up slowly, and pulled a third revolver from his boot.

As they came to a dark intersection, one with a four-way stop but no traffic light, Lou squinted to get a better view of the scene ahead. A car was stalled in the middle of the road, blocking traffic both ways, and a pale-skinned woman in a very short dress was standing near the front of the vehicle. The hood was raised.

Already a driver from the other line of traffic was approaching to offer assistance to the attractive damsel in distress. Lou braked for an instant, watching the scene play out before him. Michael turned again and looked behind them. The headlights from the trailing white sedan were creeping closer.

All three men and the baby jumped in their seats when Melanie screamed, "Don't stop! It's a trap. Go, Lou. Go!"

Without hesitation, Lou floored the accelerator, swinging wildly off the shoulder of the road to the right and ramming into the stalled vehicle's back end as his Lincoln lurched forward. He was almost around when the woman pulled a gun from under the hood, shot the good Samaritan point-blank in the face, then turned the weapon on Lou and his special passengers.

Michael raised his revolver and fired two quick shots through Lou's open window. Both shots found their mark, striking the woman chest high and sending her reeling backward into the man she'd just murdered. He'd been quick but not quick enough. The woman—now dead—had managed to put a bullet through each tire on Lou's side.

"Get down," Michael ordered seconds before shots from behind pierced the back windshield. Shards of glass fell on Jack as he shielded Melanie and Isaac with his body.

Lou was completely around the stalled vehicle now, and he pressed on the gas as Michael fired at the car behind them. But the tires were gone. Burning steel scorched the pavement as the shredded tires—now little more than bare rims—continued to spin forward. Bullets rained on the Lincoln from behind as the sedan, and the four men in it bore down on their prey.

Michael and Lou saw the alley at the same time. "Take it!" Michael shouted above the noise.

Lou did, darting through a narrow opening between dark buildings. As he did, his heart sank. Just a few hundred feet ahead, the Lincoln's headlights bounced off a brick wall. A black sign with bright orange lettering told him what he already knew. Dead end.

He hit the brakes hard, sliding the car around sideways in the narrow street. Michael was already out, pulling the family from the back seat. "Get behind the dumpster, there on the side," he said, pointing at Jack. Isaac was screaming at the top of his lungs, but Melanie was on the move. She sprinted to the dumpster, baby in arms, as Jack followed behind.

The sedan rounded the corner, headlights on high beam. The driver slowed, then stopped. He smiled at his three colleagues. "Got 'em trapped now," he snarled. "Don't waste time. Let's take care of business and be on our way."

Michael and Lou crouched behind the car and watched as all four doors on the sedan opened at once. They were outnumbered, two-to-one, and each man realized they didn't have the firepower to withstand a lengthy shootout.

Lou reached into his car from the passenger's side and grabbed a radio from the front seat. He was able to reach a dispatcher at the fifth precinct and hurriedly gave her the rundown on their situation, including their location.

"Too late for that," Michael said.

The tone in his voice made Lou drop the radio and look up. The white sedan had been shifted into gear and was approaching them at a moderate rate of speed. Trotting behind it, shielded effectively by the four open doors, were the four gunmen. Weapons drawn, they started shooting moments before the sedan struck Lou's car, knocking the two protectors to the ground.

Michael was on his feet like a cat, a big one roaring with anger. He targeted the driver first. If he killed the head, he'd learned, sometimes the body would die too. He caught just a glimpse of the driver's head over the top of the crunching metal, but it was enough. One clean shot and the lead attacker was dead as the bullet entered through his left eye and exited the back of his head.

A bullet struck Michael in the right thigh, hitting bone and stopping somewhere inside his muscular leg. He grimaced but held his ground. He searched for the source of the gunfire but could not locate a target in the darkness.

Instead, Lou found him. Still on the pavement, he saw a pair of legs on the other side of the wreckage. Quickly and calmly he put a bullet in each leg. Shrieks of pain told him the bullets had found their target. When the man fell, Lou fired again. The third bullet mortally wounded the second attacker.

Michael, now crouched low, searched for another target as the wheels of the sedan continued to churn ahead, pushing against Lou's parked vehicle. The smell of burning rubber, gunpowder, and blood filled the air, yet above it all, he could hear the high-pitched cries of Isaac from behind the dumpster.

Two down and two to go, Michael thought. *Maybe we've got a chance.*

Lou crawled to his feet just in time to see a third attacker—a black man in a dark sweat suit—hurdle the rear of the Lincoln and land on Michael. He was firing a revolver while still in the air, and two of the shots found their mark, striking Michael twice in the stomach.

Melanie, watching from her poor hiding place, screamed in anguish as Michael fell backward with the attacker still on him. Lou rose to go help his friend when a bullet ripped through his right shoulder, shattering the bone and knocking him to his knees. He dropped his revolver in the darkness and heard two more shots ring out as Michael and the attacker struggled on the other side of the alley.

His heart sank at the thought of his friend dying, but as he turned to face the fourth attacker, now standing over him with gun in hand, he felt even more despair over having failed the holy family.

As he waited for the man to pull the trigger, ending his life, thoughts of Trina filled his head. Would she be disappointed in him?.

The attacker smiled before pulling the trigger. The moment's hesitation cost him his life. A large shadow crossed between Lou and the gunman, and he stared wide-eyed into the darkness as Michael tackled the man from the side.

"Aren't you dead?" Lou asked to no one in particular. He then glanced across the alley and saw the third man lying face up in the street. His head rested against the pavement at an odd angle, the result of a broken neck.

The fourth attacker was even more surprised than Lou. Gone was the grin as Michael dug his fingers deep into the man's throat. Moments before he passed out from lack of oxygen, he pressed his gun into Michael's side, and put a fourth and final bullet into the big man's body. Slowly Michael released his grip and slumped to the ground, his breathing coming in jagged and raspy spurts. The attacker stood and prepared to finish off these ridiculously courageous protectors.

First Michael, then Lou. He rubbed his throat and slowly squeezed the trigger. But before his weapon discharged, another gun rang out in the now quiet night. The bullet sent the man backward, and he dropped his weapon. It made no difference.

Jack, now holding Lou's revolver, continued to point it at the final attacker. There were four rounds left in the gun. He used them all, emptying the weapon into the man and bringing an end to the savage attack.

He dropped it and knelt over his fallen friends. Melanie, with Isaac safe and sound in her arms, rushed to her husband's side. She gasped at the scene. Lou's arm hung limply against his side, and blood was streaked across his face as he attempted to sit up and help Michael.

Poor, poor Michael. His body was covered in blood, and his left eyeball appeared ready to burst. A combination of blood and spit streamed out of the side of his mouth, and he could feel life leaving his body. He was in extreme pain, but the shock caused by his trauma was beginning to dull the agony. And he was losing consciousness.

Tears were streaming down Jack's face as he held his friend's hand. In the distance, he could hear the welcome sound of sirens as both police and ambulance personnel made their way to the blood-stained alley. "Hold on, buddy. Please, Michael, hold on. Help is on the way."

Melanie was hysterical. Sobs poured from her shaking body in great bursts, taking her breath and causing her to hyperventilate. She put Isaac in Jack's arms and carefully lifted Michael's head into her lap. Within seconds, she too was covered in blood.

"I'm so sorry, Michael," she screamed. "Don't do this, God. Don't take him. Not now. Not this way."

Michael opened his eyes for the last time. "Take my hand," he whispered.

Melanie, still sobbing, held it tight.

"It had to be this way," he said. "As part of the plan, someone had to be willing to shed blood in order for the Holy Child to live and complete his work. I was the appointed one, and this is the appointed time."

He shifted his head slightly so he could see Lou and the parents he'd protected so well.

"Take care of Isaac. This is not the end. And don't despair," he said, looking deeply into Melanie's sorrowful eyes. "I will be watching over you, protecting you and your son, always."

Then Michael died.

Jack tried to resuscitate him. But with the first push on his sternum, blood came gushing out of the wounds.

"Don't," Melanie said in a soft voice, still crying and with the baby now in her arms. "Don't put him through that. He's been through enough."

Jack nodded and went to Lou. He took his belt off and tied it in a tourniquet around the badly injured arm. "You'll make it, Lou. As soon as they get you to the hospital, they'll give you something for the pain. Can you hold on?"

"Damn straight," he said, tears flowing down his cheeks as he continued to look at his fallen friend. "I've got to. Can't let my partner down. He's the best one I ever had."

* * *

For two days, Melanie was bitter. Bitter and angry. In fact, she was more angry than she'd ever been in her life. She listened to all the things everyone had to say. Jack, Doris, and Reece, even Lou, recovering from his hospital bed. Everything they said made sense. Every word was true.

Yes, they were lucky to escape with their lives. Yes, Isaac was safe, and yes, that was the main thing. And yes, they had to go on because, of course, that was what Michael would have wanted.

But despite it all—every true, sincere, heartfelt word—anger and bitterness burned in Melanie. And her heart ached for him. God how she missed his soulful eyes and huge heart. She had thought it impossible for anyone to be that brave and strong, yet he did it so easily and with so much kindness.

It wasn't right to take him so soon and so savagely. And for two days, she didn't much care how anyone, even God, felt about her anger. If he didn't like it, too bad. She didn't ask for much. When she asked for Michael's life—on her knees in that dark and bloody alley—she'd expected her prayer to be answered.

God had answered no, and she didn't like it. Most of all, she didn't understand.

All that changed when Matthew Benoit arrived from Kentucky.

CHAPTER 41

July 6, 2001

Reece and Doris picked Matthew up at O'Hare. He'd flown in to receive the body of his dead nephew. It was a little past seven in the evening when the old monk, having taken care of the necessary transportation arrangements, arrived at the Russell home.

As soon as he walked through the back door, Melanie burst into tears. By now he'd seen Michael, seen the horrific condition of his body. And Melanie was ashamed—ashamed of what had happened to him—and full of guilt because it had happened, all of it, as a result of his efforts to protect her and her son.

Yet somehow she felt better the moment she laid eyes on this man of God. Matthew smiled when he saw her. Led through the door by Reece and Doris, he paused to shake hands with Jack.

"It's an honor to finally meet you, Dr. Russell."

"The honor is mine, Brother Matthew. I'm so sorry it had to be this way. We're all sorry for your loss. We owe our very lives to your nephew."

"Thank you," Matthew said. As he did, he turned his eyes to Melanie. He lowered his head reverently and walked across the room to her. As he neared her, she lunged forward and threw her arms around his weathered neck.

"Forgive me," she said. "Forgive me for taking so much from Michael, for taking his life. It's because of me that he's dead now."

Matthew raised his hands and placed them on each of Melanie's elbows. Tenderly yet forcefully, he pulled her arms down and pushed her far enough away so that his elderly eyes could focus clearly on her beautiful face.

His words were steady and true. "No. It's because of you that Michael has been saved. It's because of you and Isaac and your family that he became a man of God before his death. He found the light in you, and soon he will be in heaven, seated at the right hand of the Father."

Matthew's goodness and honesty filled the room. They could all feel it, even through their pain, especially Melanie.

She looked into his eyes, and he smiled. "That's the truth. To believe otherwise is wrong, Melanie. The sorrow we feel in losing our beloved son is real, and it will be everlasting. But Michael is in a better place, for eternity. It is time for us to accept his death and celebrate his life."

Doris was sobbing now. Jack and Reece both stared at the floor, trying to control their emotions. Even Isaac, asleep in the nearby playpen, awakened and began to cry.

"I'm leaving in two hours. Taking Michael home to Montessori. Tomorrow my brothers, and I are going to have a mass to celebrate his life and say goodbye. If it will help you accept what has happened, you can join us. You and your friends are welcome."

Melanie hugged Matthew again, this time tighter than before. And this time, he didn't stop her. He held her warmly as she cried on his shoulder. He shed tears for his nephew too. But his were tears of pride and great hope. Michael, the great guardian, was coming home.

CHAPTER 42

July 7, 2001, Abbey of Montessori

The small chapel was filled to the rafters. Every member of the monastery—almost one hundred total—were in attendance. So were thirty grim-faced men and women from the Dallas Police Department. They'd lost one of their own—one of the best they'd ever known—as part of a brutal attack in a faraway northern city.

They were frustrated and confused and angry, with only sketchy information made available to them concerning the attack and Michael Starr's death. Most of all, they were deeply saddened. Everyone liked Michael. Everyone respected him. The price of round-trip tickets to Kentucky was a small price to pay for one last chance to say goodbye and to pay their respects. And so they had come.

Brother Matthew was seated in the first pew of the abbey chapel. Beside him were Melanie and Isaac, followed by Jack, Doris, Reece, and despite all protests to the contrary, Lou Dodson. He was here against doctors' orders. He was weak and still in a lot of pain, but he refused to listen to reason. He checked himself out of the hospital in time to catch the flight to Louisville with the others.

Jack, in particular, had encouraged him to stay behind, but even he finally relented as Lou made his case.

"What if things were different?" he asked. "What if I were the one dead and Michael were in my shoes? You know he'd make the trip, not only to pay his respects, but to keep doing his job—to protect the family. I'm giving you everything I have. Now please, allow me this. Don't deny me the chance to say goodbye."

How could anyone argue with that? Case closed. Lou had made the trip, and to tell the truth, Jack was glad to have him along. Lou felt like family, and it was good to have family together at a time like this. It was going to be tough to say goodbye to a loved one, especially Michael.

Jack was particularly worried about Melanie. She'd taken Michael's murder harder than anyone, much harder. At first, she was bitter and angry, but she'd softened considerably since hearing Matthew's honest and sincere words. Now she was showing hardly any emotion at all. She was quiet and reserved and said very little on the trip down. Jack was concerned his wife was slipping into the black hole of depression. And though he felt selfish for even thinking it, he was worried about survival since Michael's death. Without Melanie and her great inner strength, they didn't stand a chance, any of them, especially Isaac.

His thoughts were interrupted when the abbot at Montessori—a tall, lean man in his sixties—rose from his chair on the small altar and addressed those in attendance. He opened with a short prayer, his deep voice echoing inside the silent chamber. As he finished, he raised his head and, with kind, gentle eyes, looked at his close friend and spiritual advisor—Matthew Benoit. With a simple wave of his hand, he summoned the monk to the altar.

Matthew went to Michael's casket, which was closed, and knelt before it. As he did, the others in the chapel slid from their seats and knelt on the floor with him.

As they prayed together in silent tribute to the fallen hero, Melanie looked at the two photographs placed on top of the casket. Although she was drained, both mentally and physically, the images frozen in the pictures brought tears to her eyes.

The first was of Michael as a baby, dressed in a beautiful baptismal gown, held lovingly in the arms of his mother and father. Melanie marveled at the resemblance between Michael and Mrs. Starr—the same dark hair, the same deep blue eyes. His father was a huge man, almost as big as Michael, and he looked so proud in the picture.

The second photo was of a grown Michael, dressed in a dark suit and holding a young Asian girl in his lap. Captain Pete Walker, Michael's supervisor at police headquarters, had brought the picture with him from Dallas. According to Walker and many of the other officers who had worked with Michael, it was a fitting tribute to the man. The girl in the photo, age twelve, had been kidnapped several years ago and held ruthlessly for more than eighteen months. Many in the crime center and even her parents had given her up for dead.

But not Michael. He continued to investigate the case on his own time and eventually found her in Mexico, working in a sweat shop that produced black-market prescription drugs. He'd found her, brought her home, and returned her safely to her parents. The kidnappers were brought to justice, and he'd received a citation for his work, but his real reward could be seen in the photograph that now crowned his casket. As the little girl gazed up at her hero, the gratitude in her eyes had been forever captured on film.

Matthew spoke briefly about Michael, celebrating his life and all he had overcome despite losing his parents when he was still a young man. Captain Walker also spoke, citing his many fine accomplishments in law enforcement. As he did, many of the officers in the chapel, several of them seasoned veterans, wept. So did Walker, breaking down just as he finished his remarks.

Finally, it was Melanie's turn. She handed Isaac to Jack, pulled a piece of paper from the pocket of her black dress, and walked to the altar. She hugged Matthew, went to Michael's casket, and kissed it. Then she turned to face those in attendance.

"Michael Starr was the bravest man I've ever known—and probably the most unselfish. But you already know that. In fact, there's no words I can say that will do his life justice. He was larger than life. And he gave his away, willingly, protecting me and my family."

Jack was crying, as were the others. But astonishingly, Melanie was in complete control. Her voice was firm and steady. Her words filled with confidence. She was determined not to let Michael down. Not today.

"Instead of talking about what kind of man he was, I want to share a story with you. And although I know it's probably unusual—

in this beautiful, reverent place—I will conclude with a tribute of song to my beloved friend. I'm an average singer at best, but it comes from the heart, and I think Michael would like it."

She looked back at Matthew, and he nodded his head in approval. The abbot did the same. Jack was dumbfounded. He hadn't expected this. Melanie, though blessed with a wonderful voice, hated to sing in public. She'd last performed three years ago when Jack's younger brother married, and only then after he'd begged her. He didn't know if she could pull this off, distraught as she was, but then again, maybe she could. Melanie certainly seemed calm and determined.

"About two months ago, when my husband was working, Michael and my good friend Mr. Dodson volunteered to take me and my infant son to the doctor's office for his checkup. On the way home, a song came on the radio, and I remember being surprised when Michael turned it up. Lou and I quit talking as he became enraptured with the song, and we were shocked when he started singing along with the lyrics."

The memory saddened Melanie, and she paused to regain her composure. "The song was written and performed by a popular folk singer, Sarah McLachlan, and it is entitled 'I Will Remember You.' When it ended, Michael turned to us, embarrassed that he'd been caught up in the moment. It was his favorite song, he explained. When I asked him why, he said it was because it reminded him of his mother."

The chapel was completely silent, and behind Melanie, Matthew's heart ached at the thought of his beautiful niece and her husband killed at such an early age.

"Now every time I hear the song, I think of Michael and his relationship with his mother. In many ways, the song also describes the way I feel about my very special friend."

Melanie opened the piece of paper and, without further comment, began singing the words to Michael's favorite song. With no music. And no practice. Still her voice was steady and strong, filled with raw, powerful emotion. Jack had never heard his wife sing more beautifully, and as he listened to the words, he realized they did carry a very special meaning. And for the first time, he truly understood the strength of the unique bond between the two.

> I will remember you,
> Will you remember me?
> Don't let your life pass you by, Weep not for the memories.
> I'm so tired but I can't sleep,
> Standing on the edge of something much too deep.
> It's funny how we feel so much but cannot say a word,
> We are screaming inside but can't be heard.
> But I will remember you, Will you remember me?
> Don't let your life pass you by, Weep not for the memories
> Once there was darkness, deep and endless night,
> You gave me everything you had, oh you gave me light. And I will remember you,
> Will you remember me?
> Don't let your life pass you by, Weep not for the memories.
> Weep not for the memories.

When she finished, there wasn't a dry eye in the chapel, except for Melanie's.

She turned toward the casket and blew a kiss. "Goodbye Michael. I'll will remember you forever. And love you always. May you enjoy eternal peace and happiness in the company of our God."

CHAPTER 43

August 14, 2001, Chicago, Illinois

Melanie was a nervous wreck. It was the first day of school in the Chicago Public School System and, of course, the first day of classes for students at Mercy Elementary. More importantly, it was Melanie's first day away from Isaac since the day he was born.

Jack was home with him. And Lou. But still she was deeply concerned about the prospects of leaving his care to others, even those two. She simply felt naked without her son. And alone.

Helpless was another accurate description. The list of adjectives, she suddenly realized, could go on and on. But she didn't have time for that. Kids were already starting to filter in, kindergarten students. And this was a big day for them too—the first day of school. It was an emotional time for five-year-olds, not to mention their parents.

Melanie was distracted from her own worries and concerns and instead focused her energies on welcoming the new students and helping separate them—a few kicking and screaming—from their moms and dads. It wasn't easy, but it was part of her job.

In fact, the hustle and bustle associated with opening day kept her busy, and her mind occupied for the next several hours. She thought about Isaac often, especially during lunch when she had a few moments to sit and relax with Doris and some of the other teachers. But each time she started feeling apprehensive, one of the little tykes would tug on her skirt and pull her mind back to the present.

Before she realized it, the end of the day had arrived, and students were scurrying out the front door, headed for the big yellow buses and, ultimately, home.

Doris popped her head in Melanie's classroom just as she was turning out the lights. "I bet I know where you're going," she said, laughing as her friend made an ugly face. "How was the first day?"

"Bad. But not as bad as I thought. I've been worried sick about what's going on at home, but at least being back at work has kept my mind busy, not to mention my feet and hands."

Doris laughed and gave Melanie a quick hug. "Get out of here," she said. "I'll make sure everything is put away so you won't have that facing you in the morning. Then I'll stop by a little later to see if everything is okay. I'm sure it is."

"Thanks, Doris. Like always, you're a real lifesaver. And do stop by. I want to talk and unwind a little...and maybe drink a bottle or two of wine."

They laughed together, and Melanie was out the door. Thirty minutes later, when she walked through the door at home, she was greeted by her three smiling men.

"Congratulations!" Jack and Lou shouted together when Melanie burst through the rear entrance.

Isaac, sitting comfortably in his daddy's arms, appeared no worse for wear. In fact, Melanie was impressed. Isaac was clean and well dressed, and even the small patch of brown hair on his head had been neatly combed to one side. He grinned at the sight of his mother.

Melanie dropped her bag and ran to him. "How's my baby boy?" she said, taking him from Jack and holding him in the air above her head. Isaac laughed as she pulled him down, kissed his belly, then pushed him back into the air. He laughed again and again. So did Jack and Lou.

"See? We did fine," Jack said. "No problems at all."

"Is that true, Lou?" she asked.

"Pretty much. But I think Jack's getting a little cocky. He changed a poopy diaper, got Isaac to eat most of his carrots, then kept talking about how easy this was. I think he's getting a little carried away, if you want to know the truth."

Jack looked at Melanie and winked. "Well, I'm glad to hear you say that, Lou. Glad to see you're keeping your feet on the ground, keeping a level head about all this. That's what we like to hear when we're interviewing a prospective employee."

Lou was confused. "What do you mean? What in the heck are you talking about?"

Melanie handed Isaac to Lou, and the baby reached out for him as she did. She smiled, then took a long, deep breath. "Jack's going back to work next week. That's what he means, Lou. And we're going to need help with Isaac, special help. You probably understand that better than anyone. We're both going to take a lot of time off, as much as we can, and Doris and Reece are going to help out a lot too. But we need…"

Lou's eyes grew wide. He was obviously nervous, shaken by the direction Melanie's words had taken. Suddenly, she felt terrible. She was about to place a heavy burden on this elderly gentleman, a much greater burden than he deserved.

"I know it's asking a lot, Lou. And we will understand, completely, if your answer is no. But what we'd like for you to consider— at least for the next few months—is taking care of Isaac for us."

Lou looked at Melanie, then at Jack, and finally, into the delicate face of Isaac. There were tears in his eyes. "You'd trust me alone with your child? Trust an old hack like me to take care of this precious little angel?"

Melanie stepped closer to Lou and kissed him gently on the cheek. "You're the only one we trust, Lou, the only one."

* * *

Melanie finished brushing her teeth, rinsed, spat, rinsed, and spat again. She wiped her mouth with a clean towel, turned out the bathroom light, then joined Jack in the bedroom. She looked in on Isaac—asleep in the crib—then climbed under the sheets with her husband.

Jack took her hand, and she smiled. "I'm so relieved," she said. "I feel so much better now that Lou has agreed to watch him for us. I still feel terrible for asking, but I didn't know what else to do."

"I know. I feel better too. Lou seemed to be okay with it. Actually, he seemed quite honored. He's a good man, one of the finest I think I've ever known. It was a blessing—a miracle, really—when he came to us."

Melanie nodded. "We've seen a lot of miracles in the last year or two, haven't we? I just hope they keep happening so that somehow we can get through this. It still feels like I'm dreaming sometimes. That all this is not really happening. Then I look at Isaac, look into his eyes, and I know for sure it's real. And that's when I feel happy and scared, all at the same time. Do you ever feel that way?"

"About a thousand times a day. Every day. But it's easy to understand if you think about it. I mean, we've been given the greatest gift of all, a son, but with it comes the constant worry and fear of losing him. I guess all parents experience those same highs and lows, but our world is so much different because of the battle of good versus evil."

Melanie closed her eyes, trying to relax so that sleep eventually might come. "What we need is more help," she said softly. "Or less trouble. Some kind of break in all this trauma. If the attacks keep coming, we're eventually going to lose, especially now that Michael's gone."

Jack looked at his wife, almost asleep and resting so peacefully. "Let's not talk about that now," he whispered. "Maybe something good will happen for us. Until it does, we'll just keep taking it one day at a time."

* * *

In the Russell's guest bedroom—where Lou now spent almost all his nights—a prayer was being offered up for a helping hand. Lou, kneeling beside the bed, had been praying for more than twenty minutes.

"Give me the strength I need, O Lord, to complete your work. I fear I am not strong enough for this, but I believe in you and will follow your word to the end. If it is your will, then it shall be done."

He started to rise, then stopped, and returned to his knees. He smiled before whispering the final words of his prayer.

"And hey, big fella, I know you're up there. I could use a little help from you too. Help keep my head clear, Michael. And give me some of your strength, because I'm getting awfully old for this. Help me protect this child, because I fear I can't do it alone."

* * *

Melanie's parents came to her during the night. James and Martha appeared to her in a dream, and like the visions before, the sequence was so real that she could feel the warmth in her mother's body and strength in her father's arms as she hugged each of them.

The message was good news. Melanie sensed it immediately. The Wades were both smiling, happy to see their daughter again and even happier to deliver a much-needed ray of hope.

"You've had a hard time of it, haven't you?" Martha asked, beaming with pride as she looked down at Isaac in his crib. "You and Jack and this little angel and all of your dear, brave friends."

Melanie sat on the edge of her bed, holding hands with her father. Jack was asleep beside them. She felt like crying, but didn't. Was it possible to cry in dreams? She wasn't sure.

"I'm scared, Daddy. Not so much for me. I'm not afraid of dying anymore, now that I've seen what awaits us after we're gone. But I'm so afraid for the baby. I know how important it is that he survives, yet it's more than that. I'm his mother. I want him to enjoy his time on earth. It doesn't seem like he's ever going to get that chance. He's not even eight months old, and he's been in almost constant danger. Will he always be running for his life?"

James smiled at his daughter and squeezed her hand tightly. "God, I'm so proud of you. You've grown into a strong, wonderful woman. And you have the kind of honesty and integrity that most people only dream of. Look at you. Even now, in your darkest hour, all you ask for is the safety of your child and a bit of hope for the close group of loved ones who have been drawn to you."

Martha pulled a soft blanket higher on Isaac, tucking him in tightly as he slept peacefully in the night. Then she joined her husband and daughter at the edge of the bed.

"The answer to your question is no," she said. "This child will no longer be in constant danger. It will come and go throughout his life, but it will not be constant. That is not part of God's plan—for you or your child."

"What do you mean, Mother? I don't understand."

Martha smiled and held Melanie's face between her hands. "I'm afraid I don't completely understand it myself, dear. But look at it like this. When Christ appeared once before, it was not the Holy Father's intention for the son to suffer his entire life. Suffer, he certainly did. But he also enjoyed many of the beautiful aspects of human life, including the great love of earthly parents."

After a moment's hesitation, Martha continued, "The message we bring to you tonight is this. Your child is safe for now. There will be no more attacks on his life, at least for a time. The Father will see to that. He will be your protector for now. He is giving you and Jack and the others respite.

"It will not last forever. There will always be danger and, eventually, more attempts on Isaac's life. But the Father stands on guard now. He will hold the dark side at bay with his mighty hand so that you and Jack can raise the Holy Son and give him a good, strong beginning. This is the Word of the Lord, and we bring it to you with happy hearts."

Melanie felt relieved, greatly relieved. Temporarily, at least, her prayers had been answered. Suddenly, she longed to have other questions answered. "What happens after that? When the danger returns, how will this end? Will my baby survive? And what of the world? Do we have a future? Any of us?"

James spoke this time, and there was much pain in his voice. "I'm afraid we don't have the answer to that. It is still unclear. If Isaac is meant to survive, he will. When he is old enough, he will use his great wisdom to evaluate the condition of the human spirit. Then he will take the information back to the Holy Father, and together, they will decide."

Her parents stood, preparing to leave. Melanie reached out to them. "I wish you were still here so you could spend time with your grandson. I want him to know you."

James smiled at his daughter. "He does know us, sweetie. He knows us all."

* * *

In the morning, when she awoke, she told Jack and Lou about the dream. "We must always be on guard, but I think Isaac will be safe for a time. We should use this respite to enjoy time with him and celebrate his miracle life."

And so they did.

They laughed and cried as he learned to walk, then talk. They read him stories and took him to the zoo. Melanie bought him pretty clothes, while Jack brought home toys and games and even a small baseball glove.

It was a wonderful time, and the family unit grew together and formed a strong bond. Lou joined Doris and Reece and the McKenzie children as a warm, protective extended family.

And all was well. For a time.

Almost three years passed before Isaac and his mother found themselves in grave danger once again.

CHAPTER 44

October 22, 2003

It was a small party but certainly a special one—Jack and Melanie, Doris and Reece and their three sons, and of course, Isaac.

Lou was surprised and deeply moved when Melanie and Doris unveiled the birthday cake. The message on the cake, written handsomely in orange icing, was simple but heartfelt: "Happy 61st Birthday! We Love You, Lou!"

When Jack discovered that Lou's daughter and her family would not be able to visit for her dad's birthday, he passed the news along to the others.

"We should do something for him," Doris decided. "Where would any of us be without him?"

Everyone agreed, but Lou was a proud man. Proud and humble. His loving friends wanted to honor him on his special day, but certainly they wanted to avoid embarrassing him. So they came up with the cake and ice cream and a few special and meaningful gifts.

Lou enjoyed the cake. It was his favorite—chocolate with chocolate icing. And a big scoop of vanilla ice cream on the side. He ate a large piece, then didn't protest when Doris slid another slice onto his plate. When he finished, he rubbed his stomach ruefully. "I've got to quit eating like this," he said. "Becoming a senior citizen is hard enough without packing around a ton of extra weight. My diet starts tomorrow."

Everyone laughed, then laughed again at the sight of Isaac, sitting in his high chair and eating a small piece of cake with both hands and very little diplomacy. He was covered in chocolate—it was even in his hair—but he was enjoying Lou's birthday almost as much as Lou was.

"Is it my birthday, Mommy?" he asked, taking center stage as always with his baby voice and crystal blue eyes.

"No, not yet," Melanie answered. "Today is Lou's birthday. Can you say, 'Happy birthday'?"

"Yes, I can. Happy birthday, Lou. Isaac loves you."

Lou went to Isaac and kissed him on top of the head, chocolate icing and all. "Thank you, little man. Old Lou loves you too."

Reece brought in three small boxes from the other room, all wrapped in beautiful silver paper, and put them on the table. Melanie took a damp cloth and wiped most of the cake off Isaac's face and hands. She'd wash his hair later. They all watched as Lou opened his presents.

The first gift was an elegant gold wristwatch. It was from Doris and Reece.

Lou had cracked the crystal on his old watch during the attack that claimed Michael's life over three years ago. Stubbornly, he'd refused to replace it. "You shouldn't have," he said, looking at the McKenzies. "It's much too expensive."

"Not really," Reece said. "It's nothing compared to what you've given us."

Doris reached across the table and put her hand on the broken watch Lou was wearing. "I know it brings back painful memories. But we hope you'll wear the new watch. Sooner or later, you have to let go of the past. All of us do."

Lou nodded and removed the old watch. He smiled as he slid on the new model and marveled as it shined brightly beneath the kitchen light. "Thank you. I will cherish it always."

The other two gifts were from Jack and Melanie. The first was a small framed photo. It was a picture of Lou and Michael with Isaac, just a few months after he was born. Lou was holding the baby awkwardly in the backyard on a magnificent spring day. Michael was at his side, laughing as Lou complained about having his picture taken.

"I remember that day clearly," he said, visibly shaken by the fond memory. "I can hear Michael's laughter even now."

"That's what we wanted," Melanie said. "We wanted to give you something to commemorate the good times."

Lou gently rubbed the glass covering the photograph with his thumb. "It's a lovely thought. I've got the perfect spot for it on the nightstand in your guest room. Thank you so much."

The last gift was in a slender box. It was so light Lou decided it must be a gift certificate or perhaps even money. *I hope they didn't do that*, he thought as he unwrapped the package. *I'll feel terrible if they've given me their hard-earned money.*

The paper inside the box wasn't money or a gift certificate. It was a roundtrip airline ticket to Hawaii for a party of five. At the bottom of the airline package, under the stamp that indicated the expiration date were printed the words: "Unlimited Access—Good Anytime."

Lou looked at Jack and Melanie, his mouth open wide. "I don't know what to say," he finally managed. "This must have cost you a fortune. I…I can't accept it. It's too much."

Melanie stood, walked around to Lou's side of the table, and put her arms around his neck. "Please, Lou, don't say that. Allow Jack and me and Isaac the honor of doing this for you, your daughter and son-in-law and those two lovely grandchildren.

"Someday all this is going to end, and you're going to survive it, Lou. I just have a feeling about that. When it ends, your unique assignment will be complete. And it will be time for you to enjoy your life on your own terms, with your own family. It will be time for a well-earned vacation with your loved ones to a place where it is warm and beautiful and stress-free. We've never been to Hawaii, but they say it's that kind of place. Paradise on earth—that's what they call it, and that's what we want for you."

Lou was quiet for several minutes. The others also remained silent. Finally, he smiled and carefully put the airline tickets back into the cardboard envelope. "I'll take it, on one condition—that is, when this is over and we've saved the world, you all come with us. Everybody. We all go together. What do you say?"

Melanie looked at Jack, and for a brief terrible instant, they shared the same thought. The mental image was death for both of them before Isaac's journey had been completed. Jack winked at Melanie, and the thought vanished as quickly as it had appeared.

"It's a deal old friend," Jack said, looking at Reece and Doris. "What about you guys? Are you in?"

"Absolutely," Reece said as Doris signaled her approval with a big grin and slap of the hands. "By the time all this excitement is over, I'd say everyone will be ready for some rest and relaxation."

Everyone laughed and then sang "Happy Birthday" one more time to Lou. Isaac stared intently at the singing adults before him, no longer playing with the cake on his tray. Had anyone noticed his serious demeanor, they would have wondered what thoughts were going through the child's head.

The answer, had he been able to give it, would have chilled them all to the bone.

CHAPTER 45

May 5, 2004

It was an unusually warm day in Chicago, even for late spring. The temperature was eighty-six degrees. Lou, taking advantage of the summer-like conditions, was sitting in a kiddie pool in the back-yard of the Russell home. He watched carefully as Isaac splashed and played, sticking his head under the cool water before coming up in search of air and clutching for a towel to dry his face.

Each time he surfaced, Lou laughed loudly, then looked around yet again to make certain no one was watching as an old black man dressed only in boxer shorts played in the tiny pool with a three-and-a-half-year-old white child.

Good Lord, Lou thought. *If anyone happened upon us, they'd call the police. And with my luck all, the old gang from headquarters would show up—at once—to arrest me. I'd never live that down.*

He looked at his watch, which he was careful to keep dry, and noted the time. Almost three. Melanie would be home from school within the hour, while Jack, on duty at the hospital, should be home by seven.

"We'd better get out and get dried off, little man. If your mommy caught us in this pool, she'd probably have a heart attack. Just the sight of me alone would be enough to give her one."

Isaac obediently stepped out, and Lou handed him a Mickey Mouse towel. "That's a good boy. Have you had fun today?"

Isaac hesitated before answering. "Yes, I did," he finally said. "Thanks for getting the pool out for me."

Lou looked at his small charge. "What's the matter, little man? Is something bothering you?"

"Maybe."

"What is it? Maybe old Lou can help."

"I'm afraid I'll hurt your feelings if I say it."

An odd feeling struck Lou. Isaac seemed so serious. Almost sad.

"That's one thing you never have to worry about, at least with me," he said. "I'm a tough old goat. If something's bothering you, I want you to tell me. Always. Now what is it?"

Isaac looked at Lou with those deep blue eyes. His brown hair, still wet, was curled into little ringlets on his head. Suddenly, he blurted it out. "How come I don't have any friends?"

The words struck Lou like a thunderbolt. He wasn't ready for the question and certainly wasn't ready with an answer. Instead, he stalled for time.

"Of course, you have friends. Jordan's your friend. And Jacob and Josh. And what about me? I'm your friend, aren't I?"

Isaac frowned. "See? I knew I'd hurt your feelings. I know you're my friend, and so are the boys, but that's not what I'm talking about. How come I don't have any friends my age? How come no one ever comes to play with me?"

Lou's heart was breaking. But he was thankful Isaac was asking him this awful question instead of posing it to his mother or father. It would kill them to see him now, his eyes filled with sadness.

Again he stalled before answering. "Well, most of the time, children don't have a lot of friends until they start school. You'll be in kindergarten pretty soon, and I'm sure you'll meet lots of nice boys and girls and make lots of friends then."

Isaac had harbored these thoughts for quite some time, and now the floodgates were open. He pressed on with his questions. "But how come I don't have any friends now? Someone to play with or swim with me?"

"Your age, you mean? Not like Jordan or the other boys?"

"Yes. Someone the same size as me."

"I see. Well, it's hard to meet people when you're so young, and I don't think I've seen any boys or girls your age in this neighborhood. That's one reason. Another problem is that you're an only child, no brothers or sisters. Lots of times, kids play with their brothers and sisters until they start making friends. And it's just bad luck, I guess, that you don't have any. You shouldn't let that bother you though. I was an only child too, and look what a great guy I turned out to be."

Lou laughed at his inside joke. Isaac didn't. Instead, he looked at Lou hard, afraid to say what he was thinking. Always the detective, Lou was hot on the trail. Now he was asking the questions.

"You're wanting to say something right now, aren't you?"

Isaac slowly nodded his head.

"Well, tell me. I can keep a secret."

"You promise, Lou?"

"I give you my word. Now what is it?"

"I have a brother."

Lou almost laughed, but didn't. Isaac would clam up completely if he laughed now. So he decided to play along. It was probably one of those invisible friend kind of things.

"You have a brother? I didn't know that. Where is he? Is he here now?"

"No. He's not here. He's never here with me, although sometimes he talks to me. Sometimes he tells me things."

"He does? Then where is he?"

"Promise you won't tell?"

"Promise."

"My brother's older. He's grown, I think. Anyway, he's in heaven—you know, with my other father."

Lou, standing just outside the pool while drying himself with a towel stopped moving. His smile, so warm and understanding just seconds earlier, was now frozen on his face. He could feel the tiny hairs on the back of his neck and on his arms standing on end. He was speechless. He simply stood there in his wet boxers, staring down at the small boy.

Isaac stared back. "Did I say something wrong? Are you mad at me?"

Lou quickly came out of his trance, dropped to one knee, and hugged the boy. "No, little man. Lou's not mad at you. I was just thinking about what you said."

He paused, trying to decide how to continue the conversation without scaring Isaac. "Let me ask you something. You said your brother and your other father are in heaven. Do you know about heaven?"

"Yes. Don't you?"

"Yes, I know about it. But I'm a lot older than you. How do you know about heaven already? Has your mom talked to you about it?"

"No, me and Mommy talk about lots of things, but not about heaven. I already know about heaven."

"How?"

Isaac made a face, obviously thinking hard on the matter. Then he shrugged. "I just know about it."

Lou patted him on top of the head and placed the towel around his little body. Then he lifted the plastic pool and dumped out the water. Carefully, he continued the conversation. "So what can you tell me about your older brother and your other father?"

Isaac frowned again. "You know about them. Everybody knows about them, even though some people pretend like they don't. My brother came before me…a long time ago. He was very brave. When he talks to me, he tells me to be brave too."

Suddenly, a horrible thought occurred to Lou. Did this small boy know who he was and why he was here? Already? And if so, did he understand the fate that awaited him?

"You are a very smart boy, Isaac. You know a lot of things for someone so young. Let me ask you one more question, then we'll go in and get dressed before your mom gets home."

"Okay."

"Do you understand why you are here?"

Isaac smiled, but it was a sad smile. "Sure I do."

"Why?"

"I'm supposed to live here with Mommy and Daddy and learn as much as I can about all the other people—not just you and Aunt

Doris and Uncle Reece, but everyone. Then after I learn about them, I'm supposed to go home to be with my other family."

Lou was fighting back tears now, and he pretended to wipe his face with the towel. The two were holding hands as they walked toward the house. Isaac spoke again, and this time, the words did more than chill Lou. They made him want to scream.

"I need to learn about people as fast as I can. I don't think I have that much time."

Lou nodded his head, pretending to understand. But he said nothing. What could he say? Besides, he felt as if someone had just kicked him in the stomach.

Before they entered the house, Isaac tugged on Lou's arm and looked up at him. "Is it okay if we don't talk to Mommy about this? I think it might make her sad."

Again Lou nodded in agreement. And again he pretended to wipe his face.

This time, it took even longer to dry his eyes.

CHAPTER 46

December 24, 2004

"What is it? What did we get Mommy?"

Jack smiled at his son and opened the box. Inside, nestled against a thick pad of cotton was a beautiful strand of white pearls.

Isaac looked confused. "Did we get Mommy marbles?"

Jack laughed and put the top back on the box. He looked over his shoulder one more time, making sure Melanie was still in the kitchen, then placed the smaller box into a bigger one. "No, buddy, we didn't get Mommy a set of marbles. It's a necklace—a very expensive necklace. Do you think she'll like it?"

He measured a piece of wrapping paper, then cut it carefully with scissors. He and Isaac sat on the floor together under the Christmas tree, Jack waiting for an answer as he wrapped the season's last package.

"The little balls sure are pretty. I think she'll like it. What do you think?"

"I think so too. First of all, Mommy likes anything we get her. She's just that kind of person. Most women are really hard to shop for, but not Mommy. She always appreciates the gifts she receives, which is one reason I love her so much."

Jack taped the final edge of paper to the box, then selected a bright red bow to go with the green paper. "Besides, I think she's really going to like this because she's always loved pearls. Pearls are the little white balls you thought were marbles. They will look beautiful on Mommy when she wears them with one of her fancy dresses."

"Can't she wear them all the time?"

"Sure she can. But women are different than us guys when it comes to things like that. They like to save really nice things, like this necklace, for special occasions."

Isaac was perplexed. "What are special occasions?"

Finished with the box, Jack slid it carefully under the tree with the remainder of the Christmas gifts, then picked Isaac up from the floor, and carried him over to the couch. His son was adorable in his red-and-white Santa pajamas.

"Special occasions are when grown-ups go out and do something really fun, like maybe a party, where we would hang out with other adults, or maybe someone's wedding or some other nice, fun event."

"I know what a party is," Isaac said proudly.

"You do?"

"Yes. It's when people all go to the same place and stand around and talk and drink wine."

Jack laughed again and rubbed his son's head, messing up his freshly washed, curly brown locks. "You're watching too much TV, mister. Are you and Lou still watching those afternoon soap operas?"

Isaac didn't answer. Instead he asked a question of his own. "How come you and Mommy never go to any parties?"

The question and the unspoken message included with it startled Jack. How long had it been since he and Melanie had been out for an evening of fun? Be it a party or anything else? *Too long*, Jack reluctantly admitted, *way too long*.

"I don't know. We're getting a little too old for all that stuff. Besides, we'd rather spend time with you, either here at home or at McDonald's or in the toy store. And you know what? I never really did like drinking wine. It makes my head hurt."

Isaac laughed, and for a moment, Jack thought he'd escaped his son's pointed line of questioning with just a minimal amount of damage—almost, but not quite.

"Then when will Mommy get to wear the pretty necklace?"

255

Before Jack could answer, a third voice carried across the room. "How about if I wear it tomorrow when I go to church with my two favorite guys?" Melanie, standing in the doorway, smiled in an effort to hold back her tears.

Isaac slapped his little hand across his mouth and looked wide-eyed at Jack. "Oh no, Daddy! She knows. Mommy knows what we got her for Christmas. I was talking too loud." He began to cry.

Melanie ran across the den and scooped Isaac into her arms. "It's okay, baby. Mommy didn't hear you. I always know what Daddy gets me for Christmas. He's terrible at keeping a secret. He's been hinting around about pearls for months now, so it never was a surprise."

Jack looked at his wife and noticed the pain in her eyes. "How long have you been standing there?"

"Long enough to hear those difficult questions. And your superb answers." Then, while still holding Isaac, she kissed Jack warmly on the mouth. Isaac shrieked with delight, relieved that Mommy was still happy even though the surprise had been ruined.

"I've got a great idea," Melanie said. "Why don't we go ahead and open it? Then I can put it on. and you two can tell me how wonderful I look."

Isaac nodded enthusiastically.

Jack then one-upped his wife on the excitement meter. "I've got a better idea. How about we go ahead and open them all tonight? Even Isaac's Christmas presents. Then tomorrow we'll have more time to celebrate his birthday."

This time, Isaac nodded so vigorously it seemed his head would pop off. Melanie went to get the video camera, and all three settled under the tree.

Jack handed his son a package. "You first, buddy. Let 'er rip."

Before he tore off the paper, unveiling one of his favorite action figures, he looked at each of them. "I love you," he said. "I know you give up a lot of things for me. You both make me so happy."

Jack and Melanie looked at each other, struck deeply by the remarkable words of their young son. And as they watched him open the rest of his packages, both were beaming with pride.

CHAPTER 47

April 2, 2005

It was a little past two in the morning when Melanie opened her eyes. Immediately, her first concern was Isaac and his safety. She sat straight up and looked wildly around the room. Even in the darkness, she could make out the small figure of her son, sitting on the end of the bed.

Though alarmed, Melanie managed to keep her voice steady. "What is it, baby? Is something wrong?"

"No," Isaac whispered, trying not to wake Jack, who was sleeping beside his wife. "Nothing's wrong."

"Are you sick? Does your tummy hurt?"

"No, ma'am."

Melanie took a deep breath and slowly released it. She was relieved to find her son physically fit. Yet something was bothering him. She sensed it. Perhaps he'd talk more openly in a different setting. She crawled out of bed and slipped into her robe.

"Come on, baby. Mommy's thirsty. Walk down to the kitchen with me, and let's have a glass of water."

Isaac nodded but said nothing. Melanie's heart was starting to race again. It was not as fast as it had been moments earlier, but that familiar, dreadful feeling of concern was creeping back inside her head, just like it always did whenever her son seemed troubled. As he grew older, his troubled feelings seemed to come more frequently. It would only get worse, she realized, as she led him down the stairs.

She pulled out a chair, and Isaac climbed into it. Then she went to the refrigerator, took out a bottle of water, and brought it, along with two glasses, to the table. She poured a small amount into each glass, twisted the plastic top back on the bottle, then looked down at her son.

"Okay, Isaac. I know why I'm awake. Now the question is, what about you? Maybe Mommy can help if you tell me why you're awake."

Isaac hesitated before answering. He placed his little hand around the glass and took a big gulp. He sat the glass down, looked at Melanie, then picked it up again, and took another drink. His mother continued to wait for him patiently, looking at him with warm, gentle eyes as he struggled to find the right words. As always, he felt safe and secure just being with his mother.

But she was hard to fool. He'd discovered that already. Whenever something was bothering him, like now, she always seemed to know. Sometimes he kept things from her, only because he hated to see sadness on her beautiful face.

But most of the time, he'd open up with the truth, like now.

"I had a bad dream. When I woke up, I was still scared, so I came into your room. I'd only been there for about a minute when your eyes opened. I was getting ready to go back to bed when you saw me."

Melanie was relieved to find Isaac's problem was not a serious one. Yet she found herself disturbed by his mention of the dream. *Did he dream often?* she wondered.

"Do you remember your dream?"

Isaac fidgeted in his chair, then took another drink of water. "Some of it," he said. "Not everything."

"What was it about? Tell Mommy."

"It was just a bad dream."

Melanie waited patiently for more. She sat as still as the untouched water glass before her, giving her son all the time he needed.

"I know it was just a dream, but it seemed real," he finally said. "When I first woke up, I thought it was really happening. That's why I came into your room. I felt better as soon as I saw you and Daddy."

Another long silence filled the room. Finally, Melanie pushed back her chair and tapped her palms against her thighs. "Come sit in Mommy's lap. I need a little snuggle before we go back to bed."

Isaac smiled and rushed around the table. As he hopped into her lap, Melanie marveled at how big he was getting. He was growing up fast. *Too fast*, she thought, which made every moment important, including this one. With that in mind, she decided to push further in hopes of finding out more about her baby's dream.

"I have a lot of dreams," she said. "Some good, some bad. Sometimes I remember them, and other times, I don't remember anything about them. But if you have one of those dreams that really stick out in your mind, I think it helps to talk about it. I do that with your dad sometimes. And if I tell him about a bad dream I've had, I usually don't have it again."

Isaac, curled into a small ball in his mother's lap, nodded his head slowly but said nothing. Melanie kissed the top of his head and rubbed her right hand from side to side across his back. She could feel his heart beating rapidly and realized he was still upset. She wanted desperately to help him.

"Please, baby, tell me about the dream. Tell me what scared you tonight."

He lifted his head and looked into his mother's eyes. "If I tell you I'm afraid, you'll be scared too."

Melanie smiled and hugged him tighter. "Maybe. But that's okay. That's what mommies are for. That's my job. It doesn't matter if I'm afraid of something. I just don't want you to be upset. So tell me. Please."

Isaac looked back down, and the words came pouring out. A couple of times, it seemed, the little boy was fighting hard to hold back tears.

"I was in a dark place—someplace strange—and I was all alone, except for the people in dark clothes. I didn't know them, and I couldn't see their faces. But I could hear them laughing. They kept telling me not to run. They were telling me they wanted to help me, take me back to you and Daddy. But they weren't telling the truth. They were trying to trick me, so I started running."

Melanie was grateful her son was looking down. It prevented him from seeing the anguish in her eyes. She continued to rub his back softly and managed to keep her emotions in check. She dared not interrupt now. Instead, she let Isaac continue with his troubled tale.

"I ran faster and faster, but they kept getting closer to me. I looked back once, and they weren't running behind me—they were flying! And they kept laughing and laughing, and I was getting so scared, Mommy. I could feel one of them reaching out to grab me. He was so close I could feel him breathing on my neck. I started to scream, but before I did, I woke up."

Isaac's voice was tight and his breathing more rapid as Melanie tried to comfort him with reassuring words. "It's okay now, baby. The bad dream is over. No one's chasing you, and you're not alone. We're here together, safe in our home, and no one is ever going to take you away from me. Ever."

Melanie continued to hug her son and rock him back and forth in the kitchen chair. Slowly, his tense body relaxed, and she felt his breathing return to a more regular rate. In fact, he was remarkably calm considering the words that followed.

"When I woke up and looked around my room, the people in dark clothes were still there. They said they'd be back to get me when the time was right. They laughed at me and called me names. Then they disappeared into the darkness. I waited until I was sure they were gone, then I ran to you as fast as I could."

It was Melanie's heart that was beating hard now, and she pushed Isaac an inch or two away in hopes that he wouldn't notice. The thought of dark forces in her little boy's room took her breath away, and it was with much determination that she finally managed to steady her voice.

"Listen to me, Isaac. It was all just a bad dream. All of it. Sometimes dreams seem so real that you think something really bad is happening, but it's not. It's just a dream. That's all. Just a dream. Do you understand me?"

"Yes, Mommy. I understand."

As they sat in the kitchen, holding each other, each knew the other was lying. But it was okay. It was the kind of lie that made both of them feel better. And now, in the still hours of the early morning, that was enough. It would get them through until dawn and a new day.

With the new day came renewed hope, and the bitterness of events from the night before—either real or imagined—vanished. When Isaac awoke, his mother was still sitting at the table, and he was still in her protective embrace.

CHAPTER 48

August 19, 2006

Another opening day of school meant another fresh batch of students coming through the front door at Mercy Elementary, wide-eyed and bewildered, anxious about the world that awaited them inside the large brick building.

But this wasn't just any opening day, at least not for Melanie, because enrolled in the kindergarten class of 2006–07 was her only son. It said so right there on the registration form: Isaac James Russell.

Melanie had been looking forward to this day since Isaac was born—and also dreading it, dreading it for several reasons, really, some of which were the same reservations all parents endured when their offspring first strode off to school.

Of course, she had reason for added concern. Although the past few years had been very pleasant—wonderful times, really—the fear of losing Isaac to the dark side was never far from her mind or Jack's or the others', for that matter.

How could any of them forget he was a special child with very special needs, particularly the need for constant protection?

School was going to make protecting Isaac more difficult and more dangerous. Lou couldn't guard him constantly. Neither could Jack. As a result, most of the school day protection must be provided by Melanie and Doris.

Melanie had never been more thankful for being a teacher than she was today.

At least Isaac would be nearby, in the next classroom, each and every school day. And she was also extremely grateful that Doris had agreed to serve as her son's kindergarten teacher. She had done the same for Doris just a few years prior with Jordan, and the teacher-student relationship had proven to be very successful.

But Melanie was giving up more than instructor responsibilities. She was also turning over—at least for the most part—protection duties to Doris during the school day. She would not have entrusted anyone else with these two critical assignments, and Melanie again counted her blessings for having a friend like Doris.

They had all planned for this day—Isaac's first day of school. And both she and Jack were in complete agreement that he must attend school. He was so inquisitive, constantly seeking knowledge and information about people and places. They could not deny him a proper, formal education, no matter how severe the risk.

And the time had finally arrived. The education of Isaac James Russell would begin today, in the kindergarten class at Mercy Elementary.

So even though Melanie was happy and excited for her son, she was also terribly nervous, even more so than she had imagined. And Jack. He certainly wasn't making things any easier. He'd been up all night, pacing the floors, worrying about Isaac and what school might bring his way. And even though he wouldn't admit it, Melanie could tell he was reluctant to turn protection duties over to her and Doris.

It wasn't that he didn't trust them or respect their resolve. On more than one occasion, Jack had marveled at the determination and tenacity Melanie and Doris displayed when it came to watching over Isaac. Just last month, he thought he was going to have to pull Melanie off an older boy—and then his mother—when the other child slammed a cart, not once, but twice, into Isaac's back at the grocery store. And both he and Melanie had to restrain Doris after a group of rowdy teenagers kept pelting Isaac and Jordan with ice the night they took the boys to the movies.

No, they were fierce and protective guardians, but they were still amateurs, at least compared to a wily police detective like Lou. And try as he might, Jack could not completely suppress his reservations about taking Lou out of the equation, even for a few hours each weekday, although the poor soul certainly deserved some rest and at least part of his regular life back.

The burden placed on Lou had more than doubled with Michael's death, leaving him as the lone professional watching over Isaac. He'd performed admirably—tirelessly and without fail—for the past five years. But Lou was getting older. And even though he showed little signs in slowing down, emotionally he was drained. A few hours of rest each day would certainly do him good. There was no denying that. Still, it only added to the anxiety suffered by Jack. And by Melanie.

Yet it had to be this way. And now the time was at hand. As she welcomed her own students into the classroom, her thoughts were never far from Isaac, who was seated happily in the second row just across the hall.

Melanie almost laughed out loud when she pictured her son as he was this morning, standing in the hallway at home, washed, dried, and ready to go a full hour before she was to leave. His backpack was fully loaded, and as he waited for his mother, he could barely stand still.

"Come on, Mommy," he complained. "We're going to be late. I can't be late for my very first day of school."

When they arrived at Mercy, Melanie's car was the second one in the lot. The shortage of vehicles and people failed to deter Isaac. Melanie had to run to keep up with him as he rolled out of the car and headed for the school building.

"What's the hurry?" she called after him.

His answer was short and to the point. "I've been waiting for this my whole life."

The first day of school went smoothly for Isaac and fairly well for his mother, as did many of the days that followed. From time to time, Melanie would forget about the enormous burden that accompanied the two of them as they left the house each day. And she grew to enjoy having him at school with her. In fact, the young student was a wonder to behold.

"I've never seen anything like it," Doris said after the first week. "He's a sponge. He's so far ahead of everyone else—anyone else I've ever had—that it's all I can do to keep up. Your baby is sure keeping me on my toes."

Melanie was concerned. "Is his enthusiasm causing problems for any of the other children? Most kids prefer to start out slowly. I'll talk to him if you think I should. I'm sure I can get him to tone it down a little."

Doris laughed her familiar hearty laugh, and Melanie was instantly relieved. "I bet you can't slow this guy down. Nor should you. He's a joy to teach, really. And he's great with the other children. If they ask for help, he's quick to give it. But he never forces it on anyone. He's very considerate and understanding of the children, all of them. They're gravitating to him already."

The two women looked at each other for a moment. Then Doris concluded her brief summary. "I guess that should come as no great surprise, huh? But it's still amazing to see it in person."

Things went very well for the first few weeks of school. One day Isaac awoke with a sore throat, and since Jack was working, Lou came to the house and stayed the whole day. Melanie was also ill once and decided at the last minute to keep Isaac home with her, much to his dismay. She called Doris with the news and felt better when she agreed with the decision.

Everything seemed to be under control. One month later, they almost lost Isaac.

CHAPTER 49

October 7, 2006

"Hi, my name's Melanie Russell. I know this is your second day subbing for Charlotte, but I missed you at lunch yesterday. If I can be of any help, don't hesitate to ask."

The young attractive woman sitting across the long lunchroom table extended her hand to Melanie. "It's nice to meet you. I'm Jennifer Bryant. And thanks for the offer. I feel like I'm jumping into the frying pan with these first graders. They're smarter than me, and they know it. That's the scary part."

Doris, just taking her seat next to Melanie, laughed and shook hands with the substitute teacher. She quickly introduced herself and the conversation continued. "I noticed Charlotte was out. I hope it's nothing serious."

"No, I don't think so. They told me it was the flu and asked if I could help out for a couple of days. So here I am."

"Are you new to this district?" Melanie asked. "Ever subbed for us before?"

"No. This is my first job ever. Anywhere. I just got my teaching certificate this summer, and Mercy was my first call. I'm new in town and hope to do quite a bit of subbing this year."

"That shouldn't be a problem," Doris said. "Some principal in this system needs a teacher all the time, especially in elementary education. You'll probably be able to work as much as you want to—more than you want to, probably."

"Where are you from?" Melanie asked.

"Out west. Several places, really. But no place as big as Chicago." With that, Bryant hurriedly placed her leftovers in a small brown bag, crumpled it easily in her hand, and rose from the table. "I've got to run. I need to make a call before the children return to the classroom. It was nice to meet you both."

Both women waved as she turned abruptly and walked out of the cafeteria.

"They get younger every year," Melanie said.

"Sure do," said Doris. "And stronger. Did you get a load of that handshake? Girl nearly made me cry uncle before she finally released that death grip."

Melanie laughed and took a bite of her sandwich. She smiled at Isaac, who was sitting with friends two tables over. He and Paul Greenwell were in the process of exchanging fruit. It seemed like a fair trade—an apple for an orange.

* * *

It was a little past one in the afternoon, and Doris was working quietly at her desk. It was rest time for the kindergarten class, and all the students had taken their places on the soft mats in the back of the room. A few of them were still squirming on their towels—fighting the good fight against fatigue—but most rested quietly.

Doris, with her back to the classroom door, looked up to take a quick peek at Isaac. It was something she did subconsciously hundreds of times each day, like watching a small child in the ocean. She shifted her eyes from her prized pupil often, but never for long. Always, as was the case now, she returned her attention to Isaac.

She could tell by the deep, regular breathing that he was asleep. Isaac was different from most children, different from most people, really. He worked hard, played hard, and even rested hard. Everything was full speed ahead with him, even rest time. He was usually asleep just a few seconds after spreading out his towel. Today was no different.

A few minutes later, Doris heard someone enter the room and turned to offer a hushed greeting. She'd barely turned in her chair, making out the figure of Jennifer Bryant, when a blinding flash of light exploded inside her head. Her body went numb, and her voice failed as she tried to cry out. Instead, all that emerged was a slurred whimper.

Bryant caught Doris before she fell to the floor. She pulled her easily from behind the desk and dragged her limp body to the corner of the room. When Doris stirred, trying to free herself from the painful grasp, Bryant violently brought the nightstick down on her head again. The dull thud of hard wood against skin and skull made a sickening sound, but not a loud one. None of the children in the room stirred as Doris blacked out, blood streaming down her face from the deep gash near the top of her scalp.

Isaac could feel someone shaking him and reluctantly emerged from a deep sleep. He rubbed his eyes with the back of his hands and tried to focus on the face above him. As he looked at the young woman, two questions occurred to him almost immediately. Who was she? And where was Doris?

He didn't ask them out loud because the woman was holding her finger against pursed lips. "Shhh," she said. "My name's Jennifer. I'm a friend of your mom's. She wants to see you and asked if I'd stop by and pick you up."

Bryant reached out her hand, and after hesitating for a brief moment, Isaac took it.

"Let's not wake the other children. Nap time isn't over yet. Just walk with me, and we'll be back before the others know we're gone."

Isaac looked at the desk, searching for Doris. Jennifer seemed nice, but something didn't feel right. Every single day since the beginning of school, he'd awakened from his nap to find Doris seated behind her desk, smiling at him, except today. Suddenly, Isaac sensed danger. Confused and in the grasp of a stranger, he was afraid.

"Where's my teacher? Where's Doris?" he asked quietly.

Bryant led Isaac through the classroom door, careful to keep her body between the child and his fallen teacher. "She got sick and had to go home. Your mommy went with her to help her."

Isaac stopped in his tracks about thirty feet down the hall from the classroom door and pulled slightly against Bryant. His mother had never left him, ever, with anyone other than his father, Lou, Doris, or Reece. Something was wrong. She would never leave him, even if Aunt Doris was sick. She would have taken him with them.

"I want to go to Mommy's room. I think she's in there. Let go of me please."

She didn't release his wrist. Instead she gripped it harder, so hard that it hurt. Then she jerked Isaac forward and bent over, placing her face inches from his. "Listen to me, you little shit. I said she's gone. Do you understand me? Gone. And I'm doing her and you a big favor by picking you up. But I don't have time to listen to your pathetic whining. Now come with me or I'm going to whip your ass."

She pulled Isaac harshly down the hall. He was crying now, but despite the shock of all that was happening, he was still thinking.

If he screamed for help, someone in the school would hear him and come running. But what would the woman do? Would she turn and kill him on the spot?

Probably. If she was here to kill him—and Isaac had no doubts about that—then she'd do it here and now if need be. Escaping, getting away with murder, was secondary. Even at this young stage in his life, Isaac understood that.

So he didn't scream. He kept looking frantically behind him, down the empty hallway, as Bryant pulled him closer and closer to the side exit. Once they left the building, it was only a few hundred yards to the parking lot. Isaac realized what awaited him there. She'd put him in a car, drive away, and it would be the last time he'd ever see anyone again.

They were no more than ten feet from the door when Isaac reached a decision.

He was going to scream. His reasoning was sound. He hoped the woman, so close to freedom, would decide to make a run for it rather than kill him right away. Maybe she'd get greedy and try to accomplish both her goals. It was his only chance now.

But Isaac didn't scream. He didn't have to. Just as he opened his mouth, ready to yell at the top of his lungs, the fire alarm sounded inside Mercy Elementary. Doris had struggled to her feet long enough to reach the red lever just outside her door and managed to pull it down before collapsing in a bloody heap.

* * *

"Godammit!" Bryant spat, twisting her head around in anger and surprise. "Move it, you little Jesus wannabe. Move your ass. Now!"

Isaac resisted. And even though the effort felt as if it was ripping his arm off, he pulled hard against Bryant's death grip. Her hand was sweating, as was his, and he was shocked to find himself suddenly free. He turned and started running down the hall, toward safety, and had traveled almost fifty feet before she overtook him.

She grabbed him violently by the back of his shirt and lifted him completely off the floor. Isaac's little legs were still churning, helplessly in the air. She put him down, twisted his body around, and slapped him harshly across the face. The force of the blow took Isaac's breath, and he was unable to move as she threw him over her right shoulder and started back—running—for the exit.

* * *

The moment Melanie heard the alarm sound, her nervous system went to full alert. Something was wrong. She sensed it. And it was no fire. So instead of lining up her children, she shoved open the door rushed into the hallway. She gasped when she saw Doris, now on her knees, trying to fight her way to her feet.

Melanie ran to her side and helped her stand. Her eyes were glassy, her white blouse and navy blazer soaked in blood, but Doris managed to speak before falling again to the floor.

"The substitute—she's got Isaac."

Children and teachers alike were now filling the hallway, following the school's fire drill to the letter. "Help!" Melanie screamed. "Call an ambulance. Call the police. Please, someone come and help Doris."

Two teachers, a man and woman, came running to help. Melanie stood and rushed back into her classroom, running to the windows on the east side of the building, the windows that faced the parking lot. She screamed again—this time, in agony and fury—as she saw Bryant carrying her son across the lawn and toward the parking lot.

A sudden sinking feeling overwhelmed Melanie. There was no way to catch the woman fleeing with Isaac. It was too far down the corridor, around the side of the building, and across the property to the parking lot. She simply didn't have enough time.

Melanie had to make time and reduce the distance between her and her horrified son. Instinctively, she reached down and grabbed one of the children's desks—the kind with the tabletop and chair and steel legs—and heaved it powerfully against the large plate-glass window. The glass buckled, part of it falling onto the grass outside, and the desk bounced back into the room. Melanie picked it up and grunted as she hurled it against the broken glass again. This time, the desk kept going, landing outside, as did most of the shattered window.

She was through it in an instant. As soon as she hit the ground, she jerked off her shoes, wincing as a piece of glass jabbed into her bare heel. Then she was on the move. A track star years ago, Melanie was now in the race of her life. The finish line was Bryant's red Ford Explorer, parked in the lot's closest space, and hanging in the balance was the life of her only child.

Bryant, with Isaac sobbing hysterically over her shoulder, was nearing her vehicle. She'd reach it in a matter of seconds, she realized, and a feeling of euphoria was overtaking her.

I'm going to make it, she thought without slowing down. *I'm going to be the one to bring the kingdom down.*

But Melanie was covering ground in great strides, closing the gap quickly. Unlike her quarry, Melanie's motivation stemmed from fear—the fear of losing a precious loved one. There was no greater motivation. It was something Bryant would never understand. And because of that, she slowed down—not much, just a little. It was to catch her breath and fumble for her keys, which she finally pulled from her pocket. But it was enough to cost her. And it cost her dearly.

She pulled open the door and threw Isaac inside, tossing him recklessly across the front seat and into the side of the passenger door. As she lifted her leg to jump inside, Melanie tackled her from behind.

Even as she attacked, Melanie thought of Michael.

"No mercy," he'd once told her. "I know it sounds terrible, but you need to understand the kind of people we're dealing with. Always remember. No mercy."

Even though she'd never before, even as a young girl, struck another person in anger, Melanie proved to be a quick study. She was on Bryant like a vicious animal, pulling her from the vehicle and driving her right forearm savagely into her neck and against the back of her head. The abductor turned, trying to shield herself with both arms, but the feeble attempt had no effect. Melanie punched her in the face repeatedly with both fists, knocking her quickly to the ground. From there, the assault switched to her bare feet as she kicked her in the stomach and ribs.

Blood was oozing from the sides of Bryant's mouth. "Stop it!" she shrieked. "You're killing me!"

No mercy. Melanie's knuckles were raw and already bleeding as she dropped to her knees and straddled the assailant. She grabbed her by the hair, one hand on each side of her head, and was still pounding Bryant's head into the concrete surface when two more teachers arrived. Scott Turner, the school's gym teacher, finally managed to pull Melanie off, kicking and screaming all the way.

"Not today," she raged, looking down at the beaten woman. "Not any day. You'll never get him, do you hear me? You'll never get my son. You tell them that. Tell them all. You'll never win. Never!"

Bryant didn't hear the words. She was out cold.

"It's okay, Melanie. It's okay." Turner kept whispering the words into his colleague's ear. "It's over."

Slowly her fury began to subside. Melanie took her eyes from Bryant and looked for Isaac, still in the car. He was no longer crying. Instead, he was now looking at his mother with more than a touch of wonder in his eyes. The vehicle door was still open, and he reached out his arms to her.

"Oh, my sweet baby. Come to Mommy. Mommy's here now. Everything is going to be okay, Isaac. Everything is going to be okay."

Isaac jumped into his mother's arms, and she hugged him tighter than ever before. A crowd of children and faculty members had gathered around the parking lot, and they parted, making way for Melanie as she carried Isaac back to the school. She could hear ambulances in the distance, and she walked quickly, limping slightly as she made her way back to Doris.

Before they entered the building, Isaac pulled himself high in Melanie's arms and placed his mouth against her ear. "That was cool, Mommy. I didn't know you were so tough."

Despite the fear and anxiety that still engulfed her, the strange words made her smile. "Me either, baby," she said. "Me either."

* * *

They found Doris still lying in the hallway, but she was awake, and the school nurse was with her, holding a compress against her head, which had stopped the bleeding. Although still groggy, Doris reached out her hand as Melanie and Isaac approached.

"Thank God," she murmured, even as the nurse urged her to remain quiet. "Thank God he's safe."

Melanie sat Isaac on the floor then knelt beside her friend. Tears streamed down her face as the two women held hands.

"I'm so sorry," Doris said. "I almost lost him for you."

"Don't you ever say that again. Do you hear me, Doris? Never again. If it wasn't for you, he'd be gone now. You saved him. I love you so much."

Melanie wanted to wipe some of the blood from her face but was afraid to touch Doris until the medical technicians arrived. Instead she squeezed her hand a bit tighter. "Now stay still and be quiet. We've got to get you to the hospital so Jack can do his magic. I hate to say it, but you look like crap."

Doris smiled and closed her eyes.

* * *

Jack was ready and waiting by the time EMTs wheeled Doris into the emergency room. It took twenty-four stitches to close her wound, and she stayed two nights in the hospital for observation. Although the concussion was classified as severe, her injuries did not cause any long-term effects. It would, however, be almost four weeks before she returned to a warm reception at Mercy Elementary.

Melanie took a week off to recover from the traumatic experience while also helping Reece and the boys care for Doris. Despite her return, she decided to leave Isaac at home with either Jack or Lou until Doris returned to school.

"I just don't feel safe trusting him with anyone else," she explained to Jack.

"I couldn't agree more," he said. "Between the two of you, I don't think any other unwanted visitors will be turning up at school."

Bryant also spent time in the hospital, although EMTs were smart enough not to bring her to Jack's emergency room. She was arrested upon her release and charged with assault and attempted kidnapping. Her case never made it to trial. She was killed by two inmates in a medium-security holding facility one month after her arrest. The news came as no great shock to members of the inner circle.

By the time Christmas and Isaac's sixth birthday came and passed, things were almost back to normal. At least as normal as life could be. Isaac was getting bigger and stronger. And those charged with his security were also growing in both confidence and experience. With each passing day, the odds for success and survival were increasing.

CHAPTER 50

February 1, 2007

Lou was seated on the sofa in the Russell den, watching bits and pieces of the evening news. On the floor in front of him, playing with his Lego set, was Isaac. Jack and Melanie were in the kitchen, preparing dinner for the four of them.

Watching the news was old habit for Lou. *And why is it,* he wondered, *that old habits are so hard to break?* What difference did it make to him that the stock market in China was falling steadily or that civil unrest continued in the former Russian Empire? Especially now. For the true future of the world was sitting on the floor, right in front of him. Lou shook his head at the absurdity of it all. But he kept watching. Old habits and all.

What he didn't notice, at least for a while, was that Isaac had quit playing with his building toys. He was watching the television also, deeply enthralled by the news stories as they flashed across the screen.

A twenty-eight-year-old Iowa man, apparently infatuated with the sixteen-year-old girl who lived next door, was charged with shooting her to death as she walked past his home on her way to school. The talking head on TV delivered the alarming details: "Police have charged the suspect with aggravated murder after he apparently became upset when the girl rebuffed his advances. He approached her today on the quiet street of Hazleton and shot her six times at close range. Following the shooting, according to police reports, the man then walked back into his home and had breakfast."

The next story came from Reno, Nevada. Isaac stared at the screen as the newsman reported, "A man accused of taking part in the kidnapping, rape, and mutilation murder of fourteen women was executed by lethal injection. He had been sentenced to death for one of the killings, a 1998 murder, after horrifying details of what authorities described as a cult killing were presented during trial."

Lou muttered under his breath, then looked at Isaac to make sure the boy had not heard his negative remark. But Isaac was oblivious to Lou. He was listening intently to another report by the newscaster.

In Johns River, New Jersey, two brothers were charged with the killing of a twelve-year-old girl and her mother as part of a scheme designed to keep the youngster from testifying against one of them in a murder case. "The girl had been scheduled to testify against one of the brothers after allegedly witnessing a drive-by shooting one year ago. Yesterday's slayings prompted sharp criticism of New Jersey's witness protection program."

Isaac frowned when Lou stood and clicked off the television with a remote control. "What'd you do that for?" he asked. "I thought you liked the news?"

"Not really. It gets depressing after a while. Besides, let's go check on your mom and dad. Maybe we can help them set the table."

Isaac rose and followed Lou into the kitchen, but as he did, he looked back at the blank television screen.

CHAPTER 51

February 12, 2007

Melanie, her attention diverted by early morning traffic, paid little attention to Isaac as he punched program buttons on the car radio. They were making their regular commute to school, and he seemed intent on finding a particular station.

Finally, he settled on one that was airing a morning news report.

A teenager in Riverport, Washington, was sentenced to sixty years in prison for strangling a ten-year-old boy who had appeared at his door, selling magazine subscriptions. "The teenager—who robbed, raped, and strangled the boy with a piece of nylon cord—must serve at least forty-nine years of the sentence before becoming eligible for parole," said the voice on the radio. "Police found the body after it was discovered by a city worker in the dumpster at a nearby business."

"What on earth are you listening to?" Melanie asked, her attention back on Isaac now that traffic was starting to untangle. "Why don't you put on some music?"

Isaac shook his head. "Please, Mommy. It's the news. Can I listen?"

Melanie said nothing. Instead she watched the expression on her young son's face as more reports filled the car.

"Four Amish teens were arrested yesterday near Shandon, Ohio, and charged with vandalism. Authorities reported that the teens smashed more than forty windows, then beat an older man after he apparently tried to stop them. According to a spokesperson with the local sheriff's department, the man was admitted to the hospital with multiple injuries."

They were just a mile from school, and Melanie could hardly wait. *The sooner, the better*, she thought. "Does this guy ever report any good news?" she asked.

The answer, at least today, was yes.

"And finally we end our report on a positive note," said the voice. "A man in Decatur, Alabama, has reached an amazing milestone as his donations to area charities have now topped the $1 million mark. The seventy-five-year-old maintenance worker has been earning as much overtime pay as he could for the past forty years, just so he could give most of it away. He didn't reach his donation goal by hitting the lottery or collecting an inheritance. He did it by working hard, saving, and investing his money. When asked why he wanted to give most of his money away, the philanthropist said simply, 'It makes me sleep good at night.'"

Melanie put the car in park and turned off the engine.

Isaac grabbed his backpack from the seat and opened his door. "See, Mommy? Some of the news is good. You just have to look for it."

She looked at her son but didn't answer. She was afraid to ask the questions that were now on the tip of her tongue. *Yes, honey, but is there enough good news? And enough good people?* As she followed Isaac across the parking lot a depressing thought came to her. *Maybe we've reached the point where we just aren't worth saving.*

CHAPTER 52

September 5, 2007

It was a little past ten at night, and Eddie Weaver was resting comfortably in the moth-ridden recliner inside his apartment—or at least resting as comfortably as he possibly could. His breaths came in ragged short spurts, and he pursed his lips each time as he pushed the precious oxygen from his lungs, exporting it as quickly as possible so he could gulp in another fresh dose.

Pushed back in his chair, his shirt unbuttoned and revealing ample white flesh, he resembled a fish out of water, and he thought for an instant of the crappie and perch he used to hook as a young boy. He had left the catch on the bank, and he had watched their gills labor furiously for the oxygen that would never come on dry land.

He was in the final stages of emphysema. At least that was what the doctor told him two weeks ago. And the one before that. And the one before that. Money wasn't a problem and never had been, since he'd shafted that foolish William Bingham and collected the vast majority of the payoff from the *National Exposé* seven years ago.

So he'd been to see all the doctors, even two specialists. Each time the diagnosis was the same. He'd be dead in less than a year, his lungs ravaged by cigarettes, a seedy lifestyle, and time.

He found it odd, almost funny, that none of the experts he'd visited could give him a definitive answer concerning how much time he had left. Couldn't or wouldn't—he wasn't sure which. The last doctor, when pressed and cursed by the angry Weaver, at least managed to put his illness in perspective.

"If you have anything important to do, don't put it off," he'd said. "You need to take care of anything like that soon. As soon as possible."

With each passing day, his inability to breathe became more unbearable and painful. So tonight, he'd decided, he did have one more important thing to do.

He looked at the portable oxygen tank in the corner of the room and snarled wickedly at it. He took one last puff from his cigarette, then flicked it across the room without even snuffing it out. It landed on the carpet near a pile of dirty clothes.

"Oh my," he whispered to no one. "That could catch fire."

He tried to laugh, but couldn't. Instead, he lifted his right hand and placed the barrel of his one and only pistol inside his mouth. Quickly and even as he thought about changing his mind—maybe smoking just one more—he squeezed the trigger.

A few minutes later, as his spirit hovered in the air just a few feet above the nearly headless corpse that was once Eddie Weaver, the dark forces came for him. As they pulled him, kicking and screaming into the black recesses that were even more horrible than his worst nightmares, one last image crossed his mind.

There would be no peace for him, even in death. The evil, torturous life he had endured was nothing compared to the eternity he now faced. And as he plunged into the darkness, he screamed again and again.

CHAPTER 53

May 28, 2009

As always, the last day of school was a joyous occasion for the students at Mercy Elementary. It was joyous too for members of the faculty, although most of them tried not to show it. It was considered bad form by teachers to smile too much on the last day of school. But they were looking forward to summer vacation every bit as much as the student body.

Melanie was especially pleased for one simple reason—summer meant more time with Isaac. And nothing, she realized, was more precious than time.

The last students had evacuated the building, either catching the school buses, riding with parents, or walking to any of the three nearby neighborhoods. Isaac waited for her in the hallway, just outside her door. He would be in fourth grade next year, and sometime during the course of the last few months, he'd discovered that it was both fun and cool to stand around in the hall.

Usually he talked with friends. Today he was alone, leaning slightly against the wall, a fully loaded backpack at his feet. Melanie stood in the doorway and gazed at her son. She was struck by how handsome he'd become. And how big. He was growing up much too fast. And she made a quick promise to herself that this summer would be even better than the others.

She and Jack had talked about taking Isaac to Disney World and to the beach.

This would be the perfect time. He was the perfect age. If everything went according to plan, they'd make the trip before school reconvened in late August. Yet they were both nervous about the plan. How could they not be?

Even though the attacks had stopped, Jack and Melanie still feared for his life. As did Lou and the others. But not Isaac. He never appeared to be afraid—inquisitive, passionate, driven, and always on the go, yes, but never afraid.

Perhaps he sensed something, and maybe he would know if danger surfaced again. Melanie hoped so. She also believed she would know if the dark side returned. The faith in the power God had given her calmed her to some degree, but not completely.

Still, she thought again as he looked at him, *time is passing too quickly. Fear will have to take a back seat this summer. There are so many things I want to do with him while he's still young.*

"Yahoo!" came a shrill cry from down the hall.

Melanie and Isaac both looked up to see Jordan and Doris walking toward them. Jordan was grinning from ear to ear. In six more weeks, he'd turn twelve, and next year, he'd be moving to the upstairs section of the school with the rest of the sixth-grade class. In two more years, he'd graduate from Mercy and follow his brothers to Holy Trinity High School, the large Catholic facility located about two miles away.

Today, though, school was the last thing on his mind. He too had big plans for the summer. Swimming, baseball, skateboarding, and regular visits to the movie theater were already on his agenda, not to mention spending time with Cassie Bishop, the pretty girl who lived just down the street from the McKenzies. Jordan used to pick on her. Lately, though, he'd taken to calling her on the phone and walking past her house as much as possible. He could really make his move now that summer vacation had finally arrived.

"You guys going to hang around here forever?" Jordan asked. "Come on, Isaac, let's hit the road. We've been here long enough, don't you think?"

Isaac smiled at his older friend and bent over to pick up his backpack. "You ready, Mom?"

"Yes, I am," Melanie answered. She looked at Doris, and the two women nodded their heads simultaneously.

"We're outta here," they said together.

All four of them laughed as they walked toward the door. Everything seemed right with the world.

CHAPTER 54

June 14, 2009

They sat one after another in row 22, section 104, a mere fifty feet behind the home team's dugout on a beautiful, sunny day at Wrigley Field. The men were sandwiched between Melanie in seat 12 and Doris in seat 20: Jack, Isaac, Jordan, Lou, Josh, Jacob, and Reece. The New York Yankees were in town, and the stadium was packed as the two old rivals squared off in an afternoon game.

As they waited for Jon Lester, the Cubs pitcher, to finish his warm up tosses, Lou filled everyone in with his seemingly endless supply of baseball knowledge. "This may be the last time you guys will ever see New York Yankees short stop Derek Jeter play in person because he is nearing the end of his hall of fame career." Lou reminded them. "Watch how our fans applaud him out of respect when he comes to the plate. And it's an honor to get to see the Captain play in person."

The boys all nodded in agreement. Jack and Reece did likewise. Melanie and Doris leaned forward in their seats and looked at each other, then laughed.

"I thought you guys were big Cubbie fans," Doris said. "Shouldn't we be pulling for Jeter to make an out?"

Lou smiled and continued to stare at Jeter as he stepped into the batter's box. "We're up eight to two," he said. "Bases are empty. It won't hurt much if he happens to smack one out now, will it, fellas?"

No one spoke, but the answer was clear. Everyone in the park was leaning forward on the edge of their seat. Jeter worked the count full, then fouled off two pitches before striking out. The crowd groaned, then applauded anyway as the future hall of famer strode back to the visitors' dugout.

But in section 104, the fans were going crazy. The second foul ball had risen high into the air before falling into the outstretched hands of a tall man in row 20. Perhaps it was the pressure of the moment or maybe just a bad pair of hands, but the ball bounced away and landed squarely in Isaac's lap. He gripped it tightly and jumped excitedly to his feet, holding the keepsake treasure aloft.

"I got it, Dad! I've got one of Jeter's balls. Can you believe it?"

Jack hugged his son, and they jumped up and down together, oblivious to the applause from nearby fans or the continuing action on the field. Jordan and the older boys all pounded Isaac on the back. They were almost as excited as he was. Lou, still in his seat, beamed with pride.

When the inning ended a few minutes later and everyone settled back into their chairs, Lou leaned over and whispered into Isaac's ear, "If you're lucky, he might sign it for you after the game. Then that ball will really be worth something."

No one knew it at the time, but Isaac already had plans for the ball. He would wait outside the locker room after the game, for almost two hours, and eventually would secure the most precious autograph in baseball. Then later that night, after Jack had dropped everyone else at their respective homes, he asked his dad to take him to the children's ward at the hospital.

Silently they walked to the third floor, to the wing where the terminally ill children stayed, waiting for miracles to happen and hoping against hope that they would be allowed to return home to their families.

Isaac said nothing. He didn't have to. The minute he'd asked Jack to bring him here, the plan had become clear. They were going to see Ryan Mason, Isaac's friend from third grade. The boy had been diagnosed with leukemia last Thanksgiving, and after two failed bone marrow transplants, his life was rapidly and painfully drawing to a close.

Ryan's eyes, so sick and dull looking as they entered the room, brightened just a bit as Isaac held out the ball. Jack watched them brighten even more as Isaac told Ryan and his mother about the story behind the ball and the famous autograph. Susan Mason turned and wept as the two boys talked.

Jack, as proud as a man could ever be, smiled at her before leaving the room.

He too was crying and was determined not to let his tears put a damper on this very magical moment. It was the last time he or Isaac would ever see Ryan alive.

CHAPTER 55

July 23, 2009

Isaac slowly opened his eyes and turned his head to the left, looking out the window at the puffy white clouds that stretched for miles and miles into the distance. He'd been napping for fifteen minutes, and for a brief instant, he couldn't remember where he was.

Quickly, it all came rushing back to him. He was in an airplane, with his mom and dad, heading back to Chicago after a week's stay at Disney World. Isaac smiled as he thought of his first real family vacation. It had been the best week of his life.

Just the three of them made the trip. They'd asked Lou to come along, but he politely declined. "No way," he said. "That crowd and that heat would kill me. Besides, I have a good feeling about this. It's going to be a safe trip. You guys go together as a family, and I'll be here when you get back."

So they'd gone. Isaac had never seen so many people in one place. They visited the Magic Kingdom, Universal Studios, MGM Studios, and the Animal Kingdom. They'd even managed to squeeze in a trip to nearby Sea World. Each stop had been wonderful. But the Epcot Center had been his favorite. The mountain of information at Epcot had overwhelmed Isaac. He learned about space, technology, science, engineering, and history, and he also witnessed first-hand many of the cultural aspects of not only the United States but of countries all over the world.

They'd visited Epcot on the second day of their trip, and Jack and Melanie finally dragged him away after the fireworks and closing ceremonies ended late into the night. Isaac insisted on going back again, just yesterday, and the couple watched in amazement as their son scurried all across the learning center, soaking up information at every stop. Again, they stayed through the closing ceremonies.

Today was travel day, and they were back in the air after a half-hour layover in Atlanta. It was now a little past eleven, and the flight attendants would be serving lunch momentarily. Isaac was glad. Fully awake now, he was hungry and thirsty. He looked at Jack beside him and Melanie one seat over. Both of them were tilted back, their eyes closed, dozing. He'd have to wake them in a few more minutes. But for now, he decided to let them rest.

They deserve it, he thought. And as he turned again to look out the window, at the beautiful scene stretching before him, he offered up another silent prayer. *Thank you, Father, for giving me such wonderful parents. They've given up their lives for me. And their love and devotion will not be forgotten.*

The food came a few minutes later.

CHAPTER 56

September 10, 2009

The best thing about fourth grade, at least in Isaac's estimation, was computer class—more specifically, his introduction to the internet.

From the moment Mr. Cole, the computer teacher, demonstrated the wonders of the internet to Isaac and his classmates, he was hooked. And he took the newfound knowledge home with him. For the next several months, both Jack and Melanie were hard-pressed to find time on their home computer. Their son was engrossed with the information available on it, and since it wasn't interfering with his homework, eating, and sleeping, they decided to give him free reign on the computer.

* * *

From time to time, Melanie checked his activities for content, but after a talk with Isaac, she decided to curb her maternal instincts and simply trust her son's remarkable judgment.

"I've got to learn, Mom," he said. "About everything. The good and the bad. And this gives me the opportunity to learn so much without leaving home."

His argument was not only valid; it was true. So night after night, he spent time on the computer, listening and reading, accessing information on people and places from all over the world.

Much of what he discovered was troubling—death, destruction, crime, illness, famine, drugs, pornography, poverty, and so much more. In fact, he was sickened by some of what he saw. But at the same time, his spirits were lifted after reading articles and finding websites devoted to good, kind causes. Each piece of information gathered was important and would one day soon help him make an evaluation on the future of human life.

* * *

Police fired warning shots outside a large city in Indonesia to separate rival Christian and Muslim gangs after three days of rioting left more than twenty people dead. The mobs were enraged by reports that mosques and churches near the nation's capital had been set on fire. In addition to the deaths, at least one hundred others were injured, and as many as fifty homes were destroyed.

* * *

Four employees were shot to death at a fast-food store near Snowmass, Colorado, as they were preparing to close for the night. According to police reports, the store was not robbed or vandalized, but the killer, or killers, urinated on the victims before leaving the scene of the crime.

* * *

Advocates for the homeless in Philadelphia lay on the streets of a busy shopping district to protest a new ordinance allowing police to fine and sometimes remove vagrants from sitting or living on sidewalks. Some two hundred protestors staged a rally at the city hall before walking to the popular business district. People of all ages, race, and religion took part in the protest on behalf of the poverty-stricken.

* * *

Nigerian soldiers restored an uneasy calm to a southern oil town where a five-day street war between rival ethnic groups left ninety people dead. Armed soldiers and riot police chased militants out of the stronghold by the end of the fifth day, and a dusk-to-dawn curfew was put in place by military leaders.

* * *

One man died after valiantly protecting dozens of others from an escaped bull during a rodeo in Austin, Texas. The bull escaped from his pen and tore through a concourse before being roped and secured by event officials. The man, who worked as a rodeo clown, lured the bull away from several startled crowds before finally being attacked and trampled. Witnesses said the man's bravery most assuredly kept others from being killed or maimed.

* * *

The bodies of a missionary and his three daughters were laid to rest in a wooden coffin amid a wave of outrage at their killings, the first in a string of attacks on Christians in India. Police arrested forty-five Hindu radicals suspected of burning the victims to death as they slept in their home.

* * *

A seventy-year-old man in Omaha, Nebraska, whom neighbors described as a loner, left a surprise behind when he died—$400,000 in donations to a church he never joined and a hospital where no one remembered him. He passed away after spending two years in a nursing home. Apparently, he had no living relatives.

* * *

A woman in Little Rock, Arkansas, ambushed her ex-husband, his female friend, and their two young children and killed all four of them outside their home with a shotgun. According to a man who witnessed the shootings from the street, the woman then reloaded the shotgun and killed herself.

* * *

A couple who installed a video camera so they could watch over their disabled four-year-old daughter captured a nurse hitting and abusing the child. The girl's parents watched the tape then called police, who arrested the registered nurse on charges of assault and child endangerment. The camera was not hidden, police said, but the nurse apparently did not realize it was there.

* * *

A woman taken hostage by a man suspected of robbing a gas station in Gatlinburg, Tennessee, said she felt sorry for her captor and held the man's hand as he cried and asked God for forgiveness. The fugitive allegedly robbed a gas station attendant at gunpoint before fleeing on foot to the woman's home.

"The more I was with him, the more sorry I felt for him," the woman said. "He never threatened me in any way and said he's become desperate for money because he was out of work and his wife and children were in need of food and clothes."

She walked with the man, hand in hand, to the law enforcement officials who surrounded her home during the three-hour ordeal and promised not only to visit him in jail but to help his family through their financial crisis.

* * *

"Time for bed, buddy."

Isaac frowned at the familiar sound of his father's voice.

"Shut that thing down and brush your teeth. We'll be right up to tuck you in."

Isaac switched off the computer and walked to the bathroom. His mind was racing, and he was filled with mixed emotions. He was now old enough to realize that the line between good and evil was seldom clearly defined.

CHAPTER 57

February 20, 2010

"Mommy, wake up. I had a bad dream. I'm scared."

Melanie recognized her son's voice and rose from bed immediately. "What's the matter, baby? What's wrong?"

Isaac was near tears. He looked at Jack sleeping peacefully, then motioned to his mother. "Come with me. Come to my room with me."

Gingerly she slipped out of bed, and together they tiptoed across the hall and into Isaac's room. Melanie could hear Lou snoring soundly in the guest bedroom, so she pulled the door closed behind her as she and Isaac made their way to his twin bed.

She put her arm around him and could feel him shivering. "Tell me, baby. Tell me what's wrong."

"It's nothing really. Just a bad dream. I've had them before, but this one was worse. Usually, I can go back to sleep after I wake up, but not this time. I wonder if you'll stay with me for a while."

Melanie smiled and put her hand against Isaac's beautiful face. She used her fingers to push the brown curly locks from his forehead and noticed that his hair was damp and sticky.

Must have been some dream, she thought. Then she asked about it. "What was the dream about? Do you want to tell me about it?"

Isaac hesitated before answering. "Not really. Kind of the same as always. I was being forced to leave you and Daddy, and I was really scared. I felt more alone this time, that's all. And more scared."

"I've got an idea," Melanie said. "How about if I sleep in here the rest of the night? I think there's room for both of us, don't you?"

Isaac grinned and scooted to the edge of his bed. "Sure, Mommy. You're skinny, just like me. There's plenty of room for both of us." He giggled, but she could still see the terror in his crystal blue eyes and feel the tension radiating from his body.

"You close your eyes and try to go back to sleep, and I'll sing to you while we're waiting. When you wake up in the morning, I promise you'll find me right here and Daddy and Lou down in the kitchen, making breakfast for the queen and her handsome prince. What do you say?"

"Okay, Mommy. Thanks for staying with me tonight."

Melanie opened the small drawer of Isaac's nightstand, pushed away several small race cars, then pulled an old hymnal from its hiding place. She squinted in the darkness while thumbing through the songbook. Finally, she found one she knew. Good old number twelve, "Be Not Afraid."

How appropriate, she thought. She sang the song softly, over and over again, until Isaac slowly drifted to sleep. It was a song and a scene that would be repeated often during the middle of the night for the next few years.

CHAPTER 58

May 1, 2012

Isaac walked ahead of Melanie as they made their way to the car. He was walking stiffly and was clearly upset about something. She held her tongue when he slammed the door shut. Then she walked around to the driver's side and climbed behind the wheel.

For several seconds, she said nothing. Finally, she started the engine, turned the air conditioner on high, and turned to face her son. "Maybe this will cool you off," she said.

Isaac stared straight ahead. Melanie gave him ample time to speak his mind, and when he didn't, she forced the issue.

"Listen, young man, if you think I'm going to leave this parking lot and fight traffic all the way home with you boiling like a teapot, then you're sadly mistaken. We're not going anywhere until you tell me what's going on."

"Come on, Mom. Let's just go. I don't want to get into it."

Melanie didn't respond, and the car remained in park. After almost five minutes, Isaac gave in. He might as well, he realized. He'd learned the hard way that his mother could be stubborn.

"They're idiots," he finally said. "Pure idiots. I don't know why I let it bother me. They don't even realize what they're saying."

"Details, Isaac. I need details. Who are you talking about, and what where they saying?"

"Nick and Alex and Timmy. I get sick and tired of listening to them shoot their mouth off, talking about things they don't even understand."

"More details, please."

Isaac relented completely. "We were in the hallway, waiting for final bell to ring, and they were cursing and saying bad things. I told them to be quiet. They told me to shut up."

Melanie frowned. The teacher in her was coming out now. Maybe she should report the boys to the principal.

"What were they saying?" she asked. "You want me to repeat it?"

"Yes. You have my permission. I need to know how bad it was."

Isaac shook his head in frustration. "Bad enough. They were saying 'goddamn this' and 'goddamn that.' And Timmy kept saying, 'Jesus frigging Christ.'"

Melanie suddenly understood his frustration. "What did you say to them?"

"I asked them why they wanted to talk like that. How come they kept taking the Lord's name in vain? They just laughed. Then Alex said he didn't even believe in God or Jesus. Then he told me to mind my own goddamn business."

Mother and son sat in the car in silence. She was waiting for him to reveal his feelings while he tried his best to hold them back. Eventually, he lost the battle.

"Don't they understand?" he yelled. "Don't they know that God sent his Son for them to die like a dog on a wooden cross? They can't begin to imagine the pain and suffering that was endured—for them! And all they do is laugh and make fun of the Father and the Holy Son, cursing their name and all that they did. How can they do that?"

Tears pooled in Melanie's eyes, and she wanted to reach out and hug her son. God's second child. But she didn't. This was a battle only he could truly understand and one that he had to reconcile on his own.

After several more minutes, she sensed that Isaac's internal struggle was subsiding. "It's okay," he said. "I'm okay now. Let's go, Mom. I've got a lot of homework tonight."

Melanie nodded and put the car in drive. As they pulled out of the parking lot, Isaac offered a few more words. "Maybe someday they'll change. Maybe they'll learn to appreciate all that was done for them. I hope so, for their sake."

CHAPTER 59

December 23, 2012

Sometime in the early morning hours of December 23, Melanie received her final message from heaven. It came not in the form of a dream nor from her mother or father. This time, the message was from God.

When Melanie awoke, she found herself in the bedroom. She was seated on the edge of the bed, and the room was filled with a bright, intense light. It was so powerful she had to shield her eyes with her hand.

As she stared around the room in bewilderment, she felt a hand on her shoulder and turned to find Jack also awake. He too was shielding his eyes.

"What is it?" he whispered. "Are we dreaming?"

"I don't think so," Melanie said. She was neither alarmed nor afraid. Instead, she realized she was completely at peace with whatever it was that was now taking place.

Isaac appeared in the doorway, followed moments later by Lou. Isaac joined his parents on the bed, while Lou remained in the doorway.

"What is it, baby?" Melanie asked.

"It's God. He's come to talk with us."

Melanie heard Lou gasp and watched as he slowly dropped to his knees. She took Isaac's left hand, Jack took his right, and together they listened intently to the message.

It was not delivered orally. Rather, the four people in the room could hear the words spoken in their minds. The words and the power of the light almost lifted them from the floor.

"You are no longer in danger, my son. The dark side has been defeated. For now. You will not encounter them again, any of you. You have done well, as have your friends. You will never again be asked to face the legions of darkness."

Their hearts raced, but the mortals were incapable of speaking. Only Isaac responded.

"Thank you, Father. Thank you for protecting me and my family."

The voice filled their minds again. "Time is drawing near, my son. Soon you will have to return to us, leaving this world behind. Are you prepared for that?"

"Yes, Father. I am prepared."

"Are you afraid?"

"Yes, Father, afraid and sad. It will be so hard to leave my family and friends, especially my Mom and Dad. I'm afraid to leave them alone."

Melanie and Jack, nearly immobilized, managed to squeeze Isaac's hands tighter. Lou was crying quietly in the doorway.

"That's why I've come to you. I want you to know you have nothing to fear. This time, when you come to me, there will be no pain and suffering. You are not being asked to die for the sins of others, unlike the one who came before you. You will not bear that cross. But you must take your rightful place in heaven, with me and your brother. Then together, we will make our decision concerning all our children."

"When will it be?" Isaac asked.

"The time is almost at hand. Not now. There is still work for you to do. You and your family still have time together."

Isaac did not speak. The others could not. The Lord offered solace to those in the room.

"You need not be afraid, my children, or saddened by all that happens. Your time on earth is but a blink of an eye. Eternity awaits you, all of you—together. And when you come to me, each of you, we shall rejoice. And for all eternity, you will be enfolded in the arms of your loved ones, past and present. Some of them await you even now."

Melanie thought of her mother and father and then, almost as immediately, of Michael. Was he there now, awaiting them? The image warmed her heart.

The next words warmed them all.

"My love for you is complete. You've been asked to give everything, and you have. Each of you. Even in your darkest hour, you were devoted to me, devoted to our Son. Your place with me is secure. You will spend eternity with me and our beloved Son."

Slowly and powerfully the light began to fade and, finally, was gone. Lou rose from his knees and quietly walked back to his room. Isaac stood and kissed both his parents.

"Don't be afraid," he said. "I'm not. When my time comes, I'll be ready. Until then, our time together will be even more special than before. The final days will be our best days."

He turned and left them alone.

Jack and Melanie talked quietly throughout the night. By morning, they'd reached a decision. If Isaac needed them to be strong, then they'd be strong. They could not imagine the pain they would endure upon his death and had no way to fathom the grief they would suffer when the time came for them to say goodbye to their only child.

But they now knew they would not be alone. God had come to them. Eventually, they would return to God. Isaac, their son, was simply going to lead the way.

CHAPTER 60

June 19, 2013

Saturday, June 19, like most summer days in Chicago, was hazy, hot, and humid, especially hot. In fact, the temperature was expected to soar to almost one hundred degrees, a record for so early in the year.

Global warming—that was the buzzword on radio and television stations. Every time temperatures shot up, people in the know started talking about global warming. Well, global warming or not, one thing was certain. It was hot.

The heat reflected and radiated from the asphalt and concrete of one of America's largest cities and tortured anyone foolish enough to venture onto the street. It was too hot to mow the lawn, walk the dog, play golf or tennis, swim, or sunbathe, which, of course, made it an ideal day for shopping—ideal for everyone but Melanie and Isaac. They were out among the masses because of necessity. Tomorrow was Father's Day, and they were still looking for a gift for Jack. So like thousands of others, they made their way through the heat and haze toward the entrance of the downtown mega mall.

Melanie and Isaac felt as if they were melting as they rounded the corner of the building, glaring against the bright sun and walking gingerly atop the scorched sidewalk beneath their feet. Finally, they made it, and both of them reveled in the cool air conditioning that greeted them as they opened the large double doors.

They stood there for a moment, enjoying the coolness, before stepping further inside and taking a look around the massive galleria. They stared in disbelief at the number of shoppers inside, then looked at each other and smiled helplessly.

"Go figure," Isaac said.

His mother laughed. "Well, maybe everybody is like us, caught a day before Father's Day without a gift for Daddy. This is what we get for putting it off until the last minute."

They slowly and carefully threaded their way through the maze of storefront shops and checkout lines, then stopped near a sporting goods store. "Want to look in here?" Melanie asked. "Jack needs a new pair of running shoes."

"Sounds good," Isaac answered. "I know which brand he likes best."

* * *

Cindy Sanders was pissed, and it wasn't just the heat and humidity that had her dander up, although weather conditions certainly weren't helping matters. Her dark hair, freshly colored to hide the few follicles of gray that were creeping in even at age twenty-eight, was damp with sweat and starting to take on a life of its own.

And her baby-blue blouse, starched and freshly pressed before leaving the house this morning, was now wrinkled and wet in all the wrong places, including down the middle of her back and under each armpit. The plaid skirt, clinging neatly to her trim figure, was still in good shape, but her pantyhose were killing her—hot and uncomfortable. Surely a man had come up with the idea of securing a woman's crotch, legs, and feet in such a hideously designed garment.

I don't know why I bother, she thought. *The camera only shows me from the neck up, anyway. And viewership will be about 10 percent for this piece of trash.*

All these combined made her angry again.

"Get your ass over here," she snapped. "Let's get this over with and get back to the station."

Cameraman Jeremy Andrews was young, just twenty-four, but he'd worked long enough with Cindy Sanders and dozens of reporters like her to know when to keep his mouth shut.

She was hotter than a Fourth of July firecracker, but he wasn't the target of her anger. Thank God. No, that honor went to program director Barbara Alexander. She was due to get an earful when they returned to the Channel 4 Studios.

Not that Andrews cared. He got paid the same no matter which reporter he was paired with, and Sanders certainly wasn't the worst of the lot nor the best. She was just another in a long line of television hopefuls that worked long odd hours—paying their dues, as they liked to call it—while always keeping a watchful eye for the one story that would lead to their big break, something exciting, titillating, or even sickening enough to catch the attention of a hardened public and move them into an anchor's chair or on to a national network position.

Besides, he liked his job. And he was good at it. He had an uncanny ability, almost a sixth sense, when it came to getting just the right shot at the right angle.

His work spoke for itself, as did the half-dozen video and production awards he'd already earned and the job opportunities—a couple of them very good offers—that he'd already turned down. He'd leave when the time was right, but for now, he was happy at Channel 4, even when he had to spend a Saturday afternoon with Cindy Sanders, even when the assignment was, as she had so elegantly put it during the ride over to the mall, lower than gopher dung.

He stood beside Sanders but kept his camera pointed at the throng of weekend shoppers. He panned back and forth across the mall, watching and waiting for something, anything, that might add depth or insight to the feature assignment. "What is," he said to himself more than to Sanders, "this year's perfect Father's Day gift?"

"Who gives a shit?" his partner answered. "I don't. I bet you don't. More importantly, probably no one in Chicago does either, especially not the day before the day and not in this heat. Babs ought to have us doing a story on air conditioning. That's the only thing anybody cares about right now."

Andrews laughed. He couldn't help himself. Sanders did have two things going for her. She was attractive—drop dead gorgeous, in fact. And she was sharp. Both of these qualities made his job as a video specialist easier. Sometimes, like now, she even displayed a witty sense of humor.

"Laugh all you want, but you know it's true. The only way anybody's going to watch this piece is if I accidently pour ice water down the front of my shirt. That would get us some viewers now, wouldn't it?"

He lowered the camera and looked at the reporter. "Yes, it would," he said, taking great pains to keep his eyes straight ahead instead of letting them stray down to gaze at her ample chest. "But it would get you fired. And with my luck, they'd throw me in for good measure. So why don't we see if we can both keep our jobs and find something interesting to shoot?"

She smiled, and for a brief instant, Andrews thought he'd broken through her cold outer shell. He was wrong.

"Knock yourself out, camera jockey. I'm going to the rest room, where I can rip these pantyhose off without getting arrested. Then I'm going to call Babs and rip her a new asshole. Then if all that makes me feel better, I'll come back and interview a few of these losers for you. How does that sound?"

Without waiting for an answer, Sanders stalked off. "Sounds like a plan to me," he said, waiting until his partner was well out of earshot. "To tell you the truth, I prefer working alone."

He lowered the video camera to the floor, made a couple of lighting adjustments, then replaced the bulky piece back on his right shoulder. His battery pack and audio wiring were held neatly in place with a special belt around his waist.

With all systems go, he started moving slowly around the massive main lobby, which stretched outward in a huge circle for sixty or seventy yards. Four escalators and an elevator allowed shoppers to access all three levels of the mall, and Andrews squinted into the bright sunlight that glimmered through the towering skylight located high above the ground floor.

Instinctively, he started shooting videotape. The escalators, crowded with patrons in varying degrees of undress, would make a good visual. He zoomed in on a pair of teenage girls moving from the first floor to the second. They wore bikini tops with their short blue-jean cutoffs, and each sported a belly ring. One of the girls had a butterfly tattoo on her stomach, just above the waistline of her shorts, and the other had dyed her hair bright orange.

"I'll bet Cindy would love to interview you, ladies," Andrews muttered to himself. "She really enjoys getting to know new and interesting people." He laughed and continued moving the camera.

As usual, he was able to pick up several nice shots: a young blind man walking through the center of the lobby with his dog, carrying several packages under his arm; a woman with five children under the age of ten (what a trooper she must be!); and an elderly couple, sharply dressed in shorts and matching T-shirts, sitting together and enjoying a pair of ice cream cones. This story might not be so bad, after all.

"All right. What have you got? Anything that might have some potential?" He pushed the pause button and turned to face Sanders. She looked better.

The pantyhose were gone, revealing long tanned legs, and so was the frown. She'd washed her face and reapplied fresh lipstick and eye shadow. Her hair was pulled back in a tight and much neater ponytail, and she had that look. Finally, she was ready to quit complaining and get to work. He was greatly relieved.

"Yeah, I've got several things lined up. Let's start with the old couple there on the bench. The ones with the ice cream. They look interesting."

Sanders reached down into their travel bag and took out two microphones.

She clipped the small one onto her blouse and put the large one into her right hand, taking care not to tangle the cord. "Good deal," she said, walking toward the couple. "Stay with me now."

* * *

Isaac emerged from the sporting-goods store with a broad smile on his face. Melanie, walking a few feet behind him, was equally pleased. They'd found a real bargain—popular running shoes, three pairs of athletic socks, shorts, and a stylish T-shirt, all for less than a hundred dollars. The sign had said 50 percent off everything in the store. The sign was right.

"We did good, didn't we, Mom?"

She'd caught up with Isaac, and they stood together near the center of the mall's bottom floor.

"No," she said, rubbing him playfully on the head. "We did well. Or rather, you did well. He's your dad, not mine. But he'll love it. Jack will just love it."

Melanie glanced at her watch. It was almost one o'clock. "I'm hungry. How about some lunch?"

"Sure. We can eat here, and then we won't have to stop on the way home. I can't wait to get home and wrap these up for Dad."

Together they walked across the wide expanse of lobby toward a fast-food cafe.

* * *

Cindy Sanders was wrapping up her interview with the young blind man. As a perfect ending to their story, she'd managed to get the seeing-eye dog to bark right on cue after putting the large microphone near his head and asking—in dramatic fashion—if he enjoyed being inside as compared to the outdoor heat.

Andrews, still working the camera, smiled. She was good, he admitted to himself, terrific when she put her mind to it, which was one reason station managers and program directors like Barbara Alexander put up with her sharp tongue and negative attitude. She knew how to deliver a story.

Sanders thanked the young man for his time, patted the dog gently on the head, then walked toward Andrews as she carefully recoiled the audio wire.

"How good was that?" she asked, flashing a sassy grin. Before he could open his mouth, she answered her own question. "Too good. Admit it. Too damn good."

He nodded his head but flicked the video camera back on. He'd decided to pan for a few closing shots. He didn't really need more footage, but it was always better to have too much than too little. Besides, Sanders was gloating—and flirting just a little. And if he continued working, he wouldn't have to look directly into her inviting eyes.

"What are you doing now? We've got the shot. We've got the story. Quit stalling, and let's grab some lunch. Your treat. And while we're waiting, you can tell me how good I am."

He started to lower the camera, but just before he killed the power switch, he noticed movement in the upper left hand corner of his viewfinder—unusual movement. He panned slightly to his left and up and then saw a woman in a blue uniform running through the mall. He pulled his right eye from the lens for just an instant, attempting to get a look at the big picture. The woman was a security guard, a mall employee, and she kept running even after hitting the escalator.

"What is it?" Sanders asked. "What do you see?"

"Something...I don't know. Check out that security guard. Something's wrong. She's running up the escalator."

"Shoot it," Sanders snapped, then realized the command was not needed.

Her young cameraman was already on top of the action.

Andrews walked slowly across the crowded floor, keeping the camera glued to the woman on the run. Sanders, her right hand on his back, cleared a path in front of him, waving her left arm wildly and stopping unaware shoppers in their tracks with a look that could kill.

"Help me with the full scene, Cindy. She's heading for the top floor now."

"Where's she going? What's up there?"

Sanders lifted her eyes from the security guard and searched the upper terrace frantically for some sign of trouble. Maybe someone had suffered a stroke or a heart attack. Better yet, maybe some form of violence had broken out. Now that would make for an exciting story.

Suddenly she stopped, clutching the back of Andrews's shirt. "Oh my god…" she whispered. "Oh my god!"

* * *

Isaac tossed the empty bag and hamburger wrappers into a trash can, then came back to the table, and took the large shopping bag from his mother. "I'll get it. It's pretty heavy."

"Why, thank you, my strong lad," Melanie said in a mocking voice. Yet even as she did, she again noticed the growing muscles in his shoulders and forearms and the facial hair that was beginning to emerge across his upper lip and down the sides of his face. He was rapidly becoming a man. "I've raised a true gentleman."

As they cut a path across the center of the mall, an intense wave of concern washed across Isaac, and abruptly he stopped and looked at Melanie. Her eyes grew wide as she felt something too. "What is it?" she asked. "I feel danger."

"I don't know," he said. "Something is—"

His words were interrupted by a shrill scream from high above them. They looked up just as Andrews was raising his camera to the four-foot safety wall that surrounded the third-floor shopping concourse. There, hanging over the edge of the wall, small feet kicking wildly, was a little girl in a yellow summer dress. She had slipped from the edge of the wall and was now clinging desperately to a support cable that went from one side of the concourse to the other. Brightly colored mall flags hung from the cable, which was now the only thing between the girl and the floor almost sixty feet below.

Melanie gasped, as did the other shoppers who had heard the scream. A hush fell over the massive mall as every head tilted backward and people of all ages looked skyward, mouths open and hearts pounding like pistons.

Isaac dropped the shopping bag and started walking toward the girl.

* * *

309

Andrews quickly pulled his camera away from the security guard, now almost to the top floor, and panned across to the girl. Her small body was turned away from the wall, directly at the camera, and his heart sank as he zoomed in and saw the sheer panic on her face. She couldn't be more than seven or eight years old.

He started to lower the camera. He wanted to drop it and run to the girl.

Help her. He had to somehow help the man in the dark business suit—obviously her father—hanging over the edge of the safety wall and reaching for his daughter, tears streaming down his face as he pleaded for her to hold on.

"Don't look down, Rachel. Look at Daddy. Daddy's coming, baby. Please hold on."

He was lifting the camera from his shoulder when Sanders softly patted him on the back. "Don't." She said, and although he couldn't see her, he could tell by her voice that she was choking back tears. "We'd never get to her even if we tried. There's no time."

Andrews zoomed in again to capture the anguish on the face of the father. He was sick to his stomach, but Cindy was right. The girl was going to fall. All that was left for him to do was to stand steady and perform his job. And never had his job been more painful than at this very moment.

The security guard had reached the father, who was now all the way over the rail, holding on with one hand while reaching out in desperation for his little girl. The guard was trying to pull him back to safety, but gave up when she realized it was no use.

"He's going to fall too," Sanders whispered into her cameraman's ear. "They're going to die together."

The man's hand was six inches from his daughter's, but try as he might, he could get no closer. The girl was no longer screaming but was rather sobbing softly, too weak to generate much noise. Yet in the deathly stillness of the huge mall, even those on the bottom floor could hear her pitiful words.

"I'm sorry, Daddy. I shouldn't have climbed over. I thought it would be fun. I should have stayed with you, Daddy. I'm so sorry."

The man strained harder with his left hand, easing his right hand lower off the edge of the wall. He was supporting his full weight with little more than his fingertips now. But he was closer to reaching one of his daughter's hands, both of which were clamped around the support cable. He was just four inches away when she fell.

* * *

Andrews was ready for the shot. He'd already pulled back, opening his lens to a wide angle in order to capture the entire gruesome scene. At the top of his viewfinder was the man and girl. At the bottom of the tiny screen was ground level, the floor where the girl would land, followed soon—he expected—by her father.

He could feel bile rising in his throat as the girl's weary fingers slowly released the cable.

Or at least they seemed to release the cable. She appeared to be dropping to her death, even screaming as her hands fell away from the wire, yet somehow the gap between she and her father suddenly narrowed, then closed completely.

Defying all laws of gravity, the girl appeared to rise, and her father clutched her wrist with his left hand.

The additional weight caused him to lose his grip, and for an instant, it looked as if they would fall together. Gasps echoed through the massive structure as the security guard and two teenage boys held tightly to the father's right arm.

Together they pulled as others reached over the wall, grabbing the father from every conceivable angle. One woman even clutched his necktie. Slowly, painfully, they pulled him close enough to reach the girl. The guard pulled her over the wall, and within seconds, the father was also lifted to safety.

As the man hugged his daughter, collapsing to the floor with her, thousands of spectators inside the mall started clapping their hands hysterically.

People—complete strangers—were hugging and jumping up and down, many crying tears of joy.

A man standing next to Andrews and Sanders screamed and yelled at the top of his lungs, "Almighty God, you've given us a miracle!"

He continued rolling tape. Sanders grabbed the microphone and audio cable as she prepared to get the interview of all interviews. "I don't know about any miracle, but we just witnessed the story of the year—that's for sure. And it's all ours."

As she ran for the escalator, Andrews finally lowered his camera and looked at the boy and woman standing on the ground floor, not thirty feet away from him.

He watched them intently as they turned, arm and arm, and headed for the exit doors. The woman hugged the boy and kissed him on the cheek. But as she looked over her shoulder, eyes searching for something unseen, a cloud of worry crossed her face. She seemed concerned for the boy.

After they walked through the door, Andrews turned his camera on and quickly rewound the tape to double check his footage. It was there—everything, including the one scene that no one else had noticed. In slow motion, he played it again and again, peering silently into the camera's small viewfinder.

Just as the girl's fingers slipped from the cable, the boy on the floor lifted his right arm in a powerful, dramatic gesture. His hand was open, palm stretched skyward, as if holding a small bird, gently lifting it back to safety.

It wasn't an invisible bird he'd lifted. It was the girl. The slow-motion replay showed the girl's hand slipping away from the cable, dropping several inches in what should have been a deadly freefall, then reversing direction, and actually rising to meet her father's desperate grasp. It was on the tape, clear and in living color.

It was hard to believe and difficult to comprehend, but there was no denying what had just happened inside this huge mall on a hot, summer afternoon.

Jeremy Andrews had not only witnessed a miracle. He'd captured it on film.

* * *

In the frantic moments that followed the amazing rescue, as Sanders moved quickly to secure interviews with the joyous father and his badly shaken daughter, Andrews thought about destroying the videotape. It was a fleeting thought but one he gave serious consideration.

Despite having fallen away from the church several years ago, he still considered himself a Christian. He believed in God and still remembered many of the things he'd learned in Sunday school. If nothing else, he knew a miracle when he saw one.

Because of his deep-seated religious convictions, his heart told him to do the right thing. By destroying the tape, he would not only preserve the sanctity of the blessed event he had just witnessed; he might also preserve the life of the young man who had performed it. Without the tape and public scrutiny, the boy might continue to walk the streets of Chicago in obscurity. He would be left alone to save more lives and souls and perhaps perform even more astounding miracles.

Once the videotape was placed into the hands of Cindy Sanders and the managers at the television station, the secret would be out. There would be little doubt about what had just happened in this huge mall. Andrews was just too good and, in this case, too lucky. The entire mesmerizing scene was shot at the perfect angle. The slow-motion replay, which would be shown over and over on every television set in the world, clearly depicted the girl's hands falling from the cable before miraculously rising to meet the outstretched hand of her father.

Everything would change if the tape made it on the air—for him, Cindy, everyone associated with the station, the father and his daughter, the security guard, and everyone else who had witnessed the event. For people everywhere, really, especially those with true religious faith. Most of all, it would change everything for the young miracle worker and the woman with him. She was his great protector—that much was certain. And Andrews thought again about the look of concern on her face as she'd led the boy from the mall.

He pulled the tape from the video camera, his right hand shaking as he looked at it, so many thoughts and conflicting emotions racing through his mind. He gripped the tape harder and harder, half hoping it would disintegrate in his hand, alleviating him of the burden he now bore.

It didn't. Instead Sanders's hand suddenly appeared on the tape. She jumped up and kissed him, and he looked at her in bewilderment. "They're willing to talk about it," she said, trying hard to keep her voice at a normal level. "Put that tape back in, and let's roll. This is it, Jeremy. This is our ticket to the big time. We're looking at a Pulitzer here, my friend. A Pulitzer! Come on, don't just stand there. Let's move."

He hesitated for a moment, then reluctantly slid the cassette back into the camera. It was his job, after all. He was a newsman, and what had happened today was definitely news—good news even, which was getting harder and harder to find.

But as he followed Sanders up the escalator, he moved with a heavy heart. "Forgive me, Lord," he said in a hushed, almost silent whisper. "I didn't know."

* * *

It was worse than he imagined. Not the story. The story was great. Sanders was all over it. Her interviews with the father and daughter were breathtaking. She knew what an audience wanted, and she knew how to give it to them. Every question was perfect. And the answers, pouring forth from the emotional father and his daughter, were better than anything ever written for a screenplay.

The only thing lacking was a live remote feed. No one at Channel 4, especially Cindy Sanders, had expected the piece from the shopping mall to turn into a major late breaking story. But they had plenty of time to get back to the station, edit the piece, and get it on for the day's first big newscast at five o'clock.

In fact, the additional time gave everyone at the station time to review the tape.

Sanders gasped when she saw the shot from the ground floor. So did the two editors. One of them, Vince Galloway, froze the picture with the girl's hands inches below the cable and Isaac's arm raised high into the air.

He twisted around in his seat and stared at Andrews. "Did you know you had this?"

Everyone else in the room was also staring at the young cameraman. He shrugged his shoulders. "I thought so. But to be honest, I'm not sure what I have."

Sanders walked to the large editing screen and put her finger on it, pointing to the gap between the girl's fingers and the thick wire. Then she pointed to Isaac's hand raised high into the air, directly beneath the girl. She was grinning from ear to ear.

"Are you shitting me?" she asked. "Look at this thing. I mean, really look at it. Unless that little girl is a miniature version of Wonder Woman, then what you've got here is the biggest miracle since Moses parted the Red Sea. Jesus Christ, Jeremy, you've got it! On tape! It's the greatest shot in the history of television, and you're standing there like some kind of idiot. Snap out of it, will you?"

Andrews shook his head and walked out of the room. Sanders followed but turned to Galloway before reaching the door. "Make at least two copies of that before you start screwing around with it. And call Barbara at home, and get her ass down here. She's going to wet her pants when she gets a look at this exclusive."

* * *

She caught him in the hallway. "What's the matter, Jeremy? Am I missing something? You act like you don't care about shooting what will be the hottest piece of videotape ever produced."

For a few depressing minutes, he tried to reason with Sanders. "I do care. That's the problem. Don't you understand what happened today? It was a miracle, Cindy, not some high-tech, special-effects miracle created by a movie studio, but a real miracle. The genuine article. I don't think it's the kind of thing we should mess around with. We shouldn't have been there. We shouldn't have captured it on film. And I don't think we should use it now. Let's go back in there and try to talk them out of it. Will you help me?"

Sanders stared at him with her mouth open. She was flabbergasted—and repulsed. He was serious. He wasn't kidding. For a moment, she didn't know how to respond. For the first time in her life, she was speechless.

"Hogwash," she finally managed. "Pure hogwash from a blabbering idiot. And you call yourself a newsman. I thought I knew you better than this, Jeremy. You're asking me to sit on a story. The biggest news story of my life! Well, let me say it as simply as I can. You can go to hell."

She turned to walk away, but he grabbed her arm. "You know what it will do to him. The boy. It will ruin his life. They'll flock to him like he's the Messiah, and in their rush to worship him, they'll destroy him. Do you want his blood on your hands, Cindy? Think about that for a minute."

Her face was pale, and the arm in his hand was clammy. She jerked away and staggered against the wall. "Get your filthy hands off me, you lunatic. I can't help it if this ruins his life. I didn't perform the miracle—he did. Besides, if he really is some kind of messenger for God, then surely God will take care of him. Isn't that what gods are supposed to do?"

With that, she was gone.

Andrews left the building and walked slowly to his car in the parking lot. The sun was beating down on him with ferocity, and a steamy haze seemed to rise from the asphalt. The temperature had climbed at least five degrees during the past hour. As he opened the door and sat down inside the vehicle, the heat that greeted him felt like a blast furnace.

"I wonder if this is what hell is like," he asked himself.

CHAPTER 61

June 20, 2013

The story had been running on Channel 4 virtually nonstop for almost twenty-four hours. The national networks and every major cable news channel in the world had already picked it up. Since it was an exclusive, reporter Cindy Sanders was already something of a celebrity.

But the real story was in the videotape. The scene was both shocking and amazing, and already the controversy was growing. Real or fake? Religious miracle or optical illusion? Was the boy sent from heaven, or was he a dark angel trying to fool the masses with this so-called act of heroism?

The debate raged back and forth on television and radio talk shows and in churches before and after Sunday services, and would undoubtedly fill the columns of every newspaper in the world come Monday morning.

Already the search for the boy was on. Who was he? Where did he live? How old was he? And who was the woman with him?

By noon on Sunday, Father's Day, all the questions had been answered. The mother of one of the students at Isaac's school recognized him and also Melanie. She quickly called the television station and reported her information. By early Sunday evening, dozens of satellite trucks were lined up outside the Russell home. Everyone, including Cindy Sanders, was fighting for an interview with Isaac, the boy wonder.

Only the police force, contacted by Lou shortly after the piece was aired, kept people from knocking down the doors and barging into the home. If the crowd kept growing, even they wouldn't be enough.

Lou, his weapon holstered under his arm, glared out the front window at the horde of reporters, gawkers, and would-be stalkers. "We're going to need the National Guard," he said, sadness in his voice. "Anybody know the governor?"

The room behind him was silent. Melanie and Jack and Isaac sat together on the couch. Doris, caught in the crunch of uninvited guests while visiting the night before, stood behind them. She held a small radio in her hand, which she used to communicate with Reece and the boys at home. Jack had pulled the phones out of the wall hours earlier before the constant ringing could drive them all mad.

Isaac was disconsolate. Not only had he brought this on himself, he'd brought it on his loved ones. They deserved better. Certainly, they didn't deserve this. They were trapped in their home like caged animals, with no escape, all because of his actions at the mall.

"I'm sorry," he said suddenly. "I didn't mean for this to happen. You've all worked so hard to keep me safe and protected, and now this. It's all my fault."

As he spat out the last words, he covered his head with his hands.

Melanie was the first to him. "Please, baby, don't cry. We're okay as long as you're okay. And there's nothing to be sorry for. You did what you had to yesterday. You saved two lives. This other stuff, this publicity, isn't important. Maybe it's supposed to be this way. Maybe it's finally time for people to know you are among us. This might be a sign. It might be part of God's plan."

Isaac wiped away the tears and looked at his mother. His next words sent a chill down her spine.

"If that's true, then the end must be near."

CHAPTER 62

June 23, 2013

After three days, the throng surrounding the Russell home had reached incredible proportions. The entire neighborhood and even adjoining neighborhoods were swamped with members of the news media and thousands of other people. Helicopters, sometimes two and three at a time, circled the area from high above.

Two National Guard units had been activated, and with the help of police, fire, and rescue teams, as well as other city employees, they had managed to erect temporary barricades around the house. At one point, the guardsmen had been forced to load their weapons with tear gas canisters before police warnings to move away from the barricade were finally heeded.

Lou had been drafted to serve as spokesperson for the family. Aside from staying in constant communication with those who were protecting them, he continued to vigorously deny all requests for interviews. With no one to talk to, members of the media dug deep for new information. And by week's end, everything was out.

Much of what was reported was only rumor, but the truth emerged also—the attempted kidnapping of Isaac at Mercy. The bloody shootout, including the murder of Michael Starr, on Independence Day when Isaac was just a baby. His amazing birth on Christmas Day, year 2000. And even the tabloid article concerning Melanie and her miracle baby, all but forgotten during the past dozen years. The information came pouring forth, and with each new revelation, the intensity surrounding Isaac continued to mount.

There was no turning back now. People knew who he was, or at least thought they did. Most dismissed him as a fake and fraud or, at the very least, as an unfortunate boy caught in a whirlwind of controversy.

Others believed this boy to be the long-awaited Messiah, and that certainty only fueled the fires of speculation on several other important fronts. If he was God's Son, then why was he here? Was he here to save the world? Or to destroy it?

Euphoria was quickly turning into panic. Was Armageddon finally at hand?

Had the prophesied End of the Age arrived? Many believed the answer to all these questions was yes. God was going to strike down upon the earth, and Isaac was his lightning rod.

All of this placed him in grave danger once again. And this time, the danger would not come only from the dark side. Those who truly believed would also come to him, drawn to his power like moths to a flame. And in their eagerness to worship him, Isaac would be crushed.

It was Lou who finally made the decision.

"We've got to go," he said. "There's no other choice. We must get Isaac out of here, give this thing a chance to die down. Maybe it will, and maybe it won't, but he's not safe here. Not now."

He looked at Melanie and Jack. "It's your decision. You're his parents. Do you have any ideas?"

Neither said a word for several minutes. Finally, Melanie looked up and smiled. She went to Isaac and hugged her son tightly. Then she turned to face the others.

"It's time to go home," she said. "I know the one place where we'll be safe."

CHAPTER 63

July 1, 2013, The Abbey of Montessori

Brother Matthew Benoit met the car at the monastery's front gate. It was four in the morning, and the small country road leading to Montessori was quiet and deserted, just what the doctor ordered for the four weary travelers inside the car.

Jack was at the wheel with Melanie at his side. Lou was in the back seat with Isaac. The boy was asleep, his head resting comfortably in Lou's lap.

Matthew waved his hands as the headlights of the car splashed bright beams on him, and even in her weariness, Melanie marveled at the old monk's appearance.

He was near ninety now, and they hadn't seen him for several years. Melanie had kept close contact with her secret confidant—the bond between them was incredibly strong—but their interaction had been by telephone and letter. Yet despite the years that had come and gone, Matthew looked virtually the same, a tad more weathered perhaps, and as he walked toward them, his familiar limp was more pronounced. But everything else was the same, even the crystal clear eyes. Especially the eyes.

Melanie jumped from the car and ran to greet him. She threw her arms around her old friend and let the emotions inside her spill out. His embrace was warm and loving, and it felt good to be back in his pure presence.

"Oh, Matthew, it's so good to see you again. I've missed you so much. Thanks for letting us come."

The old man didn't speak for a moment. His throat was dry and coarse as he too welled up with emotion. He was honored and humbled to once again hold the Holy Mother in his arms.

Finally, he managed some words. "I just thank God you made it safely. I take it the escape plan worked?"

Jack joined them, and he gave Matthew a mighty hug. Isaac was still asleep, so Lou remained with him in the car. "Everything worked just like we'd hoped," Jack said. "Lou came up with a great plan."

Melanie smiled when reminded of the escape plot. Lou hatched the plan two nights ago with the help of some of his police buddies. Under the cover of darkness, the Russell vehicle pulled out of the driveway and quickly headed for the interstate—a mother, father, and boy all in the front seat, driving southwest toward St. Louis. Their departure caught everyone, especially the media, by surprise.

And despite a full police escort, the satellite trucks and other media vehicles quickly fell in behind the Russell family.

As Jack and Matthew talked, a funny thought came to Melanie. How surprised they all must have been when the "fake" family, a policeman who looked remarkably like Jack, along with his wife and their son, finally emerged from the vehicle in St. Louis.

By that time, of course, the real Russell family, with Lou also on board, had been smuggled out in the trunk of two police cruisers. Once outside the mass of humanity that continued to surround their home, they switched cars and drove south, down I-65, to Louisville, Kentucky. Forty minutes later, with no followers in sight, they'd arrived at the abbey.

A wave of sadness washed over Melanie as she thought of the secret evacuation. The most difficult part had been saying goodbye to the McKenzies. It had been painful, more painful than any of them had imagined.

They were all at the house in the hours leading up to the escape, even the boys. A sense of urgency hung heavy in the household because of the uncertainty of when the Russells might return. The hardest part for Melanie had been watching Isaac say his goodbyes.

He hugged his friends—Jacob, Josh, and Jordan—then Reece and Doris.

Each of them had cried, but no one more than Reece. Doris, as always calling upon her deep faith, had been strong. She'd even managed to smile through her tears and offer Isaac some wonderful words of encouragement. Reece, crying unashamedly, could find no words of consolation. He'd grown to love Isaac like one of his sons. Letting him go to such an uncertain and dangerous future was almost more than he could bear.

This was why Isaac delivered only to Doris the message he had so long dreaded. As he prepared to leave the house, he hugged her one last time and whispered into her ear, "I won't be back, but I will be with you always. Know that and know how much I love you, all of you. Tell them from time to time how much I love them, and keep me in your heart until we meet again."

* * *

Melanie hadn't heard the words whispered in secret to Doris. She didn't need to. She realized the time left with Isaac was drawing to a close. Yet she still wasn't prepared—and perhaps never would be. How does one make ready for the death of their only child?

But she was glad to be out of Chicago, out of the spotlight, and back home in Kentucky. She was especially grateful to be at Montessori with her friend and holy advisor, Matthew Benoit. If it had to end, she was certain this was the right place.

She reached out and hugged Matthew again, even tighter than before. "Thank you for letting us come. We had no place else to go."

Isaac had awakened, and Jack returned to the car to help him out. In their brief moment alone together, Matthew looked deep into Melanie's eyes. "This is where you are supposed to be. Montessori is where you will make your final stand and spend your final precious days with the Holy Son."

Melanie's shoulders sagged, but the old monk grabbed then gently and quickly bolstered her spirits. "Don't despair, my child. All is not yet lost. We will enjoy some grand days here together with

Isaac, especially you and Jack. You deserve that. It is your reward from our Heavenly Father."

The others joined them, and Jack introduced his son to Brother Matthew. The boy smiled broadly and held out his right hand. Matthew accepted it, then dropped to his knees, and hugged the Holy Child. Isaac hugged him back, and the many years between their ages slowly melted away.

CHAPTER 64

July 3, 2013

Everyone at the monastery, from the abbot on down, was aware of the new guests, especially of Isaac. They knew who he was and, more importantly, what he was. Yet it made little change to their daily structure. These were, after all, men who had devoted their entire life to God. They were honored to be in the presence of the Holy Family, but they afforded all three of them, and even Lou, complete privacy. Matthew had not asked for it. It was simply granted to him and his guests out of respect, and no words were necessary. When the monks passed them in the garden or chapel or cafeteria, they only nodded and moved on.

Montessori was precisely what the Russells needed. For the first two weeks, they did little but rest and relax. And meditate. Each of them, in their own way, was beginning to prepare for the difficult days ahead.

And while they waited, they embraced life with newfound gusto. The days at Montessori were the best and happiest of their collective lives.

CHAPTER 65

July 20, 2013

Isaac entered the dark and sacred chapel, standing in the back until his eyes adjusted to the dimly lit room. Four monks were kneeling in silent prayer near the front, and he instantly recognized Matthew as the second from the left. Slowly he walked up the narrow aisle, then gently eased himself into the old wooden pew directly in front of the holy men. He closed his eyes and offered his own prayers in silence.

One by one, the monks made the sign of the cross with their right hand, touching first their forehead, then chest, then both shoulders. Then each kissed the small plain cross hanging at the end of their beaded rosary. With slight grimaces, each man pushed himself from his knees, exited the pew, then walked out of the chapel—all but Matthew. Instead of leaving, he moved forward one pew and joined Isaac on his knees. Isaac said nothing, but rather, he remained silent until Matthew opened his eyes and looked at him.

Matthew smiled, then leaned back into the creaky seat. "You want to talk?"

Isaac nodded slowly. "Yes, Brother. I have some questions I'd like to ask—if that's okay. I mean, if you have the time…"

Matthew smiled, and his crystal clear eyes sparkled. "I have nothing but time, my son. And I can think of no better way to spend it than with you." Isaac grinned, slightly embarrassed, then joined the old man in his pew. "Ask your questions," Matthew said. "I'll do my best to answer them."

The boy sat silently for several minutes, thinking hard about what to say and how to say it. When he finally asked his first question, the floodgates opened. He asked Matthew about everything—God, Jesus Christ, heaven, the good and evil he had encountered during his many years on earth. Questions and answers. The conversation continued on and on, and although they didn't realize it, almost three hours had passed before Isaac finally approached the one subject he was most curious about.

"Can you tell me some things about Michael? Your great nephew. I know so little about him, yet I feel as if I've known him all my life, even though he died when I was just a baby. I never ask Mom about him because I think it hurts her so much. Lou too, really. Dad has told me a few things, showed me some old pictures. But he told me once that you were the only one who really knew Michael well. Do you mind talking about him?"

The image of his nephew—his fall from grace and his meteoric rise into the Heavenly Father's arms during his final precious months on earth—warmed Matthew's heart. It had been many years since he'd spoken of Michael, but not a day went by that he didn't think of him, and he prayed to him often. It made him feel good that the Holy Child wanted to know more about him.

He shook his head and smiled. "No, I don't mind. I'm honored, really. He was a brave and honest man. Perhaps the bravest I've ever known."

For the next hour, Matthew told Isaac stories about his great protector. He described Michael as a young boy, then a man. He included everything, even the bad parts, and Isaac listened intently as the old man's facial expressions revealed the depth of love he felt for his beloved nephew. The pride in his voice was particularly evident when he talked of Michael's arrival in Chicago and in describing the devoted service he bestowed on the entire Russell family.

"He saved your life more than once, young man. He and Lou together. With your parents and the McKenzies. But Michael showed them the way, really. He told them what to expect and taught them how to prepare for the dark side."

Isaac felt like crying. Matthew had told the entire story, filling in every last detail, and now that he had a clear picture of Michael, he felt the full impact of the lost life almost as if it had just occurred.

"I'm so sorry he had to die—just for me. Why did it have to be that way, Brother Matthew? Why did he have to die just for me?"

Matthew reached over and pulled the boy closer to him. As he did, Isaac pushed his face into the chest of the wise old man and burst into tears.

Matthew stroked his head as he answered the final question. "Michael didn't give his life just for you, my son. He did it for us all."

CHAPTER 66

August 1, 2013

Lou was sitting on the edge of his bed. He was in a small dormitory room located just down the hall from the double rooms shared by Jack, Melanie, and Isaac. The room was neat and clean yet simple. In addition to the bed, the only contents were a desk and chair, two lamps, and an old couch.

Having finished his reading for the night, he was just about to turn in when he heard a soft knock on the door.

"Yes? Come in."

Isaac stuck his head around the corner, revealing a huge grin. "You still up?" Lou laughed and looked at his watch. It was ten minutes to ten. "Sure I am. I'm a night owl. I make sure my head never hits the pillow until at least ten o'clock. Come on in, big guy. What's on your mind tonight?"

"Oh, nothing really. Dad fell asleep in the chair, and Mom's taking a bath. I'm not sleepy yet, so I'm just wandering around the halls."

"Well, quit standing in the doorway and come on in. Let's rap a little. You know how to rap, don't you?"

Isaac laughed and joined Lou on the bed. He looked at his shoes, then reached down and untied one, then retied it. He started to do the same to the other one, but Lou reached over and rubbed him on the back.

"Come on, big guy. Quit stalling. You're gonna hurt my feelings if you don't spit it out. Have I ever revealed one of your secrets?"

"No. Never. It's not that, Lou. I just want to make sure Mom doesn't hear about this. I need to talk about some things, but I don't want to worry her. I think she's worrying enough already—she and Dad both."

Lou nodded his head. He'd been sleepy just a few minutes ago. Now he was wide awake. This was going to be a serious conversation. That much was obvious. But he said nothing. It was up to his young friend to make the first move.

Finally, the question came. "Do you ever think about dying?"

"Sure I do," Lou said without hesitation, "especially at my age. I mean, no matter how good my health might be at the moment, it can't go on forever. You know what I'm saying?"

He expected Isaac to laugh. He didn't. Instead he reached down and retied the same shoe. Lou frowned. Maybe that hadn't been such a good answer.

He decided to try again. "Let's see. What was the question again? Do I ever think about dying?"

Isaac simply looked at him, waiting for another answer.

"Sometimes. But not too often. It's weird really. I think when a person is busy living, they hardly ever think about dying. But if they're just kind of sitting around, letting life pass them by, then it seems to me like they spend a lot of time—more than they should—thinking about death. I know I did."

His answer was followed by a puzzled look from the boy. "What do you mean?"

"Well, the truth is, everything changed when you were born. I guess things changed for everyone in a way, but they changed a lot for me. Until I found out about you and went to meet your mother and father, I wasn't doing much with my life.

"My wife had passed away, I was retired from my police work, and my daughter and her family had moved away from Chicago. I wasn't able to see them much, and I guess I spent a year or two just feeling sorry for myself. During those times, I thought a lot about dying."

He leaned back on the bed and propped a pillow between his back and the wall.

"Were you sad?" Isaac asked.

"Sad and depressed. More than I realized, I guess. But my life took on a whole new meaning when you came along. Watching over you gave my life purpose. Just like when I used to be a detective. I felt needed again. It's important for people to feel like they're making a difference in the world. And with you, of course, I was definitely making a difference."

Lou looked at the boy, now realizing what was on his mind. He wondered if Isaac would have the courage to say it.

"I worry a little—about dying, I mean. We all know it's going to happen, and I really think I'm prepared for it. But sometimes...I...I don't know. Sometimes I'm—"

"Scared." Lou finished the sentence for him. "Sometimes the thought of death scares you. Right?"

Isaac returned his gaze to his tennis shoes. "Yeah. I'm not worried about the pain or anything. That's not what scares me. I just worry about leaving you guys, being without Mom and Dad. And you. And the McKenzies. It's scary to think about not being here anymore, not being with all of you."

Lou's eyes were moist, and he struggled to remain composed. The boy needed him to be strong now. He needed understanding, certainly, but he also needed reassurance—reassurance that in the end everything would be all right.

"I think it's perfectly normal for you to be scared. Passing on is a pretty big thing, you know. Like birth, it's one of the few things in life that happens only once. So nobody really knows what it's like until it happens. That's probably what makes it so scary."

He pulled Isaac over onto his lap and gently rocked back and forth with the boy held warmly in his arms.

"But that's the one thing you don't have to worry about, the unknown. Your entire life has been pointed toward this moment. God sent you here to do a job, and you've done it wonderfully— better than anyone could have ever asked, I'll bet. Soon it will be time for your reward, your eternal reward, Isaac. Soon you will be in heaven with those who came before you—your father and brother. And in due time, the rest of us, maybe even me, will follow. We will join you there, and we will be together for the rest of time."

Isaac snuggled against Lou. "I want you all to be with me," he said. "Do you really think that will happen? Even after I'm gone?"

"I do, son, with all my heart. You'll be the one to lead us there. And the thought of that makes me feel good. Safe and secure. The sorrow I'll feel when you leave will be replaced with unimaginable joy when God brings us together again."

They sat silently for several minutes, rocking back and forth together. Finally, Isaac rose and prepared to leave. "Thanks, Lou. Thanks for talking with me. I feel much better. I'm not so scared now."

Lou smiled. "Good. Just one more thing, though, big guy. I need you to do me a favor."

"What? I'll do anything for you."

"When you get to heaven, I want you to find my wife. Her name is Trina. I know she's there, so don't you quit looking until you find her. Tell her I love her now even more than the day she died. Tell her I'll be coming home soon, following not long after you, and that I look forward to being with her again.

Forever.

"Can you do that for me?"

"It's a promise," Isaac said. "And I'm going to tell her about what a brave and kind man you are. And how much I love you."

With that, he was gone.

It was many hours before Lou, weeping in silence and gratitude, finally found sleep.

CHAPTER 67

August 19, 2013

"Have you ever seen a more beautiful sight?"

Jack and Isaac were on a knoll near the end of a large field, looking over the vast acres of corn and tobacco that would soon be harvested by the monastery's neighboring farmers. Isaac held his hand, salute-like, across his forehead to reduce the sun's bright glare on his eyes. A city boy his entire life, he'd never before seen the majestic beauty of well-nurtured farmland. To the right, near the horizon, they could see cattle and horses grazing on the other side of a black wooden fence. And beyond the livestock were woods that seemed to stretch forever.

"It's green and gold as far as I can see," Isaac said. "No buildings. No cars. Not even people. This is so much different than the city."

Jack plucked a thick blade of bluegrass from the ground, placed it strategically between the palms of his two hands, and blew hard against it. The resulting sound was a long shrill whistle, almost a bird call.

Isaac looked at his dad in amazement. "I didn't know you could do that. How'd you learn?"

Jack walked down the hill a few steps and made himself a seat on a slab of flat white limestone. He patted the rock beside him and motioned for Isaac to join him. They sat together, looking out across the wide, spacious fields and shared the best father-and-son talk of their lives.

"I wasn't always a city slicker. When I was young, my family lived on a farm in southern Indiana—not too far from here, in fact. It was a small farm, nothing like what you see now, but it was beautiful and peaceful, a wonderful place to grow up. I still have fond memories of it."

Isaac stared at Jack as he spoke. "Anyway, my dad taught me how to make a whistle from a blade of grass. Here, let me show you."

After several weak attempts, Isaac finally did it. The whistle was long and shrill. He clapped his hands excitedly and giggled as the grass tickled his lips and nose. Jack roared with laughter.

"You're a quick learner. Of course, you always have been."

They sat quietly for a time, watching the animals below feed on the thick pasture.

"I didn't know you were from Indiana," Isaac suddenly said. "Sometimes it seems like there's so much I don't know about you and Mom. Tell me some more things. Tell me about Mom."

Jack grinned. "You sure? You sure you want to know about your mother? She has a very dark and dangerous past."

Isaac's eyes flew open wide. For a moment, he was shocked. Then Jack, unable to control himself, rocked with laughter and rubbed his belly. Isaac, obviously relieved, laughed too.

"Let's see. What can I tell you about Melanie Wade Russell?"

The son sat anxiously on the slab of rock, waiting for his dad to continue.

"Well, the first thing you notice about her is her beauty. I know it's hard to believe—as beautiful as she is now—but once, when we were a little younger, she was even more beautiful. Breathtakingly beautiful. And not just on the outside. Her warm and gentle personality made her the most special person I've ever met, even to this day."

Jack's eyes danced as he thought about his wife. His face filled with expression, and his hands moved rapidly as he spoke. Isaac noticed the passion and love in his father's voice as he realized once again how much he loved her.

"When your mother walks into a room, she owns it. And it doesn't matter who else is there—movie stars, models, millionaires. *She* owns it with her beauty and style and elegance. There's just an aura that surrounds her. It's a glow almost. It's grown brighter and stronger as our days together have passed by."

He looked at Isaac and smiled. "She was her most beautiful right after you were born. We had waited so long for a child, and finally, we were blessed with you. You completed her, really. Completed us both. You were the best thing that ever happened to either of us, and still are."

The words were followed by another long pause, broken finally when Isaac asked a question that had been troubling him for many months.

"Will you and Mom be okay, you know, after I'm gone? I think I worry about that more than anything."

Jack's heart melted. He was proud of his son. What a brave young man he'd become. Even as his darkest hour approached, his concern was not focused on his impending death but rather on the parents he would leave behind. This was his one chance, Jack realized, to make him feel better.

"I can't lie about it. Letting you go will be so hard. It's the most difficult thing any parent faces—losing a child. And losing you, such a wonderful boy, will be the hardest thing of all."

He felt tears beginning to pool in his eyes but forced them away. Tears would come later. Now was the time to be strong.

"Time will help. It always does, or at least that's what they say. I believe staying busy will be the key for your mom and me. I love my work, and I plan to devote a lot of time and effort to it. Saving lives is the greatest thrill on earth. And I work with a lot of good, dedicated people at the hospital. Everything is fine with my leave of absence, but when I return, I plan to make up for lost time. I owe them that. I'll probably work another fifteen years, then retire, if the good Lord doesn't decide to take me sooner. Maybe you can put in a good word for me, huh?"

Isaac, despite his sadness, grinned. Like always, talking with his dad made him feel better.

"What about Mom? Do you think she'll be okay?" Jack thought for a moment before answering.

"Yes, I do. With time. Your mother is a strong woman, Isaac. She has an inner strength that few others understand. And I'm sure she'll be busy when she returns to school. She'll be around children she loves all day, and that will help. Plus, she'll have Doris. Doris has the faith of ten people, and she will stand with Melanie each and every day. As will I. I'll be strong for her, Isaac. I promise you that."

The man and boy hugged tightly—father and son sharing the most special of a lifetime of special moments. Finally they stood, wiped away tears, and laughed at themselves before turning back toward the monastery and beginning the long walk home.

"You've always been my dad," Isaac said, holding Jack's hand. "And you always will be."

Jack squeezed his small hand with a devoted fierceness. "I know, son. I know."

CHAPTER 68

August 24, 2013

Melanie lay in bed, staring at the ceiling. She could tell by the sound of birds chirping outside the window that morning had arrived, yet the sun was just beginning to peak above the rolling hills to the east. Jack was gone, even at this early hour. He slept little of late, preferring instead to make the most of each day with Isaac.

And so she was surprised moments later when her son crawled in beside her, pulled the light blanket over them both, and cuddled close to her.

"Good morning," she said, kissing him on the ear. "You're up early."

"I was talking with Dad, but he left a little while ago. I think he was going to the chapel. I'll bet he's praying again with Brother Matthew."

Melanie stroked Isaac's soft brown hair. It had grown longer since they'd left Chicago a month ago. "Well then, I hope he'll say a few for me. Lord knows, I need all the help I can get."

Isaac turned sharply in his mother's arms. "Don't. Why would you say something like that? You know we're all going to be together. Don't ever say something like that again. Please."

He was upset, and Melanie was immediately sorry she'd made the lighthearted remark. She was still groggy from the poor night's sleep. The last thing she wanted to do was upset her son.

"You're right, baby. It was a dumb thing to say. You know I didn't mean it. Forgive me?"

He nodded and snuggled close to her again. His long, lean body was warm against her. They lay together for almost another hour, not a word spoken between them. There was no need for words. Their bond was incredibly strong—and unbreakable. Even death would never separate these two.

Finally, they rolled out of bed together. "I love you, Mommy," he said, smiling warmly at her. She kissed him lightly on each side of his face, then hugged him with all her might.

"I love you too, my sweet baby. And I will be with you until the end of time."

Six weeks later, Isaac developed the cough.

* * *

It was a normal cough at first. At least that was what they hoped. Somewhere in the back of their minds, however, Jack and Melanie knew better. The cough became more jagged and raspy over the course of several days. And it was accompanied with several episodes of breathlessness, weakness, and some puffiness around Isaac's feet and ankles.

After a week, Isaac experienced heart palpitations. Jack recognized the symptoms. He'd seen them before in people of all ages but rarely in children. He asked Matthew for medical supplies, and when they were made available, he examined his young son.

As Melanie, Lou, and Matthew looked on, Jack took his son's blood pressure and listened to his chest with a stethoscope. He could hear crackles in the lungs and a heart murmur. He also tapped against Isaac's chest with his fingers and, by carefully listening to the percussion, was able to determine that the heart was enlarged. Carefully, he traced his index finger along the distended veins in Isaac's neck. His findings revealed to him what he already knew. His son was dying.

"What is it?" Isaac asked. "I want to know. The truth, please, Dad."

Jack looked at the others, then looked directly into his son's eyes. "It's called cardiomyopathy. It's a disease of the heart, one that eventually leads to congestive heart failure. I'd need a CT scan and an echocardiogram to be absolutely positive, but I'm almost 100 percent sure even without them, especially knowing what we know about the way all this is going to end." Tears flowed down his face as he sat on the edge of his son's bed. "Cardiomyopathy is correctable only if the underlying disease can be cured. Most of the time, symptoms do not surface until the disease is quite advanced. Hospitalization may slow the process, but usually, the only cure is a successful heart transplant."

Isaac took a long, deep breath then sat up in bed. He reached over and wiped the tears away from his father's face. Lou and Matthew wiped away their own. Melanie, her face gentle and reassuring, sat down beside him.

"Is it painful?" she asked without taking her eyes off Isaac. She rubbed his hands and smiled warmly at him.

"Not usually," Jack said. "All things considered. There is some discomfort with the shortness of breath and chronic fatigue. I can help him with that, though. I'll take good care of you, Isaac."

He smiled at his mom and dad, and there was no sadness in his eyes, not even a touch. They both looked hard for any sign of despair and were surprised and encouraged upon seeing none.

He's taking it, Jack thought to himself, *like a real man.*

"Looks like it's time, then," Isaac said. "Let's just ride it out, and do the best we can."

Matthew walked to the edge of the bed and knelt beside it. Instinctively, Lou did the same. There, in the quietness of the Holy Child's room, he led them in prayer. As they prayed together, each of them felt better and stronger. They were beginning the final journey.

* * *

Over the next two weeks, Isaac's condition worsened. He was weak and tired most of the time, and his appetite was almost completely gone. Jack traveled to a small community hospital—and with the help of Matthew—was able to secure an oxygen tank and some mild pain medication.

"It's hard to say no to a colleague," the doctor had told them, "especially one accompanied by one of our fine brothers from Montessori."

The oxygen helped a great deal, at least for a while, and the pain medication kept him groggy and sedated most of the time. The last few days were not pleasant, but all of them took heart knowing Isaac was not experiencing much pain.

Lou and Matthew sat with him one afternoon, watching him sleep. "I guess there's just no good way to die, is there?" Lou asked, thinking of Trina as well as Isaac. The old man looked at his friend with a sharp eye.

"No, there's not," he finally said. "But this sure beats being nailed to a cross. Before, the need for suffering and public execution was vital to God's plan. This time, there is no need. Our merciful Father will let his Son pass in relative peace this time. We should thank him for that."

Together, in their own way, both men did.

CHAPTER 69

October 30, 2013

The time was at hand.

Isaac, pale and weak on his bed, was fighting for every breath. His mother and father were with him, kneeling on each side of the bed. Lou, the great protector to the end, stood guard outside the door. Matthew had gathered the other monks in the chapel, where they prayed together.

Jack and Melanie were both in tears. They'd promised each other and Isaac that they would not cry. But now that the time was at hand, their sorrow could not be controlled. They wept quietly, almost silently, as their son tried to speak.

Isaac was hallucinating. His fever was high, and he was badly dehydrated. The damaged muscle that was once his heart was barely beating. Still he managed to whisper the final, uplifting words that would comfort his parents until their own deaths many years later.

"Someone's coming for me. It's…a man—a strong man reaching out for me with his giant hands. I think it's Michael…Mommy. It is. It's Michael. He's come for me…to take me to heaven."

Melanie and Jack cried out in both joy and anguish. But Isaac's words were giving them great hope.

"I'm not scared anymore, Daddy. I'm not afraid, Mommy. Michael is with me. I'm in his arms. He's going to show me the way home."

Isaac took one more breath, then gave up his spirit to his father and brother in heaven.

* * *

Outside the window, as Jack and Melanie held their son's lifeless hands, the bright orange leaves of October fell to the ground.

In the distance, escaping from the small confines of the Montessori chapel, the beautiful, prayerful chanting of the Abbey monks rose through the air, lifting the Holy Child and his special guardian as they ascended to a better place.

CHAPTER 70

November 1, 2013

The funeral Mass and burial were both held at Montessori. The only guests were Doris, Reece, Jacob, Josh, and Jordan.

The family members and friends were in too much pain to speak. Instead they suffered in silence as Matthew led the short, simple service. He spoke for them all in offering up the final words for Isaac James Russell.

"You brought him to us, Father, so that we could be saved once again. You entrusted these special people with his care, and in so doing, you afforded us the opportunity of a thousand lifetimes. You graced us with the chance to walk hand in hand with the Holy Child. And you gave us time—almost thirteen glorious years to love and learn from him.

"In your greatness, we ask for one last thing, almighty God. Let us not forget what he taught us. Help us to go forth and teach others so that we can somehow make this world a better place to live. Your son sacrificed so much for us. Give us the strength and courage we need to make certain those sacrifices were not made in vain.

"Until we meet again, help us cope with the pain in our hearts as we say goodbye to our human son. It is difficult to let go of such a brilliant star."

* * *

The small unmarked headstone adorned the simple grave located beneath a great oak tree in the far corner of the Montessori cemetery. It was alone, separated completely from the good men who had come and gone at the monastery over the many years.

Each evening, shortly before dark, the old monk would make the long trek up the hill, just to sit, rest, reflect, and talk with the Holy Child. He talked of many things, but most of all, he thanked Isaac—and his brother and father—for saving the world and for giving mankind one more chance to find the right path back to God.

Matthew would make the trip for almost three years. On the last day he curled up beneath the old tree and, without a sound, offered up his own spirit and joined his loved ones in heaven.

CHAPTER 71

December 25, 2013, Honolulu, Hawaii

The crystal blue water of the great Pacific splashed against the brilliant white sand of Honolulu beach. The color of the ocean reminded Melanie of Isaac's beautiful eyes, and despite her best effort to push it away, pain filled her heart.

She dabbed at her eyes with a tissue, but just as she'd done each and every day since her son's death, she willfully forced the hurt aside. After all, it was what he'd asked her to do.

Melanie put her sunglasses on and looked out across the sun drenched water.

Jack, Reece, and Lou were standing in the ocean, waist deep, as Josh and Jacob tried their hand at surfboarding. Both boys were big and strong now, men really, and they were lean and muscular just like their father. She smiled as she watched them fall head over heels into the ocean, only to resurface moments later with smiles almost as wide as the beach.

She looked at Jack and realized yet again how much she loved him. He was her rock. His dark hair was beginning to turn gray, and there were a few more wrinkles around his eyes now, but he was as handsome as ever.

And Lou, past seventy now, was still as healthy as a horse. He was finally getting the chance to relax and enjoy retirement. His daughter, Virginia, and her husband, Thomas, were sitting together at the edge of the surf, using buckets and rough carving tools to build an elaborate castle in the warm sand. Their daughters, nearly college age, pretended to help but mostly watched as handsome young men jogged up and down the beach.

Jordan, almost sixteen and sprawled full-length on a towel, lay motionless under the bright sun just a few feet away from Melanie. He was working on his tan and had lemon juice sprayed on his hair, harboring high hopes that his blond locks would turn even lighter by the time this special vacation ended in another four days.

Doris, seated beside her in an identical beach chair, was with her friend again. As always. Emotionally as well as physically. She frowned slightly as she remembered the funeral, especially how Doris and Jack had both held her while Matthew spoke.

Suddenly, Doris reached over and gently touched her on the hand, bringing her attention and her aching heart back from the past.

"Come on now. He wouldn't like that—seeing you sad. You know he wouldn't like that."

Melanie smiled and turned to her friend. "I'll never understand how you do that. It's like you can read my mind."

Doris laughed and grinned mischievously. "I guess you think you're the only one with special powers? Some of us mere mortals are pretty special too, you know. So don't ever try to fool me, sister. I know your every thought. That's my job."

Melanie laughed, and this time, it wasn't forced. The laughter was sincere, and greatly needed.

"That's better," Doris said. "Now that's what he had in mind."

Melanie looked out over the beautiful ocean again. "I'm really glad we decided to take the trip now. Spending Christmas here is a good idea. I think it makes today a little easier for all of us."

The two sat quietly for a time, enjoying the warm weather and the majestic scenery of the island paradise, before the others finally came in for a cold drink and relief from the sun. Everyone huddled together under a pair of large umbrellas that provided a considerable amount of welcome shade.

Against the beautiful backdrop, with friends both old and new, it was Jordan who finally asked the question. His plea was to hear another account of the modern-day Savior.

"Aunt Melanie, will you tell us another story about Isaac? Tell us about the exciting times when he was just a baby. Or tell us again about the miracle he performed in the mall. I get chills every time I hear that one."

Melanie smiled, sat up straight and tall in her chair, and removed her sunglasses so everyone could see her expressive eyes. As always, her heart filled with pride when they asked again to hear about her baby.

In a steady and even voice, she recounted another chapter in the story of the Second Coming—and of the brave child who came at the appointed time to save the world again.

ABOUT THE AUTHOR

Randy Burba is an award-winning writer and editor whose work appeared monthly as part of Kentucky Living Magazine. A retired communications specialist for a large energy company, he received over 45 national awards. An honor graduate of University of Kentucky's School of Journalism, Randy previously worked as a staff writer for *The Kentucky Standard*, a Scripps Howard Community newspaper located in historic Bardstown, Ky. During his 5 years at *The Standard* he captured nine awards as presented by members of the Kentucky Press Association, including the top award for writing in 1985. His work includes an article on the Abbey of Gethsemani in Nelson County, Kentucky, the 150-year old monastery which served as home to famous poet and author, the late Thomas Merton. Other religious related topics he has written about include historical pieces on St. Joseph Proto Cathedral in Bardstown, Kentucky, which in 1819 was the first Cathedral built west of the Alleghenies, and also a story on the religious community of Nazareth, home of the remarkable congregation of women known as the Sisters of Charity. Today, Randy continues to write in Bardstown, Kentucky where he lives with his wife.